This Book Belongs
Gerig Ranch

Paper Roses

PAPER ROSES

A Novel

TEXAS DREAMS, BOOK 1

Amanda Cabot

Revell

a division of Baker Publishing Group
Grand Rapids, Michigan

Published by Revell
a division of Baker Publishing Group
P.O. Box 6287, Grand Rapids, MI 49516-6287

Printed in the United States of America

ISBN-13: 978-1-60751-543-2

In memory of Jean Ellen Mayer,
whose journey to the Light
changed the direction of my writing.
Adieu, mon amie.

1

"It'll be all right." Sarah Dobbs wrapped her arms around the child, wishing with all her heart that she could believe the words she'd uttered so often. The truth was, it didn't matter what she believed. All that mattered was keeping Thea safe. And so Sarah knelt on the hard-packed dirt of San Antonio's main street to wipe the tears from her sister's cheeks. The child was hot, tired, and excited by the unusual sights, a combination that turned normally sweet-tempered Thea querulous.

"Let me see, sweetie." Sarah reached for her sister's hands, giving each of the tiny palms a kiss. Thank goodness, this time Thea had not hurt herself. When she'd run and tumbled, trying to chase a burro, all she'd done was torn her hem again. The dress could be repaired far more easily than the skinned hands and knees that had been almost daily occurrences since they'd left the train.

"It'll be all right," Sarah repeated, rising as gracefully as she could. *It* will *be all right*, she told herself, *when Austin arrives*. The journey that had been more difficult than she had dreamt possible was almost over. Once she and Thea reached Ladreville and the Bar C, the past would truly end. The old Sarah Dobbs would be gone forever.

"Walk?" Thea gave Sarah a look only a curmudgeon could refuse. Sarah was not a curmudgeon. She was a woman whose right leg was protesting the exercise and whose common sense was shouting that she and Thea should not remain in the hot Texas sun. She was also a woman who knew how desperately Thea needed to expend some of her seemingly endless supply of energy.

"A short walk." Sarah smiled as a grin crossed the child's face. It took so little to please Thea. *How could anyone have . . . ?* Deliberately, Sarah bit the inside of her cheek. *That's all past*, she reminded herself. She wouldn't think about the past. Instead, she walked slowly and deliberately, trying to minimize her limp as she looked for the man who held the key to her future.

Where was he? Where was Austin Canfield? Sarah kept a tight grip on Thea's hand as they made their way down the street. Her tumble forgotten, Thea giggled at the sight of oxen with almost unbelievably long horns pulling two-wheeled carts.

There was no denying the differences between this city and Philadelphia. They were as real as the warmth that felt more like midsummer than the last days of winter, as real as the smells of dust and dung and dried leaves. But the greatest difference was sensed rather than seen or heard. There was a contagious vitality about this frontier town. Sarah saw it in the way men swaggered rather than strolled; she heard it in the shouted greetings. Whether they spoke Spanish or English, enthusiasm was evident in every word. Texas was young and brash and exciting. It was everything she sought, or it would be if Austin were here.

But he wasn't. There was no doubt about that, just as there had been no doubt the previous dozen times she had looked for him. Though the center of San Antonio bustled with life, there was no one who fit his description. *I'm four inches over six feet*, he had written, *with sandy hair and blue eyes, and when I see you, I'll be wearing a grin as big as the state of Texas.* Sarah had smiled when she had read his words. Texans, she had heard, were prone to exaggeration. She wasn't smiling now. The last of their traveling companions had departed half an hour ago, leaving Sarah and Thea alone, more than a thousand miles and a lifetime away from home. She shook her head slowly, negating her last thought. Philadelphia wasn't home. Not anymore.

"Papa!" Thea tugged Sarah's hand and started to run across the road. Though they hadn't been there a moment ago, two cowboys had emerged from the saloon on the opposite side of the street and were lounging in the doorway.

"No, sweetie." Sarah wrapped her arms around her sister, restraining her. Neither of those men was the new father who had promised to meet them, the man who was now an hour late.

As if they had heard Thea's cry, the cowboys approached Sarah. "Might we be of assistance, ma'am?"

Sarah shook her head. When it had been apparent that Austin Canfield wasn't waiting for the stagecoach, the other woman who had traveled with them had advised waiting inside the town hall, which Texans referred to by its Spanish name, *cabildo*, but Sarah, knowing that Thea would hate being cooped up in yet another small space, had remained outside. She had believed her mourning garb and the presence of a small child at her side would discourage unwanted attention. That had been the case on the train and the stagecoaches. But San Antonio was different. Texans were as friendly as Philadelphians were reserved.

"No, thank you, gentlemen. My fiancé will be here momentarily." She hoped it wasn't a lie.

Though the men exchanged amused glances, they retreated. With a sigh of relief, Sarah looked at the clock tower. She would wait for five minutes longer. If Austin hadn't arrived by then, she and Thea would go inside.

Where was he? Sarah looked around for what seemed like the hundredth time, hoping that a tall, sandy-haired rancher would appear. He didn't. She took another deep breath as she considered the reasons he might not have come. Perhaps his horse had gone lame. Perhaps a wheel had fallen off the wagon. Those were possibilities, and they were far more palatable than the alternative. Surely Austin hadn't changed his mind. Surely he hadn't been lying when he'd written those wonderful letters. Surely he wasn't going to abandon her and Thea the way everyone in Philadelphia had. Or was he?

"No, sweetie. No skipping." Though Thea wanted to run, running was one of the things Sarah could not do. Was that the reason Austin was not here? She paused as doubts assailed her. Had Austin reconsidered and realized he had no desire to wed a woman whose right leg was twisted and scarred and an inch shorter than her left?

Sarah reached into her reticule and touched the packet

of letters, trying to reassure herself. *"You speak of your imperfections as though the rest of us bore no blemishes."* There was no need to open the envelopes and withdraw the pages, for she had memorized the words Austin had written, just as she had engraved upon her mind the appearance of the brash handwriting that was somehow at odds with the eloquent phrases. *"My dearest Sarah, if there is one thing I have learned, it is that no one is perfect. But you, my sweet wife-to-be, are closer to perfection than you know."*

She wasn't perfect. Far from it. Still, her heart had soared with happiness when she'd read that sentence. It was Austin who was perfect, for he had somehow known exactly the right words to woo her. Sarah hadn't expected to be courted. This was, after all, a business arrangement. But there was no denying the fact that she had reveled in Austin Canfield's letters. They had been the one ray of light in those horrible months after Mama and Papa's deaths.

Reverend Lang claimed they were proof that God loved her and was watching over her. Sarah knew otherwise. God had deserted her and so, it appeared, had her bridegroom.

❧

What else could go wrong? Clay Canfield bit back an oath as he stared at the mare. It wasn't her fault. When he had come into the stable to harness the horses, Clay had discovered Nora ailing. If the fact that instead of greeting him eagerly as she did each day wasn't enough, the sorrel mare lay curled in a ball. Those big brown eyes lacked their normal sparkle, and her nose didn't even twitch when he pulled a carrot from his pocket. Clay clenched his fist, snapping the carrot from the force of his grip. He didn't need this. Indeed, he did not.

The last thing he needed was an ailing horse, particularly today. But he had one.

"Miguel," he called when he heard the stable hand's heavy tread, "Nora's sick. You'd better look at the others before you feed them." Clay knelt next to the mare and checked her gums, nodding when he saw they were still pink. "C'mon, girl." He reached for Nora's halter. "It's just a touch of colic." Clay wasn't certain of that. It was, he had discovered over the past year, easier to treat people than animals. Humans told you what hurt, while horses could only look at you with mournful eyes. Nora might have colic; she might have something else. The one thing Clay knew for certain was that another innocent being could not die. Ladreville, Texas, had been the site of far too many Canfield deaths.

Clay glanced at his black armband and shuddered as waves of pain and anger swept through him. The man responsible for that would pay. Unfortunately, not today.

"C'mon, Nora." Clay spoke softly as he slid the halter over her head. "We're gonna get you on your feet and walk a bit." That had helped the last time the mare had had colic. With a little luck, it would work again. Clay's lips twisted in a wry smile. He was the last person on earth who should expect luck to favor him.

"I'm taking Nora out." Miguel knew what to do in the stable. Clay walked, slowly at first, leading the mare around the paddock, trying not to look at the horizon, where the sun was even now tinting the sky. He should have been on the road by now. Instead . . .

As Nora whinnied, Clay stopped and laid a reassuring hand on her muzzle. "It's all right, girl. We'll get you feeling better soon."

14

With her flaxen mane and tail and the white blaze, Nora was a beautiful horse. Despite her advanced age, Clay had received offers to buy her, offers that he'd refused without a second's consideration. He'd never sell Ma's horse. Nora deserved to live out her days on the Bar C. That was why Clay was taking endless circles around the paddock, trying not to think of how much time had passed since he'd discovered Nora lying in her stall, trying desperately not to think of the last time Nora had left the Bar C and how she'd returned, a lifeless body draped over her back.

Clay forced himself to take a deep breath. They'd keep walking. And they did. It was only when Nora's digestive tract was once again functioning normally that Clay returned her to the stable.

"Good news, boss," Miguel called out as Clay led Nora to her stall. "The others are all fine."

"That is good news." The first of the day. The first in a long time. Clay rubbed Nora's nose again before giving her a ration of bran.

"I thought you were going to San Antonio today." Miguel's voice came from the other end of the stable, where he'd started to muck out stalls.

Clay shrugged his shoulders. "I was. I am." He looked down at his sweat-stained shirt and wrinkled his nose. He couldn't go looking or smelling like this. As he headed for the pump, Clay glanced up. The sun was now above the horizon, staining the sky a bright red that promised unseasonable warmth. It would be a good day for travel, if a man wanted to travel. Clay did not, at least not when that traveling involved a return trip to Ladreville and the Bar C. Unfortunately, what he wanted didn't change anything.

He dipped his head under the pump, then walked toward the house. As he pulled out his watch, Clay frowned again. He'd be late. There was no way around that. Caring for Nora had taken more than two hours. Though he had planned to arrive in San Antonio before the stagecoach, now he would be late. Very late, and that meant Miss Sarah Dobbs and her little sister would have to wait.

Clay climbed into the wagon that Miguel had harnessed. It wasn't fair. The woman had traveled all the way from Philadelphia, expecting to be met by her bridegroom. Instead, she would be forced to wait, and when that waiting ended, the only things she would have were Clay and a message he would have given almost anything not to be delivering. It wasn't fair, but life, Clay had discovered on far too many occasions, wasn't fair.

He tightened his grip on the reins. If he'd been able to ride Shadow, he could have made up lost time, but riding wasn't an option, not when he needed to transport Miss Sarah Dobbs and all her earthly possessions to Ladreville. So here he was, driving the wagon, while the sun's inexorable rise reminded him of just how late he was and how many miles he had yet to cover before he met his brother's bride.

And the child. Mustn't forget the child that Austin had claimed was part of God's plan. Some plan. Clay clenched his fists, trying to fight back the pain. *Why?* he demanded. *Why did you let it happen? Austin believed in you. He said you were a loving God.* There was no answer. It appeared God was not listening. No surprise there. God hadn't listened to Clay Canfield in a long time. And, it appeared, he had not been listening to Austin, either. That was why Clay was on his way to San Antonio to meet the Canfield bride. And the child.

What would she do when she learned the truth? Clay tugged on his hat brim, trying to block the sun. As the red ball lit the horizon, the horses continued to lower their heads. Clay wished he could follow suit, but—unlike them—he needed to watch more than the road. This country held hazards far more serious than potholes, including marauding Comanche. And at the end of the road was the greatest hazard, at least to Clay's equilibrium: Miss Sarah Dobbs.

How would she react? How would any woman handle the announcement he was forced to make? Clay lowered his chin in another vain attempt to keep the sun from blinding him. If Patience had been faced with the news, what would she have done? Would she have swooned or simply wept buckets of tears? Clay had seen her do both when she had been upset. He squinted, and this time it was not in response to the sun's rays. Odd. He could not conjure the image of his wife's face. That had never happened before. Clay shook his head, trying to clear it. What mattered today was Miss Sarah Dobbs, the woman whose stagecoach was even now lumbering into San Antonio.

How was he going to tell her? An hour later as he drove the wagon into the heart of the city, Clay was still searching for the words to make the announcement easier to bear.

He stared at the woman who stood in front of the *cabildo*, a small child at her side, looking at the town hall's clock tower with what appeared to be barely controlled impatience. Though he could see only her back, there was something about the tilt of her head that spoke of anger. Clay couldn't blame her for that. In a similar situation, he doubted he would have bothered to mask his impatience. The stagecoach had arrived over an hour earlier. Austin should have been here,

17

ready to help her alight from the coach, showing her that he was as eager to marry her as his letters had claimed. Instead, Miss Sarah Dobbs and her sister had been left alone in the middle of San Antonio, as out of place as a piece of mesquite in a Boston parlor.

The woman turned slightly, revealing her profile. There was no doubt about it. This was Sarah. Clay would have known her, even without the miniature she had sent to Austin. *"Medium height, medium brown hair, medium brown eyes,"* she had written in one of her letters. This woman was all that, and more. Though her fancy clothing was the first clue, the slightly imperious tilt of her head and the proud angle of her shoulders announced to the world that this was a lady, an Eastern lady. She turned again, and this time she looked directly at Clay, her eyes flickering from the top of his hat down his dusty clothes before she dismissed him. The action surprised Clay almost as much as the fact that she had remained outdoors rather than seeking the sanctuary of the *cabildo*. Sarah Dobbs was no shy miss. Instead, she appeared to possess more self-assurance than he had expected, certainly more than Patience had. Clay clenched his jaw at the knowledge that he would be the one to destroy that confidence.

Trying to control his anger, he jumped out of the wagon and approached his brother's fiancée. "Miss Dobbs," he said softly as he doffed his hat, not wanting to startle her. Two cowboys on the opposite side of the street appeared to be keeping watch. Clay suspected that if Miss Dobbs let out a cry of alarm, their protective instincts might result in a brawl. He most definitely did not need that. "Miss Dobbs," he repeated, a bit louder this time.

18

Austin's mail-order bride had moved and was once more staring at the town hall, her hand placed protectively on the little girl's shoulder. At the sound of his voice, she turned to face Clay. For a second, her eyes were brilliant with hope. But as quickly as it had been ignited, the hope faded. "I beg your pardon, sir. May I ask who you are?"

"Papa!" The child grinned and raised her arms toward him.

Clay's hand tightened on his hat brim. "No," he said, forcing his voice to remain even, though he wanted to shout his denial. "I'm not your papa." *Thanks to Austin's God, I'm not anyone's papa.*

He raised his gaze to Sarah. "I'm Clayton Canfield, ma'am. Clay for short," he said as calmly as he could. In case she had forgotten the part of the letters where Austin had described his family, Clay added, "Austin's brother." As she nodded, Sarah looked past him, clearly expecting his brother to appear. The poor woman. She didn't deserve this. While his heart balked at pronouncing the words, Clay couldn't let her continue to believe that Austin was in San Antonio. "I've come to take you to the ranch."

Sarah Dobbs's composure seemed to slip. "But . . . I thought . . ." The woman who had seemed so self-assured now appeared vulnerable. Silently Clay railed at the events that had put uncertainty in her eyes. Sarah swallowed before she asked, "Where's Austin?"

The taller of the two cowboys straightened and took a step into the street, glaring at Clay. Seconds later, apparently reassured that Sarah was not being coerced, he returned to the shelter of the doorway.

"I'm sorry, ma'am." Clay took Sarah's arm and led her

toward the wagon. "There's no easy way to tell you this." He lifted the child onto the seat, then assisted Sarah, waiting until she was settled before he spoke. Only then did Clay take a deep breath and force himself to utter the words that haunted him. "My brother is dead."

❧

Austin was dead. Sarah stared at the man who now would never be her brother-in-law. Austin was dead. It couldn't be true. But it was. The man with the black armband had no reason to lie. Austin was dead.

"Take another sip," Clay Canfield urged. Obediently, Sarah raised the tin cup to her lips and swallowed the lukewarm water. He must have thought she was going to faint. That was why he had insisted she sit before he told her the news. That was why he produced the canteen and cup. That was why he counseled her to take deep breaths. But she wasn't going to swoon. She wasn't even going to cry. Fainting and tears solved nothing.

Sarah closed her eyes for a second, grappling with the fact that the man who had written those beautiful letters asking her to marry him was gone before she had had the chance to meet him, to hear his voice and to see whether his smile really was as big as the state of Texas.

"What happened?"

"Drink, Sarah?"

Thea's words interrupted whatever Clay might have said. Instinctively, Sarah clutched her sister. Precious, precious Thea. She was all Sarah had left. Losing her was unthinkable. But so was the loss of their parents. Mama had been so happy when Thea had been born, so excited about the grand tour of Europe she and Papa planned for all of them, so eager to hold her first grandchild. And then . . .

Thea yipped.

"I'm sorry, sweetie."

"Drink." Thea grabbed for the cup.

Loosening her grip on her sister, Sarah held the cup while Thea sipped.

"What will Thea and I do?" The words tumbled out. An instant later, Sarah wished she could retract them. How selfish! This man's brother had died, and all she could think about was her own situation. Hers and Thea's. She was being as unkind as the parishioners who had shunned her, lest the scandal of her parents' deaths taint them.

"I'm sorry," Sarah said. "I can't even imagine how I'd feel if something happened to Thea."

"God willing, you'll never know." Clay Canfield recapped the canteen and stowed it behind the seat, then flicked the reins, setting the wagon in motion.

"Where are you taking us?"

He shrugged, as if that should be evident. "To the Bar C. You must be fatigued from your travels. I imagine you'll need a week or two of rest before you take the stagecoach East."

Sarah shuddered at the enormity of her dilemma. Return to Philadelphia? Impossible. "We can't go back," she said, wincing at the desperation she heard in her voice. There was nothing for them in the City of Brotherly Love other than ridicule, ostracism, and humiliation.

As Thea started to doze, Sarah took a deep breath, trying to find words to explain the situation without revealing too much. Had it been less than an hour since she'd assured Thea everything would be all right? How wrong she'd been.

Her mind whirling with unhappy thoughts, Sarah looked at the town that had seemed so appealing as the stagecoach had lumbered its way toward the center. Instead of the stone edifices that marked her hometown, San Antonio had adobe buildings, a vivid reminder of the city's Spanish heritage. Those were startling enough, but even more surprising was the juxtaposition of those graceful buildings with shops of rough-hewn wood and mismatched brick, shops whose almost casual architecture bore witness to the exuberance of the Americans who had built them, just as the curved lines of the adobe buildings spoke of the more formal society that had first established the city.

When she'd entered San Antonio, Sarah had been filled with anticipation. The man she had promised to marry would be waiting for her, and soon she and Thea would begin their new life. Thea would grow up never knowing shame. Now the anticipation was gone, destroyed by the brutal reality of death. In place of anticipation came the knowledge that once again Sarah and Thea were alone, their future as uncertain as it had been the day the attorney had told Sarah nothing remained. Their father's disastrous investments had resulted in the loss of not just Sarah's dowry but everything he owned, including the house she called home. That was the reason Papa had taken her mother's life and then his own, leaving Sarah and Thea alone and destitute, shunned by the people who had once pretended to be friends.

"We can't return," she repeated.

Clay nodded slowly, as if he understood the reason for Sarah's refusal. "I will, of course, pay for your tickets."

He didn't understand. Lack of money was only one of Sarah's problems. "Mr. Canfield, I have no reason to return to Philadelphia. Ladreville is my home and Thea's. Or it will be, once we arrive there."

Though she wouldn't have the protection of Austin's name and the respectability that came with being a married woman, somehow Sarah would find a way to build a new life for her sister. Nothing—nothing on earth—was more important than keeping the promise she'd made the day their parents died.

They were outside San Antonio now, with the two ruts that served as a road stretching straight in front of them. Clay turned toward Sarah, his face reflecting his surprise. "It pains me to state the obvious, ma'am, but you no longer have a husband waiting for you. While it's true there are single men in Ladreville, I can't guarantee . . ."

"I don't need a husband. I am certain I can find a way to earn my room and board." Sheer bravado propelled her declaration. The truth was, Sarah had no salable skills. Playing the pianoforte and being able to capture a flower's beauty in watercolors were important assets in Philadelphia society; however, she suspected there was little calling for those particular skills in Ladreville, Texas.

"The offer of passage home still stands."

His words were meant to be kind. Sarah knew that. They shouldn't have stung like a rose's thorns, and yet they did. It was obvious Clay Canfield did not believe she could play a useful role in his hometown. The thought that he might be right rankled, for Sarah had no other choices, not if Thea was to have the life she deserved.

They rode in silence. In a desperate attempt not to think about the future, Sarah darted glances at the man on the opposite end of the seat. Though his eyes were the same deep blue Austin had claimed, Clay Canfield's hair was blond, not

Austin's sandy brown. Clay was a few inches shorter than Austin, perhaps an even six feet tall. Were his facial features the same? Sarah would never know. She glanced at the hand that had held the canteen. Odd. When he'd removed his glove, it hadn't looked the way she thought a rancher's hand would. There were none of the calluses she imagined ranching would create. Those heavy leather gloves must protect hands well.

Sarah choked back a nervous laugh. How could she be thinking about gloves when her fiancé had died? She didn't even know the cause of his death.

"What happened?"

"Do you mean, how did Austin die?"

Sarah nodded. She had heard that horrible diseases swept the Texas countryside, making the yellow fever that plagued Philadelphia seem mild in comparison. Wild animals and poisonous reptiles roamed the land, seeking human prey. And then there were the Comanche, whose moonlit raids struck fear in the settlers' hearts. Texas, she had heard, was no place for a gentlewoman. It seemed it also was not a place for Austin Canfield, since something had killed him.

Clay's lips thinned, and Sarah saw his hands tighten on the reins. "Someone shot my brother. A single shot, point-blank in the heart."

2

Night had fallen, bringing with it both a welcome respite from the sun's glare and a new set of dangers. Though the moon was not full, there was always the possibility of a Comanche attack, and a coyote's unmistakable call provided a reminder of the presence of nocturnal animals.

For what seemed like the thousandth time, Clay glanced at the woman on the other end of the seat. She appeared drowsy, with her head slumped to one side, but her arms remained tightly wrapped around the child. He hoped they were both asleep, for they needed rest. So, for that matter, did he. Clay frowned as he scanned the horizon, looking for predators. Today had been a difficult day. He frowned again. Today was only the culmination of a difficult two weeks. Why stop there? The truth was, nothing had been normal for the past year. Clay's life had been irrevocably changed the day Pa had his stroke.

The horses plodded down the road, oblivious to the knot

tightening Clay's stomach. A year ago he had been a happily married man, renowned in Boston society for his skills as a physician. A year ago he had been convinced that he could employ those skills to restore his father's health. A year ago, Austin had had no intention of marrying. And now? Clay clenched the reins. In the space of a year, he had lost his wife, their unborn child, his brother, and all hope of curing Pa. Now, instead of cradling his child, Clay was transporting Sarah Dobbs and her sister to the home Austin had built for them, a home his brother would not share.

It wasn't supposed to be like this.

As an owl hooted, Clay tried to bite back his anger. There was naught to be gained by dwelling on all that he had lost. He couldn't bring Patience and the baby back. He couldn't restore Pa's faculties. But he could—and he would—ensure that Austin's murderer received his just deserts as soon as he had Austin's mail-order bride and his ready-made daughter settled on the Bar C.

Clay reached for the canteen and took a swig, remembering how he'd offered water to Sarah when her face had grown alarmingly pale. He'd been certain she'd keel over, but she hadn't. She hadn't swooned or screamed, and as far as Clay could tell, she had shed not a single tear. It wasn't that she hadn't been affected by the news of her fiancé's death. Sarah hadn't even tried to hide her sorrow. It was simply that the way she dealt with it revealed an inner strength Clay hadn't anticipated. The letters she had written Austin had only hinted at resilience, just as the miniature she'd sent had failed to do justice to her face.

Sarah Dobbs was not beautiful, at least not beautiful in the way that Patience had been, but she had a quiet dignity

26

and a surprising amount of . . . Clay searched for the word. Spunk. That was it. Miss Sarah Dobbs was spunky.

Was that the reason Austin had insisted she was the bride for him? Clay forced his gaze back to the road. A man could not be too vigilant, particularly at night. Had Austin let down his guard for an instant? Was that the reason the killer had gotten so close? Clay would probably never know, just as he would never know why Austin had chosen Sarah.

Clay had disagreed with his brother's decision, vehemently, in fact. Why, he had asked, should Austin saddle himself with a woman who not only limped but was also burdened with the raising of a small child? The only advantage Clay could find, besides her being obviously well educated, was the fact that her parents had died during an influenza epidemic. Clay didn't wish that fate on anyone, but being an orphan meant that Sarah Dobbs would be less likely to flee when life in Ladreville became difficult, as it surely would.

Austin could have done better. He had shared the letters from all the prospective brides with Clay, and it had been clear to Clay that there were other women far better qualified to become his brother's wife. But Austin had been adamant. God, he had insisted, intended Miss Sarah Dobbs to become the Canfield bride. Either Austin had been wrong or God had changed his plan, because that hadn't happened. The new house was ready. The bride was here. But there was no bridegroom, and there never would be.

Clay's gaze returned to Sarah. He wasn't surprised to see that she was sleeping. Darkness and quiet often had that effect. Night had fallen hours earlier, but even before then, they hadn't spoken much beyond agreeing to dispense with the formalities and call each other by their given names.

Then they'd retreated into private thoughts. At first Clay had known Sarah wasn't asleep. The irregular breathing and the occasional shudder led him to suspect she was trying to understand everything that had happened. As if anyone could! Understanding meant finding a reason, and there was no reason Clay could imagine that anyone would want to kill his brother.

Now Sarah slept, her position decidedly maternal as she kept Thea cradled next to her. She was as fierce as a bear sow protecting her cub, and that, too, was something Clay had not expected. Spunky Sarah Dobbs was full of surprises, not the least of which was her apparent determination to remain in Texas. She wouldn't, of course. No matter what she said, Clay knew that once Sarah experienced the reality of Ladreville, she would want to return to Philadelphia. As for the notion of paying him for her room and board, anyone could see that she had no way of earning a living. In Philadelphia she might have become a companion or a governess, but those positions didn't exist in Ladreville. No doubt about it. She'd be headed East within a month.

As the horses splashed their way into the river, Sarah wakened. Clay's heart clenched as she dropped a kiss on her sister's head. It appeared Austin had been correct claiming Sarah Dobbs would be a good mother for the next generation of Canfields.

"We're almost there." Clay kept his voice low as he gestured toward the water. "This is the Medina River. If we'd continued for another mile on this side, we'd have reached Ladreville. The Bar C is on the opposite bank." Clay wasn't certain why he was explaining all this to Sarah. She wouldn't be here long enough to care.

"I appreciate your coming to meet us," she said. "I know this has been a difficult time for you. Having to see me probably didn't help."

As understatements went, that one would win a prize. She had no way of knowing that the sight of a woman holding a child was painful for him, and when Thea had called him "Papa," he'd been almost blinded with rage. Where had Austin's loving God been the day Patience and the baby had died?

Clay swallowed deeply, fighting to regain control of his emotions. "I could hardly have left you and Thea in San Antonio."

"You could have sent someone else."

That was something Clay had not considered. "Austin would have wanted it this way."

"Thank you." Though the moon was only a crescent, it provided enough light for Clay to see the way Sarah smiled. She hadn't done it often, but when she smiled, Miss Sarah Dobbs was downright pretty. "I'll try to ensure that Thea and I are not a burden to you," she said, her smile fading.

They wouldn't be, not because of her efforts, but because Clay would not allow it. "The ranch keeps me so busy that I doubt you'll see me very often." From the day he and Patience had returned and Clay had been forced to assume some of his father's responsibilities, he had resented the amount of time the Bar C demanded. Pa and Austin might find the work satisfying. Clay did not. But tonight for the first time he acknowledged one advantage to the endless chores: they would keep him away from Sarah and Thea and memories of what might have been.

They'd reached the road and were approaching the lane

that led to the Bar C. Recognizing the familiar landmarks, the horses increased their pace. They were anxious to be home. So was Clay, for once he had Sarah and Thea settled in their temporary abode, he would be able to relax, knowing they were safe.

He wasn't the only one who'd been vigilant, Clay realized when he saw Pa's light still burning. Since the night of Austin's death, his father had refused to sleep until he knew Clay was home. It was as if Pa somehow thought that staying awake would ensure the safety of his remaining son.

After the most cursory of introductions when Miguel emerged from the barn to care for the horses, Clay helped Sarah out of the wagon, then reached for the sleeping child. The sooner he got them settled, the sooner he could reassure Pa. Carefully he lifted Thea into his arms and turned toward the house.

As Sarah extended her own arms, Clay shook his head. "I can carry her. You must be tired."

"I told you we wouldn't be a burden." There was an asperity to Sarah's tone that surprised him, for he'd noted her unfailing politeness.

Clay continued walking. "I hardly think carrying a child up six steps and into the house constitutes a significant burden."

The lantern on the porch revealed Sarah's surprise. "In that case, thank you."

Why was she so unwilling to accept even the slightest help? The combination of fatigue and her limp could have caused her to stumble, injuring her sister. That was why Clay was carrying Thea. It certainly wasn't because he longed to hold someone else's child in his arms. But spunky Sarah had turned as prickly as a cactus. Why? Nothing in her letters to Austin had hinted at this side of her personality.

Clay had reached the porch and was about to open the door when Thea stirred. "Papa?" she asked, her eyes widening as she stared at Clay.

"No, sweetie, that's not Papa." At the sound of her sister's voice, Thea squirmed and stretched her arms toward Sarah. "You might as well put her down. She'll only be cranky if you don't."

When it was evident that Thea would no longer tolerate being carried, Clay complied. "I'll take you to the cabin." Though he could have walked around the perimeter of the main house to reach the cabin that would have been Austin and Sarah's home, the shortest distance was through the house.

Sarah gave him a rueful smile. "I'm afraid Thea won't sleep for a while now." She held the child's hand in an obvious attempt to restrain her enthusiasm. "If he's still awake, I'd like to meet your father."

Clay tried not to frown. He had hoped to postpone the inevitable, at least until morning. Now even that slight reprieve was impossible. A difficult day had just grown worse.

"My father's room is this way." Clay ushered Sarah into his home. Though constructed of rough timber like the neighbors', the house his parents had built was smaller than either neighbor's, containing only one large central room that served as a gathering space as well as a place to eat. That room was flanked by a modest cooking area and two bedrooms, one on each side.

Hoping he was successful in concealing his worries, Clay led Sarah to the bedchamber on the right. This was where

Pa had spent most of his life for the past year, the walls imprisoning him as surely as a Mexican jail once had. And now this woman—this stranger—would see him and pass judgment on him.

As they stood in the doorway of his father's room, Clay tried to view it from Sarah's perspective. Though the massive bed and bureau dominated the chamber, Clay was certain Sarah's attention was drawn to the man in the chair. A year ago he had been a tall, sturdy man with gun-metal gray hair and blue eyes that sparkled with enthusiasm when he spoke of his beloved ranch. Today, only the hair was unchanged. The blue eyes were dull with pain, and the rancher who once strode confidently across a room or a paddock now sat slumped in the chair, the right side of his face twisted in a horrible caricature of a once vibrant smile.

Though he wished with every fiber of his being that he could spare his father the indignity of the next few minutes, Clay could delay no longer. He gestured toward the woman who stood on his right, her hand clasping Thea's. "Pa, this is Miss Sarah Dobbs, the woman who was going to marry Austin." Not wanting to see pity or revulsion on her face, Clay refused to turn toward Sarah as he continued the introduction. "Sarah, may I introduce you to my father, Robert Canfield?"

There was a moment of silence before Pa spoke, his words so badly slurred that Clay was certain only he understood that Robert Canfield was welcoming Sarah to the ranch. Stiffly, Clay waited for Sarah's reaction. Would she turn and run, as Patience had that first day? Would she mutter words of sympathy to Clay, as if Pa had lost his hearing along with his ability to speak? The neighboring ranchers had done that.

Would she simply stand immobile, frozen with horror? That had been the response of the churchwomen.

Sarah did none of those things. Instead, she murmured something to Thea, something that made the little girl smile. Together they walked across the room, Sarah's limp more pronounced than ever. Clay stared, astonished, as Sarah knelt next to the wheeled chair and took Pa's left hand in hers. "I'm happy to meet you, Mr. Canfield, although I wish the circumstances had been different." Her voice, low and melodic, sounded sincere. "You see, I lost both of my parents less than a year ago, and I've been looking forward to having you as my new father."

For the first time since Austin's death, Clay saw a spark of hope in his father's eyes. But Pa wasn't looking at Sarah. His attention was focused on the little girl at her side.

"Grandpa!" Thea punctuated the word with a giggle.

Sarah probably thought it was a grimace, but Clay knew the truth. By some miracle, his father was smiling.

❧

Clay wasn't smiling the next morning, but, then again, he couldn't recall smiling very often in the past year. The notable exception had been the day Patience had told him her suspicions were confirmed and they were going to be parents. For days afterward, Clay hadn't been able to wipe the grin from his face. He hadn't even tried. But today, other than the fact that Nora seemed completely recovered, Clay saw no reason to smile.

"C'mon, girl," he said, leading the mare out of her stall. "Another day of rest, and then I'll let you run." Clay was reaching out to give Nora a gentle pat when he heard it. A shriek. Definitely human, but so brief that he could not tell whether it reflected pain or pleasure. He spun around, his eyes widening in surprise at the sight of Thea running toward him. What on earth was she doing? Her pigtails sailed behind her, and beneath the white skirts of what had to be her nightclothes, Clay saw bare feet. Bare feet! Surprise turned to fear, and Clay's own feet flew as he raced across the ground to sweep her into his arms.

"Papa!" Thea laughed and touched his face as if they were playing a game. This was no game.

"No, Thea," he said sternly. "My name is Mr. Canfield."

She shook her head. "Papa," she insisted, tightening her grip on his neck.

There was no reasoning with a two-year-old. Clay wasn't sure why he had even tried. Thea was Sarah's responsibility. He would let Sarah explain that Clay was not and never would be Thea's papa. Though Austin had been eager to assume the role of adoptive father, reminding Clay that they'd both recognized Pa's need to know the ranch would be passed on to another generation of Canfields, Clay did not share that enthusiasm. Those pudgy arms and those brown eyes so like her sister's might have melted another man's heart, but they had no effect on Clay's. Thea was Sarah's responsibility and Sarah's alone.

Where was she? Miss Sarah Dobbs had a lot to answer for this morning, starting with the fact that she had let her sister come outside clad this way.

"Horsey!" Her attention now focused on Nora, Thea was flailing her arms. Though her vocabulary might be limited, there was no doubt that she wanted to touch the horse.

"She *is* a horse," Clay said as he started walking toward

the house. "Her name is Nora." And the little girl in his arms was not going into the corral. No, sirree. A horse, even one as gentle as Nora, was not an Eastern child's plaything. Texas children were raised around horses. They knew the dangers. Thea did not. Sarah should have realized that. She should never have let Thea go outdoors alone.

"No-rah." Thea tried out the new word, giggling as she repeated it. As Clay continued striding away from the paddock, Thea batted his face with a tiny fist. "No-rah. Want No-rah."

"Thea!" Though alarm and relief mingled in Sarah's shout, Clay felt nothing but relief when he saw her emerge from the cabin. Her limp more pronounced than normal, Sarah hurried across the yard, her gaze never moving from Thea's face. Sarah's feet, Clay noted, were sensibly shod, but why on earth was she wearing a heavy woolen cloak? The temperature was close to eighty. As the cloak parted slightly, revealing a froth of white ruffles, Clay had his answer. Like her sister, Miss Sarah Dobbs was still in her nightclothes. Thea must have escaped while Sarah was asleep.

"Oh, Clay, I'm so sorry." The palpable relief that her sister was safe had changed to regret. Clay could almost hear Sarah's thoughts, thoughts in which the word *burden* figured prominently. When she reached him, Sarah extended her arms. "Come, Thea. Come to Sarah." Thea had other ideas. Turning her head into Clay's neck, she ignored her sister. Sarah frowned slightly, then continued her apology. "I must have been more tired than I realized, because I didn't hear her waken." As Thea began to babble about horses and papas, Sarah raised her voice slightly. "She's never done that before—leave me, that is."

Sarah touched Thea's shoulder again. Though the child protested, she drew her into her arms. Clay was surprised at how empty his own felt. Perhaps that was why his words were harsher than he'd intended.

"She came to no harm, but that's not to say that she couldn't have. You should never let a child go outside with bare feet," he continued. "We have rattlesnakes and the occasional cottonmouth." Clay tried not to picture Thea's leg swollen with venom. "Texas is far more dangerous than Philadelphia." Not just because of the snakes. Texas also harbored murderers.

Sarah's face paled and she tightened her grip on her sister. "It won't happen again, I assure you."

After a quick glance at the sky, Clay pulled out his watch. "Martina should have breakfast ready in a few minutes." That was Sarah's cue to return to the house and leave him to more pleasant thoughts than small children being bitten by poisonous snakes and brothers being shot by friends.

She must have missed the cue, because instead of hurrying back, Sarah turned to Clay. "Will you be joining us?"

He shook his head. "I already ate." For some reason, she seemed disappointed. That surprised Clay as much as the question itself. "Was there a reason why you wanted me to join you, other than the dubious pleasure of my company?"

Sarah nodded. "I wanted to talk to you." She gave her attire a rueful glance. "This isn't quite the time or place I would have chosen."

"All right. A second helping of Martina's flapjacks sounds good."

As he watched Sarah return to the small house Austin had built for her, Clay considered the possible reasons she wanted to talk to him. If he was lucky, it would be because she had come to her senses and realized that the best option—the only reasonable option—was for her and Thea to return to Philadelphia on the next stagecoach.

Less than half an hour later, Clay realized that luck was not with him. As Sarah cut Thea's food into small pieces, she asked, "Is there a general store in town?"

Clay nodded. Though it wasn't the question he had expected, perhaps there was still hope. Perhaps she required supplies for the return trip.

"I need some thread and a few other things," Sarah said as she passed the plate to Thea. "I wondered if there was anything I could get for you while I was there."

It was a thoughtful offer. Going to the mercantile was not Clay's favorite activity. "I can't think of anything," he said, "but Martina may need some staples. You might ask her. As soon as we're finished here, I'll have Miguel saddle a horse for you." Judging from the way she had reacted yesterday, Clay was confident that, whatever other skills Sarah possessed, driving a wagon wasn't one of them.

Though her eyes widened slightly with something that, had he not known better, Clay would have called alarm, Sarah's voice was even as she said, "That won't be necessary."

Perhaps he'd been wrong. Perhaps she could handle a team of horses. "Then you'd prefer the wagon."

Sarah paused, a piece of pancake halfway to her mouth, and shook her head. "Thea and I will walk."

"I beg your pardon." His ears must have deceived him. Surely she wasn't proposing what he thought he'd heard.

"A walk," she said, her lips curving into a sweet smile. "It's a fairly basic concept. You put one foot in front of the other."

"I'm familiar with the concept. It's just that . . ." He tried not to look in the direction of Sarah's feet. How did a man refer to an obvious physical impairment without seeming callous?

Sarah's brown eyes met his, the amusement in them startling Clay more than her request. What kind of woman would laugh at her own infirmity? Patience certainly would not have. "You mean because I limp?" Sarah shrugged. "I know I lurch when I walk, but it doesn't hurt. In fact, exercise is good for me." She helped Thea spear a morsel. "I believe you said it was about a mile into Ladreville. That won't be a problem. I've walked farther in Philadelphia."

She didn't understand. "This isn't Philadelphia. Besides the snakes and the occasional alligator, there's the not inconsequential matter of the sun. To put it bluntly, walking anywhere in Texas is not like a casual stroll in a Philadelphia park. The sun and heat can be as deadly as the reptiles. And then there's the river. Were you planning to wade across it? We have no bridges." Clay looked from Sarah to the child. He wasn't sure which surprised him more, the fact that a woman with her obvious disability thought she could walk or that someone as protective of her sister as Sarah would even entertain the notion of taking the child that distance. "Horse or wagon," he said firmly. "The choice is yours."

The blood drained from Sarah's face, leaving it even whiter than it had been earlier when he'd enumerated the dangers to Thea's bare feet. Perhaps Sarah finally understood how different life was in Texas.

"I'll walk."

Though her voice signaled determination, she was no match for Clay Canfield. "You will not," he countered. "Do you prefer to ride or take the wagon?"

Oblivious to the tension that flowed between the adults, Thea continued spooning pieces of pancake into her mouth. Somehow she managed to leave at least half the food on her face, a fact that appeared to please her. Had he not been so annoyed with Sarah, Clay might have found the child's obvious satisfaction amusing.

"I'm not trying to be difficult," Sarah said. "I told you that we wouldn't be a burden, and I meant that. It's simply that I don't know how to drive a wagon. As for riding . . ." She hesitated, and something about her expression told Clay she was choosing her words carefully. "Did Austin mention that my limp is the result of a riding accident?" When Clay nodded, Sarah continued. "I haven't been on a horse since then."

She didn't have to spell out the reason. The tremor in her voice was more eloquent than a thousand words would have been. Sarah was afraid. Had he suffered the same injury, he probably would fear horses too. Fear was a normal reaction. What amazed Clay was that she had admitted it. That wasn't normal, not for Sarah. For a woman as determined to be self-sufficient as Sarah Dobbs was, admitting any weakness had to be difficult.

Clay thought quickly. She couldn't walk; she wouldn't ride; that left only one option. "I'll teach you to drive the wagon," he told her. That would accomplish two objectives. She'd be independent, and he would be able to avoid seeing her and Thea. "For today, though, I'll take you into town. There are a couple things I need to do there." Foremost of which was learning whether Michel Ladre had made any progress in finding Austin's killer.

Today, since he wasn't expecting Clay, that miserable excuse for a mayor and Ladreville's only pretender to the title of sheriff might be in his office. Whenever they had an appointment, by some strange coincidence, Michel always left on an important errand mere minutes before Clay arrived. Perhaps today would be different.

꼭

Sarah took a deep breath, trying to quell the fear that had been a frequent companion for the past six months. It would have been different if she'd been alone. Sarah knew how to care for herself, but caring for Thea changed everything. A small child demanded constant attention, a combination of entertainment and vigilance. Though it was more exhausting than she'd dreamed possible, Sarah thought she'd been successful. Until this morning. How on earth had she slept through Thea's waking?

"Horsey." Thea giggled as she pointed toward the animals pulling the wagon. Clay had apologized for the absence of a buggy, explaining that when it had fallen into disrepair after his mother's death no one had seen a need to replace it.

"That's right, sweetie." Sarah kept her arm around her sister. Though her heartbeat had returned to normal, the memory of waking and realizing she was alone in the cabin lingered. She'd been fortunate. Thea had not been in danger. When Sarah had found her sister, Thea had been giggling and holding onto Clay as if she belonged in his arms. But she didn't. Clay's expression and the unmistakable way he'd avoided looking at Thea during breakfast told Sarah the man did not like children. That was one reason she kept Thea close to her. She had promised not to be a burden, and that was a promise she intended to keep. Somehow she'd find a way to earn money, to prevent Thea from bothering Clay and, most importantly, to ensure her sister's safety.

Sarah took another deep breath, forcing back the fear of failure. The future—her future and Thea's—was waiting across the river in Ladreville, Texas.

"Look, Thea. Houses."

The town was not what she had expected. Of course, Sarah had to admit, nothing in Texas had been what she had expected. She had expected a bridegroom and a peaceful existence in the house he'd built for them. Instead . . .

Sarah forced a smile onto her face. She couldn't change the past. All she could do was create a future. And she would. She'd find a future for her and Thea in this town that was so different from San Antonio, Philadelphia, and every other city she'd seen.

Sarah's smile became genuine as she realized that Ladreville looked like a storybook come to life. The two-story half-timbered buildings with their steeply pitched roofs made her think she'd stepped into the pages of one of her German books.

Sarah's smile broadened as she remembered how often Mama had spoken of taking her and Thea on the Grand Tour. The family would not make that trip, but it appeared that Sarah and Thea would be living in a small piece of Europe. Surely that was a good sign.

"Pretty."

It was indeed. Though Austin had written that the town had been founded by Alsatian immigrants, he'd neglected to mention that the settlers had replicated their European architecture in Texas.

"This is the Hochstrasse," Clay said. He'd been silent for

most of the trip, preoccupied, Sarah surmised, with thoughts of whatever it was he hoped to accomplish in town. "That's 'high street' in German," he added. "From what I've heard, almost every German town had a Hochstrasse."

Sarah saw no reason to tell Clay she didn't need the translation and that she was familiar with German street names. Instead, she smiled again, then looked down the road. Ladreville, although considerably smaller than San Antonio, was spotlessly clean and appeared to be prosperous, its main street lined with houses, shops, and two gleaming white steeples.

Though she wouldn't have expected a town this small to have two churches, Sarah suspected that was the result of the centuries-old enmity between France and Germany, an enmity that had resulted in wars and in Alsace, the townspeople's former home, being traded back and forth between the two countries. Ladreville, Sarah could see by the names on the storefronts, had both German and French settlers. Those settlers, she guessed, worshiped in separate churches.

As Thea bounced with excitement, Sarah pulled her onto her lap, pointing out early blooming flowers and a sausage-shaped dog. The town was not only a mélange of France and Germany, it was also a mixture of Europe and America. Older women dressed in European-style garb walked briskly toward the center of town, some accompanied by their daughters. The younger girls, unlike their mothers, wore clothing that would not have been out of place in Philadelphia.

Sarah and Thea, it appeared, would not be shunned for their attire. Even more importantly, as San Antonio had, Ladreville exuded an unmistakable air of vitality. Looking at the town and seeing Thea's excitement, Sarah felt her fears subside, replaced by the sweet taste of hope. Perhaps their future, though far different from the one she'd imagined, would be a good one.

While Clay remained silent, Thea chattered as the wagon rumbled further down the street, stopping in front of a store with a large plate glass window. No sign was necessary, for the merchandise in the window announced that this was Ladreville's mercantile. The proprietors, Clay had told Sarah, were named Rousseau. A small plate on the door confirmed that.

When he'd helped Sarah and Thea alight, Clay touched the brim of his hat. "I'll be back in an hour."

As soon as her feet touched the ground, Thea started to skip. Had she been able, Sarah would have joined her. Instead, she grabbed her sister's hand and opened the door.

"*Bonjour, madame.*" Though both a man and a woman stood behind the counter, it was the petite brunette who greeted Sarah.

As her eyes adjusted to the darkness, Sarah smiled at the young woman. A few inches shorter than her own five feet four, she also appeared to be several years younger. A quick glance at the woman's ringless hands told Sarah she was unmarried. Her own gloves and the presence of Thea, who was young enough to be her daughter, had made the proprietor believe Sarah was married.

"*Bonjour, mademoiselle,*" Sarah said in the French she'd perfected during those long years when everyone had feared she'd never walk again. "*Je suis Mademoiselle Sarah Dobbs.*"

The brunette's eyes widened in surprise. "Miss Dobbs, of course." She switched to only slightly accented English. "Austin told Léon about you." Gesturing toward the man who remained behind the counter, she said, "Léon, come meet Austin's . . ." The woman's voice trailed off, and the flush staining her face told Sarah she wasn't certain how to categorize Sarah, since the word *fiancée* no longer applied.

"Isabelle, tais-toi."

Isabelle glared at the man whose resemblance, not to mention the familiar way he addressed her, marked him as her brother.

"I'm so sorry for your loss, Miss Dobbs," she said. Despite her brother's admonition, it was obvious she had no intention of remaining silent. "Austin was a wonderful man."

"And a good friend," her brother chimed in. "We all miss him."

Clearly bored by the adults' conversation, Thea reached toward the counter, her small hands grabbing at a glass jar. Sarah captured both hands in hers and nodded at Isabelle and Léon. "Perhaps some other time you can tell me more about him. Today I need . . ." Thea jerked her hand free. "No, Thea. You can't touch that."

"What can I get for you, Miss Dobbs?" As Isabelle gestured toward the shelves lining the back of the store, two women entered the store. Though they conversed softly, Sarah realized they were speaking German. "We have almost everything you could want," Isabelle continued. As she stationed herself behind the counter, Sarah noticed that Isabelle was wearing a small gold cross around her neck. Instinctively, Sarah touched her own collar. It wasn't there, of course. She'd removed the cross the day Reverend Lang had told her Papa could not be buried in hallowed ground.

Blinking rapidly to keep her tears from falling, Sarah said, "I need some thread." Thank goodness her voice did not betray her sorrow. "I'm afraid I used my entire supply mending Thea's clothing on the journey West."

Though she knew all too well the dangers of eavesdropping, Sarah couldn't help noticing that when Léon approached the women and attempted to serve them, his command of the German language appeared to consist of nothing more than a greeting. The women's English was equally limited.

"What color would you like?" Isabelle pulled out a tray of thread.

As Sarah selected a spool of black, she gave the brunette another smile. Isabelle appeared friendly, and as someone who worked in the store, she was in a position to overhear many conversations. Perhaps she could help with Sarah's other needs. "There is something else," she told the young Frenchwoman. "Austin's death changed my situation, and now I must find a way to earn my room and board. Do you know of anyone in Ladreville who might be looking for help?"

Isabelle's expression was doubtful. She fingered the cross around her neck, then smiled. "I'll ask Maman. She knows everyone's business." With a nod toward the door that Sarah surmised led to the Rousseaus' dwelling, Isabelle said, "It'll take only a moment."

Sarah bent down to ruffle Thea's hair. Thank goodness the child appeared content to sit on the floor and play with her doll. Above them the conversation between the German women and Léon continued. Everyone, it was clear, was frustrated, and the women appeared to be on the verge of leaving the store.

A glimmer of an idea danced before Sarah's eyes. Carefully she rose and turned toward the women. "Perhaps I might assist you," she offered in fluent German.

A smile lit the older of the two women's faces. *"Sie spricht deutsch!"* she announced to her companion.

"Ja. Ich spreche deutsch." Sarah smiled at the potential customers. "I would be honored to help you." Excitedly, the two women began to speak at the same time. Sarah held up a cautionary hand to slow the barrage of words, then relayed their requests to Léon one by one. By the time Isabelle and her mother arrived, Léon had a large pile of purchases assembled on the counter.

Madame Rousseau stared at her son. "What happened?" she demanded in French. "Frau Bauer and Frau Kentzel have never bought so much."

Léon nodded toward Sarah. "Miss Dobbs helped them. She speaks German."

"Evidemment." Madame Rousseau gave Sarah an appraising look. It was only after the two German women had left, their arms filled with purchases, that Isabelle's mother addressed Sarah. "My daughter told me you were in search of work. I regret . . ."

Sarah could see the older woman searching for the correct English word. "I also speak French," she told Madame Rousseau in her native tongue.

"That is most unusual for an American." Madame Rousseau managed a small smile before her face turned serious again. "I regret that I have no suggestions for you, mademoiselle. Ladreville is a small town. We have simple needs."

Thea, who had been sitting quietly at Sarah's feet, chose that moment to scramble to her feet and run toward the door. "Excuse me, madame," Sarah said as she grabbed Thea's arm. "My sister is still excited about being in a new place."

"I understand." Madame Rousseau shook her head slowly. "I wish I could help you."

The thoughts that whirled through Sarah's mind began to crystallize. "I believe, madame, that I could help you." When the woman looked skeptical, Sarah said, "This is Ladreville's only store, is it not?"

Madame Rousseau nodded.

Sarah gestured toward the front door. "I assume from the fact that this street has a German name that German residents outnumber the French."

Another nod, this one accompanied by an expression of curiosity.

"Correct me if I am wrong, but it appears that no one in your family speaks German."

A third nod.

Sarah's confidence rose. This could be the solution to her problem. "As you've seen, I speak both French and German. If you would hire me to work here, the increased sales should more than offset the wages you would pay me."

Before Madame Rousseau could reply, both of her children began to speak.

"Then you wouldn't need me, Maman." Léon grinned as he touched his mother's arm. "I could work for Karl Friedrich."

"Don't you see, Maman," Isabelle said, her expression more earnest than her brother's. "Miss Dobbs is the answer to our prayers."

Madame Rousseau raised an eyebrow as she looked first at Isabelle, then at Léon. "I will have to ask your father." She turned toward the interior door.

"That means yes," Isabelle whispered. "Papa always does what Maman wants."

Though she gave no sign that she had heard her daughter's words, Madame Rousseau halted, her hand on the doorknob. "If my husband should agree, and mind you, I'm not saying he will, but if he should, you must make arrangements for the child. The store is no place for her."

Sarah nodded slowly, her initial excitement starting to ebb as she realized she had solved one problem only to create another. What had she expected? Nothing had been easy since that day in September. Only a fool would have thought her luck would change. Sarah Dobbs, it appeared, was a fool.

3

"Good morning, Mayor." As Clay had hoped, since Michel Ladre hadn't been expecting him, the man who'd transplanted a bit of Alsace into the heart of Texas a decade before was in his office.

"Good to see you, Clay." The older man rose from behind his desk. Though of modest height, he was still a commanding presence, his brown eyes intense, his dark hair only slightly mottled with gray. At forty-eight, he was the same age as Pa. The years, however, had been far kinder to Michel Ladre than they had to Clay's father.

Clay looked around, his lips tightening. The town's founder, mayor, sheriff, and self-appointed arbiter of every dispute kept a map of Alsace on his wall, along with pictures of the succession of rulers who'd invaded, conquered, and oppressed Alsace's citizens. They were, he claimed, reminders of all the townspeople had overcome. Austin had scoffed every time he'd spoken of those pictures, declaring that the colonists hadn't bettered their lives the way they'd hoped but had merely exchanged one form of despotism for another.

Clay's lips tightened again. His brother had worried about the townspeople. Clay did not. He had enough worries of his own, starting with why Michel Ladre was treating Austin's murder as if it were nothing more than a petty crime.

Before Clay could speak, the mayor pulled out his watch and frowned. "Unfortunately," he said in a tone that sounded anything but regretful, "I was on my way out. I'm afraid that the matter is urgent."

Since Ladreville's founder had been sitting with his boots propped on the desk, the picture of indolence, when he arrived, Clay doubted the story was true.

"This will only take a moment." Michel had not invited him to sit, and Clay preferred not to. Some things were best discussed standing up. But he did position himself in front of the door to keep the mayor from leaving. "I want to know what progress you've made in finding my brother's murderer."

"*Je regrette.*" Michel frowned, then reverted to English. "These things take time."

That was the same thing he had said when Clay had seen him three days ago. "How long can it take to talk to seven men?"

The mayor frowned again and shook his head slowly. When he spoke, his words were deliberate, his tone one Clay imagined he would have used when speaking to a small child or a not-very-bright adult. "If only it were that simple, Clay. Austin's murderer could have been anyone, even a Comanche."

Biting back his anger, Clay forced himself to respond calmly. There was no point in alienating the town's only lawman. "My brother would not have allowed a Comanche to come that close to him. Austin didn't even pull his gun. That means the man who killed him had to be someone he knew and trusted."

"Many more than seven men fit that description. It could include everyone in Ladreville. Your brother knew everyone."

While that was true, Clay wasn't certain Austin had trusted them all. He knew for a fact that Austin hadn't trusted the man standing next to the desk, at least not with the town's finances.

Keeping his voice as even as if he were discussing the weather, Clay said, "It makes sense that the killer was someone Austin was playing poker with." Those men were the ones closest to him. They were the ones who knew where Austin was that night and what time he left the Brambles' barn.

"It may make sense to you, Clay," Michel said in that infuriatingly condescending voice, "but let me remind you that I'm the one who's conducting this investigation. I need to consider all possibilities."

"What harm would there be in starting with the last people who saw Austin alive?"

"None, other than to waste my time." The mayor picked up his hat. "As much as I regret being unable to continue this conversation, I must leave."

It was as Clay had suspected. Michel Ladre had no intention of questioning the other poker players, perhaps because his own son had been one of them, perhaps because Michel himself had few regrets that Austin was dead.

"If you're not willing to talk to those men, I will."

The mayor clenched his fist. "I'm afraid I cannot permit that."

"I'm afraid you cannot prevent that." Clay had already

spoken to the men, but he'd kept the conversations casual. In doing that, he'd learned nothing. Each of the seven had the same story: they'd all remained in the barn from the time Austin left until well past the hour when Nora had arrived back at the Bar C, Austin's body slumped over her back. Clay didn't believe them. One of them had killed his brother, and if Michel Ladre wasn't willing to find out who it was, Clay had no choice but to do it himself. Austin's murderer would pay for his crime.

"You might be on the lookout for Austin's watch," Clay told the man who claimed he was investigating the murder. "Austin had it when he left that night, and it wasn't in his pocket when he—"

Michel didn't let him finish the sentence. "He probably lost it," the mayor said, dismissing Clay's suggestion.

Clay shook his head. "That watch was Austin's most prized possession, especially that day. He'd just put Sarah's miniature in it and was planning to show it to his friends." Though he doubted Michel would take any action, Clay continued, "Like I said, Mayor, someone needs to question those men. Thoroughly."

Michel took a step toward Clay, his position menacing. With a gesture toward the side door, he hissed, "If you interfere with my investigation, you'll find yourself sitting inside that cell."

"Then do your job."

The man's face flushed as the implication registered. "I am, and I'm doing it far better than you could." Michel's voice seethed with anger. "Face it, Clay. There's a reason why I'm the mayor and sheriff of this town, and you're a doctor. If you're wiser than your brother, you'll do your job and leave me alone to do mine."

Clay stared at the man who held the power of life and death over the citizens of Ladreville. Michel Ladre was wrong on many counts. He was wrong about who had killed Austin. He was wrong about his own abilities. And he was wrong about Clay. Clay wasn't a doctor. Not any longer.

❧

They were waiting for him, just as they had been a day earlier. The wagon was the same. The passengers were the same. He was even late again, although for a different reason. Today he had chosen to be late, deliberately waiting until his temper cooled before he headed back down Hochstrasse. That wasn't the only difference. Today, instead of standing on the street, her annoyance clearly apparent, Sarah was smiling and talking to Isabelle Rousseau as if they had been friends for years, while Thea appeared to be joining the conversation.

Clay never had understood why the females of the species spent so much time jabbering. Even Patience had talked more than Clay would have liked. Fortunately, Sarah hadn't subjected him to that same degree of chatter on the ride from San Antonio, and she'd seemed to sense his need for silence when they'd driven into town this morning. That was good. What was even better was that once today was over, she'd have limited opportunities to say anything to him.

Clay halted the wagon in front of the mercantile, then climbed out to assist Sarah and her sister.

"Papa!" He'd no sooner put his feet on the ground when Thea raised her arms toward him. She was a child, Clay reminded himself, but surely even a child could learn that he was not her father. Apparently oblivious to Clay's frown, the little girl giggled. Then, when he did not immediately pick her up, she wrapped her arms around his leg. Clay's frown deepened.

With an apologetic glance at him, Sarah untangled the child's arms. "That's Mr. Canfield, sweetie." She knelt next to her sister. "Say it: Mr. Canfield."

Thea looked up at Clay, those brown eyes so like her sister's glowing with happiness.

"Papa Clay," she announced.

Though Sarah frowned, Clay heard laughter. He glared at the source and said slowly, "Good morning, Miss Rousseau." Unlike Thea, Isabelle Rousseau understood anger when it was directed at her. Her face red with embarrassment, the young woman bade Sarah farewell and returned to the store.

Once Clay had Sarah and Thea settled in the wagon, he flicked the reins. The sooner he was across the river, the better. During the time he strode along the Medina's banks, trying to beat his anger back to manageable levels, Clay had decided to give Michel Ladre one more week. If the man had made no progress in finding Austin's killer by the end of that time, Clay would take matters into his own hands. And— with only a modicum of luck—within that week Miss Sarah Dobbs and her sister would have realized that Ladreville was not their home.

"Were you able to find everything you needed?" he asked Sarah as the horses started to ford the river. The package she'd stowed in the back of the wagon was smaller than he'd expected. Perhaps she'd already realized how unsuitable Ladreville was and had purchased only what she needed for the return journey.

Sarah nodded. "In fact, I accomplished more than I'd hoped." There was no ignoring the excitement in her voice.

That was not a good sign. She was supposed to be discouraged and disillusioned. Instead, Clay had a feeling that he would not like her next sentence. He did not.

"The Rousseaus have hired me to work in their store."

Clay kept his eyes on the river while he tried to dislodge the large, immovable lump that had settled in his stomach. Luck—even the tiny bit he'd hoped for—was not with him. Clay knew, as surely as he did that Austin hadn't deserved to die, that if Sarah was employed and became part of the community, she and her sister might not leave Ladreville. Ever.

"Are you certain you want to do this?" he asked, searching for a way to dissuade her.

"You mean, remain in Ladreville?" When Clay nodded, Sarah smiled one of those smiles that made her almost beautiful. "Yes," she said. "I want this to be our home." With a self-deprecating shrug, she continued, "I'll admit I've never worked in a store before, but I'm confident I can do it."

Clay wouldn't dispute that. The letters she'd written to Austin had revealed a good measure of determination. So, too, had her actions in the past day. If the knowledge that her bridegroom was dead hadn't made Sarah flee, Clay suspected that not much would discourage her. Still, he'd hoped she would come to her senses and return to Philadelphia.

She was silent for a moment, and Clay could see the indecision on her face. "There is a small problem," she admitted at last. Her voice told Clay the problem was larger than she wanted to acknowledge.

"What kind of problem?"

Sarah hugged her sister, then stroked the child's head. "I can't take Thea with me. Madame Rousseau was adamant about that."

After watching them together, Clay knew that was a very large problem. Sarah did not like to let her sister out of her sight, even for a few minutes. She wouldn't, as Pa used to say, take kindly to the idea of being separated for the entire working day. On the other hand, Clay understood the Rousseaus's position. He had been inside the mercantile and could not imagine as active a child as Thea spending hours there. What would Sarah do?

When Austin had learned of Thea's existence, he had told Clay the presence of a child was another part of God's plan. They had both discussed the fact that, although a bride would normally be in charge of the household, Martina could not be displaced from her position as housekeeper. Not only was their father dependent on her, but he had promised Martina and Miguel positions on the Bar C for the rest of their lives. That was the crux of the problem. Although no one expected Austin's wife to work on the ranch, both Clay and Austin knew she would require something to occupy her days. Caring for Thea, Austin had declared, would give Sarah something to do while they waited to be blessed with a child of their own. That was God's plan, he claimed. Unfortunately, the plan was not working out the way Austin had envisioned.

"Martina's too busy to watch Thea," Clay told Sarah.

She nodded. "I assumed that. I'm hoping to find someone in town who'd be willing to keep Thea during the day. Isabelle mentioned a woman named Frau Reismueller."

The Reismuellers had six children of their own. While Clay doubted they'd object to caring for another, he was not certain it was the best place for Thea. She was accustomed to a lot of attention, and that was something Frau Reismueller could not provide.

Stop it! Clay told himself. *This is Sarah's problem, not yours. If Thea's unhappy here, maybe they'll leave.* But, despite his admonitions, Clay could not stop thinking about the child.

As the wagon rolled by the Bramble ranch, he stared at his neighbors' home. "There may be another answer." Clay gestured toward the two-story house and adjacent barn. "Mrs. Bramble might be able to help you. She doesn't do any of the ranch work, so she'd have time. And"—this was the trump card—"her son David was Austin's closest friend. She might consider caring for Thea an act of friendship."

Sarah appeared pleased by the suggestion. "Could we stop there now?"

Clay had no intention of spending time listening to two women chatter. "Wait until tomorrow. Today's your first lesson in driving a wagon." And, if Clay was a good teacher, her last. Once she could control the wagon, they could go their separate ways, and he wouldn't be bothered by a woman and a little girl who reminded him of dreams that would never come true.

◦◦◦

He didn't mind the horses, Clay reflected as he smoothed wrinkles from the saddle blanket and reached for Shadow's saddle. Although he disliked almost everything else associated with the ranch, he didn't begrudge the time he spent with the horses.

Clay tightened the cinches and led Shadow out of the stable. The sky was the faultless blue that he associated with the happy days of his childhood. It would be the perfect weather for a ride, if Clay were a child again. But he was not a child. Those carefree days were over, replaced by adult responsibilities, the foremost of which were hundreds of what Pa used to call "gold on the hoof." Clay had other, far less complimentary, terms for the cattle. To him, the animals Pa thought were so valuable were nothing but a source of endless work. The roundup was bad enough, but there was also the branding, the constant culling out of the sick and injured, the feeding of orphan calves, and the worry that a sudden storm, drought, or rustlers would wreak destruction.

"No, sirree," Clay muttered as he mounted Shadow. Raising steers was not the life he would have chosen, no matter how lucrative it could be. He never had understood why Austin and Pa found ranching so rewarding. They spoke of freedom, of the wide-open spaces, of not being at someone's beck and call. Ha! What was ranching other than being at the beck and call of a herd of ornery black steers? There was more satisfaction to be found in setting one broken leg than in all the money that the Bar C reaped from selling those critters.

Shadow whinnied, as if he agreed. "Who do you suppose set Sarah's leg?" Clay asked. It was probably crazy, talking to his horse, but there was no one else around. A man might not crave the constant chatter females provided, but he did like to exercise his vocal cords occasionally. "Whoever it was, he must not have been very skilled. She shouldn't limp that much."

Clay shook his head while his eyes searched the horizon, looking for anything out of the ordinary. There was no point in thinking about Sarah Dobbs. Even if she did remain in Ladreville for more than a week, it wasn't as if Clay could do anything about her limp. Not now. He had read about rebreaking and setting bones that hadn't knit properly, but it was reported to be a very painful procedure with no guarantee of success. Clay wasn't the man to try that or any other surgical procedure. Not anymore.

Cattle were his future, and they would be until the day Austin's murderer paid for his deeds. On that day, Clay would pack up Pa and head East, knowing that his brother's death had been avenged. When Clay shook the dust of Ladreville from his boots that day, it would be for the last time. Then and only then would he think about doctoring.

He flicked the reins to turn Shadow. "Let's go, boy." When he reached the highest point on the ranch, Clay slowed the horse to a walk. Though Shadow loved to run, there was no point in exhausting him when they had another section of the ranch to cover before dinner. They'd rest here on Clay's favorite vantage point for a few minutes, then continue in search of those pesky cattle.

Clay needed to clear his head, and this was one spot that never failed to do exactly that. From here, he could see the road, the neighboring ranch houses, and the entire town of Ladreville. From this distance, there were no cattle in sight. From this distance, the town and countryside appeared to be a scene of perfect tranquility. Best of all, from this distance, there was no hint that a murderer walked the streets or that ancient rivalries divided the townspeople.

Taking a deep breath, Clay started to turn, then stopped. When he had first arrived on the bluff, he had noticed the doctor's buggy crossing the river. It was such an ordinary occurrence that Clay had attached no significance to it. But now, if the horse's casual grazing was any indication, the buggy wasn't moving. That was odd. Normally Herman drove quickly, knowing that even apparently mild symptoms could turn dangerous in a short time and that when people summoned the doctor, they wanted him there that very moment. Clay squinted. There was no doubt about it. The horse, the buggy, and Dr. Herman Adler were going nowhere.

"C'mon, Shadow." Clay's horse needed little encouragement to gallop, and within a few minutes, he had reached Ladreville's only practicing physician. As Clay had feared when he'd seen the motionless buggy, something was wrong. Herman was slumped in the seat, the reins fallen from his hands.

"Herman, are you all right?" The older man's face had lost its normal ruddy hue, and his gray hair was disheveled, as if the doctor had run his hands through it. That bothered Clay almost as much as his colleague's pallor, for Herman was a notorious dandy.

The man winced. "It'll pass. It always does."

With a trained eye, Clay assessed the man's color, the grip he maintained on the edge of the seat, and the way he refused to open his eyes. "Where is the pain?" Clay asked, seeking confirmation of his diagnosis.

Herman winced again. "Behind my eyes." He took a deep breath in an obvious attempt to lessen the pain, then added, "It's worse today than before."

Repetitive incidents. Increasing severity. Clay frowned, grateful that Herman's eyes were still closed. One of the first rules he had learned in medical school was the importance of allaying patients' fears by never showing them your concerns. Herman was a good enough doctor that he probably recognized the symptoms, but if he didn't, the middle of an episode was not the time to discuss diagnosis and prognosis, especially when both were grim. If what Clay thought was true, it wasn't only he and Herman who should be concerned. All of Ladreville would suffer when its doctor could no longer practice.

"We're going to the Bar C," Clay said in a voice that brooked no dissent. "You can rest there." Quickly dismounting, he tied Shadow to the back of the buggy and took the reins from Herman.

"I can't," the older man muttered. His shuttered eyes and the creases bracketing his mouth attested to the pain's intensity. "Mrs. Bramble is expecting me."

"Mrs. Bramble is the healthiest person in the county." Far healthier than Herman at this moment, although Clay forbore mentioning that particular fact.

A faint smile crossed the older man's face. "It's true that I've never found anything wrong, even on her most urgent calls." The color was returning to Herman's face, and he had lessened his grip on the seat. Though it appeared the worst of the attack was over, the man still needed to rest, especially if his next patient was Mary Bramble.

"I reckon she's set her cap for you."

Herman's eyes flew open, revealing an expression of pure terror. "That's absurd!"

"Is it?" The diversion was having its desired effect. "Everyone in the county knows Mary Bramble doesn't like being a widow. She used to bring my father cakes and pies practically every week until Pa told her he had no intention of remarrying." Clay chuckled at the memory of the woman's scarlet face the last time she had come to the ranch. "I hate to say this, Herman, but it looks as if you're next on her list."

Dr. Herman Adler grimaced, and this time Clay knew

it was not from physical pain. "And to think I believed the headaches were my worst problem."

❦

Clay was right, Sarah mused. Driving the wagon wasn't difficult. The horses seemed not to mind that her grip on the reins was tentative. They moved in the directions she wanted; they stopped when she told them to. The hardest part of driving was controlling Thea. That was why, in anticipation of her sister's inclination to squirm, Sarah had tied her to the bench. Though Thea protested not being able to peer over the edge of the wagon, she was safe.

Fortunately, it wasn't much further to the Brambles' ranch. Once they reached it, Thea would be able to run. Then would come the hardest part of the visit—seeing whether Mrs. Bramble was willing to care for a child as active as Thea and whether Thea would like the woman.

Sarah had hardly slept last night, thinking about everything she'd seen in Ladreville and how, if she saved her money carefully, she would be able to buy one of those fairytale houses for herself and Thea. They'd be independent then, and there'd be no need for a horse, even one attached to a wagon. But no matter how much Sarah might want to work at the mercantile, Thea's needs came first. If Sarah couldn't find the right woman to care for her, she would have to find another way to earn the money they needed.

"We're almost there."

Larger than the house at the Bar C, the two-story building that formed the center of the Lazy B ranch was also surrounded by more outbuildings than the Bar C. According to Clay, Mrs. Bramble had once tried to be self-sufficient and had employed a farrier as well as ranch hands and enough men to till the acres she'd devoted to farming. Though she'd abandoned farming once Ladreville's residents began selling their produce, the extra buildings remained.

As the wagon rattled its way up the lane, the front door opened and a woman stepped onto the porch.

"Come in, my dear." Mrs. Bramble greeted Sarah with such enthusiasm that it appeared she and Thea had been expected. It wasn't the welcome and the broad smile that gave Sarah that impression but, rather, their neighbor's clothing. Sarah didn't claim to be an expert on Ladreville fashion etiquette, but surely the navy silk with white lace trim wasn't something a woman wore unless she was going to church or expecting important visitors. Perhaps Clay had stopped by the ranch earlier this morning to say that Sarah would be coming.

"Good morning, Mrs. Bramble." Sarah climbed down from the wagon and lifted Thea into her arms. "I'm—"

"Sarah Dobbs, Austin's fiancée." The tall woman whose dark hair was only lightly threaded with gray gave Sarah an appraising look, her brown eyes seeming to take in every detail of Sarah's appearance. "I reckon you're even prettier than your miniature," she said at last. "And this must be Thea."

To Sarah's surprise, when Mrs. Bramble reached for Thea, her sister went willingly into the older woman's arms. At home—in Philadelphia, Sarah corrected herself—Thea was normally shy with strangers, but she'd displayed no reticence around Clay and now with their neighbor. Sarah felt the knot of tension that had caused her head to ache begin to unravel. The first hurdle was passed. Thea had not taken an immediate dislike to Mrs. Bramble, and the older woman appeared to like children.

"Your sister's gonna be a beauty when she grows up, just like you."

Sarah blinked in surprise. Mama had been beautiful. Papa told her that every day. But not once had anyone claimed Sarah was beautiful. When people described her, it was as "that girl with the unfortunate limp."

"Don't fret none. You'll find yourself another suitor soon," Mrs. Bramble continued. "Why, my David will be sorry he missed you. There ain't many pretty girls in Ladreville, you know."

Sarah didn't want another suitor. Though love hadn't been part of the plan, on the long journey West, she had admitted to herself that she was more than halfway in love with the man who'd written those wonderful letters, the ones she called her paper roses. As she'd traveled, she'd dreamed of happily-ever-after. Sadly, those dreams had died along with Austin, and now that she'd had a brief taste of love, Sarah knew that marrying someone else was something she'd consider only if she could find no other way to protect Thea.

She gave Mrs. Bramble a noncommittal smile.

"What kind of neighbor am I, leaving you standing on the porch?" Mrs. Bramble ushered Sarah inside. "Come and visit for a while. I have some cool tea and a coffee cake ready." It hadn't been Sarah's imagination that Mrs. Bramble had been expecting visitors. Clay must have been here.

"Your home is very pretty," Sarah said as she took a seat in the parlor. To Sarah's relief, Thea seemed content to sit on the floor and play with her doll, leaving Sarah to admire her surroundings. Unlike the Bar C, which was a purely masculine abode, this room bore feminine touches. Crocheted antimacassars protected the chairs; a bouquet of dried flowers graced an end table; delicate watercolors hung on two walls.

Mrs. Bramble smiled. "Thank you. It's too big for just David and me, but it's our home. Now," she said, "if'n you wait a moment, I'll be back with refreshments."

"Please, don't bother on our account."

The older woman shook her head. "Nonsense. I'm glad to have the chance to meet you before you go back East."

Before Sarah could explain that she and Thea would not be leaving Ladreville, Mrs. Bramble left the room. When she returned, she was carrying a silver tray laden with a pitcher, glasses, and a plate of delicious-smelling cake. How on earth was Thea going to manage such adult fare without making a mess? Seeing Sarah's worried look, the older woman shook her head. "Don't you fret none about crumbs. They'll clean up."

The coffee cake was as delicious as its aroma promised, the tea cool and refreshing. Though Sarah savored both, what pleased her most was the way Mrs. Bramble regarded Thea. Though she'd provided a tin plate for Thea instead of the delicate china one she'd used for Sarah's cake, she did not flinch at the inevitable crumbs. Sarah started to relax. It appeared that Mrs. Bramble enjoyed the company of children and that, as Clay had indicated, her days were not filled with work. If she agreed to Sarah's proposal, Thea would be well cared for here.

Sarah kept the conversation light while they ate. It was only fair to give Mrs. Bramble time to observe Thea before she made any decisions. If anything about her sister's behavior appeared to annoy the older woman, Sarah would say nothing. This would become a purely social visit.

Once her cake was finished, Sarah cleaned Thea's hands and encouraged her to play with her doll. That ploy worked for only a few minutes. Obviously bored, Sarah's sister climbed onto the settee next to Mrs. Bramble.

"Pretty." She smiled and stretched her hand toward the older woman's gold locket.

"No, Thea." Sarah knew from painful experience that Thea would try to pull the necklace off. Shiny objects allured her sister, and the oval pendant with its filigreed surface would be almost irresistible to her. "Your locket is beautiful," Sarah told Mrs. Bramble as she settled Thea back on the floor where she could do no harm.

The older woman's smile was bittersweet. "It's very dear to me, a gift from my late husband. He was killed in the war with Mexico, you know."

"I'm sorry." What else could she say? Sarah knew all too well the sense of loss and loneliness caused by the death of a family member.

"If Mr. Bramble had lived, David's and my lives would have been different." Mrs. Bramble's eyes flashed with something Sarah thought was pain. She closed them for a second, as if trying to control her emotions. When she opened her eyes again, Mrs. Bramble shook her head slowly. "Forgive me for speakin' of death when you just learned of Austin's." She reached over to pat Sarah's hand. "It's downright dreadful that you come all this way for naught."

"It wasn't for naught. I plan to make Ladreville my home and Thea's."

Mrs. Bramble's confusion was obvious. "I don't understand, unless . . ." She gave Sarah another of those long, appraising looks. "Has Clay offered to marry you?"

"No, ma'am." This was the opening Sarah needed. It was time to tell Mrs. Bramble her plans and see whether she was willing to be part of them. "I don't expect to marry, but I do want to stay and make a home for myself and Thea." Mrs. Bramble raised an eyebrow, encouraging Sarah to continue. "The Rousseaus have offered me a job in their store."

For a moment the only sound was Thea's conversation with her doll. At last Mrs. Bramble spoke. "I see."

Though the words were simple, Sarah thought she detected disapproval. Perhaps the older woman was so opposed to the idea of Sarah's working that she wouldn't agree to help her. There was only one way to find out.

"I have a problem, though. The store is not a good place for a child of Thea's age." As Mrs. Bramble nodded, Sarah took a deep breath. "I wondered whether you would consider caring for her during the day. I'd pay you, of course."

The older woman's expression was guarded. She looked at Thea and then back at Sarah. "It's been more than twenty years since I had a child that age."

She wasn't going to agree. The tone of her voice told Sarah that. She hoped her own expression didn't reflect her dismay. There were other women in Ladreville, Sarah reminded herself. But would any of them have the same rapport with Thea that she'd seen here?

Mrs. Bramble stared out the window, her indecision clear. Her left hand covered her mouth, then dropped to touch her locket, and still she said nothing. Sarah clenched her fists. She'd never been good at waiting. At last Mrs. Bramble looked at Thea, then raised her eyes to meet Sarah's gaze. "I reckon it would be like having a grandchild," she said with a smile that made Sarah's worries melt faster than spring snow. "Yes, I'll do it." Mrs. Bramble continued. "Thea and I will get along fine, won't we?" She opened her arms and welcomed Thea into them. "But there won't be no money involved. Is that clear?"

Sarah felt tears of joy sting her eyes. This was so much more than she'd expected. If she didn't have to pay Mrs. Bramble, she would be able to buy a house that much sooner. When that happened, not only would she and Thea be truly independent, but they'd no longer be a burden to Clay. "I don't know how to thank you."

Mrs. Bramble's eyes shone. "My pleasure. I figger it's a neighborly thing to do."

A clock chimed, and Sarah's hostess frowned. "I reckoned he'd be here by now."

As the words registered, Sarah realized her instincts had been accurate. Mrs. Bramble had been expecting someone, but it wasn't her and Thea. She started to rise. "It's time for us to go back to the Bar C."

"Nonsense. The doctor is sometimes late."

Doctor? Sarah tried not to be alarmed. Though Mrs. Bramble appeared healthy, if she had some ailment, she should not be caring for Thea. It would be too much of a strain. "I hope it's nothing serious."

As if she understood Sarah's concerns, Mrs. Bramble shook her head. "A touch of nerves. It ain't nothing that would stop me from taking right good care of your sister."

Sarah let out the breath she hadn't been aware she was holding. "I'm glad to hear that, and not just for selfish reasons. I could find someone else to care for Thea, but I'd hate to lose a friend, especially one I've just met."

Mrs. Bramble started to place the plates and glasses back

on the tray. "I hope we will be friends. Out here, a woman cain't have too many friends." She looked up at Sarah. "This here's a bit of advice from a friend. If'n you and Thea ever need a doctor, make sure and call Dr. Adler. You might be tempted to ask Clay, seeing as how he's right there, but that would be a mistake."

"Clay?" Sarah didn't understand.

Mrs. Bramble pursed her lips. "The townspeople are mighty impressed by his degree from the Massachusetts Medical College. To my mind, that ain't nothing but a piece of paper. What counts is experience. For all his fancy training, Clay ain't a very good doctor. He cain't help his father, and he didn't save his wife when she was dying."

Clay had been married? His wife had died? Sarah felt the blood drain from her face. No wonder he seemed angry. He had lost almost everyone he loved. The poor, poor man!

❦

Sarah's mind was still reeling as she tried to swallow the food Martina had put in front of her and Thea. Though her sister was eating with relish, Sarah barely tasted the dishes. Poor Clay! How had he borne the pain? Sarah's happiness in finding someone to care for Thea during the day was tempered by the knowledge of what Clay had endured. When her parents had died, for the first few days Sarah had blamed herself, believing there must have been something she could have done to stop Papa. Gradually, though, she had realized that nothing she could have said or done would have changed his mind. That was when her sorrow had turned to anger.

Sarah took a sip of water before she broke another piece of cornbread for Thea. The visit with Mrs. Bramble, although brief, had been filled with revelations she was still trying to understand. Clay was a doctor. No wonder he'd been so solicitous when he'd told Sarah of Austin's death. No wonder he'd been so concerned about Thea's being bitten by a snake. No wonder his hands weren't as callused as Sarah had expected.

Being a doctor was wonderful. It meant easing pain and saving lives. It also meant accepting responsibility when things went wrong. A doctor's family wasn't supposed to die, yet Clay's had. What had he done? How had he felt? If Sarah had been filled with remorse after her parents' deaths, believing she should have saved them, how much greater must Clay's suffering have been? He was trained to preserve life, and he'd failed those closest to him.

Another sip of water did nothing to dissolve the lump in Sarah's throat. Poor Clay. The thought was becoming an endless refrain. Though the death of his wife and brother was a heavier burden than anyone should have to carry, that was not the full extent of Clay's suffering. Every day he had to face his father and admit that all his schooling and the fancy diploma that impressed Ladreville's citizens hadn't been enough to cure him. It was no wonder Clay was angry.

If only there were something she could do to assuage that suffering. Sarah pushed back her chair and rose, stumbling ever so slightly. As she did, she nodded. Perhaps that was the answer. She couldn't restore Clay's wife or Austin. No one could. But maybe, just maybe, she could help his father.

"I want to spend some time with Mr. Canfield," Sarah told Martina as she wiped her sister's hands. Clay had not joined them for the meal, but that, Martina had explained, was normal. When he was riding the ranch, Clay was gone from sunup to sundown. That was just as well. Since Sarah doubted Clay would approve of her plans, she was glad she could start without him knowing. Thea's nap was the ideal time.

"I don't want to leave Thea alone in the cabin," Sarah explained. She gestured toward the closed door on the opposite side of the main room. It was, she guessed, a second bedroom. "Can Thea nap there?"

"Oh no, Miss Sarah." Martina shook her head vigorously, lest Sarah misunderstand her words. "That was Mrs. Canfield's room. The younger Mrs. Canfield," she clarified. Sarah nodded, realizing that the housekeeper was speaking of Clay's wife. "Mr. Clay won't let anyone go in there, not even to clean. Why, he took to sleeping in the barn loft the day Mrs. Canfield died."

Martina's words confirmed what Sarah had feared, that Clay's grieving continued unabated. If, as she suspected, he blamed himself for his failure to save his wife, it was understandable that he didn't want to face daily reminders of that failure by entering the room they'd once shared. And so Thea slept on the floor of the main room where Sarah could hear her when she stirred.

Straightening her shoulders, Sarah took a deep breath. The next hour would be a difficult one. She knew that. But she also knew it was something she had to do. She took another deep breath, mustering her courage. It was one thing to dream of helping Clay's father, another to make those dreams come true.

"Good afternoon, Mr. Canfield."

Sarah walked briskly to the wheeled chair. Today, since it was daylight, Clay's father was facing the window. Though the view over the rolling grassland was beautiful, Sarah turned the chair and, wanting no distractions, closed the heavy drapes. Mr. Canfield murmured something that might have been a greeting. Sarah couldn't distinguish any words, but she did see curiosity reflected in his eyes. That was a good sign. Yesterday when she and Thea had stopped in to see the older man, he'd barely looked at them.

She pulled a chair next to his. "I can't pretend to know what you're feeling. My injury was much less severe than your illness." Sarah gestured toward her right leg, wishing she dared show him how poorly it had healed. "Still," she continued, "I remember how I hated being confined to bed or a chair. I wanted to walk and could think of little else, even though the doctors told me I'd never be able to."

The left side of Mr. Canfield's face twisted, and he mumbled a few words that Sarah took to be agreement. She leaned forward. It was vital that he understood what she was proposing. "I believe you can walk again." There was no doubt about it. His eyes registered confusion, followed quickly by hope. "It won't be easy," Sarah cautioned. "It will be painful, and it will take time, but with your permission, I want to try."

This time the mumbled words were louder. Though Sarah could not understand them, she chose to believe they signified assent.

"The first thing we have to do is strengthen your legs. They've weakened from the months of not being used." Trying not to wince at the memory, Sarah recalled the first time she had tried to stand. She had expected her right leg to trouble her, but she hadn't anticipated that her left leg—the uninjured one—would buckle under her weight.

"All we're going to do today is straighten them a little." On her last visit she had seen that both feet were extended with the toes pointing down. No one could walk in that position. She would start with the feet, trying to restore flexibility, then move to the legs themselves.

Sarah reached for Mr. Canfield's left foot, sliding off the carpet slipper. This side of his body, she had observed, had suffered less damage than the right. She grasped the ball of Clay's father's foot, then slowly, gently massaged his toes. An intake of breath was followed by a groan. Though Sarah knew pain was an inevitable part of the process, she hated being the one to inflict it.

"I'm sorry," she said softly. "It'll get better. I promise."

Mr. Canfield grunted. When he groaned again, Sarah replaced his slipper and turned her attention to his right foot. Though Clay had told her that his father had no feeling in his right side, she kept her touch soft, massaging the ball of the foot before moving toward the toes. But when she reached his toes, Mr. Canfield cried out in pain.

Sarah's eyes widened. She hadn't expected that. Her heart began to race as she considered the possible reasons. Surely it was a good sign that Clay's father retained some feeling in his foot. Perhaps the healing had already begun. Sarah touched his toes again. Another cry confirmed that Mr. Canfield's toes registered sensations.

An instant later, Martina raced into the room. "What's wrong?" she demanded, looking at her employer. Clay's father mumbled something that the housekeeper appeared to understand. Whatever it was, she was not alarmed. Still, she did not leave, and the look she gave Sarah was filled with distrust.

"That's all for now," Sarah told Mr. Canfield as she rose to stand at his side. "The next time will be a bit longer." Sarah turned her gaze to Martina. "It might be best if you didn't tell Clay what I was doing here." Sarah doubted any doctor would appreciate a layman's attempts to help, no matter how well-intentioned those attempts might be, and a man as riddled with guilt as Clay would see this as yet another proof of his failure. Since Sarah's goal was to help, not hurt, that meant keeping him ignorant of her efforts until she knew whether they would succeed.

She touched Mr. Canfield's hand. "I'll be back. It'll be easier next time." That was a lie. The pain would grow more intense as they proceeded. "You'll walk again," she said softly. And that, Sarah was determined, would not be a lie. It was a promise. Somehow, some way, she'd make that promise come true.

4

"You see," Isabelle said as she settled onto one of the store's stools, "it's not as difficult as you feared."

Sarah nodded, grateful for the momentary lull and the opportunity to rest her leg. Today was her third day working at Rousseaus' Mercantile, and though she was surprised at how quickly she had become accustomed to the routine, there was no doubt that standing for long periods took its toll on her leg.

"You're the one who's making it easy," she told the woman who in a few days had become more friend than employer. Isabelle had displayed infinite patience, showing Sarah where everything was located, helping her with the prices, and seasoning almost every lesson with a heaping dose of humor. "I doubt I'll ever be ready to handle the store alone."

Isabelle wrinkled her nose. "This week I couldn't do it alone, either, not with all the extra customers." She gave Sarah a warm smile. "Maman and Papa are more pleased than they'll ever admit that you brought us so much new business."

Sarah felt a flush of pleasure color her cheeks. The steady ache in her leg hardly mattered when compared to the undeniable satisfaction of knowing she was useful. It was the first time in her life that she'd worked for wages, and while there was nothing glamorous about helping women select thread or pointing men toward the barrels of nails, it brought her more pleasure than playing a perfectly executed Chopin prelude or creating another still life watercolor.

Sarah's smile faded as Isabelle continued. "Truly, it was God's hand that brought you to Ladreville."

"I thought it was Austin's letters." Perhaps if she turned it into a joke, Isabelle would cease what Sarah thought of as her "God talk." The young woman's unfortunate need to share her beliefs with Sarah was the one cloud in an otherwise sunny workplace.

"Who do you think was responsible for those letters?" Though Isabelle's words were soft, there was no doubt they were deeply felt. "I heard Austin say God meant you to be the Canfield bride."

Austin and his God had been wrong. The journey Sarah had begun, believing marriage to a lyrical Texas rancher was the solution to her and Thea's problems, had ended with every hope dashed. There would be no wedding, for there was no bridegroom. There would be no happy ending in Ladreville, for Sarah and Thea were as alone as they'd been in Philadelphia. "There won't be a Canfield bride now."

Knowing there was nothing to be gained by arguing with Isabelle, Sarah tried to shift the conversation. "What was Austin like?" Perhaps it was foolish, like probing an open

76

wound, but Sarah wanted to learn more about the man she had promised to marry.

"He resembled Clay, but—unlike Clay—I never saw Austin without a smile." Isabelle's own face was somber. "He didn't always agree with people; in fact, he got into more than his share of arguments, but Austin could usually find a way to convince folks that his way was the right way."

"And yet someone killed him." Sarah took a deep breath, trying to block the image of a man who looked like Clay lying on the ground, a bullet in his chest. How she hated guns! Her father had used one when he had ended his life and Mama's. She took another deep breath in an attempt to eradicate memories of that night from her mind, though she knew they were indelibly etched. "Austin's death seems so senseless." As senseless as her parents'. Papa was a clever man. Surely he could have found a way to rebuild their fortune. Surely he should have realized how defenseless he was leaving her and Thea.

Isabelle shook her head slowly, and for a second Sarah feared she'd read her thoughts. But when Isabelle spoke, she was referring to Austin. "The Bible teaches us to trust that good can come out of even the worst of days. Do you remember the story of Joseph?" Without waiting for Sarah's reply, Isabelle continued. "His brothers were so jealous of him and his coat of many colors that they sold him into slavery. No one could claim that was anything other than evil, and yet good came from it. Joseph was able to save many people—including his own family—during the great famine. He wouldn't have been in Egypt—and he couldn't have done that—if his brothers hadn't tried to hurt him."

Though it had been a long time since Sarah had read the

Bible, she remembered that story. It was one her mother had told her when she'd been a small child. At the time, it had seemed a wonderful tale. Today it did not. "As I recall, it took many years before the good things happened. I can't wait that long." She doubted Clay could, either. The man had suffered so much.

No benefit could come from Austin's death, just as there could be no good outcome from her father's sins. Because of Papa, two people were dead, and Sarah and Thea's lives had been changed irrevocably. She could not undo that. All she could do was hope that they'd traveled far enough to escape the shame. She would be careful that no one in Ladreville ever learned what had happened last September. That way Thea would not suffer ostracism.

Sarah shifted on the stool, trying to find a comfortable position at the same time that she sought another topic of conversation. Speaking of Austin had done nothing to deflect Isabelle's fervor. The way she spoke of God and the way she acted made it seem as if he were a real person, a part of her daily life, not someone who resided in a church and was to be worshiped once a week. Sarah had never met anyone who acted that way about God, and it made her uncomfortable.

"Is it always this warm?" Mama had claimed that the weather was a safe subject.

Isabelle gave Sarah a long look, her expression telling Sarah she recognized the ploy and was ignoring it. "I don't mean to preach," Isabelle said with a self-deprecating smile, as if she realized how often she'd done exactly that, "but faith is what has helped me through difficult times. When we were . . ." She bit off her words as the door opened.

The man who entered the store stood a few inches shorter than Clay, with broader shoulders and more heavily muscled arms. When he removed his hat, revealing hair that was almost as dark brown as his eyes, something about him tugged at Sarah's memory. That was odd, for she knew she'd never met him.

"Good morning, David." Isabelle's voice was once again cheerful. Whatever she had been on the verge of revealing had been relegated to the recesses of her mind. She gave Sarah a questioning look. "Have you met?" When Sarah shook her head, Isabelle began the introductions. "May I present David Bramble?"

As Isabelle pronounced the name, Sarah realized why the man had seemed familiar. Now that she knew to look for it, the resemblance to his mother was clear. Though his face had more masculine contours, David had inherited Mary's nose and chin.

"I reckon it's my pleasure, Miss Dobbs," he said when the formalities were complete. "Ma claimed you was the prettiest gal to enter Ladreville in a long time, and she don't exaggerate." David gave Sarah an appraising look before he added, "It's plain as the rattles on a snake why Austin picked you for his bride."

Sarah bristled, even though she suspected he meant the words as a compliment. It wasn't the first time a man had regarded her as if she were an object for sale. That had happened far too often in the years before Papa's death when she'd been an eligible heiress, albeit one with a limp. That should not have caused her hackles to rise. Perhaps it wasn't the appraisal but the subtle alteration in David's tone when he spoke of Austin, almost as if he begrudged Austin his mail-order bride. Whatever the cause, Sarah felt a moment of discomfort. Mindful of her manners, she bit back the caustic reply that had been on the tip of her tongue, saying only, "I'm deeply indebted to your mother for agreeing to care for Thea."

"It's good for her." There were no undercurrents in David's voice when he spoke of Mary, simply filial love. "I ain't seen Ma this happy in a long time."

As the conversation turned to ordinary things and Sarah's uneasiness faded, she told herself it had been nothing more than her imagination. Certainly Isabelle appeared to have no reservations about their customer, for she bantered with David, treating him as if he were a friend as well as the source of potential sales, and seemed genuinely regretful when he left.

"Papa will need to order more poplin." Isabelle made a note as she returned to her seat behind the counter. So far this afternoon had been the busiest of the week, with three women waiting outside when the store reopened after the midday break. They'd soon been joined by half a dozen others, none of whom left with empty arms.

"I was surprised at how many yards Frau Reismueller bought."

"You're responsible." Isabelle chuckled. "When you mentioned that Madame Ladre had chosen that fabric for her new frock, every woman in town wanted it, especially the Germans. Frau Reismueller was probably ensuring that no one else could have a dress with as many flounces as hers."

"I'm glad to make the sales, but I don't understand the reasoning behind them." Far from wanting the same pattern as another woman, when she and Mama had frequented the dressmaker's shop, they'd been careful to ensure that the bolts of fabric were recent arrivals and that no one else in Philadelphia would have gowns like theirs.

Isabelle shrugged, as if the logic should be apparent. "Some people call it the curse of Alsace that its citizens came from two countries who've been at war more often than not. According to my parents, there have been problems for centuries. Maman and Papa had hoped the differences would be put aside when we emigrated here, but that hasn't happened." Isabelle sighed. "In good years, we see nothing more than rivalry between the French and the Germans. Most of the time it's friendly. People brag about who has the largest crops or who ordered a pianoforte. In bad years, there has been outright hostility with fights. My guess is this is a good year, and Frau Reismueller plans to make a fancier dress than Madame Ladre."

"Are you boring Sarah with tales of our ancestors' battles?" The door to the Rousseaus' residence opened, admitting Léon. Though he'd begun working on Karl Friedrich's farm, today had been a half day for him, and he'd joined the family for dinner. His refusal to explain the reason he could not work in the store until late afternoon had convinced Isabelle her brother was courting someone, and she'd spent most of the meal teasing him. Now it appeared Léon was returning the favor.

"No, you foolish boy. If you'd listened, you would have realized I was talking about recent events." She turned to Sarah. "Beware of my brother. He likes to eavesdrop."

"Only when there's something interesting to learn. Which, I must admit, is a rare occurrence when you're concerned."

As Isabelle made a moue, Sarah grinned. This was a

continuation of the sparring that seemed to characterize Léon and Isabelle's conversations. Unlike the hostilities Isabelle had been describing, the siblings' taunts were good-natured.

"I always wondered what it would be like to have a brother," Sarah said. "Now I know."

"They're horrible. Truly dreadful pests." Isabelle winked at Léon.

He twisted his mouth into a grimace. "Little sisters who follow you everywhere and want to play with your friends are the worst creatures God put on this earth."

Sarah raised an eyebrow, disputing Léon's assertion that being followed was the worst thing possible. "Did Isabelle ever waken you by trying to pull your eyelids open? That was one of Thea's favorite tricks."

As his hands covered his eyes in apparent fear that Sarah might attempt to demonstrate her sister's technique, Léon groaned. "No."

"You were fortunate. It took me a full week to teach Thea that a young lady does not do that."

Extending a hand to his sister, Léon said, "I retract every nasty thing I've ever said about you. You're a perfect sister."

"And you're a miracle worker." The smile Isabelle gave Sarah underscored her words. "Even if he didn't mean it, I can always remind Léon that he once called me perfect."

Her brother walked slowly, studying each of the shelves. "All right, perfect sister, what have you and Sarah done with the store? It looks as if I need to restock."

"If you hadn't been so busy trying to convince Karl Friedrich he should hire you, you'd know that we've had more customers in the past three days than we normally do in two weeks."

The momentary truce was ended, and Isabelle's voice held a hint of asperity. "I told you and Maman that hiring Sarah would be good for all of us."

Sarah grinned. "Are you ever wrong?"

"Only about a hundred times a day."

"If that's true, I'm Napoleon Bonaparte." Sarah pretended to slide her hand inside her bodice, imitating the portraits she'd seen of the French emperor.

"I beg your pardon, mademoiselle, but you don't look like Napoleon Bonaparte."

Sarah blinked at the sight of the newcomer. Surely he was one of the most handsome men she had ever seen, blessed with classic features, dark brown hair, and eyes that reminded her of Madame Rousseau's hot chocolate.

"Of course she's not Napoleon," Isabelle declared. Though her expression remained guarded, she slid off her stool and emerged from behind the counter, her hand tugging Sarah's so that she had no choice but to follow. "Sarah, may I present Jean-Michel Ladre?" No further introductions were necessary, for Isabelle had already explained that this man's father, Michel Ladre, was the town's founder, who'd purchased property and water rights from both the Canfields and the Texas government, then convinced a group of Alsatians this was the Promised Land.

Jean-Michel bowed, his courtly gesture more suited to a ballroom than the frontier. "It is my pleasure to meet you, Miss Sarah Dobbs who does not look like Napoleon Bonaparte." His eyes sparkled with mirth. "You're even prettier than your picture. Almost as pretty as Isabelle."

"That's the first time I've heard you speak the truth." Sarah turned to stare at Léon. Gone was the friendly bantering that had characterized his conversation with Isabelle. This time his words were laced with venom.

Jean-Michel made a show of sniffing the air. "What is that odor? Can it be a skunk? But, no, it is the peasant who works in the fields."

"Farming is good honest work." Léon's face flushed as he defended himself.

"For a German. I should have known to expect nothing more from you. You may bear a French name, but you're a dirt-digging German at heart." Jean-Michel gave Sarah a brief bow. "My apologies, mademoiselle. I shall return when we can converse without interruptions."

"What was that all about?" Isabelle demanded when the door closed behind Jean-Michel. She took a step toward her brother, her eyes flashing with anger. "You started the fight. Why?"

"I don't trust him, that's why." Léon adopted a pugilistic stance. "Last week he was here, making eyes at you, and now he's doing the same to Sarah. He's like that old coon dog, always sniffing around."

Though Sarah expected a vehement reply, to her surprise, Isabelle laughed. "Oh, Sarah, Maman always warned us to be careful what we asked for." The anger had vanished, replaced by amusement. "You said you wanted a brother. I give you my deepest condolences, for it appears Léon has adopted you."

❦

Clay paused at the top of the hill, his spirits rising as he recognized the rider fording the river. Though he hadn't planned to start his questioning today, he couldn't ignore the opportunity that had just presented itself. Perhaps this was an omen, a good one. It was about time. "Let's go," he said to Shadow.

"Good morning, David." Clay waited until he was close enough not to shout. "How was your trip into town?" He cared not a whit, but only a fool would blurt out the questions that were foremost in his mind.

David grinned. "Mighty fine. I met Miss Dobbs. That is one mighty purty woman. She'll be a real looker when she gets out of them ugly clothes." The grin was almost a leer as David added, "I reckon anyone can see why Austin picked her."

The words shouldn't have rankled. The truth was, black was not the most becoming color for many women, Sarah included. She needed brighter shades—perhaps the deep pink of a sunrise or the vibrant blue of the Texas sky—to flatter her. But the woman was in mourning. She wore the drab garments for the same reason he was wearing this confounded armband: respect.

Clay tried to bite back his annoyance. There was no point in alienating David, not when he needed answers about something far more important than Sarah's clothing. But he couldn't let the insinuation that Austin had been swayed by her beauty stand. "Miss Dobbs's appearance had no bearing on my brother's decision. He knew she was the bride he wanted months before he received her miniature."

Though the hat shaded his eyes, Clay saw his neighbor nod. "Yeah, Austin told me that. He said God had led him to her."

"The same God who let him be killed." Clay clenched his fists. "That's not the God I want in my life."

David's head jerked up and he stared at Clay, his expression stern. "I reckon your ma woulda washed your mouth out with soap if she heard you say that."

"I suppose she would have." His anger faded as quickly as it had flared. "The fact is, Austin tasted soap more often than I did."

As his horse pawed the ground, eager to move, David let him walk. "That temper of his got Austin in trouble more than once."

It was the opening Clay sought. Though his heart began to pound, he kept his voice as even as Shadow's steps. "Is that what happened the night he was killed? Did Austin argue with someone?" Eight men had gathered in the Brambles' barn for their weekly poker game. Only seven had gone home.

David shook his head. "I don't reckon nothin' coulda bothered Austin that night. Fact is, he was happier than I ever seen him. He kept showing us all Sarah's miniature and talking about how glad he was she was comin'."

That sounded like an encore of Austin's supper conversation. Clay hadn't bothered to do much more than nod at appropriate times. "Something must have happened. After all, someone killed him."

"It weren't any of us. Austin left early, but no one else did. The rest of us stayed and had another glass of beer. Truth is, I reckon we were all a little envious of your brother, what with Sarah being so pretty and all."

Clay didn't want to hear about beer or even envy. He wanted to know who was responsible for Austin's death. "The killer had to be a friend or someone he trusted. Austin wasn't careless. No matter how preoccupied he was with thoughts of his bride, he wouldn't have let a stranger get close to him." Some things were instinctive, and in this country, self-preservation was one of them.

David gave him a long look, then turned to stare into the distance. "I reckon you're not gonna like my advice, but you oughta stop trying to find the killer. It don't matter what you do; you can't bring Austin back. Why try? You oughta be thinking about the future. In a couple months, you'll be out of mourning for Patience. You could marry Sarah then."

Marry Sarah? What a crazy idea! David was right. Clay didn't like his advice. Not one bit. He wasn't going to marry his brother's fiancée, and he most definitely was not going to abandon his search for Austin's killer. In fact, he was going to redouble his efforts.

"Will you join us for dinner?" white-haired Frau Friedrich asked half an hour later when Clay knocked on his other neighbor's door.

Though the aroma of chicken and dumplings was enticing, Clay shook his head. "I'm sorry, but I can't. I came to see Karl. Do you know where he is?"

His mother nodded. "*Ja.* He said he'd be working in the north field. I'm surprised you didn't see him on your way here."

There was only one road on this side of the river, extending south from the Lazy B, past the Bar C, and ending at the Friedrich farm, its sole purpose connecting the three ranches. Clay retraced his path, his eyes searching the farmland, looking for Karl. When he saw him, he cut into the plowed fields.

"I'm glad you're here," Karl said as Clay approached. Several inches shorter than Clay, Karl had the same blond hair and blue eyes. Only his stocky build kept him from being mistaken for Clay's brother. "I've got something to show you." Wordlessly, Karl led the way to the fence marking the boundary between the Friedrich farm and the Bar C. Though most of the land was open range, when Karl and his parents had bought the Preble ranch and decided to turn it into corn fields, they'd erected a fence line. Today that fence had a gaping hole.

"You know anything about this?" Karl asked. "Some fifty head of your cattle got through and trampled my corn." Justifiable anger tinged his words.

"I don't understand. I checked all the fences earlier this week." It was true that the Bar C's being shorthanded kept him from riding the fence line weekly the way Austin had, but Clay had been here only four days ago. He dismounted for a closer look. Though it was not unheard of for cattle to damage a fence, it was unlikely. He frowned. There was no doubt about it; the barbed wire had been cut. "Why would someone cut it?"

Though he'd meant it to be rhetorical, Karl appeared to be pondering Clay's question as he leaned back in his saddle. "Some would say it's a way to save on cattle feed."

A bolt of anger shot through Clay. "Are you accusing me of cutting the fence?"

"Nope. Just pointing out one possibility." Karl glared at the fence once more before he dismounted and joined Clay. As they worked to repair the wire, he said, "I reckon the person who did this is the same one who's responsible for the other problems—the salt in Granny Menger's well, Gunther's cracked millstone." He tugged the wire taut. "I tell you, Clay, I don't like it. Ladreville used to be a peaceful town."

"And now it harbors a murderer."

"You don't know that."

"All the evidence points to it. He could even be one of your poker group."

Karl stared at Clay, his blue eyes hot with anger. "Are you accusing me?"

"Just making an observation."

"I didn't do it. Mind you, I'm not saying your brother didn't rile me. Everybody knows we had our differences. But I didn't kill him, and for the life of me, I can't figure out how any of the others could have, either."

That was not what Clay wanted to hear. It was hard to believe all the men who'd been with Austin that last night would lie, but the other possibility—that the killer was a stranger—was even less palatable. Clay took a deep breath, reminding himself that today was almost over. Tomorrow would be better. It had to be.

That thought buoyed his spirits until he reached the Bar C and found Martina waiting for him, her face lined with concern. "She asked me not to tell you, but I thought you ought to know."

When the housekeeper finished her story, Clay's fists were clenched. What else could go wrong?

⚜

"All right, sweetie." Sarah gathered the crying child in her arms. When she'd entered the Bramble house, she'd found Thea sitting in one corner of the parlor, her eyes and nose reddened from tears. The same scene had greeted her the previous two days.

"Go home." Thea clutched Sarah's neck and repeated the phrase.

"Yes, we're going home. Soon." But first Sarah needed to talk to Mary. She lowered herself carefully onto one of the fancy chairs, mindful of her leg's ache and fearful of dropping Thea if it buckled. "Has she been crying all day?"

Though she'd said nothing while Sarah maneuvered herself, Sarah saw a hint of pity in Mary's eyes. Whether the pity was for Sarah or Thea wasn't clear. Mary shook her head. "Less than yesterday. She was cheerful as could be when we made biscuits." The bits of flour in Thea's hair confirmed the biscuit baking story. "I reckon she's just tired now," Mary continued. "Take a mother's advice and don't fret so much. It's normal for a child to miss her mama. She'll adjust."

Sarah hoped so. By the time they reached the ranch, Thea's tears had dried and she was bouncing on the seat, her arms stretched out toward the horses, acting as if nothing had bothered her. If she'd been tired, she'd caught her second wind, for all traces of the petulant Thea were gone, replaced by a child with more energy than Sarah could ever match. As Mary had predicted, Thea was resilient.

Sarah was smiling as she and Thea joined Clay for supper, but the smile faded when she realized Clay was in what Mama would have called a thunderstorm mood. He frowned when Thea called him "Papa Clay" and studiously ignored her for the rest of the meal, despite her attempts to catch his attention. Even more significantly, his responses to Sarah's attempts at casual conversation were monosyllabic. Though no one would ever call Clay garrulous, he was not usually taciturn.

"What's wrong?" Sarah asked when she could bear the silence no longer. Perhaps Clay had learned something about Austin's killer and that was the reason he seemed morose.

His eyebrows shot up, as if he were surprised by the question. "We'll discuss it later, once you've put Thea to bed."

Sarah tried not to sigh at the realization that whatever he wanted to discuss, it was not pleasant. Though the cabin Austin had built for her and Thea was cheerful and normally made Sarah smile, tonight she was so worried about what was bothering Clay that she took no notice of it and could barely keep her mind on the story she was reading to Thea. It was with a sense of foreboding that Sarah reentered the ranch house.

Clay rose. "I heard something today that disturbed me," he announced without preamble.

"Is it about Austin?" As she sank into a chair, she noticed the door to Robert Canfield's room was closed. Though the older man did not join them for supper, normally the door was left open so he could hear the conversation. It made him realize he was still part of the family, Clay had explained. For some reason, he was being excluded from this discussion. That could only mean that whatever Clay had learned was too painful for his father to endure.

Clay shook his head. "No. It's not about Austin. It's about you." He clenched his fists, then spat the words, "Martina said you've been torturing my father."

Torture? Sarah recoiled as if she'd been slapped. Though her leg protested, she rose and took a step toward Clay, unwilling to let him continue to tower over her. "I have not been torturing anyone." She enunciated each word carefully. Though she'd known Clay might not approve of her efforts, she'd not expected this reaction. "I would never torture anyone." Her denial was as vehement as Clay's accusation. "What I have been doing is exercising your father's feet. That's the first step toward helping him walk again."

91

Clay was silent for a moment, and Sarah sensed he had only a tenuous grip on his temper. "Why would you do that? My father will not walk again. There is no reason to subject him to pain."

"I beg to differ with you. I believe he will be able to walk."

The raised eyebrows told Sarah Clay felt otherwise. "On just what do you base this opinion?" Now his tone was condescending. "I am a trained physician, and I know otherwise."

Perhaps she should have backed down. This was, after all, Clay's father they were discussing. He loved him and wanted only the best for him. But so did Sarah. She hadn't been mouthing platitudes the day she'd met Robert when she'd said she had been looking forward to having a new father. She needed him and, though neither he nor Clay might admit it, Robert needed her.

Sarah took another step toward Clay, deliberately softening her voice in the hope he'd understand. "Half a dozen doctors—some of the finest in the country, I might add—told my parents and me the same thing when I broke my leg. No one offered me the slightest hope, but I'm walking now." She gestured toward her right leg. "Even though I'll always limp, at least I'm not confined to a chair. If I could escape the chair, so can your father. I can show him how."

Clay shook his head. "This is different. Pa suffered from apoplexy, not a fall from a horse."

Clay sounded like all the doctors her parents had consulted. He might have gone to medical school, he might have helped many patients, but this time he was wrong. "That's all the more reason to think he can regain the use of his legs. Nothing was broken."

The look Clay gave her was filled with pity. "You don't understand."

"You don't, either. The human spirit can overcome more than you imagine. The doctors said it would be a miracle if I walked. I don't believe it was a miracle. I'm walking because of my determination."

"And you believe your determination will let my father regain use of his legs? That *would* be a miracle. Unfortunately, I don't believe in them any more than you do. Stay away from my father."

But she would not.

5

It reminded her of Philadelphia. Though smaller, the building was filling with people. As she settled Thea on her lap, Sarah heard murmured conversations, the rustle of pages as others opened their hymnals, the occasional cry of a baby. She took a deep breath to calm her nerves and inhaled the scent of candle wax mingled with the stronger fragrances of toilet water and hair oil. It was Sunday morning, only a few minutes before the service was to begin, time for the faithful and those who wanted to be counted among them to gather.

If she closed her eyes and pretended the parishioners were speaking English rather than French, Sarah could believe she was once again in Philadelphia. But she wasn't, and for that she was supremely grateful. In Philadelphia, she would have been sitting alone. In Philadelphia, she would have been subjected to stares, to whispered comments, to outright snubs. Here she faced none of that. Instead, she was greeted with genuinely welcoming smiles. Oh, there was curiosity. She had expected that. But there was no condemnation and no pity. Since no one knew her past, there was no one to judge her for her father's actions. The only judge was the voice deep inside, reminding her that she who'd been so quick to accuse the Philadelphia congregation of hypocrisy was guilty of the same sin.

Thea patted Sarah's hand, urging her to turn another page. Though she managed a smile for her sister, Sarah could not dismiss the feeling that she was an imposter. The others had come to worship God; Sarah had not. She was here because she knew it was what Mama would have wanted for Thea. That's why they were sitting in a pew with Isabelle's family. That's why Sarah was holding Mama's Bible so Thea could pretend to read it. This was an obligation, nothing more.

When the organist paused, the whispering ceased, and a sense of anticipation rippled through the congregation as a slight, black-robed man entered the sanctuary, his hands urging them to rise. This was, Sarah knew, Père Tellier.

"Let us pray."

Sarah moved mechanically, standing and kneeling at the correct times. Though the service was in French, the words were similar to those she'd heard every Sunday of her childhood. There had been a time when those words had touched her heart, when she had felt a joy so great it had brought tears to her eyes. But that time had ended. The joy had evaporated the day she'd heard two churchwomen discussing her. It was God's will, they had said, that Sarah would not walk again. *How could that be?* she had wanted to scream. *How could a loving God want me to remain an invalid?* There was no answer save one: he was not a loving God. If she had had any lingering doubts, they were destroyed the night he allowed

95

gunshots to kill her parents. Nothing remained. Were it not for Thea and the need to create a normal life for her, Sarah would not be in church today. That was practicality, not hypocrisy, she told herself. She would not feel guilty.

As the service continued, Sarah marveled at how well her sister behaved. Though she had expected her to be fussy, Thea seemed fascinated by the people around her, her head swiveling as she regarded the parishioners. The thought assailed Sarah that this might be the reason her sister was unhappy staying with Mary Bramble. Perhaps she missed the company of others. It was true that Thea's short life had been spent surrounded by many people. At home, there had been numerous servants bustling around the house, always taking time to spend a moment with the youngest member of the family. The journey West had involved crowded trains and stagecoaches. Perhaps Thea longed for the company of more than one person.

As if in response to Sarah's thoughts, Thea's eyes lit on a small girl two pews ahead of them. For the first time since the service began, the little girl turned and was staring toward the back of the church. Thea smiled, waved and gurgled, then started to talk. "Shush, sweetie." Sarah laid a finger over Thea's lips, admonishing her to be silent, and glanced around to see how many people her sister had disturbed. When she turned in her direction, Isabelle shook her head, as if to say no one minded. But surely that couldn't be. Sarah continued to look around, anticipating the angry expressions, the lips pursed with disapproval that she would have encountered in Philadelphia. There were none. Instead, she saw indulgent smiles. This congregation, it appeared, did not subscribe to the belief that children should be seen and not heard.

For the first time since she'd entered the sanctuary, Sarah began to relax. Perhaps Isabelle had not exaggerated when she'd said that Sarah and Thea would be welcome in either church.

As Père Tellier climbed into the pulpit, the parishioners settled back into the pews, anticipating a long sermon. For Thea's sake, Sarah hoped that was not the case. Her sister's behavior had been amazingly good, but all good things ended.

The black-robed pastor looked at his congregation, smiling as his eyes moved from one pew to the next. It was only when he'd silently greeted everyone that he spoke. "For today's sermon, I have chosen one of the Ten Commandments: thou shalt not . . ."

The blood drained from Sarah's face as he pronounced the final word. *Kill.* How had he known? Instinctively, her arms tightened around Thea, squeezing her sister so tightly that she squirmed. *Oh, Thea. I thought I could protect you. I was wrong.* Somehow, the past she had believed they had escaped had followed them. Sarah closed her eyes, wishing she could simply disappear. But, of course, she could not, for nothing was simple. She took a deep breath, willing her hands to stop trembling. When at last she'd regained a modicum of composure and opened her eyes, Sarah darted surreptitious looks around her. She'd expected contempt, perhaps even condemnation. Instead she discovered no one was looking at her. Their attention was focused on the minister, who continued to expound on his chosen commandment. Sarah exhaled the breath she hadn't realized she was holding. How foolish could she be? It was her imagination that had caused those moments of panic. No one knew what had happened. No one would ever know.

When the service ended, Isabelle touched Sarah's arm as they waited to leave the church. "I'm so glad you decided to come. I hope you'll attend services here every week."

"I'm not sure." Sarah thought she would visit the German church next Sunday. If the congregation was equally welcoming, she and Thea could alternate between them.

Isabelle's eyes darkened. "Please don't think it was intentional. I'm sure he didn't mean to upset you."

Before Sarah could ask what Isabelle meant, Thea batted her hand against Sarah's cheek.

"Down!" she demanded. "Down."

Accepting the inevitable, Sarah lowered her sister to the floor but refused to relinquish her hand. Thea could squirm all she wanted, but she would not run through the group of people waiting to greet the pastor.

"I'm sorry." She faced Isabelle again. "You were saying . . ."

"The sermon. Père Tellier had no way of knowing you'd be here today. I'm certain he didn't mean to remind you of Austin's death when he chose 'thou shalt not kill' as his subject."

Austin. Of course. If anyone had seen Sarah's distress, they would have believed she was mourning him. How shocked they would be to learn she had not thought of him once. Sorrow for the man who should have been her husband came at unpredictable times; today had not been one of them. Sarah managed a brief smile for Isabelle. "I know that. I'm fine now." And she was. As they stood in line, waiting to greet the minister, Sarah chatted with her friend as if nothing unusual had happened.

After accepting the pastor's warm welcome, Sarah stepped into the sunlight. Though Isabelle's parents had invited her and

Thea to join them for Sunday dinner, this was one meal at the Bar C she could not miss. Sarah headed toward the wagon. Unfortunately, progress was slower than she would have liked, for it seemed that everyone wanted to greet her. Though she'd met many of the women and children when they'd shopped at the mercantile, the men were strangers. Dutifully, they doffed their hats and muttered a welcome, their sidelong glances making it clear they'd rather be part of the group of men standing in one corner of the churchyard, despite the fact that that conversation was provoking scowls and clenched fists. Sarah herself was anxious to go home—to the Bar C, she corrected herself.

She and Thea had almost reached the street when Jean-Michel Ladre approached them.

"I'd like you to meet my parents." He nodded toward the older couple standing behind him. Even without the introduction, Sarah would have known the trio was related. Jean-Michel had inherited his father's coloring and regal posture, but his face was a masculine version of his mother's. It was no wonder Jean-Michel was such a handsome man, for his mother was one of the most beautiful women Sarah had ever seen. She bit back a smile at the thought of all the women who tried to surpass Madame Ladre by creating more elaborate gowns. This woman would be beautiful dressed in rags.

"Welcome to Ladreville. I trust your stay here will be pleasant." As the man who founded the town spoke, Sarah understood why he'd had no problem recruiting emigrants to populate his dream. Monsieur Ladre's voice was low but compelling, imbuing even a simple greeting with charisma. It appeared that he was what her father would have described as a born leader. It also appeared that he was laboring under a misunderstanding. Sarah was not visiting.

"You chose a beautiful location for the town." She accompanied her words with a smile. "This is a fine place for Thea and me to make our home."

Madame Ladre gave her son a long look before she returned her gaze to Sarah. "Then Jean-Michel was correct. We thought he'd misunderstood when he said you plan to remain here. After Austin . . ." Her voice trailed off as the townspeople's frequently did when they spoke of Austin. What could one say to a woman whose fiancé was killed before she'd had a chance to meet him?

"We plan to stay."

"Then I hope you'll find everything you seek here." Madame Ladre gave Sarah another appraising look, as if assessing her sincerity. "If there's anything you require, you need only ask." She nodded at her husband, but he had turned aside, drawn a few feet away by one of the men who'd been part of the animated conversation in the churchyard corner.

"It's time to do something about those Germans," Sarah overheard the man say. "My best rake was taken right out of my barn last night, and Albert said someone stole his wife's silver bowl two days ago. I tell you, Mayor, this thievery has got to stop."

Michel Ladre frowned. "Let's discuss this tomorrow. Today is the Sabbath." He turned toward Sarah and managed a small smile. "I'm sorry you had to overhear that, but even a place as close to heaven as Ladreville has its serpents."

❦

If one thing in Ladreville was heavenly, it was Martina's Sunday dinner. Though all of her meals had been delicious, she had told Sarah that cooking Sunday dinner was her way

100

of giving thanks for her blessings. Today, perhaps because of Sarah's announcement that Pa Canfield would be joining them, she had made a greater variety of food than last week and had enlisted Miguel's aid in bringing the bowls and platters to the table. Succulent beef, tender baked potatoes, the lightest biscuits Sarah had ever eaten, and green beans cooked with bacon and a spice she could not identify were accompanied by relishes and salads.

This was not a meal but a feast, and—judging by the amount of food that had made its way into Thea's mouth rather than coming to rest on her cheeks—Sarah's sister was enjoying it as much as she was. So, too, was Clay's father. Though he normally took his meals in his room, accompanied only by Martina, Sarah had suggested to Clay that he join them for dinner. Clay's reluctance had been palpable, but something—perhaps the memory of how he'd forbidden her to help his father walk—had caused him to agree.

"All right. We'll try it this Sunday." He nodded slowly. "But only if you agree to call him Pa." When Sarah had raised an eyebrow, Clay continued his explanation. "I know he'll never be your father-in-law, but I think he'd like it. I've seen him smile when Thea calls him Grandpa."

And so Pa was seated at one end of the table with Sarah at the other. She wasn't certain who watched him more carefully, herself or Clay. She didn't know how Clay felt, but from Sarah's perspective, the experiment was a success. With his food cut into tiny pieces, Pa was able to eat almost as well as Thea, and though he did not speak, it was clear that he enjoyed the conversation.

"Everything is delicious," Sarah said when Martina entered the room to refill their tea glasses.

Clay nodded his approval. It was only when he'd helped his father drink that Clay asked Sarah about her morning. "Did Père Tellier preach fire and brimstone?"

"Not exactly." His words had been powerful despite the gentle delivery. "He spoke calmly, but he left no doubt about his beliefs." Or about the fact that anyone who broke one of God's commandments would suffer.

"More, Pa?" Clay gestured toward his father's empty plate. When Pa shook his head, Clay turned back to Sarah. "What was today's sermon topic?" The casual way he phrased the question told her he was only being polite, that he had no genuine interest in how she and Thea had spent the morning. When she'd asked if he would be accompanying them to church, Clay had said his family did not attend services, that his parents and Austin had always worshiped at home. There was no mention of his own religious attendance, leading Sarah to suspect that—unlike her—Clay was not a hypocrite.

"Père Tellier spoke about one of the commandments: 'thou shalt not kill.'"

The change was instantaneous. One second Clay was cutting a piece of beef. The next he was glaring at her, anger turning his features harsh. "Our good pastor was a little late with that warning," he said. "Three weeks and one day late, to be precise."

The uninjured side of Pa's face moved as he struggled to speak. Though the words were unintelligible to Sarah, the anguish in his eyes told her he was reliving the moment he'd learned his younger son had been killed.

"Don't worry, Pa," Clay said, touching his father's hand. "I'll take care of it." His lips twisted in scorn. "The pastor's preaching wouldn't have made any difference. The truth is, someone wanted Austin dead. Now it's up to me to find the man and make sure he never again kills anyone."

A shiver of dread raced down Sarah's spine. Could Clay really mean what he had implied? She looked at Pa and saw her own fears reflected in his blue eyes. "Isn't it the sheriff's job to find the killer and a jury's to determine the punishment?" she asked as calmly as she could. At her side, Thea whimpered, frightened by Clay's anger. "Eat your biscuit, sweetie. It'll be all right." Sarah's words rang hollow.

Clay shot her a scornful look. "That may be the way it happened in Philadelphia, but out here, more times than not, we have to take matters into our own hands."

Sarah had heard of vigilante justice. It had, in fact, been one of the subjects Papa had introduced at dinner one day. At the time, she'd been appalled by the whole idea. Now, faced with the prospect that the man who sat opposite her was about to exact it, she shuddered. "Justice doesn't mean more killing." By some small miracle, her voice was firm, betraying none of the horror that coursed through her. "There's already been too much killing." Perhaps Isabelle had been wrong. Perhaps Père Tellier had indeed been speaking of Austin this morning. Perhaps this was what he meant. "Another death won't bring Austin back."

Sarah looked at Pa for corroboration and saw the slightest of nods.

"Maybe it won't bring him back, but his killer must pay." Clay's eyes were dark with anger. "Austin was mighty fond of quoting his God. According to him, God said, 'An eye for an eye.' That makes it pretty clear to me what has to happen. No matter how long it takes, I can promise you one thing: my brother's death will be avenged."

Sarah had never been so thankful to hear the clock strike noon. Trying not to limp, she walked to the door and turned the sign to "closed," grateful that for the next two hours, she would not have to face customers. It had been so difficult, pretending she was carefree when her mind was filled with worries over Clay and Thea. She couldn't claim she didn't understand Clay, for she did. Sarah knew what it was like to hate a murderer and to want him punished. Hadn't she prayed that Papa would burn in hell? But that was different from searching out a man and killing him. Wasn't it?

By tacit agreement, neither she nor Clay had mentioned Austin after dinner. They'd spoken of Pa and how he seemed to enjoy eating with them. Clay had even agreed that Pa could join them for supper each day. Thea would like that. If she was aware of his infirmities, she gave no sign, but simply treated Pa like a new playmate, chattering as if he cared about horses and flowers and her unfortunate encounter with a prickly pear cactus. The hours Thea spent with Pa were good ones, unlike her days.

"Is something wrong?"

The concern in Isabelle's voice told Sarah she'd failed to mask her emotions. She didn't want Isabelle to know how worried she was about Thea, for there was nothing her friend could do. "The weather must be changing," Sarah suggested. "My leg hurts a bit." Though true, that was the least of her worries.

Isabelle nodded as the two women walked across the store toward the door leading to the Rousseaus' living quarters. Madame Rousseau had insisted that Sarah take her noon meal with them, claiming it was part of her wages.

"Maybe that's why some of our customers looked so glum," Isabelle continued. "I couldn't understand them, but they didn't seem happy."

They weren't. Almost everyone who'd come into the store this morning had complained. "There've been more cut fences," Sarah said, repeating the stories she'd heard. "Some of Herr Mueller's goats got into Frau Ott's vegetable patch."

Isabelle wrinkled her nose. "And goats being goats, nothing is left."

"Precisely. No one knows how the fence was cut, but they're pretty certain it wasn't the work of the goats."

"So they suspect the French."

Sarah nodded. "I'm afraid so."

Her friend's eyes were thoughtful. "No wonder they were glaring at me."

"No one accused you." Sarah couldn't let Isabelle believe that. "They're just concerned about who's responsible for all the trouble. It reminded me of the parishioners I overheard after church, only they were blaming the Germans."

Isabelle started to climb the stairs. As was true of many of the commercial establishments in Ladreville, her family's home was above the store. "Papa's afraid tempers will flare someday and we'll have a fight on our hands."

That was not an appealing prospect. Trying to lighten the discussion, Sarah said, "Maybe we'll have a storm, and the rain will quench their tempers."

Pausing, Isabelle turned and looked at Sarah. "You haven't seen a Texas storm, or you wouldn't be joking about it. Summer rain comes almost without warning, and it's stronger than you can imagine, sweeping away everything in its path.

The last time it happened, we couldn't cross the river for three days."

Sarah blanched at the thought.

"Don't worry. You would stay with us."

Her own safety wasn't what concerned Sarah. "But Thea would be on the other side. She'd be frantic."

"Is she still having trouble adjusting?" They'd reached the landing and were inside the Rousseaus' main room where the aromas of roast lamb and garlic mingled with the lighter scent of the wildflowers Isabelle had gathered that morning.

Sarah frowned, thinking of her sister, as she and Isabelle went to Isabelle's room to remove their pinafores. "If anything, Thea's worse," Sarah told her friend. "She used to be happy in the morning when I took her to Mary's. She'd cry when I left but not before then. Now she starts pouting as soon as we get into the wagon."

Isabelle reached for the ewer on her bureau. "I wish she could stay here."

So did Sarah. "We both know that's impossible. Thea would destroy the store in a day." She unbuttoned her pinafore and laid it on the bed. "Thea will just have to get used to being with Mary."

Surely their neighbor was right, and it was only a matter of time before Thea looked forward to spending the day with her. The alternative, which had kept Sarah awake last night, was so much worse. If Thea didn't adjust, Sarah would have no choice but to stop working at the mercantile. She couldn't let Thea be unhappy. Everything she'd done—accepting Austin's offer of marriage, making the long journey West, convincing the Rousseaus to hire her—had been for Thea. Sarah had vowed to keep her sister safe and happy, and she would. But if she couldn't work, how would they live? They couldn't remain on the Bar C indefinitely.

"Maybe the problem is Mary being so much older," Isabelle suggested as she poured water into the basin. "Some little ones are frightened by gray hair and wrinkles."

"I don't think that's the case. When I'm there too, Thea loves to play with Mary. And she's happy when we're with Clay's father. She treats him like the grandfather she's never had." Taking Thea to Pa's room had been one of the best things Sarah had done. Not only did her sister and Clay's father appear to enjoy each other's company, but Pa was more cooperative when Thea was present. Though it was obvious he didn't want Sarah to work on his legs, he made no cries that would alert Martina, so long as Thea was in the room. "I thought maybe she'd be happier with other children, so I talked to Frau Reismueller when she came into the store this morning. She said she would have been glad to care for Thea, but she's in the family way again and feeling poorly. Oh, Isabelle, I worry about Thea every day."

Isabelle dried her hands. "I'll pray for a solution."

Sarah turned abruptly, wrenching her leg. "That won't do any good. God stopped listening to my prayers a while ago."

Isabelle shook her head slowly. "Let me help with your leg." She motioned to Sarah to sit on the bed and began to rub her calf while she spoke. "God never stops listening. He's always there, and he answers prayers." Isabelle looked up, her eyes darkening with concern. "Sometimes his answers aren't what we wanted, and it's hard to believe they're what's best for us."

Though Isabelle's hands were soothing the ache in Sarah's

107

leg, her words were far from comforting. "How can you claim he's a loving God when he allows so much evil?"

"He *is* a loving God," she insisted. "It's true he doesn't stop evil, but he turns it to good. The Bible promises that."

"Please don't talk about Joseph again. I know you believe it, but I've never seen good come from evil." Her father's sins had been horrible, and nothing good had come from them, nor had Austin's death led to anything positive.

"Sometimes it's hard to trust." Isabelle's eyes reflected an emotion Sarah could not identify. "The good comes in God's time, not ours."

"I'd like to believe that, but I've seen no evidence that it's true."

"It is." Isabelle straightened Sarah's skirts, then rose. When Sarah started to join her, Isabelle shook her head and sank onto the bed, looking at Sarah for a long moment before she said, "No one besides my family knows what I'm going to tell you. I'm trusting you not to repeat it." Her expression reminded Sarah of the day Isabelle had related Joseph's story and how she'd seemed on the verge of confiding something, only to be interrupted by David Bramble's arrival.

"I'm good at keeping secrets," Sarah said. Especially her own.

Despite the assurance, Isabelle seemed reluctant to begin. At last she did, saying, "I didn't want to leave Alsace. I loved our home there. It wasn't perfect, but I had friends in our town and cousins in the next one. I was comfortable there, and I didn't want to start over. If you ask them, my parents will probably deny it, but I know they felt the same."

Sarah wondered where this was leading. "Then why did you emigrate? It's a long journey, with many hardships."

She looked around the room, her eyes lighting on the cuckoo clock Isabelle had brought from her previous home. She'd told Sarah that the clock reminded her of her friends and family in the Old Country and how she had refused to have it packed with the family's furnishings. Instead, she'd carried it with her, carefully wrapped in a spare petticoat, so she could see it each day while they were traveling. "It was my link to home," she'd explained.

Sarah's hands rose to her ears, assuring herself that the earrings were still there. Like Isabelle's clock, they were her memento of happier times, her link to her mother.

Isabelle hesitated before blurting out, "We had no choice. We couldn't let Léon be jailed."

"Léon? Your brother?" As the cuckoo emerged from his house and the clock chimed, Sarah tried to reconcile the Léon she knew, the teasing young man who treated her as a second sister, with a man about to be incarcerated.

"Léon has a wild streak," Isabelle admitted, "and he let it overcome his good judgment. One night he broke into some houses, stole a few things, and was caught. The magistrate said the only way to avoid prison was to leave."

Sarah tried and failed to picture Léon as a thief. She'd seen his protectiveness toward Isabelle and his anger with Jean-Michel. He was a good brother, a loving son. He also did not appear to be a man who expected something for nothing. Sarah knew the labor he performed for Karl Friedrich was more tiring and paid less than working at the store, and yet it was what Léon had chosen. How could this be the same man who'd stolen property in Alsace?

"Why would he steal?"

Isabelle's lips twisted into a rueful smile. "He said it was fun. It was his way of proving to his friends that he was more clever than they. Some friends! When Léon was caught, they pretended they knew nothing."

The same way Papa's friends disavowed him. It was no wonder the Rousseaus had left their home. Like Sarah, they'd had few choices.

"Maman and Papa prayed for guidance," Isabelle continued. "A few days later, when they heard about Michel Ladre's search for emigrants, they knew that was what we were meant to do."

Just as Austin's advertisement had resolved Sarah's dilemma. She hadn't realized she and her friend had so much in common. "So you came here. I understand why you came, but I don't see how that changed evil into good."

"I haven't finished. I was miserable the whole trip." Isabelle managed a smile. "I must have been a real trial to my parents. I hated everything. I complained about the slightest mishap. And, of course, I blamed Léon for it all."

"Isabelle, Sarah, dinner's almost ready," Madame Rousseau called.

"In a moment, Maman. This is important." Isabelle took Sarah's hands in hers. "I was so filled with bitterness that I couldn't see anything good."

It was as difficult to reconcile the story Isabelle was telling with the young woman Sarah knew as it was to believe Léon a thief. "What changed?"

Her answer was simple. "I did. I realized that my anger toward Léon was hurting me, not him. I was the one who was in prison, but it was a prison of my own making. It was only when I forgave him for his role in our emigration that I freed myself."

Isabelle tightened her grip on Sarah's hands. Though her eyes were dark with emotion, her smile reminded Sarah of paintings of saints she'd seen at the Museum of Art in Philadelphia. Isabelle was no saint, she knew, and yet she had the same peace-filled look on her face as she said, "If you've never experienced it, you may not believe me, but I felt like a new person. I was finally able to see how good our life here is. My parents have more opportunities. Léon has a new life, and so do I. Don't you see, Sarah? God used Léon's sin to give us all a better life."

Sarah nodded slowly. It was a touching story, and there was no doubt that Isabelle believed it was true. But, no matter what Isabelle believed, nothing good could come from murder. As for forgiveness, Sarah would never, ever forgive her father. What he had done was unforgivable.

❦

As days went, it was far from the best. Admittedly, it wasn't as bad as the day Patience had died or the night Austin had been killed or when he'd learned of Pa's stroke, but it wasn't much better. Clay let the reins slacken as he reached the opposite bank of the river. Shadow knew the way home, and the horse was so attuned to Clay's moods that he'd realized this was not a day for galloping. Though speed might soothe him momentarily, what Clay needed this afternoon was time to think.

He'd gone into town, looking for answers, and he'd found them. Unfortunately, they were not the ones he'd sought. Michel Ladre, wearing the smirk that seemed to be part of his wardrobe whenever he saw Clay, had declared the investigation complete. Austin had been killed by a stranger; the case was closed, or so the mayor claimed.

The mayor was wrong. He'd also lied when he claimed he'd checked every possible lead. Clay doubted that Michel had conducted more than a perfunctory investigation into Austin's death. Why would he? Anything that resembled a true inquiry would have required him to look closely at the men who'd played poker with Clay's brother that evening—a group of men that just so happened to include Michel's son. Everyone in town knew that the Ladre name was sacrosanct and that not even the slightest insinuation was allowed to taint a member of the family. They were perfect, at least in Michel's eyes.

Clay shook his head. That was a lesson Austin had refused to learn. He'd mockingly called the Ladres the town's royal family right before he accused Michel of appropriating some of the community's funds for his own personal use. It was no wonder Ladreville's mayor and self-appointed sheriff cared little for finding Austin's murderer. He had probably toasted his good fortune with several glasses of ale when he learned that the gadfly who dared to question him would question him no more.

Oh, Austin, why did you let your temper overrule your good sense? It was a question Clay had asked himself repeatedly that morning. Though he'd known that Austin had come close to fisticuffs with the mayor on more than one occasion, he wasn't aware that the same statement could be made about Austin and a number of other people in Ladreville. Clay knew how quick Austin's temper was, but not how often it flared, particularly on the last day of his life.

He had come to town hoping to retrace his brother's steps, convinced that something had happened that day to trigger—literally—the killer. He'd hoped to narrow the list of suspects. Instead, he'd learned that Austin had argued with everyone he'd met. He'd accused Gunther Lehman of overcharging for the flour he'd milled. He'd been belligerent when Albert Mueller had told him the price of a dairy cow. He'd argued with William Goetz over the design for the chest the carpenter was making for Sarah's bride gift. According to the men, these had not been casual disagreements, but violent arguments which Austin threatened to resolve with force. The men had all sworn that they'd backed away rather than fight with him. Though Clay knew they had a vested interest in protecting their own reputations, their words rang with truth. Austin could be hotheaded. On a bad day, even seemingly trivial events had been known to provoke Austin to fight. Clay knew that. What he did not know was what had caused his brother's spate of anger that morning.

From what he could piece together, the only person who'd seen Austin smile was the postmaster. Steven Dunn reported that Austin had stalked into the post office, his fists clenched as if he were spoiling for a fight, and demanded the Canfields' mail. But his mood had changed the instant Steven had handed him a package. When he'd seen the sender's name and realized he'd received a gift from his betrothed, a smile had wreathed Austin's face, chasing away the storm clouds.

Clay knew what had happened next. Austin had raced home, waiting until he was at the Bar C to open the box. Then he'd strutted around the ranch, as proud as the proverbial peacock over the miniature Sarah had sent him. Clay had seen only the happy side of Austin that day, the exuberant, almost playful part of his brother. The euphoria hadn't faded by suppertime. If anything, it had increased as Austin had boasted of how envious the other poker players would be when they saw just how lovely his bride was. Clay didn't doubt that the men had felt twinges of regret when they realized that their own brides—if they were fortunate enough to find them—might not be so beautiful, but mild envy was not a cause for murder.

"Who hated Austin enough to kill him?" Clay hadn't realized he'd spoken the words aloud until Shadow whinnied. "You're right, boy. It doesn't make any sense." While Austin's temper might provoke anger, even a brawl, surely nothing he had said or done was serious enough to warrant death. But the fact remained: someone had killed his brother.

When he reached the ranch, Clay splashed water on his face and hands, washing off the road dust. He'd delayed so long that there wasn't time for more complete ablutions, but at least he wouldn't look totally unpresentable at the supper table. It was odd how he found himself looking forward to the last meal of the day. It must be because Pa was joining them every day now. Clay had been surprised when Sarah had suggested they would all benefit by having Pa there. Patience hadn't wanted him to sit at the table, claiming it only served to remind Pa of all that he could not do. Though he'd said nothing, Clay had suspected it was Patience who preferred not to be reminded of her father-in-law's disability.

Sarah was different. Clay suspected that if he lived to be a hundred, he would not understand her. A sensible woman would have gone back to Philadelphia and the comfortable life she'd led there. Not Sarah. A sensible woman would not have chosen a position at the mercantile where hours of standing could take their toll on her leg. Sarah had. Though he knew she was in pain, she would not surrender. Instead, she continued to insist that working at the Rousseaus' store was the key to creating a new life for herself and Thea. Stubborn woman!

Clay frowned as he tried to picture her as Austin's bride. How would she have dealt with his mercurial moods? Would she have been the steadying force he needed, or would she have grown frustrated by her unpredictable bridegroom? Would her independent streak have annoyed Austin, or would he have been charmed by it? Clay didn't know. What he did know was that from the very first letter he'd received from Miss Sarah Dobbs, Austin had been convinced that she was the bride he wanted, and nothing Clay had said had dissuaded him.

"More chili, Pa?" Sarah smiled and offered the man who should have been her father-in-law another serving of Martina's spicy stew. It must have been Clay's imagination, but it seemed that Pa was having less difficulty eating. The strangest thing was, he seemed to watch Thea and imitate her motions. It was almost as if he were learning to eat along with Sarah's little sister.

That was another part of the puzzle that surrounded Sarah. Her sister. Clay hadn't wanted her here, serving as a reminder of the child he and Patience had dreamed of, the unborn child who'd died with his wife that hot August day, but once again Austin had been adamant. And now that Thea was here, Clay had to admit it wasn't as painful as he'd feared. And even if he would prefer having no reminders, it was clear that Pa enjoyed the little girl's company. Clay would do almost anything to bring his father a few moments of happiness. If Thea could accomplish that, surely Clay could overcome memories of his own losses.

"Is something wrong?" The meal was over, and Pa and Thea were seated at the far end of the room, seemingly content to look out at the pasture. Sarah had remained at the table, drinking a final cup of coffee.

"Why do you ask?"

Though she gave him a small smile, her brown eyes were somber. "You appear troubled."

Clay let out a sigh. He never had been good at hiding his feelings. That was a fault he and Austin shared. The difference was, Clay rarely acted on his emotions the way his brother did. "It was a bad day," he admitted. Though he hadn't planned to, Clay found himself recounting how he tried to retrace Austin's steps, keeping his voice low so that Pa would not overhear. "All I've learned is that he fought with everyone he saw the day he was killed."

"Austin?" There was no disguising Sarah's surprise. She laid down her coffee cup and looked at Clay, her eyes wide. "That doesn't sound like the man who wrote my paper roses."

It was Clay's turn to be surprised. "Your what?"

"Oh . . ." She smiled, a full smile this time, a smile that transformed her face into one of the prettiest Clay had ever seen. "That's what I call the letters Austin sent me. He told me once he wished he could send me roses. Though he was apologizing, there was no reason. The letters were so beautiful that I thought they were flowers—perfect roses made of paper." Sarah stared into the distance, her eyes focused on something Clay could not see. "When I answered Austin's advertisement for a bride, all I expected was a business arrangement, but then the letters came, and I felt as if I were being wooed." Her face softened again, and when she looked at Clay, he felt his breath catch at the emotion blazing in her eyes. "I fell in love with your brother without ever meeting him. His letters told me so much: that he was a gentle man, a sensitive man. That's why I was so surprised by your story. The Austin I loved was not someone who'd fight with everyone he saw."

A mule's kick to the stomach would have hurt less than her words. Sarah was wrong. Dead wrong. But so was he. Clay lowered his eyes hastily, lest Sarah somehow guess the reason for his distress. He should never have written the words he had. That was clear now. He should have kept everything purely businesslike. But he hadn't.

Clay swallowed, trying to dislodge the lump that had settled in his throat. When Austin had asked him to woo his bride, pointing out that he himself was incapable of using pen and ink to create a coherent sentence, Clay had agreed. It was no less than he could do, since Austin was giving up his dream of travel to ensure that the Canfield line would not end and that Pa would spend his final years at peace.

Clay had written the words, and Austin had copied them over so that his bride would have letters in his own penmanship. At the time, the arrangement had made sense. Austin had his letters, and Clay . . . Clay had gotten far more than he'd bargained for. Not even Austin knew how much he'd looked forward to reading Sarah's letters and planning his response. The world had seemed bleak and his life a shambles after Patience's death, but when he sat at this table and composed what Sarah called her paper roses, Clay had been able to forget all that was wrong in his life. For a few minutes, he'd been transported to a world where love and happiness flourished.

It had been a mistake. A huge mistake. Clay could see that now. Perhaps if he hadn't written the letters, Sarah would have been more willing to return to Philadelphia. Perhaps she would have considered this a business arrangement that hadn't turned out the way she'd expected. But the damage had been done. Sarah believed herself in love with a man who didn't exist.

Clay drained his coffee cup as he considered the enormity of what he'd done. He could tell Sarah the truth. The Bible Austin was so fond of quoting claimed the truth would set a man free. Clay didn't believe that. She was happy now, believing she'd been wooed by Austin. In her eyes, Clay's brother was a hero. The truth would destroy her memories of him, leaving nothing in return. Surely that would be cruel. Let her keep her illusions. They were all she'd ever have.

6

"Why don't you come in and sit for a spell?" Though the words were framed as an invitation, Mary's tone made them little less than a command. The reason wasn't hard to find. When Sarah had arrived at the Lazy B, Thea had flung herself at her, grabbing her legs and sobbing, "Me wanna go home." Nothing Sarah did, not even gathering the child in her arms and murmuring soothing sounds, quelled the tears.

"I don't know if that's a good idea." Sarah doubted her sister would sit silently in Mary's elegant parlor. The last time they'd been there, Thea had wanted to climb the stairs and had succeeded in scraping her hands when she'd tumbled, precipitating more tears. She bore no cuts or bruises today, but the tears continued to flow for reasons that weren't clear. Sarah might have blamed her sister's mood on the weather— even Martina, who'd lived here her whole life, admitted it was unusually hot for early April—had she not known how frequently Thea cried.

"We'll sit on the porch," Mary announced. "It's cooler there, anyhow. Thea, I have milk and cookies for you."

Though Thea's eyes brightened at the prospect of her favorite snack, she did not release her grip on Sarah. "It's all right, sweetie. We'll go home as soon as we have our milk." Apparently convinced, Thea loosened one hand long enough to brush the tears from her cheeks.

When she and Sarah were seated on the porch swing with a now smiling Thea playing at their feet, Mary turned her attention back to Sarah. "Your sister is a puzzlement."

Sarah gulped, fearing this was the prelude to Mary's saying she could no longer care for Thea. She'd been expecting that announcement, and today's crying spate, which was little less than a tantrum, might have convinced Mary of the futility of watching a young child. Sarah folded her hands, trying not to let her dismay show.

"I ain't never seen a child cry so much. At first, I reckoned it was cuz she was a girl." Mary's expression was stern as she looked down at Thea. "I got no experience with little girls. Boys are different. The two Canfield boys spent as much time here as they did on their ranch."

"More milk." Thea rose to hand her empty cup to Sarah.

"Please," Sarah admonished. When Thea repeated the word, she poured a few ounces into the cup and settled her sister back on the floor.

"I figgered she'd get better," Mary continued, "but she ain't. She cries most of the time and keeps talking about home." Mary stared into the distance, as if choosing her next words.

For a moment, the only sounds were the creaking of the swing, Thea's slurping, and a few songbirds' trilling. Sarah gazed at the meadow, wondering if she would ever grow accustomed to the sight of an ordinary green meadow suddenly transformed into a carpet of blue. Though Isabelle had told her that this part of Texas was famous for its wildflowers, the reality surpassed even Isabelle's exuberant praise. The bluebonnets were quite simply gorgeous. With puffy white clouds drifting slowly across a sky that rivaled the flowers' hue, it would have been a scene of pastoral tranquility, if Sarah had no worries. But she did. No matter what Mary said, it was clear the situation could not continue. Thea was miserable and Mary frustrated.

When Mary spoke, her words were not what Sarah had expected. "You may not want an old woman's advice, but I reckon you should take Thea home."

"I will, as soon as she finishes her milk."

The older woman shook her head. "Not to the Bar C. Back to Philadelphia. That's the only home your sister knows."

Sarah cringed at the thought and the myriad of unpleasant memories it conjured. It wasn't Mary's fault. She had no way of knowing how impossible her suggestion was. "I can't." The words sounded as bleak as a November day.

"Why not? It 'pears to me that's the only thing that will make Thea happy."

Sarah tightened her fingers until the knuckles whitened, forcing herself to loosen her grip as she tried to repress images of the home she and Thea had once shared. Thoughts of the three-story brick residence with its leaded glass chandelier and the gracefully curving staircase brought nothing but pain, for they were inevitably followed by memories of the last time she'd entered Mama and Papa's bedchamber.

"The house is sold," Sarah said bluntly. Mary didn't need

to know that creditors had taken everything except Mama's Bible. "Ladreville is our home now."

Mary's face softened. "Forgive me for prying." She looked down at Thea. "We'll keep trying."

Sarah took a deep breath and let the relief flow through her. Perhaps she was being foolish, believing tomorrow would be better, but oh! how she hoped it would. "Thank you," she said softly, knowing there was no way she could repay this woman for her kindness.

"I'll do the best I can to make her happy. There must be something." Once again, Mary stared into the distance, a small smile crossing her face. "That's it. We'll work in the garden. Young'uns always like dirt."

As a wave of pleasant memories washed over her, Sarah nodded. "Our mother had a rose garden. While she was working on the bushes, she let Thea dig in one corner." Sarah looked down at her sister. Thea had drained her cup and was drowsing, apparently worn out by her earlier tears.

"We women love our flower gardens." A chuckle punctuated Mary's words. "Why, Clay's wife weren't here very long afore she started one of her own. I reckon she hoped the baby would be a girl, so they could work together."

"The baby?" By all rights, Sarah should be heading back to the Bar C, but she lingered, curious about the man whose home she shared. Martina, steadfastly loyal, did not indulge in gossip, and Sarah had not asked Isabelle about Clay. This was her chance to learn more about the man who might have been her brother-in-law.

Mary's eyes widened ever so slightly. "You didn't know Patience was expecting?" She shook her head, her lips pursed in disapproval. "Of course not. Those Canfields always were

122

closemouthed. Don't want nobody knowing their business. Why, they probably didn't tell you what happened to Patience." When Sarah nodded in confirmation, Mary continued. "I blame myself for the tragedy. If I hadn't taken that fish chowder to the potluck, Clay's wife might still be alive."

Mary reached for her handkerchief and dabbed at the corners of her eyes. "I shouldn't a' done it, but Patience told me she had a hankering for a stew like she had at home. You know how women who are in the family way ofttimes crave peculiar foods. Patience wanted fish. I figgered Martina wouldn't cook it, so I found an old recipe for Boston clam chowder. 'Course I didn't have no clams, so I had to make do with a fish David caught."

Thea looked up, as if intrigued by the story. Sarah doubted she'd understood many of the words, but her sister had always been sensitive to voices and seemed to sense Mary's distress.

"To this day, I don't know what spoiled. Coulda been the fish. Coulda been the cream. All I know is something went bad. Real bad." Mary touched her stomach, remembering. "The only good thing was that the other church ladies wouldn't touch the stuff. They said it smelled funny. Patience said that was the way it was supposed to smell and took a big helping. I couldn't let her eat alone, so I took some too, but only a little bit. I reckon that's why I lived and Patience didn't." Mary touched her abdomen again. "I tell you, Sarah, I ain't never been so sick in all my life. Bearing David was easy as pie compared to that."

As Thea started to whimper, Sarah reached down and drew her sister onto her lap, her own distress at Clay's loss becoming secondary to the need to comfort her sister. A quick check revealed that Thea hadn't hurt herself. Could it be that she was reacting to Mary's story and that was the reason she cried so often? Just because she had been a widow for many years didn't mean Mary wasn't lonely. Perhaps she talked about her losses to Thea. Perhaps Thea wept, not because she longed for home but because she sought to comfort Mary in the only way she knew, by crying with her.

"It was the saddest thing you ever did see." Mary's words brought Sarah back to the present. "Clay was beside himself. I never seen a man so bereaved, and I hope I never do again." Mary shook her head, her coronet of braids moving ever so slightly. "He loved that woman something fierce. I heard tell he wouldn't let no one touch her things, wouldn't even give away her clothes. It's a pity, but I reckon he let her garden go to weeds too."

Pity was not the word Sarah would have used. *Tragedy. Catastrophe.* Clay's situation deserved more than an ordinary word like *pity*. It wasn't only Thea who wanted to cry. Sarah's heart ached, and she felt tears well in her eyes for the man Clay had been and the pain he had endured. First his father had suffered apoplexy; then he'd lost his wife and unborn child; and then, in a blow no man should have to bear, his brother had been killed. It was no wonder he was bitter. Though Sarah could not condone his plans for revenge, for nothing—absolutely nothing—justified killing, she understood what had brought him to that point, and her heart wept for him.

Clay was still in Sarah's thoughts an hour later as she and Thea stood at the edge of the paddock, watching Nora graze. Lured by the sight of the vivid red flowers that Martina called Indian paintbrush dotting the field of bluebonnets,

Sarah and Thea had taken a walk to pick a few blooms for Pa's room. Now they were back at Thea's favorite part of the ranch, but while her sister seemed mesmerized by Nora, Sarah's thoughts remained focused on the horse's owner. It was logical that she'd think of Clay today, for she'd learned more of the tragedies that seemed to stalk him. Knowing that he'd been expecting and then had lost a child helped explain the apparent aversion he'd had to Thea. If Sarah was right, through no fault of her own, Thea reminded Clay of the baby he would never hold, of the son or daughter he would not raise. It was no wonder he hadn't wanted to be near her, just as it was understandable that Sarah's thoughts were focused on him this afternoon.

"Run, Sarah. Me wanna run." Thea tugged on Sarah's hand.

"All right, sweetie, but just to the corner and back." Though Sarah could not run with her sister, the exercise would help dissipate some of Thea's energy.

Sarah leaned on the railing, smiling as she watched her sister pretend to gallop. Had Clay done that as a child? She shook her head, trying to dismiss the image of a miniature Clay prancing like a horse. It was annoying that she couldn't find the reason why thoughts of Clay were such frequent companions, triggered by the slightest thing. She'd be in the mercantile, helping a woman choose the right color ribbon for her new frock, and simply looking at the shades of blue would remind her of Clay's eyes. A man would ask for a can of beans, and Sarah would wonder whether Clay ate beans when he rode the range for weeks, searching for stray cattle. Here at the ranch it was more understandable, for she was immersed in his life—his present life, at any rate. But, still, there was no reason—no logical reason, that is—for her thoughts to drift to him as often as they did.

"Papa Clay!" Thea clapped her hands with delight as he rode into the yard. "Horse. Thea wanna ride horse."

As Clay dismounted, looping Shadow's reins over a fence post, Sarah kept a firm grip on her sister. She knew from experience that Thea had no fear of horses, not realizing a well-placed kick could maim or even kill her. "I'm sorry, sweetie, but you're too little to ride a horse."

"No!" Thea wailed. "Not little. Me big girl."

Sarah tightened her grip, fearing a full-blown tantrum was imminent. Thea wasn't getting on a horse, and that was final.

"It appears your sister is turning into a genuine Texan," Clay said as he strode toward them, his long legs covering the distance in half the time it would have taken Sarah. "She's old enough to learn to ride."

"No!" The word came out as little less than a shriek. "It's too dangerous."

Clay appeared not to have heard Sarah. "She can have a pony of her own when she's a little older. Meanwhile, she ought to get used to the feel of a horse. If she'd been born here she'd have already been on one."

His voice was low and soothing. Was this the way he dealt with difficult patients? Sarah wasn't being difficult; she was, quite simply, terrified by the prospect of her sister on a horse, even gentle Nora.

Clay nodded as if he understood. "I'll take her for a ride."

"Yes, Papa Clay, yes! Thea ride." Thea stretched her arms toward Clay, entreating him to carry her into the paddock.

"What if she falls?" Though Sarah knew it was irrational, memories of her own accident and the months of excruciating pain flashed through her mind. She couldn't allow Thea to take such a risk.

"I won't let her fall." Clay's words were matter-of-fact, defying her to challenge them. "C'mon, Sarah. She can't get hurt while I'm holding her. Don't let your fears infect her."

He was right. As much as she hated to admit it, Sarah knew that. If Thea was to grow up in Ladreville, she needed to be comfortable on a horse. More than comfortable, she needed to feel as if the horse were an extension of herself. Sarah had felt that way once and had found riding wonderfully exhilarating. How could she deny her sister that pleasure, simply because she'd been injured by a horse? Slowly, Sarah nodded her agreement.

A minute later, Clay was astride Shadow with Thea in front of him, her tiny hands gripping the reins as she shouted commands to Shadow. Though her heart continued to pound with fear, Sarah couldn't help smiling at the sight of her sister sitting there, her legs splayed to the side, her face split by the biggest grin Sarah had ever seen.

"Sarah, look!" Thea cried. "Me riding!" And she was. Though Clay kept his arm wrapped around her stomach and was guiding the horse, Thea seemed to believe she was in charge of Shadow. Her squeals of delight echoed across the pasture, leaving no doubt that Thea was having the time of her life.

"Thank you, Clay," Sarah said ten minutes later when the riders had dismounted and Thea had raced to the house to tell Martina of her adventure. "That's the happiest I've seen Thea in a long time." Perhaps ever.

Clay uncinched the saddle. "I don't claim to be an expert on children, but your sister seems happy enough to me."

"She is when she's here, but Mary says she cries most of the time she's there. All she wants to do is come home."

Shrugging, Clay lifted the saddle off Shadow's back and laid it on the fence. "Ma used to claim that children went through stages. This is probably one of them. She'll grow past it."

"That's what Mary and I thought, but she's getting worse." And, if it was true that Thea was being influenced by Mary's moods, her sadness would not end as long as she was at the Lazy B. Even working in the garden might not be enough.

Clay wiped his hands on his chaps. "It seems to me there's an easy solution to your problem. You could spend your days here with Thea. And, before you argue, that's what you'd have done if you'd married Austin."

"But I didn't marry Austin. Everything is different now." Sarah wasn't a wife. She and Thea were not part of the family. At best, they were guests. At worst, interlopers. "It's very kind of you to let us stay on the ranch, but I don't want to be beholden to you any more than we already are. I told you I'd find a way to pay for our keep, and I'm doing that."

Sarah thought she heard him sigh, but when he spoke, Clay's words were even and betrayed no exasperation. "You wouldn't be a burden. Someone might as well enjoy the ranch." Frowning, he looked at the paddock where Shadow and Nora were grazing. Though it was a peaceful scene, it appeared to bring him no comfort. "It's for certain, I don't like being here. This place holds nothing but bad memories for me."

Sarah had no doubt about what had caused those memories.

Still, it wasn't fair to blame a place for what had happened there. "It's a beautiful ranch."

"That's what Pa and Austin used to say. I never could see that. To me, it's just a lot of work." Clay turned toward the house, waiting until Sarah moved before he started walking. "Pa loves this place, but that's because he and Ma were the original Anglo settlers. They came here when they were first married. According to Ma, they thought this was the promised land. It probably seemed like that at the beginning, until the promise turned into a curse."

Clay scowled as he looked at the house his parents had built. "I don't know how much you know about Texas history, but it seems as if we're always fighting the Mexicans. I was fourteen when Pa went to war. Naturally, Austin and I wanted to go with him." The furrows between Clay's eyes bore witness to remembered pain. "I think that was my first real fight with Austin. He didn't take too kindly to my telling him he was too young to go to war. When Pa broke up the scuffle, he announced neither one of us was stepping one foot off the Bar C. Later he took me aside and told me I had to stay, because someone had to be in charge of the ranch." Clay's lips tightened. "He probably said that to make me feel important, but it turned out to be the truth. Ma died soon after he left, leaving Austin and me with a few ranch hands. Instead of fighting the enemy, I was stuck herding cattle."

Though he gave his words an ironic twist, Sarah heard the pain behind them and tried to imagine what it must have been like for Clay, faced with his mother's death at the same time that he tried to run a ranch.

"It's ironic. When Pa returned home, the State of Texas called him a war hero and rewarded him with a grant of more land. Lots of land. That was what he and Ma had dreamt of, having a huge spread. The sad thing is, their dream had come true, but Ma wasn't alive to enjoy it." Clay frowned again. "The only good thing that came out of that war was enough money for me to attend school in Boston."

Sarah raised an eyebrow, uncertain how war had translated into dollars.

"When he heard Michel Ladre wanted to establish a town, Pa offered to sell him a piece of land. My share paid for college and let me escape this miserable place. Austin made an agreement with Pa that the Bar C would be his when Pa died and put his share back into the ranch."

"Now it's yours." Though his father was still alive, Clay had full responsibility.

He nodded. "This isn't a birthright. It's a burden I never wanted. That's why, as soon as I can, I plan to sell everything and move back East where I belong."

Though Sarah had come to love Texas and the Bar C in the short time she'd lived there, she understood Clay's feelings. Hadn't she chosen to leave Philadelphia and its painful memories? There was only one problem with Clay's plans. "What about your father?"

He appeared startled by the question. "I'll take him with me, of course. He can't stay here alone."

Sarah hadn't doubted that Clay planned to move his father. What she questioned was the effect on Pa. "Will he be happy away from here?" She had seen how the pain drained from Pa's face when he sat next to the window and gazed at the front yard, his eyes focused on the small stand of live oaks. Though she'd only visited it once, Sarah knew the trees sheltered the Canfield burial ground. It was there that Pa's wife and son, as well as Clay's wife and unborn child, were buried. Pa found peace, looking at the final resting place of his loved ones. How could a city, no matter how beautiful, have the same effect?

"This was your father's dream. Do you think he wants to leave it?"

Clay's lips tightened. "I don't know. All I do know is that I cannot stay in a place I hate."

Sarah started to stretch her hand out to him, then drew it back. Who was she to think she could help him? Though her heart ached with the pain he'd endured, she could not assuage Clay's anguish. She had no words. Even a friendly touch wouldn't help. Try though she might, Sarah didn't seem able to help anyone. Thea was unhappy. Pa wouldn't cooperate when she tried to exercise his legs. Clay was miserable. There was no point in pretending otherwise. Sarah Dobbs was a failure. Those prayers Isabelle had promised to send on her behalf had had no effect. Why had she been so foolish as to think they would?

⌁

The man was tall, even taller than Clay. When he entered the store, he ducked his head, then removed his hat, revealing hair a few shades lighter than Clay's and eyes the same color blue, a blue Sarah thought of as "Texas sky." Though her mind registered impressions of the man, they were fleeting, for Sarah's attention was drawn to the girl at his side. This child was unlike the others who had visited the mercantile. She was, Sarah guessed, six or seven years old, though her age was difficult to ascertain, for she kept her shoulders slumped, her head bowed, and her eyes downcast, darting only brief glances at Sarah.

Though she might have been shy, as some children were on their first foray into the store, the looks she gave Sarah were bright and filled with curiosity, dispelling the notion of timidity. Something else was making the girl literally shrink from Sarah. As the child plaited her skirt with nervous fingers, Sarah nodded slowly, realizing she was embarrassed. The reason wasn't difficult to find. The girl's blonde braids were uneven and lacked the bows others her age wore; her skirt revealed too many inches of leg; her blouse strained at the seams. In sharp contrast to her outgrown and somewhat shabby clothing, her shoes were perfectly polished and betrayed not a single scuff mark.

"*Guten Morgen, Fraulein.*" The man added, "I heard you speak German."

Before she could respond, Isabelle leaned across the counter, seeming to forget that she was counting spools of thread while Sarah waited on customers. "Shame on you, Gunther Lehman." She shook her finger at him in a parody of a stern schoolmarm. "I know you speak English."

The girl's head jerked up, revealing a sweet smile. The man's was sheepish. "Miss Rousseau is right," he said, surprising Sarah with his lightly accented English. Unlike the other immigrants, Gunther Lehman sounded almost American, as if he'd spent a great deal of time listening to the Anglo residents and imitating their accents. "I do speak English, and so does my daughter." He placed a hand on the child's shoulder, urging her forward. "Come, Eva, and meet the nice lady."

"Hello, Eva." Sarah gave her a warm smile, hoping to ease some of her distress, before she addressed the girl's father. "Your daughter is lovely." Other than the coloring of her hair and eyes, there was little resemblance between them. While

Gunther Lehman's face was square and heavily featured, his daughter's was heart-shaped with delicate features.

"*Ja*. She looks like her mother, God rest her soul." His words explained his dilemma. Without a mother, the child had no one to dress her or braid her hair. "Eva needs new clothes. I do my best, but I don't know what a six-year-old would like. Will you help us?"

The girl's imploring look confirmed what Sarah had surmised, that she was embarrassed by her outgrown clothing.

"Certainly. How many dresses did you have in mind?"

If his daughter hadn't been there, Sarah might have laughed at the horrified expression on Gunther's face. A casual observer who hadn't heard the exchange would have thought Sarah had demanded he perform some impossible task, when all she'd done was ask a seemingly simple question.

"I don't know. How many should she have?"

Sarah heard a faint twittering and realized Isabelle was enjoying the situation. Though normally she let Sarah handle customers alone, for some reason she was taking an unusual interest in this sale. "At least two complete ensembles for everyday," Sarah said firmly, "and one for Sunday."

"Fine. Frau Berger agreed to sew whatever we buy."

"Oh, *Vati*, thank you." Eva gave her father a hug, her gratitude telling Sarah she hadn't expected more than one dress. Sarah suspected that Gunther had not considered pantaloons, petticoats, and pinafores, not to mention the layers of undergarments females of the species wore. She made a mental note to select fabric for a nightdress too.

When Gunther shuffled, clearly ill at ease in what he considered a feminine environment, Sarah suggested he wait on the bench outside. Madame Rousseau had told her it was a

133

popular spot for the town's gentlemen, particularly when their wives were selecting corsets and chemises. "Eva and I will choose everything she needs. Won't we, Eva?"

"Oh yes." Her slump disappeared as the girl scampered toward the back of the store where the bolts of fabric were displayed and began to finger one. "This is pretty."

It was, though the silk was better suited to an adult. Gently Sarah steered Eva toward the calicos. When they'd selected three different fabrics, Sarah reached for a spool of soutache braid and held it against the navy blue poplin they'd chosen for Eva's Sunday dress. "I think this would be pretty around the sleeves and hem." When the girl hesitated, eyeing Sarah's unadorned gown, she added, "It's very grown up. When I'm out of mourning, I plan to get some for myself. Now, would you like some?"

Eva's eyes sparkled. "Oh yes, please. Let's buy it."

Sarah heard Isabelle's chuckle and suspected she would regale the family with tales of how Sarah had persuaded yet another customer. "All right. Now let's figure out how much you'll need." Sarah did a quick calculation. "Half a yard for each sleeve. That's one yard for both of them. And three for the hem." Sarah gave Eva an expectant look. "How many does that make altogether?"

The girl shook her head as the sparkle faded from her eyes. "I don't know," she mumbled, clearly ill at ease.

"One plus three," Sarah coached, certain that Eva would be able to do the arithmetic. The girl's eyes gleamed with intelligence. Surely she could count to ten and add simple numbers.

But Eva's expression remained bleak. "I don't know." Once again her shoulders slumped and her head drooped with shame. It wrenched Sarah's heart to know she'd been the one to destroy this child's fragile self-confidence. There must be something she could do.

"Look at me, Eva." When the girl complied, Sarah raised her hand with the fingers fisted. Slowly, she elevated her index finger. "That's one for the sleeves," she said. Lifting the other three, she held them slightly apart from the first one. "We have three more for the hem. Can you count them?"

Eva nodded. "One, two, three, four."

Sarah gave her a bright smile. "That's right. The answer is four. Three plus one is four."

Her smile once more restored, Eva raced to the front porch and dragged her father back inside to pay for her new dress materials. When they'd left, Sarah climbed onto one of the stools behind the counter, glad there were no customers. Though thankful for the opportunity to rest her leg, Sarah also wanted a chance to ask Isabelle about the problem she'd seen.

Her friend grinned. "I'm surprised it took Gunther this long to come here," she said before Sarah could raise her question.

"What do you mean?"

Isabelle gave Sarah an arch smile. "Gunther's wife died two years ago, and he's been looking for a new mother for Eva ever since. I thought he'd be here the first day you started work."

Sarah bristled. Gunther might be seeking a wife, but she was most definitely not interested in a husband. Not today. Probably not ever. Her dreams of marriage and happily-ever-after had died along with Austin. Now all that mattered was keeping Thea safe and happy. Though that had seemed

135

impossible yesterday, hope glimmered today. If what Sarah thought was true, she might have a solution. "Eva seems bright. It's odd she can't do simple arithmetic."

Isabelle shrugged, as if the reason should be apparent. "How would she learn? Ladreville has no school. The mothers teach their children as much as they can. What's Eva to do? She has no mother, and she spends most of the day with Gunther." Isabelle stopped to greet a customer, then said, "I can't recall how much I've told you, but Gunther owns the grist mill, and that means he works longer hours than most anyone else. He's a good, hard-working man with no time for a child. That's why Eva needs a new mother."

Or something else. Though she kept her face impassive, inwardly Sarah was smiling. Gunther and Eva's predicament was anything but amusing, but maybe—just maybe—solving it would help more than them. For the rest of the day, Sarah served customers. She must have said the right things and calculated the bills properly, for no one complained, but if she'd been asked who had entered the store and what they'd bought, she would have been unable to answer, for her thoughts continued to whirl. Gunther. Eva. Problem. Solution. It might be crazy. It might not work. But if it did, this could be the answer to Sarah's greatest concern.

❧

"Yeah, you're right, Shadow. I'm aggravated." Though there was no shortage of things to do around the ranch, Clay had wakened feeling more out of sorts than normal. His foul mood was not due to Daniel Morton's latest letter, asking when Clay intended to return to Boston. Though his father-in-law—his former father-in-law, Clay corrected himself—had not pressed the issue, it was clear that the older man needed someone to lighten his workload. When Clay had been in Boston, though he'd been the junior partner, he'd seen more than half the patients.

Even with the temporary assistance of a young doctor, Daniel found the practice a heavy burden. But the heaviest burden, Clay knew, was the realization that he and Prudence would never again see their elder daughter. Now they feared they were losing the man whom they'd always treated as a son, not merely a son by marriage.

Clay had responded to Daniel's letter, reassuring him and Prudence with the truth: that he would return to Boston as soon as he'd brought Austin's killer to justice. The correspondence had not disturbed his sleep. What had disturbed it had been far more insidious and dangerous.

Clay leaned forward, urging Shadow to run. When he'd been a boy, the one thing that would lighten his mood was a gallop. While there was no guarantee the old remedy would still work, he had to try something—anything—to chase away the memories of his dream.

It had come again. That was the third, maybe the fourth time. Clay had lost count. It was always the same. He'd hear the clip-clop and the gentle neighing of two horses. Then he'd see the wagon. At first he was an onlooker, watching the driver and passengers. But then, in one of those shifts that seemed logical in a dream, he became the driver on the high seat. His right arm was wrapped around a little girl who had a woman at her other side. Gradually, the faces would come into focus and he'd realize it was Thea who nestled close to him, one of her hands clasping the reins, and Sarah who cradled the baby.

The baby. Though he shuddered now at the memory, in his dream, Clay's heart filled with pride at the sight of the small boy in Sarah's arms. When he thought no one would notice, he'd sneak glances at the mother and child, feeling a warmth creep into his heart. The infant with Sarah's sweet features and Clay's blond hair had a smile that reminded him of Austin.

Each time he glanced, Sarah would catch him in the act, her lips curving into a smile as she said something that made them all laugh. And as she did, the warmth that had lodged in Clay's heart spread through him, making him feel that for the first time in his life he was complete. He was part of a family. The joy lasted only an instant. As he reached out his hand to touch the baby, the dream would end and Clay would waken, bereft and empty.

That feeling lingered. He was flying down the road now, Shadow's hooves kicking up swirls of dust as Clay bent forward, urging him to even greater speeds. This was what was important. This was real. The dream was not. Clay patted Shadow's neck, then recoiled as his fingers registered the familiar texture of horseflesh. How stupid could a man be? He was awake, not dreaming. This was a horse, not his son. Stupid! Stupid! Stupid!

Clay took a deep breath, trying to settle his roiling thoughts. It was absurd to remember how good it had felt to be with Sarah and their baby. That was a dream, nothing more. Clay didn't want dreams, and he didn't want a family, for his dreams had died last summer along with Patience.

When he returned to the Bar C an hour later, Clay was still thinking about the dream. It was annoying how the memories persisted. No matter what he did to chase them away, they were like cobwebs, clinging to the distant corners of his mind, ready to reach out and snare him. As he approached the ranch, Clay's eyes widened, and sudden fear clenched his heart. Pa. Something had happened to Pa. That was the only reason Herman Adler's buggy would be here. Someone must have called for the doctor.

"Herman." Clay leapt off Shadow and ran toward the house. As the doctor climbed down from the buggy, Clay realized he'd just arrived. "What's wrong with Pa?"

The gray-haired man shook his head. "Nothing as far as I know. How could there be when he has his own private physician in residence?"

The fear receded as quickly as it had surfaced. "Then this is a social visit. C'mon in." Clay gestured toward the ranch house. Martina would have something cool to offer their guest.

"I'd rather sit out back. I always did like the view."

Something in Herman's tone set Clay's antennae quivering, but he acquiesced, calling to Martina to bring their drinks outside.

"This is not a social visit," Herman confirmed when he'd taken a long swallow of buttermilk. "I can't ignore the signs any longer. You can pretend otherwise, but I think you know what I mean."

Clay nodded, remembering the day he'd found Herman's buggy stopped along the road and the symptoms his friend had exhibited then. The concern born that day turned to dread. "The headaches are worse?"

As he stared into the distance, as if committing the view to memory, Herman nodded slowly. "The intensity and frequency have increased. It's only a matter of time until I won't be able to see anything."

Herman was a good doctor. Clay suspected that he'd diagnosed his illness when the first symptoms had appeared, just as Clay had when he'd heard about the headaches and halos. Though he might rail at his fate privately, today Herman sounded detached, as if he were discussing a patient's prognosis, not his own.

"You know there's nothing I can do for you." How Clay hated saying that! Herman wasn't just a good doctor; he was the man who'd inspired Clay's own love of healing. "There's no cure." When he'd studied diseases of the eye, he'd learned that, though the disease might progress at different rates, it was inexorable. Eventually, the patient would be blind.

Herman turned to face Clay, the gray eyes that would one day be clouded and sightless now filled with concern. "It's true there's no cure, but there is something you can do for me. You can take over my practice."

Clay recoiled as if from a blow. As much as he respected Herman, Daniel Morton also needed him, and Daniel's needs were primary. Besides, assuming Herman's practice would mean staying here. Some things were unthinkable, and that was one. "I'm sorry, Herman," Clay said as gently as he could, "but I can't do that. As soon as I find Austin's killer, Pa and I are leaving."

"Why?" The older man appeared genuinely confused. "This is your home."

"It was my home," Clay corrected him. "Not any longer. I have no desire to live in a place where murderers go free."

"Do you honestly believe there are no murderers in Boston?" Herman fixed his gaze on Clay, as if defying him to say yes.

"I'm not that naïve, but at least no one there killed my brother."

Herman stared into the distance for a long moment, as if marshalling his thoughts. When he spoke, his voice was firm, reminding Clay of his childhood, when the doctor had served as his mentor, showing him how he treated patients. "I'm not trying to excuse anyone. Murder is wrong, but it's also wrong to let an entire town suffer because of one person's crime. If you leave, they'll have no one, and people will die unnecessarily." He looked at Clay, his eyes bright with emotion. "Stay, Clay. I beg you to stay. You could do so much good here."

Clay shook his head. "I'm sorry, Herman, but the answer is the same. No."

⸎

What would he think? Sarah looked across the supper table, trying to imagine his reaction. She wouldn't ask until the meal was finished and Pa was settled in the corner with Thea playing at his feet. That was at least half an hour from now, for both Pa and Thea ate slowly. Sarah tried not to count the minutes. She'd waited half a day; thirty minutes more wouldn't matter. Perhaps she was foolish, waiting to talk to Clay first. She could have asked Isabelle and her family what they thought. In fact, she probably should have broached the subject with them, but from the moment the idea had popped into her mind, embedding itself in her thoughts more deeply than the sand burr had in Thea's heel, she had wanted Clay to be the first to hear.

Sarah took a sip of cool tea as she tried to focus her attention on Clay, who was telling his father about the heifer he planned to buy to supplement their milk supply. On another day, she might have been interested, but today was not another day. Today she was anxious for the meal to end so she would have a chance to speak to Clay privately.

She couldn't explain why his opinion was so important. Perhaps it was because she knew he would be honest. He had nothing to gain or lose. The Rousseaus might not approve of the idea, because if she implemented it, Sarah would no longer work at the store. That might hurt their business. Then, too, they were partisan. They saw only the French settlers' side of any matter, while Clay would consider the entire town's needs.

Those were plausible reasons for consulting Clay, but if Sarah were to be honest with herself, she would have to admit they were not the only ones. So much had changed since the day Clay had lifted Thea onto Shadow's back. At first Sarah had thought it was her imagination, but it wasn't. Clay no longer regarded Thea as if she were a poisonous snake, coiled to strike. Now he returned to the ranch early enough to take her for a ride each day. The difference in Thea was unmistakable. Like a flower blessed with abundant rain and sunshine, she flourished under the newfound attention. Thea smiled more, and Mary said she cried less frequently. Though Mary attributed the change to the work they were doing in her garden, Sarah knew otherwise.

The change in Clay was almost as dramatic. He seemed less tense than before, and he even smiled once. Sarah smiled, recalling her surprise the day that had happened. She hadn't realized his lips knew how to curve upward, but oh! what a difference it made. Though he was handsome even when he scowled, the sight of Clay smiling literally took her breath away.

It was easy to find the reason for Thea's contentment; the changes in Clay were more difficult to diagnose. Perhaps they started the day he told Sarah his feelings about the ranch. If he'd been keeping his resentment bottled inside himself, it could have been like a boil, festering, needing to be lanced. Perhaps the change had nothing to do with that day but was merely the effect of time lessening his sorrow by healing the empty spaces inside him. Whatever the cause, Sarah wouldn't argue with the results. Life at the ranch was decidedly more pleasant now.

At last the meal was over, and Sarah was alone at the table with Clay. Before she could speak, he smiled again. "If my mother were alive, she would say you look like the cat who swallowed the canary." Clay's smile widened. "Austin and I never understood why she'd say that. As far as we knew, she'd never seen a canary, much less a cat who'd swallowed one, but she persisted in using the phrase."

A sound from the other side of the room caught Sarah's attention. She turned and was surprised to see Pa with what appeared to be a smile. Though she hadn't realized he'd been listening, it appeared he was enjoying memories of his wife.

"Tell me, Miss Dobbs, was the canary tasty?" Clay laced his words with mirth.

"Why, yes, Mr. Canfield." She imitated his faux formality and lightly teasing tone. "Those were the best feathers in the State of Texas."

"They must have been, to make you look so excited. Now, tell me the truth, what happened?"

"I may have found the answer to my problem." To ensure there was no misunderstanding, Sarah nodded toward Thea. "I'd like your opinion."

"Should I be flattered?"

"Indeed you should." Oh, this bantering was fun. It was almost as exhilarating as the idea that had taken residence in her thoughts earlier today. She paused and gave a dramatic sigh. "Gunther Lehman and his daughter came to the store this morning."

"And he asked you to marry him." Clay made it a statement, not a question.

"No!" The word came out more forcefully than necessary, causing Pa to look in their direction. "I hadn't met the man before today."

"That was a jest, Sarah," Clay said, his voice once more serious, "but everyone in Ladreville knows Gunther is looking for a new wife. Correction: he's looking for a new mother for Eva. The poor man has a hard life. He can't even play poker at night, because he needs to be home with her."

"A truly dreadful existence." Sarah decided to keep her tone light, at least for the moment. There'd been too much sorrow and gloom in this house. Each laugh, no matter how brief, was a gift. "The truth is, Clay, Gunther's plight isn't what bothers me. I'm concerned about his daughter. The child is practically ignorant."

Clay nodded. "I'm not surprised. That's another reason Gunther needs a wife."

"Maybe." Sarah made a show of licking her lips. "My, but that was a tasty canary." When Clay chuckled, she said, "I think there's another solution and a better one. Ladreville needs a school." She paused, waiting for Clay's reaction, and was disappointed when he kept his face impassive. Had she been wrong in thinking this would solve so many problems? It had seemed like such a good idea. "If all the children went to school, they'd learn more," Sarah continued, "and their mothers would be less harried. A school would be good for everyone."

"I agree. The town would definitely benefit." Though a moment earlier Clay's eyes had sparkled with mirth, now they reflected confusion. "What I don't understand is how that would solve your problem."

Relief washed over Sarah at the realization that he approved of the plan. She wasn't deluding herself. It was a good idea. "If I were the teacher, Thea could go to school. I wouldn't have to worry about whether or not she was happy. I know she would be, because she'd be surrounded by other children and would be close to me."

Clay lowered his voice, perhaps to keep Pa from overhearing. "I know you want to help your sister, and this seems like one way to do it. The question is, are you qualified to teach? It's not as simple as working at the mercantile."

"I don't have formal training, if that's what you're asking." Sarah wouldn't lie. "But I spent a lot of years at a fancy school. When I was bored by most of the classes, the teachers let me help with the younger pupils." Sarah leaned forward, hoping to convince him. "I can do this, Clay. I know I can."

He nodded slowly, his expression serious as he appeared to consider everything she'd said. "There's no question that it's a good idea. Other towns this size have schools; Ladreville probably should too." He was silent for a moment before he asked, "Have you thought about where you'd hold classes?"

That had been one of Sarah's first concerns. Though she'd heard of some rural schools being held in barns, she knew there were no empty barns or sheds or buildings of any kind in Ladreville. "There aren't too many choices. I drove around town this afternoon, just in case I'd missed any, but it seems to me the churches are the only buildings with enough space. At least they each have a fellowship hall."

Clay reached for the coffee Martina had left on the table and offered to refill Sarah's cup. When she shook her head, he emptied the pot into his cup. "So, which church would you use?"

"Both." That was another thing Sarah had considered this afternoon between helping customers. Ladreville's politics created its own set of problems. "If I picked one, the other's parishioners would be insulted, and they might not let their children attend." She couldn't let that happen, for one thing Sarah had realized was that the school might be a way to unify the town. "I know it'll be more work, moving things back and forth, but I think I need to alternate—one week in one church, the next week at the other."

The look Clay gave her was approving, and it sent a tingle of warmth through her veins. "No wonder you had the canary look. It seems as if you've thought it all out. Or, should I say, you've eaten every last feather?"

Sarah shook her head. "I've just begun. My head is so full of ideas, sometimes I think it'll burst." When his lips twitched, she said, "Don't laugh, Clay. I'm serious. I know what I want to do, but I don't know how to start."

His expression sobered, and he drained his cup before responding. "You'll need to get Michel Ladre's approval. Nothing happens in this town without that. I have to warn you, though, that he may refuse out of spite."

Sarah blinked, startled by the thought of the town's charismatic leader refusing to support something as valuable as a school. "I've done nothing to alienate him. Why would he refuse?"

"You were Austin's fiancée." Pain darkened Clay's eyes. "It's no secret that my brother didn't trust Michel. Austin didn't bother to hide his opinion that the mayor had appropriated public funds for his own use. I'm sorry, Sarah. What Austin said shouldn't matter, but it might."

Surely Michel would not let personal animosity affect the town. "I'll have to be my most charming." Sarah gave Clay a mockingly sweet smile, eliciting a chuckle.

"If you do that, the man will have no defense."

"I hope not."

Clay stared into the distance for a moment. When he returned his gaze to Sarah, his eyes were dark with an emotion she could not identify. "Michel may raise another concern. You probably know teachers cannot be married. He may not want to found a school, only to be forced to abandon it in a few months."

That would not be a problem. "I'll tell Michel the same thing I'm telling you. He should have no worries, because I have no intention of marrying."

Clay raised an eyebrow. "Not even if Gunther courts you?"

"Not even." Sarah paused, unsure how much she should say. Would she be reopening wounds that were only beginning to heal if she spoke of Austin? Perhaps it would be kinder to say nothing, and yet the way Clay gripped his cup told Sarah that for some reason he needed reassurance. She swallowed, waiting until he met her gaze before she said, "I can't imagine finding anyone as wonderful as the man who wrote my paper roses, and I don't plan to settle for second best."

Surely it was Sarah's imagination that Clay began to relax.

7

It was Sarah and Thea's week to attend the German church. Though they'd been there before and were no longer strangers to the simple whitewashed building whose two tall, elaborately carved silver candelabra seemed unusual companions to the rough-hewn cross, Sarah had dressed herself and Thea with more care than normal. If all went as planned, they would both be subject to more scrutiny than usual.

She settled Thea on the pew next to her, letting her hold Mama's Bible while the rest of the congregation rose for a hymn. Her sister seemed to take comfort from the pages that held the family history. Though she was too young to read Mama's writing, she invariably turned to the page that recorded her own birth, as if she somehow sensed that was her last connection to their mother. Thea rarely glanced at the previous page where Sarah had made the final entries for their parents, her hand shaking so badly the dates were scarcely legible. That was a page Sarah herself preferred not to read, for it served as a reminder of what she'd lost. She took a deep breath, reminding herself that Mama and Papa were part of the past, but this morning could be the beginning of the future.

When the congregation was once again seated, shifting in the pews to find a comfortable position for the sermon, Pastor Sempert climbed the steps to the pulpit. "The cross is empty," he said, gesturing toward the chancel. "Those of you who carried it know how heavy a burden it was." He looked around the congregation, nodding slightly in acknowledgment of the parishioners who had felled the live oak, fashioned a crude cross from its trunk, and borne it to the church.

It was a story Sarah had heard several times, how the congregation had chosen to take only the silver candlesticks from their church in Alsace, deciding that everything else would be made of materials they found in their new home. On Ash Wednesday of their first year in Ladreville they had gathered in the forest, choosing and cutting the tree and letting it dry until Good Friday, when they'd split the trunk and created two massive beams, lashing them together to form a cross. One by one, the men had taken turns carrying it, staggering under the immense weight, trying to envision how someone who'd been scourged could have borne it for even a few feet. That day the French settlers had joined the Germans, watching with pride as the cross was hoisted into place, a lasting reminder of the enormous sacrifice that had been made for them and all mankind.

The tale of how the townspeople had banded together that day, putting aside their differences to accomplish something that would benefit only one group, was part of the reason

Sarah believed the school would succeed. The town, she had told Clay, simply needed a reason to unite.

"Three weeks ago we sat here, rejoicing in the miracle of the empty tomb." The minister continued his sermon. "Our mission today and every day is to not forget the promises our Father made. Each year, Easter morning raises hope in our hearts. We are filled with God's love, and we know that he has prepared a home for us. Let us remember that message of hope and love every day of our lives. Let us keep Easter in our hearts year round."

As Sarah bowed her head in prayer, she found herself smiling at the realization that she once again felt hope. The eager anticipation she'd experienced when she'd received Austin's letters and had agreed to marry him had been destroyed by the reality of his death. Now that optimism was rekindled. Isabelle would probably use one of her favorite phrases and say it had been reborn. Sarah smiled again. Perhaps reborn was a better description than rekindled, for her hope had taken a new form. When she'd envisioned her life with Austin, the future had seemed nebulous. Now it was clear.

After Pastor Sempert delivered the benediction, he paused. "Before we depart, our mayor has asked to speak with you about a matter of importance to the town." A low murmur greeted his words as Michel Ladre made his way to the front.

"Thank you, Pastor Sempert." The mayor accompanied his next words with a smile. "I know you're anxious to return home to your Sunday dinners, and so I won't keep you too long, but, as Pastor Sempert said, this is a matter of importance." Michel paused, letting his words echo in the now silent church. "Our town is more than ten years old. We've grown and thrived in that decade. We've built two magnificent houses of worship. We even have a post office. But, there is one thing we do not have." Again, he paused for emphasis. "We have no school."

The murmurs resumed, louder than before. Michel waited until they'd subsided before he continued. "I believe it is time that we, the residents of Ladreville, address the needs of our youngest citizens and establish a school."

Sarah kept her face impassive, refusing to smile at the way he emphasized the first person singular pronoun. When she'd approached the mayor with her proposal, he'd greeted most of her statements with frowns, making her fear Clay had been right and Michel would not support her.

"There is some merit to your suggestion," Ladreville's founder admitted when Sarah had exhausted her arguments. "I fear, though, that the townspeople would not be receptive were you to present it. You are, after all, an outsider." Michel looked out the window, then clicked his fingers, as if an idea had suddenly occurred to him. "There may be a way to persuade them. The citizens of Ladreville trust me. If I were to tell them we needed a school, most likely they would agree." Michel had narrowed his eyes as he cautioned, "We would, of course, have to ensure that no one knew you and I had discussed this."

Sarah had nodded solemnly, though inwardly she was rejoicing. She cared not a whit who took credit. What mattered was that the town would soon have a school. Eva would receive the education she needed, and Thea would be happy.

"Is there anyone who does not agree that this is a vital need?" The mayor raised his voice slightly, almost as if defying someone to refute him. When no one did, he gave the congregation a benevolent smile. "I was confident you would see the wisdom of proceeding, and so I took the next step. I'm sure you all realize we cannot have a school without a schoolmarm. That would be like chicken and dumplings without the chicken."

As he'd intended, laughter greeted Michel's words. "We are most fortunate to have among us a young lady who's served as a teacher." Though he was exaggerating her experience, Sarah would not contradict him, for she realized the importance of gaining the community's confidence. "Miss Sarah Dobbs has agreed to assume the responsibility of ensuring that our children receive an education worthy of the great town we've founded. Please rise, Miss Dobbs."

As attention shifted from the mayor to Sarah, a round of applause filled the church. Afterward, as she'd anticipated, Sarah was surrounded by a group of women asking questions about the school. A few seemed dubious, as if doubting her credentials, but the majority appeared excited by the prospect of their children receiving a formal education.

"The mayor had a good idea," a tall woman with a strong German accent said.

Her companion, shorter and a few years younger, nodded. "I'm glad he knew you used to teach."

"That's his job," the tall woman declared. "He knows everything about everyone in Ladreville."

Everything except who killed Austin.

❧

"I knew God would answer my prayers." Isabelle gave Sarah a radiant smile. It was the next morning, and though Sarah had attended both churches' services to be present for the mayor's speeches, this was the first opportunity she had had to talk with her friend. Her concerns over Isabelle's reaction vanished when Isabelle touched her hand. "God led Michel to realize we needed a school and that you'd be the perfect teacher."

Whether it was God's hand or something else that had provided the opportunity, Sarah was happy that every hurdle was being surmounted. The mayor had agreed, the townspeople had approved the idea, and both congregations had ratified the use of their fellowship halls. The next step was to purchase books and other supplies.

"There are so many things to get ready." Sarah had tucked a piece of paper and a pencil into her pinafore pocket so she could make notes each time an idea struck her.

"I wish we had more of what you need here." Isabelle made a moue as she perused Sarah's list. Though the store was filled with merchandise Ladreville's residents needed for their daily lives, it was not an emporium designed to outfit a school.

"You have no reason to stock chalk, slates, and McGuffey readers." Sarah had accepted the fact that there were more challenges to overcome. The townspeople had agreed to provide tables and benches to serve as desks, but no one had school supplies. That was why she'd approached Isabelle.

"Maman said it would take three to four weeks if we order from San Antonio."

Sarah frowned. "I had hoped to begin classes sooner than that. I know I'll lose some pupils during the summer, because their parents will need them to work in the fields. If I start quickly, perhaps I can kindle enough enthusiasm that they'll be eager to return to school in the fall."

"You'll do it." Isabelle's voice radiated confidence. "I saw the way you helped Eva learn to add without making her feel stupid. That's a special talent."

Though praise was pleasant, in this case, Sarah knew it was undeserved. "Eva's intelligent. All she needed was some encouragement."

"That's what we all need."

❧

"Your sister is ready for the next step." Clay studied Sarah carefully. She'd done something different to her hair. Though he couldn't pinpoint the change, she looked ready for a party, not a trip to the corral. Her expression did not match the fancy coiffure. Both she and Thea stood by the fence, but only one of them was enthusiastic about the animals within.

"What is the next step?" Sarah asked.

"Riding alone."

The blood drained from her face so quickly that Clay feared she would faint. As he reached out to steady her, his hand registered the fragility of her arm. Though she was at least four inches shorter and thirty pounds lighter than Patience, Clay hadn't realized Sarah's bones were equally slender. It was no wonder her leg had been so badly shattered, no wonder she still feared horses. "Not completely alone," he said, attempting to reassure Sarah. "I'll be walking at Thea's side, but it's true she'll be the only one mounted."

A faint color returned to Sarah's cheeks. "She's too young."

The problem wasn't Thea's age, and they both knew it. "Age has nothing to do with it." Clay kept his hand on Sarah's arm, enjoying the warmth that radiated through his fingers.

"Thea's more than ready; she's eager. C'mon, Sarah. You have to have seen how much she loves riding and how she tries to pretend I'm not there. With a little encouragement, your sister will be an excellent rider." Something in his words appeared to have breached her defenses, for Sarah nodded slowly, as if she agreed with his assessment. "Trust me. I won't let her fall."

Sarah bit her lip, her indecision clear. Then she nodded again. "All right. Thea can ride alone. If she's happy about that, she won't mind so much when I leave her behind tomorrow."

"What's happening then?" Sarah left Thea at Mary's every day, yet she was acting as if something would be different tomorrow.

"Ride, Papa Clay." Thea tugged on his hand, clearly impatient with the adults' conversation.

"In a minute. I need to talk to Sarah first." Clay reached into his pocket, pulling out two carrots. "Why don't you give Nora and Shadow a treat?" They recognized Thea's youth and were gentle when she fed them. As Thea scampered toward the horses, Clay turned back to Sarah. "What's special about tomorrow?"

"I need supplies for the school, so I thought I'd take the wagon to San Antonio."

Clay felt his jaw drop. Perhaps he'd been mistaken. Perhaps his ears had deceived him. "You thought you would go to San Antonio alone?"

Sarah nodded, as if what she proposed were perfectly reasonable. "I asked a few people, and everyone said I couldn't get lost."

He had not been mistaken. The woman was crazy. With

155

an effort, Clay kept his voice even. "I wasn't worried about you losing your way. What would you do if one of the horses went lame?" She couldn't even harness them but depended on Miguel and the town's livery to do that each day. If Clay were a betting man, he would have bet his last nickel that she had no idea how to even remove a rock from a hoof. How on earth could she contemplate a trip like that? Besides, horses were only one of the dangers.

"What would you do if you encountered a thief? How would you defend yourself?" He thought she'd learned enough to be wary of her new home, but believing she could go to San Antonio unaccompanied was as ridiculous as her declaration the first day she'd been here that she and Thea would walk to town.

Anger colored Sarah's cheeks and her words. "I'm not helpless." She spat the words at him, daring him to disagree.

He did. "You might be in those situations. This is not Philadelphia. We have dangers you've never encountered."

Sarah's eyes darkened again, and Clay sensed she was wavering. Perhaps she remembered his tales of hostile reptiles and marauding mammals, some of them the two-legged variety. "The school is important. You said so yourself. I have no choice, Clay. If I'm going to have a school, I need supplies."

"Fine. We'll go together, and we'll take Thea with us. She'll enjoy the ride." Now who was crazy? Those were not the words he'd intended to speak, but somehow they'd come out of his mouth instead of the retort he'd planned. Look what he'd done. He had volunteered to spend a day he couldn't afford away from the ranch. Worse, much worse, he'd be spending that day with the last two people on earth whose company he craved. These were the woman and child who disturbed his thoughts and his dreams. A prudent man would have run in the opposite direction. Clay Canfield, it appeared, was not as prudent as he thought.

Though her relief was palpable, Sarah shook her head. "I don't want to—"

"Be a burden." He finished the sentence. "I've heard that before, Sarah. You need to trust me on this. It would be more of a burden if you went alone, because I'd spend the day worrying about you." That was the reason, the only reason, he'd volunteered to accompany them. It was not because he desired their company.

"Oh!" When Sarah's expression reflected her surprise that someone would worry about her, Clay felt as if a hand were squeezing his heart. What had this woman endured that she no longer believed anyone cared about her? Hadn't she realized that both Austin and he had been concerned as she'd traveled from Philadelphia, that each night they'd speculated where she was and what she had encountered? Austin's worries might have ended, but Clay's had not. He still spent far too much time thinking about this woman, trying to keep her and her sister safe and happy. When would it end? Clay had no idea.

"It's settled," he announced, his tone brooking no disagreement. "We'll leave first thing tomorrow morning."

❧

It had been only a month since she'd taken this road, but so much had changed. Sarah leaned back, savoring the rhythmic clip-clop of the horses' hooves and the sweet scent of fresh grass. The sun was higher now and hotter than it had been that day, the sky a more vivid blue. The trees were fully leafed, making Texas even more beautiful than her first impression. Though the fields had been green that day, today they were a riot of color. Delicate burgundy winecups, yellow daisies, and Indian paintbrush poked through the carpet of bluebonnets, creating a scene that drew Sarah's eye again and again.

A month ago Thea had clung to her, afraid to let even a few inches of space separate them. Today her sister was playing contentedly in the wagon bed. Though significant, those changes were dwarfed by what had happened inside Sarah. When she'd traveled toward Ladreville, she'd been filled with sorrow and fear. Austin's death and uncertainty over the future had weighed on her more heavily than the pails of water Thea had attempted to carry, only to discover they were far beyond her ability. Now anticipation made Sarah smile. She knew what the future would bring, and, though it was not the future that had led her to Texas, it was good.

Part of the reason it was good was sitting next to her. When he'd met her in San Antonio, Clay had been a stranger, a man who'd been forced to deliver tragic news. Now he was . . . Sarah paused, trying to find the correct word. A friend. Exactly. Clay was not her brother-in-law, but his actions had proven that he was a friend. Only a friend would have taken a whole day away from his responsibilities to help her.

"A penny for your thoughts," that friend said.

"I was thinking about Austin," she prevaricated. The last thing that Sarah wanted was to admit how often she thought of Clay, not his brother. That would only embarrass both of them. "I wish I had met him." That was no lie.

Clay's lips tightened, as they often did when he spoke of

his brother, before they turned up in a smile. "He was a fine man. Did you know he's responsible for many of the children speaking English?"

Though Sarah had wondered at the children's fluency, comparing it to their parents' halting English, she had never asked how they'd learned a new language. "How did he do that?"

"He turned it into a game."

Clay's eyes moved slowly, scanning the horizon, studying the thick brush that lined the road, his vigilance reminding Sarah of the dangers he claimed might lurk along the road. Though the rolling hills and the glossy green leaves of the live oaks appeared peaceful, Clay was taking no chances. The realization warmed Sarah's heart. Other than her parents, no one had ever worried about her. Her suitors had made it clear that they were doing her a favor by courting her and that she would be expected to care for them, not they her.

Clay's expression cleared, telling Sarah he'd seen no hint of danger. "Austin had the fanciest saddle in town," he said. "He knew all the children wanted to sit on it, so he would teach them a few words. Whoever remembered the most the next day got to sit on the horse and, if they were old enough, they were allowed to ride."

"Clever. Maybe Austin should have been a teacher."

"Hardly. He was a rancher, through and through, like Pa." Clay's smile broadened at the memory of happier times. "They both liked games, though, and would spend hours playing chess."

Because she was an only child for most of her life, Sarah's pastimes had been solitary: reading, painting, practicing the piano. "Do you play?" she asked Clay.

"Not well." He shrugged. "Austin tried to teach me, but I was never proficient. The game moves too slowly for me."

As he spoke, an idea lodged in Sarah's mind. "Will you teach me?"

Clay looked at her as if she'd asked him to tutor her in charming snakes. "Why? You need two people. I have no interest in playing, and I'm not sure who else in Ladreville knows how."

Sarah turned around, assuring herself that Thea was happily occupied in the wagon bed. At some point, she might teach her sister chess, but that wasn't her immediate concern. "I wouldn't ask you to play, once I learned the moves."

"Then why learn?" Clay was clearly mystified. "Chess is not a game for one."

The answer was simple. "I'd play with your father. You said he once enjoyed chess. Maybe he would like to try something that reminds him of his former life." Sarah forbore mentioning the resistance she met each time she tried to help Pa walk. Clay didn't need to know that she'd continued to exercise his father's legs. The fact was, healing came in many forms. Chess games would be in addition to those sessions, not a substitute for them. "Pa handles a spoon well enough that I imagine he could move chess pieces."

Raising an eyebrow, Clay gave her a quick smile. "You were right about having him eat with us, so I'm going to trust you on this. We'll start our lessons tomorrow."

"Thanks, Clay."

To Sarah's relief, they encountered none of the hazards Clay had feared, and the rest of the drive to San Antonio was spent in casual conversation while Sarah entertained her now-bored sister. Sarah would be glad when they arrived and

Thea could run for a few minutes, expending some of her abundant energy. When they reached the city and found the stores Madame Rousseau had recommended, Clay remained outside, watching Thea run and jump while Sarah purchased the needed supplies in less time than she'd thought possible. The wagon was now filled with parcels, leaving only a small area for Thea and her doll.

Sarah suspected that Thea, who regarded Clay as a play-mate, would not be content to remain in the back. Each day her sister grew more attached to Clay and Pa. Although that was good for Thea, it concerned Sarah. How would Thea react when they moved to their own house? Sarah shook herself mentally. She'd worry about that when the time drew near. First, she needed to get the school organized. Only then could she start saving money and searching for a house. It was odd, though, that the prospect of living in one of the quaint half-timbered houses no longer held as much appeal as it once had.

"Are you two ladies ready for dinner?" Clay asked when Sarah left the last store.

She nodded, welcoming the opportunity to think of some-thing other than moving from the Bar C. "Martina packed a basket of food." When Sarah started to reach for it, Clay laid a restraining hand on her arm.

"I know, but I thought you and Thea might enjoy a meal at the hotel." Clay nodded at Thea's bonnet, which had come untied for what seemed like the hundredth time and hung down her back, providing no protection against the sun's rays. "This will be a chance to spend some time out of the sun."

Sarah nodded her agreement. It wasn't only Thea who'd benefit from the shade. Her own skin was beginning to redden.

A few minutes later, Clay hitched the horses to a post and ushered Sarah and Thea into the hotel he'd chosen. Though the exterior was unprepossessing, the dining room was fancier than Sarah had expected, with linen tablecloths and fine china. She looked around, dubious, when the waiter seated them. This was not a suitable place for an active two-year-old. "I'm worried about Thea breaking something."

Clay appeared unfazed. "We'll ask for a tin cup and plate." Motioning to the waiter, who'd left them alone to consider the menu selection, Clay explained what he needed.

"Yes, sir. I'll bring your daughter's plate." The man practically clicked his heels in his eagerness to serve.

Though Clay nodded, Sarah flushed with embarrassment. "She's not . . ."

"Thank you." Clay's look cautioned her not to continue.

"You let him think . . ."

Once again Clay overrode her words. "No harm was done. Besides, there will be less gossip if everyone believes we're a family."

"I see." But they were not a family.

❧

As he lifted Thea into the wagon bed, Clay bit back a smile, knowing Sarah would not appreciate his amusement. Still, it had been humorous, watching her blush at the waiter's assumption that they were married. Though she was an attractive woman even when she wore her most serious expression, a blush and a smile turned her into downright beautiful. And that made a man consider ways to provoke a new blush. *Stop it, Clay. You have no business thinking those thoughts. You'll be leaving Texas soon, and she'll be staying.*

162

"Ride horsey, Papa Clay?"

He shook his head, thankful that Thea had remained oblivious to the currents running between him and her sister. She'd seemed to find nothing unusual, whereas Clay . . . He must have been crazy to agree to bring Sarah and Thea here. Agree? He'd insisted on it. The moment the words had escaped his mouth, he'd realized he would be creating the scene that haunted so many dreams, the image of the three of them sitting in the front of the wagon. Fortunately, Sarah had agreed when he'd suggested Thea play in back.

Perhaps that was the reason the ride hadn't triggered unwelcome thoughts. The truth was, the day had been more enjoyable than he'd thought possible. Clay couldn't recall the last time a drive had passed so quickly or when he'd laughed so much. He didn't need to search far for the reason. It was sitting next to him, in the form of a woman who jested and blushed and made him forget his sorrows, if only for a moment.

The sun had set by the time they crossed the Medina and headed for the ranch. Thea slept in the back, and Sarah, visibly tired, dozed occasionally. Only Clay needed to remain alert, watching for predators.

No predator greeted him as he drove toward the barn. Instead, he saw Martina waiting for him, her face white with strain. "Praise the Lord! You're home."

Her tense greeting sent fear rushing through his veins. Something was desperately wrong. Clay jumped out of the wagon. "Is Pa all right?"

"Yes. But Leah Dunn is not. Dr. Adler sent a message hours ago, asking you to go. He said you'd understand."

Clay took a deep breath, willing his pulse to return to normal as he helped Sarah climb out of the wagon. Pa was fine. That was what mattered. Leah Dunn was not his worry. She was Herman's patient, not his. Almost involuntarily, Clay asked, "Did he say what was wrong?"

"Something about her throat closing up."

Clay shuddered as his mind began to race, trying to imagine what had caused the symptoms and how to alleviate them. "I can't." The words were almost a whisper. *Why are you asking this, Herman?* The answer was simple. The treatment would require perfect eyesight, and that was something Herman no longer possessed. The older doctor was turning to his protégé, for he hadn't believed Clay when he'd said he would not take over his practice. "I can't." As visions of his brother's lifeless body flashed before him, Clay repeated the words.

Sarah touched his arm, then waited until he looked at her before she asked, "Why not?" Her brown eyes filled with confusion and something else—something that looked dangerously close to pity. Clay didn't need pity, and he didn't need to heal the town's sick.

"I'm not Ladreville's doctor."

"But you are a doctor. If the situation is as grave as it sounds, you're this woman's only chance. If you don't go, she may die." Sarah tightened the grip on his arm. "Oh, Clay, haven't there already been too many deaths?"

Though she did not pronounce the words, Clay knew she was thinking of Austin. So was he. The difference was, Austin's death was the reason Clay would not help Leah Dunn or anyone in this miserable town.

"Please, Clay. Life is precious." Sarah's eyes flickered toward the back of the wagon where Thea still slept, as if she feared someone or something would steal her sister's life.

Clay looked away, unwilling to face the anguish in her eyes, and as he did, he pictured Thea gasping for breath while a man stood at her side, refusing to help. "You're right." Allowing Leah Dunn to die would not bring Austin back. Barking commands to Martina, Clay saddled Shadow while the housekeeper retrieved his medical bag. Within minutes, he was racing toward town.

Don't let me be too late. Clay punctuated his silent prayer with a mirthless laugh. Why had he bothered? God wasn't in the habit of answering his prayers.

"Thank God you're here." Steven Dunn opened the door before Clay had tied Shadow to the fence. The postmaster's normally ruddy face was pale and etched with lines of worry.

"What happened?" There was no time for amenities. The two men were practically running as they entered the house.

"Leah was playing with the children, and a ball hit her in the throat."

Clay shuddered, knowing the damage a direct hit could have inflicted on the trachea. It was no wonder Herman had called for him. If what Clay thought was true, there was only one way to save this woman's life, and it demanded a steady hand and excellent vision.

Clay strode into the couple's bedroom, trying not to cringe at the sound of the thin breathing. He needed no examination to tell him how critical the situation was.

"Bring more light, and you'd better boil some water." Even without the additional lanterns, Clay saw the bluish tint of the woman's hands. Her pulse was dangerously low, her eyes open but unseeing. Unless he could restore her breathing, Leah Dunn would die within the hour. Clay touched the woman's throat, feeling the crushed bones. It was nothing short of a miracle that she'd lasted this long.

"Is Granny Menger nearby?" Clay would need an assistant, and the town's midwife was his best choice. She, at least, was accustomed to the sight and smell of blood.

Steven must have anticipated Clay's need for boiling water, for he placed a large kettle on the bureau. "Granny's out delivering a baby."

What else could go wrong? The man would probably faint at the first incision. Still, Clay had no alternative. "You'll have to help me."

Clay pulled his scalpel and a piece of rubber tubing from his bag, placing them in the boiling water. "I need a couple towels. Roll them together like a sausage." When Steven had complied, Clay positioned them between Leah's shoulders, forcing her throat upward and allowing him better access to her windpipe.

"Hold her head," he directed as he reached for the scalpel. "Don't watch if you don't want to, but—whatever you do—do not let her move."

Dimly, Clay heard the man gag when he made the incision. His eyes never wavering, Clay cut the membrane that covered the larynx, then inserted the rubber tubing. The whoosh of breath confirmed his success. With a speed that never failed to amaze him, Leah Dunn's color began to return, and with each breath she took, elation flowed through Clay. How could he have forgotten the pure joy of saving a life? This was why he'd become a doctor. How could he have ever doubted that this was what he was meant to do?

"She's going to live." Steven said the words so softly Clay almost missed them. "I don't know how to thank you, Dr. Canfield, but you were the answer to my prayers."

8

Thea was excited. Though Sarah had told her she would not be staying with Mary today, she didn't seem to understand until they passed the turnoff to the Lazy B. Then she started clapping her hands and chanting, "Stay with Sarah. Me stay with Sarah," glee evident in her smile and her sparkling eyes. It wasn't only Thea who was excited. If Sarah hadn't needed both hands to control the horses, she would have joined her sister clapping. Today was the first day of school, and while mild apprehension vied with anticipation, the anticipation was winning. Sarah had spent the last week supervising workers and planning lessons. Though she was confident everything was ready, a niggling fear that she'd forgotten something kept her from enjoying Martina's flapjacks. That was one of the reasons she and Thea had left the ranch half an hour earlier than necessary. Sarah wanted to arrive before anyone else, giving Thea a chance to run off some of her excess energy

167

while she assured herself that everything in the classroom was in order.

She was too late.

As the wagon rattled down Rhine Street, Sarah heard the sounds before she saw the children and mothers gathered in front of the German church. Half a dozen adults and close to twice that number of children were milling around the grounds, the mothers admonishing their children to keep their clothing clean, while the youngest engaged in an exuberant game of tag.

Sarah's smile turned into a full-fledged grin as she dismounted from the wagon and greeted the adults. Any lingering doubts she had about the wisdom of founding a school melted under this proof of the town's enthusiasm. Ladreville wanted a school. Her heart singing with joy, Sarah entered the classroom.

"Guten Morgen, Fraulein Dobbs," the children greeted her as they scrambled for seats. Unable to resist their eagerness, Sarah had opened the school after only a cursory check.

"Good morning, boys and girls." She smiled as she realized that, unlike the parishioners at church services who often left the front pews empty, her pupils were scrambling for seats in the first row. "I'm pleased to see so many of you." A few more children had joined the group, their conversation a mixture of German and English. So far the French contingent had not arrived.

"We will speak only English." Sarah spoke slowly and enunciated clearly as she announced her policy. Though he'd been skeptical initially, she had convinced Michel by explaining that no child would have an advantage over another, and—more importantly—use of English would emphasize the fact that they were all Americans. When several of the children's foreheads furrowed with concern, Sarah added, "I promise I'll make it easy for you. Before long, you may even be dreaming in English."

It was a poor choice of words, for it reminded Sarah of dreams that were best forgotten. She had lost count of the number of times she'd dreamt of a wedding—her wedding. It was always the same. There was never any preparation, any warning. Instead, she would suddenly find herself walking down the aisle, wearing her mother's blue satin gown, carrying Mama's Bible and a single white rose. Though the church was unfamiliar, she knew what was happening, and her heart raced with anticipation as each step brought her closer to the man whose life would soon be joined to hers. He was there. She knew it, but with the oddness that so often characterized dreams, his face was blurred, as if he were standing behind a cloud. She would take another step and then another, and then at last the cloud would lift, revealing her groom. Clay.

Each time Sarah would waken, her heart pounding, her mouth dry. Mama used to claim dreams were important and would remind her of all those recounted in the Bible. Mama was wrong. The dreams in the Bible might have foretold important events, but this one did not. No matter how often it came, it signified nothing. While it was true Sarah had been eager to marry Austin, wedlock was no longer part of her plan. She didn't want to marry, and if she did, she certainly would not choose Clay, a man mired in sorrow and thoughts of revenge. She and Clay were friends, she told herself, nothing more. Sarah sighed. It was easy to remember that when she was awake. If only she could be so sensible while she slept. If only she could stop the dreams.

169

The clock chimed eight, bringing her back to the present. She forced herself not to frown when she realized none of the French children had appeared. It was time for school to begin. Even though half her class was absent, she could wait no longer. Sarah fixed a bright smile on her face. She'd focus on the positive, the fact that she had fifteen pupils who appeared to range in age from about fourteen down to six. They sat at the tables, most of their expressions eager, a few apprehensive, one defiant, as if announcing to Sarah that he had no need for schooling.

"If you'd all stand up and form a line," Sarah said with a reassuring smile, "I'm going to assign seats." The audible protests confirmed her belief that they'd chosen places next to their friends. Sarah knew from experience that that was a bad idea. "Each one of you older children will have a younger one next to you."

As the tall blonde girl who'd introduced herself as Olga Kaltheimer moved toward Thea, assuming that she as the oldest would be responsible for the youngest, Eva Lehman raised her hand. "May your sister sit with me, Miss Dobbs?"

"Thea's not really a pupil." Sarah had planned to give her a chair in the back corner, where she could play while the others did their lessons, but the eagerness in Eva's eyes made her reconsider. Thea needed a place to sit, and this would even out the number of students. Furthermore, if Eva was as bright as Sarah thought, she wouldn't need an older child helping her. Instead, being responsible for Thea might increase Eva's self-confidence. "Why, yes, Eva. That's an excellent idea. You and Thea may sit in the last row." The child's obvious pleasure as she reached for Thea's hand confirmed the wisdom of Sarah's decision.

The day went quickly, at least for Sarah. Despite the predictable squabbles and the tears when one girl misspelled a simple word, the class was remarkably harmonious all morning. When some of the children struggled to express themselves in English, Sarah remembered how Austin had taught them, and turned it into a game. Olga, who admitted she was sixteen, quickly established herself as a leader and helped Sarah maintain order.

The afternoon was different. Soon after lunch, Sarah realized her pupils were no longer paying attention. Tempers frayed, turning one squabble into a fistfight. When she'd disciplined the offenders, Sarah dismissed school early. Perhaps they were tired from so much concentrated learning. She would have more frequent recesses, starting tomorrow.

"How was school?" Clay asked the question as he saddled Nora for Thea's riding lesson.

"Fun! Me have new friend," Thea announced.

In response to Clay's raised eyebrow, Sarah explained. "Gunther Lehman's daughter took Thea under her wing. So far it seems to be a good arrangement. There were no tears today." Instead, Thea had bounced with enthusiasm all morning, slowing ever so slightly when fatigue overtook her in the afternoon.

"Gunther?" Clay's eyebrow reached new heights. "Did he come courting?"

As memories of her traitorous dreams flashed before her, Sarah shook her head more vigorously than the question demanded. "He brought his daughter this morning. That's all. Really, Clay, you and the rest of the town are mistaken. Gunther doesn't view me in that way."

"Gunther views every woman as a potential stepmother

for Eva." When Sarah let out an exasperated sigh, Clay raised his hands in the universal signal of surrender. "All right. All right. Subject closed. Tell me, Miss Dobbs, did you have a full class?" Clay lifted Thea onto the gentle mare, keeping his arm around her waist until he was certain she was settled.

"No." Sarah had expected close to thirty students and had had tables and benches constructed for that number. It had been slightly discouraging to see the room half empty. "I don't understand why only the German children attended."

As Nora began to walk, Clay kept pace, his eyes fixed on Thea. "Don't worry," he said without turning toward Sarah. "The others will come."

But they did not. Two more German children joined the school on Wednesday, but there was not a single French-speaking student. Sarah tried not to worry, telling herself this was only the first week. Next week would be different, and it was, but not the way she had hoped. When Sarah reminded her pupils that the next week's lessons would be held in the French church, they nodded, and her spirits rose. Unfortunately, Monday morning brought a new group of pupils, all French.

"I don't understand what's happened," Sarah groused to Isabelle at the middle of the second week. She'd stopped at the mercantile after class, hoping Isabelle would know what was wrong and how Sarah could correct it. "Everyone thought the school was a good idea, but if this continues, their children will learn only half what they could."

Faced with a totally new group of students, Sarah had had no choice but to repeat the first week's lessons. That was frustrating for her as a teacher, but it was far worse for her pupils. She knew how quickly knowledge could be lost and worried that the German children would have forgotten most of what they'd learned by the time they returned to school.

Isabelle unwrapped a bolt of calico, holding it out for Sarah's approval. "The mistrust is deep. I've heard some of the French mothers say they're afraid their children will learn something bad if they go into the German church."

Though the calico was a deep rose that would flatter her coloring once she put aside mourning, Sarah could muster no enthusiasm for it. "That's absurd! This is school."

"True, but it's the parents who decide whether their children can attend that school." Isabelle drew out another bolt, this time a light green muslin. "You probably know that there've been more thefts and vandalism recently. Each group is blaming the other."

Sarah had heard the complaints. It didn't matter which church she attended; the conversations after the service were always the same. Only the language varied. "What if it's only one person who's responsible for all this trouble? The whole town is divided and the children are suffering because of one person."

"We don't know there's only one person involved, and even if there is, the enmity is deep. The fact that we've been here for over ten years and we're still two separate groups tells you that." Isabelle closed her eyes and was silent for a moment, as if she were praying. "Each time there's an unexplained crime, the centuries of hatred resurface."

How could these people who claimed to be God-fearing act this way? They were like the parishioners in Philadelphia who'd shunned Sarah. "That sounds like the sins of the fathers being visited on the children, only I thought it was God who did the punishing—not man."

Isabelle nodded. "Exodus 20, verse 5." Her expression was solemn as she said, "I love my town, but I have to admit that people carry grudges for too long and are too suspicious of each other. That's why I pray no one ever learns about Léon's past. I don't want to think what it would be like for us if they did."

For what seemed like the hundredth time, Sarah was thankful she had told no one of her past. Ladreville was a new life, a new beginning, a place where Thea would not be blamed for something she did not do.

When she left school the next day, Sarah was smiling. She might not have a full room, but for the first time, she had a mixed class. Much to Thea's delight, Gunther had been waiting at the church that morning, bringing Eva to join the French students.

"She wants to learn," he said simply. "You will help her."

Sarah would indeed. As the day passed, her pleasure increased. Though she'd feared their parents' prejudices might infect them, there had been no signs of antagonism toward the blonde girl whose English was still heavily accented with German. Instead, the other students had treated Eva like one of them. Sarah's smile turned into a full-fledged grin. This was the beginning. Perhaps next week all the students would be together.

"Horsey!" Thea clapped her hands in delight as they left the building and headed for the livery. "Horsey!" There were, in fact, two horses approaching the church, one from each direction. Instead of the sedate pace that most riders and vehicles observed in town, these horses were galloping. No wonder Thea was excited. She loved speed and rarely failed to urge Sarah to make their horses run.

Sarah felt a moment of alarm as she tried to imagine what had precipitated the full gallop. To her surprise, the riders reined in their animals and dismounted at practically the same moment. Why were David Bramble and Jean-Michel Ladre here? There was no emergency at the church.

"Horsey!" Sarah gripped her sister's hand to restrain her.

"Good afternoon, Sarah." David strode quickly toward her and Thea.

"I got here before you," Jean-Michel complained. "You should let me speak first." He doffed his hat, then glared at David, who had not repeated the polite gesture.

David returned the glare. "I reckon I can do whatever I want. I came to invite her to supper with my mother."

"My mother would like her to join us for Sunday dinner."

Sarah tried to hide her amusement. Not only were they acting as if she were not present, but the two men were facing each other, their belligerent posture reminding her of her youngest pupils.

"Good afternoon, gentlemen," Sarah said in the soft voice that frequently diffused the children's arguments. "Did you come to visit the school?" Since they'd not addressed their invitations to her, she would ignore them.

"I can't speak for David." Jean-Michel punctuated his words with another glare. "I came for the pleasure of your company."

"And I came to tell you Ma's mighty lonely without you and Thea."

Sarah felt a pang of guilt that she hadn't visited the older woman since school had begun. Though she'd been tired by the end of each day, that was no excuse for ignoring a friend. "We'll stop by on our way home tomorrow," she told David.

"Will you stay for supper?"

Sarah nodded. "If you're certain it will be no trouble for Mary."

"Ma enjoys your visits."

"As does my mother." Jean-Michel raised his voice, perhaps to compensate for the fact that he'd been excluded from the conversation. "That's why she hopes you'll join us for Sunday dinner."

"I'd be honored." Sarah knew it was a custom in many communities for families to invite the schoolteacher to Sunday dinner. She also knew that the order of invitations was prescribed by social rank. Michel Ladre, as the mayor and town founder, would be the first.

"Horsey!" Thea tugged on Sarah's hand as the livery owner brought their wagon to the front of the church.

"I need to take my sister home." Sarah bade the men farewell. She was lifting Thea into the wagon when she overheard Jean-Michel.

"It's a pity Sarah limps. She'd be a pretty woman otherwise."

"The way I see it, the child's more of a problem," David countered. "I reckon I never will understand why Austin wanted to saddle himself with one. Who'd be dumb enough to want to raise someone else's brat?"

Sarah's pleasure in the day evaporated.

༄

Frieda had always said he wouldn't notice a fire until it singed his hands. Though Gunther had to admit that his wife had been right about many things, he wasn't as oblivious to the world as she used to claim. Take today, for example. He knew there was something different about Eva. It was simply that he couldn't pinpoint it.

He stared at his daughter as she wrestled with the spaetzle, refusing to accept that the tender noodles were not readily speared with a fork. Her tenacity, which others might call stubbornness, was something she had inherited from him. Frieda had been the easygoing parent, far more amenable to spur-of-the-moment changes than he. But Frieda was no longer here. Now it was Gunther's responsibility to be both mother and father to their daughter. That was a heavy burden for a man who couldn't even figure out what was different about his child's appearance.

He chewed another bite of Wiener schnitzel, swallowing hastily when he realized what she'd done. "What happened to your hair?" he demanded. Eva had pinned her long braids into loops that coiled around her ears, a style more suited to a grown woman than a six-year-old child.

Uncowed by his brusque tone, his daughter grinned. "Olga Kaltheimer fixed it. Isn't it pretty, *Vati*? It's almost as pretty as Miss Dobbs's hair." Eva's rush of words reminded him of the water that ran his mill. On one side of the dam, the water was deceptively still, but once it tumbled over the dam, its power was released, and it became a thundering torrent.

"Oh, *Vati*, Miss Dobbs is such a good teacher. Everybody likes her, even Wilbur Menge, and he doesn't like nobody." Eva flushed. "Anybody," she corrected herself. "Miss Dobbs says that's the proper word. She says it's important to use the right words."

Eva's enthusiasm, so like her mother's, sent a pang of

longing through Gunther. A man wasn't meant to live alone. Even the animals on Noah's ark came in pairs. He cleared his throat, then managed to say, "So, you like school?"

"Oh yes. It's *wunderbar*. Wonderful," Eva amended. "Miss Dobbs says we're Americans now, and we need to speak English." His daughter had made that announcement after the first day of school and appeared to have taken it to heart. To Gunther's surprise, she'd even begun to say her bedtime prayers in English.

As Eva recounted the day's lessons, the words barely registered. Instead, Gunther watched his daughter's face, observing the gleam in her eyes and the frequent smiles, while he tried to recall the last time he'd seen her so happy. His own smile was bittersweet when he realized it had been the last summer of Frieda's life, when they'd eagerly awaited the birth of their second child. Though Eva had been only four, she'd been part of the planning, learning to care for a doll the way her mother would soon care for an infant. And then one hot night, the dreams had turned into a nightmare, taking both Frieda and their son, leaving Gunther with a void deep inside.

Though the townspeople thought otherwise, he hadn't even tried to find a substitute. Oh, it was true he'd spent time—perhaps more time than was wise—with each of the single German women in Ladreville. He'd hoped that one would make a good mother for Eva. As for himself, he knew no one could ever take Frieda's place in his heart. It appeared no one could take Frieda's place in Eva's life, either. Each time, when it had become clear that his daughter did not care for the woman, he'd abandoned the idea of courtship. Eva was what mattered. That was why Gunther had devoted his life to keeping Eva safe and fed and clothed. He'd succeeded, or he thought he had. His one continuing worry was his daughter's solemnity. When Frieda had been alive, Eva had been a smiling, laughing child. Without her mother, she'd become silent and withdrawn, and as much as he'd tried, Gunther hadn't been able to restore her sunny disposition. Now it appeared someone else had accomplished what he had failed to do. Eva was once again happy, a child apparently without cares. *Gott sei dank. Thank you, God.* Gunther translated his silent prayer of thanksgiving. His prayers had been answered.

As he buttered a piece of bread, he watched Eva's animated expression, trying to understand what was responsible for the change. Intuitively, he knew school was part of the reason. Eva enjoyed being with other children and learning to read and cipher. But that could not fully account for the change, for Sunday school had not had the same effect. Gunther suspected that Eva's teacher, whose name seemed to be part of every sentence, was the real reason for his daughter's newfound happiness. In her eyes, Miss Dobbs was perfect. That was why Eva had convinced one of the older girls to fix her hair in the same style. That was why she quoted her teacher so often.

His thoughts raced as he chewed another bite of veal. Pastor Sempert claimed that God used ordinary people to do his will. Was this the answer to Gunther's prayers? He looked at his daughter happily babbling about something. Had God sent Miss Dobbs to Ladreville to fill the hole in their lives? Gunther closed his eyes for a second, then nodded. It was possible. He had no doubt that Miss Dobbs would be a good mother. The way she cared for her sister was proof of that. And she'd been kind—more than kind—to Eva each time they'd been together.

Gunther took a long swallow of milk, nodding again as he pushed his plate aside. God had spoken; it was time for him to take a wife. The problem was, he had no idea how to do that.

❧

Dead ends. That's all he'd found. Clay waited until they'd crossed the river before he urged Shadow to gallop. Speed didn't solve anything, but it might ease his frustration. Once again he'd spoken to everyone who'd seen Austin that last day. Once again no one admitted knowing anything. Once again he'd learned nothing about Austin's pocket watch. Everyone claimed the killer must have been a stranger and that Austin had lost his watch. Both allegations were patently absurd. Clay knew that someone in Ladreville was responsible as well as he knew that the sun would rise each morning. The problem was, he could find no clues. Whoever had killed Austin had been clever. Very clever. He would have to be twice as clever to unmask his brother's murderer, but he'd do it, for the alternative was unthinkable. The man could not go free.

Clay leaned over Shadow's neck, hoping the wind would clear away his turbulent thoughts, and for a moment it did. For a moment, he remembered Austin alive, not slumped lifeless over Nora's back. When he saw another rider approaching, Clay slowed his horse to a walk. Common courtesy demanded he speak to Léon Rousseau, particularly now that he was working on the Friedrich farm.

"You look tired." The man's clothing was stained with sweat, his shoulders slightly slumped with weariness. This was a far cry from the man who favored impeccable tailoring and flashy one-of-a-kind buttons on his jackets.

"It's hard work," Léon admitted. "Austin was right when he told me farming was harder than ranching."

"Then, why are you doing it?" Clay had been surprised when he'd heard that Léon had approached Karl Friedrich, looking for work. It seemed an odd choice for the son of a merchant. The Rousseaus were a traditional old-world family, raised with the expectation that sons followed in the family business.

Léon straightened his shoulders as he said, "Anything is better than working inside. Besides, I like seeing things grow."

Clay nodded. Though that wasn't one of the things that he enjoyed, Patience had claimed working in a garden brought her closer to God than almost anything else. "I imagine Karl is glad to have a helper."

A wrinkled nose accented Léon's reply. "Most days. Today Karl's downright ornery. I wouldn't go near him if I were you. He's out for blood, and Canfield blood is first on his list."

Though Karl was not as phlegmatic as most of the German immigrants, that sounded extreme, even for him. "Why?"

"After another fence was cut last night, your cattle ate most of the corn."

"Karl thinks I was responsible?" First dead ends. Now this. What else could go wrong today? Clay and Karl had already discussed cut fences. Surely his neighbor realized Clay had no reason to resort to such tactics.

Léon stared into the distance rather than meet Clay's gaze. "Karl claims you're just like your brother. You know Austin was pretty vocal in saying this side of the river wasn't a place for farmers. He never did approve of the Prebles selling their ranch to Karl. That's why Karl's convinced Austin was responsible for the first fence cutting. He keeps muttering things about retribution and that Austin deserved what happened to him."

"Austin did not deserve to die!" Clay spat the words.

"I know that, and so does Karl." Léon's voice was conciliatory, as if he regretted having repeated Karl's accusation. "You know Karl. He can be hotheaded."

But was he a murderer? That was the question. Clay took a deep breath, trying to let his own anger subside. As much as he wanted to find clues to Austin's killer, he had trouble believing Karl was the man he sought. Perhaps the timing would prove otherwise. Perhaps the fence had been cut months before Austin died. Perhaps Karl's words had been nothing more than a frustrated man's ranting. "When was the first fence cut?"

"Two days before Austin was killed."

Unfortunately, the timing fit. Unlike Austin, whose temper died as quickly as it flared, Karl was known for holding grudges. He was also known for demanding punishments that far outweighed the crime. But death? Surely that was extreme, even for Karl. Still, Clay could not ignore what he'd learned. As farfetched as it seemed, Karl might have had a motive for wanting Austin dead. The problem was, the other poker players claimed he was in the barn at the time Austin was killed. Either they'd all lied, or Karl had hired someone to do the actual killing. If so, who?

Bidding Léon farewell, Clay resolved to start asking questions tomorrow when his temper had cooled. In the meantime, he needed to do something constructive, something that would keep his thoughts from dwelling on Austin's death. Though Martina had stopped nagging him, Clay knew the task was overdue. He had to pack Patience's belongings. They served no purpose, sitting unused in a room Clay could not bear to enter. Martina was right about that. She was also right in claiming Pa needed Clay close at night. He ought to move back from the barn, but he couldn't return to the room he and Patience once shared when it held so many memories. Removing his wife's possessions would be the first step.

As he entered the ranch house, Clay spoke to Martina and asked her to have Miguel bring in Patience's trunk. Though she smiled and nodded, surely it was Clay's imagination that his housekeeper muttered something about miracles. This was no miracle, just a chore that needed to be done.

Though he'd dreaded it for more than half a year, it wasn't as painful as he'd expected. As he'd feared, sorting his wife's clothing brought back memories, but—to Clay's surprise—they were happy ones. When his hands touched the emerald green satin, he remembered the day she'd first worn that gown. It had been at a party her parents had hosted in honor of their engagement. She'd been so happy that evening as they'd planned their life together. And they had been happy, even here in a land that was as foreign to Patience as the Sahara Desert would have been.

She'd had no opportunity to wear the gown in Ladreville, for there'd been no fancy parties. Clay would send it and her jewelry back to the Mortons. Boston was a better place for ball gowns and baubles.

He opened the small intricately carved wooden box Patience had used to store her valuables, looking at the half dozen pieces of gold that had meant so much to her. Her wedding ring was not there, for Clay had buried it with her.

Though someone, perhaps one of the women who'd come to prepare Patience's body for burial, had urged him to keep it, Clay had been unwilling to think of another woman wearing the band he'd slipped on Patience's hand the day they'd promised to love, honor, and cherish each other. He touched the emerald earbobs he'd given her for their first anniversary, remembering how she'd worn them with her green satin gown. They should go back to Boston, where her sister might wear them in Patience's memory.

Clay looked out the window for a moment, trying to clear the unwelcome moisture from his eyes before he returned to his task. Patience's parents would probably want the locket that had been their eighteenth birthday gift to her. They should have that and the box too. Clay looked at the satin-lined compartments, his eyes searching for the locket. Where was it? It should be here, and yet it was not. Clay shook his head, surprised when he did not see it. Next to her wedding ring, that had been Patience's most treasured piece of jewelry, the one thing she wore almost every day. This was the only place she would have stored it.

"Can I help?"

Clay spun around, startled by the sound of Sarah's voice. How long had she been standing at the door? The fact that she was home told him he'd been in this room longer than he'd expected. Sarah must have come to remind him of Thea's riding lesson. "I'm afraid I'll be late today."

She shook her head. "The lesson's cancelled. Martina told me you were busy, so I explained to Thea that Nora needed a rest. She's talking to your father now."

Clay smiled, imagining the torrent of words that would be directed toward his father. Fortunately, Pa seemed to enjoy the child's company. That was one thing Austin had been right about.

"My offer of help stands."

Though part of him recoiled at the thought of anyone touching Patience's belongings, the more practical part realized Sarah could help him find the locket.

"I'm no good at folding," Clay admitted, gesturing toward the two piles of gowns that now covered the bed. He pointed to the smaller one. "Could you get these ready to ship back to Boston?" Sarah nodded. "And while you're doing that, would you look for Patience's locket? It's gold and oval and has a fancy design on the front."

"Filigree?"

Clay shrugged. "You're asking the wrong person. All I know is, I can't find it."

More quickly than he'd thought possible, Sarah had placed the green satin gown and the few other dresses he'd selected into the trunk. "The locket isn't in any of the pockets," she told him. "I checked the ruffles too, thinking it might have been caught in one of them, but it wasn't."

"I don't understand where it could be." And that bothered him. It wasn't the cost, although he suspected Daniel and Prudence had paid a pretty penny for it. What bothered Clay was the feeling that if he did not send the locket back to her parents, he would be failing Patience. He hadn't been able to save her life. Surely he could do something as simple as finding a piece of jewelry.

"I'm certain it will turn up." Though Sarah's words were laced with confidence, Clay did not share her optimism. Nothing in his life had been going well. Why should he have expected this to be any different? Now, not only did he have to find a murderer, but he needed to search for his wife's locket.

"What do you plan to do with those?" Sarah pointed toward the other pile of dresses, the ones Clay thought of as ordinary.

"I'll give them away." He'd heard the churchwomen were always looking for serviceable clothing to distribute to the less fortunate. "They're not worth sending back to the Mortons."

Sarah fingered one of the skirts, her gesture oddly hesitant. When she spoke, her voice reflected the same hesitation. "May I have them?"

"You?" The harshness of his tone made her recoil, and so Clay deliberately softened his voice as he said, "They're much too large for you." That wasn't the reason he'd reacted as he did. Clay knew women could work wonders with an old dress, turning it into something far different than the original gown. The problem was, for some reason he didn't want to see Sarah wearing Patience's garments.

She seemed to sense the cause of his hesitation, for she smiled reassuringly as she said, "They're not for me. I want to teach the older girls to quilt, and these would make beautiful pieces."

Clay relaxed. "All right. There's bound to be someone in Ladreville who can use a quilt." One problem was solved. The clothes were disposed of. Unfortunately, another had cropped up to take its place. Where were those miracles Austin and Martina believed in?

❧

"You're the local hero," Herman told Clay the next morning. "Even though it's been a couple weeks, your saving Leah Dunn's life is still all anyone can talk about."

Clay frowned. He hadn't come into town to talk about himself, Leah Dunn, or anything related to practicing medicine. "I didn't want to treat your patient, and you know it."

"But you're glad you did. I can see that."

The choice of words surprised Clay. "What do you mean? You told me your eyesight was worsening."

"It is. I can still see shapes but no details. When I said 'see,' it was figurative. I heard the satisfaction in your voice. You're a born doctor, Clay. Healing people is as necessary to you as breathing."

Though Herman was right, Clay had no intention of admitting it. If he did, Herman would stop trying to lure another doctor to Ladreville, and that would be flat-out wrong. No matter how much satisfaction Clay found in healing people's bodies, he would not remain in Texas. As soon as Austin's killer was brought to justice, Clay would leave.

He fixed his gaze on Herman as he asked, "Do you remember the day my wife died?"

Herman's head jerked at the abrupt change of subject. "How could I forget? I felt as if I'd failed you."

"I'm not blaming you," Clay hastened to reassure the older doctor. "I know you did all you could." Unlike Austin's death, which could have been prevented, Patience's was as close to natural causes as any. "I can't find my wife's locket, and I wondered whether you remembered seeing it that day."

"She wasn't wearing it." Herman's voice rang with conviction. "I would have noticed if there'd been anything around her neck." Unspoken was the fact that, though Herman might have removed it in his efforts to save her, he would have returned it to Clay. "It must have come loose and fallen off.

187

Why don't you talk to Mary? They went to that meeting together."

Clay nodded, then shot his friend a mischievous smile. "Speaking of Mary, have you seen her recently?" Pa had laughed at the thought that their neighbor had transferred her affections from him to Herman.

"Thankfully, no. I suspect little Thea keeps her too busy to invent ailments."

Or perhaps she hadn't wanted the child present when she tried to attract the doctor. "I need to warn you, Herman. Thea's not spending her days there anymore. Mary may start calling you again."

"She wouldn't want a blind man."

"Don't be so sure." Clay suspected Mary was as determined to find a spouse as Gunther Lehman, and Herman, even with incipient blindness, would be a good catch. "I'll tell her you miss her," he teased.

"You wouldn't!"

"No, but it's mighty tempting." At least discussing Herman would have been more pleasant than asking about Patience's last hours. That, unfortunately, had to be done, and he might as well do it today.

When he stopped at the Lazy B on his way back to the ranch, Clay found the kitchen redolent with delicious aromas and Mary rolling out biscuits. "It appears I came at a bad time."

Mary inclined her head slightly, agreeing with Clay's assessment. "Sarah and Thea are coming for supper tonight. I wanted something special for them."

"Whatever it is, it smells delicious." Mary had a reputation for being the best cook in Ladreville, and tonight's supper would only cement that.

"If you're angling for an invitation, Clay Canfield, you ain't gonna get one." Mary's smile was conspiratorial. "I'll deny it if you ever repeat this, but I'm fixin' to try my hand at matchmaking."

Matchmaking. David. Sarah. Clay swallowed as bile rose into his throat. It must be that the idea had caught him unaware. That must be the reason for the sour taste in his mouth. It wasn't as if he had a personal interest in Sarah. Of course it wasn't. When Mary's eyes narrowed, Clay realized she expected a response. "Sarah's a fine woman," he said.

"That she is, and my David is a fine man." Mary floured the rim of a glass and began cutting biscuits. "Now, what brings you here?"

"I packed up Patience's belongings yesterday."

Mary cut another biscuit before she looked up at Clay. "You fixin' to go back to Boston?"

"As soon as I learn who killed Austin. Meanwhile, I thought I'd send Patience's things to her parents. The problem is, her locket is missing. Do you remember whether she was wearing it the day she died?" Clay couldn't recall, but women noticed that sort of thing.

Mary held the glass up, apparently checking the quantity of flour on its rim. "I don't recollect," she said slowly. "I wish I could help you, Clay, but I was sicker than a dog that day, and my memory ain't what it shoulda been." She cut another biscuit. "If I had to guess, I'd say she didn't have it on."

Clay frowned. First his wife's locket; then his brother's watch. What would disappear next?

9

The days were getting longer. Sarah smiled as she glanced out the window at the children who were chasing each other around the churchyard. Though for the most part they sat quietly during lessons, there was no doubt that recess was their favorite time of the day. It was then that they could run and shout and be children. Sarah enjoyed the respites too, for they gave her a chance to rest her voice and collect her thoughts. Normally she planned her next lesson, but today her mind refused to focus on arithmetic and spelling. Instead, it wandered, transporting her almost two thousand miles to the place she'd once called home. The dogwood and azalea buds would be swollen, preparing to dazzle the eye with the beauty of their flowers. Mama would be working in her garden, transplanting the seedlings she'd nurtured on a windowsill, singing softly as she ran her fingers through the fertile soil.

Oh, Mama! Sarah blinked in a vain attempt to hold back

the tears that came as regularly as April rain. Sarah brushed the tears from her cheeks, then closed her eyes briefly, picturing her mother's garden. Perhaps that was the answer. Though she couldn't bring her back, perhaps sharing something Mama had enjoyed would ease the pain.

When she walked to the doorway to summon the children, Sarah heard one of her pupils groan. They knew recess was coming to an end. Her tears banished, she smiled, as much at the children's predictable reaction as from the realization that only a few miles away a garden awaited her. She'd thought about it ever since Mary had mentioned it, but while Clay had been in deep mourning, Sarah hadn't wanted to speak of anything that would remind him of his wife. Things were different now that he'd shipped Patience's belongings and moved back into the house. Sarah thought he might agree to let her and Thea work in Patience's garden. She'd ask him tonight.

For the rest of the afternoon, Sarah was as bad as the children, her mind refusing to concentrate on lessons. While she was teaching the older pupils multiplication tables, she conjured images of sweet peas and daisies. As the youngest children recited the alphabet, she wondered whether Patience had edged her garden with boxwood the way Mama had. By the end of the day, Sarah was as anxious as her pupils for the final bell. As they raced outside, she slid her lesson papers into her satchel and hurried Thea toward the door.

"Good afternoon, Fraulein . . ." The man doffed his hat and shook his head in apparent consternation as they met on the steps. He backed down and waited until Sarah and Thea were on level ground before he spoke again. "I beg your pardon. Good afternoon, Miss Dobbs." Gunther Lehman

191

emphasized Sarah's appellation. "Eva has told me you insist they speak English. It is a good plan."

Thea, clearly bored by the prospect of adult conversation, plunked herself on the bottom step and began to pout. Sarah could hardly blame her. Gunther's arrival meant their trip home would be delayed.

He looked down at his hat, as if seeking inspiration from it. "I want to thank you for teaching the children. Eva has not been so happy since her mother died."

"She learns very quickly. So do you." Sarah had noted that Gunther's English was only lightly accented and that he avoided telltale German speech patterns. "Your English is excellent."

Gunther continued to stare at his hat. "I learned from Austin. He was a good teacher."

Sarah smiled. It appeared Austin had taught more than the children.

Gunther turned his attention from his hat to the sky. "It doesn't look like it will rain."

If she hadn't been impatient to return to the ranch, Sarah might have found the conversation amusing. As it was, she wondered why Eva's father had come to the school. Other than the first few days when he'd brought Eva in the morning, she'd come alone. Today's visit must not have been planned, for Eva had already left. But her father stood there, clearly ill at ease and reduced to discussing the weather. Why had he come?

"Would you like to see the schoolroom?" Sarah suggested. Gunther had not been inside. Perhaps he wanted to see where his daughter spent her days.

"Yes, please."

The palpable relief in his voice told Sarah that hadn't been his intent but that, for some reason, he appreciated the suggestion. She led the way inside and gestured toward the last row of desks. "Eva always sits here with my sister."

"*Ja*. She told me she wants a real sister." Though the words were innocuous, Gunther's face reddened. "I had best let you take Thea home," he said quickly.

As she lifted Thea into the wagon, Sarah mulled the odd conversation, trying to find a reason for Gunther's visit. She wouldn't believe Isabelle and Clay were right that Gunther considered her a potential stepmother for Eva. Surely that was not the case. If it was, surely he'd have acted differently. There must be another reason. Mothers came occasionally to inquire about their children's progress. Gunther had never done that. Relief washed over Sarah as she realized Gunther had heard what other parents did and wanted to ensure that Eva did not feel neglected, simply because she had no mother. He was being a conscientious father. Nothing more.

It was not relief but pure pleasure that Sarah felt when Clay agreed she and Thea could use Patience's garden.

"I never understood why she chose the location," he said after they'd finished supper. Though he'd been amenable to her working in it, Clay had insisted he would take Sarah to the garden while Thea remained at the ranch house, "helping" Martina wash dishes. Clay shook his head slowly, as if still trying to fathom Patience's motives. "There are other places on the ranch that are easier to reach."

Sarah had to agree. The path they were following was little more than an animal's track, almost overgrown with mesquite, and it had taken them a full ten minutes to get this far. Part of the reason for the slow progress was Sarah's unsteadiness. Clay preceded her and held the branches aside so she could pass. Though it was a gentlemanly gesture that any woman would have appreciated, for Sarah, it was more than a courtesy, for it gave her the opportunity to concentrate on her footsteps. The path was rough, pocked with piles of dirt and holes that bore witness to the presence of small rodents. An able-bodied woman might not worry, but Sarah knew that a fall could damage her leg unbearably. Unless there was something special about Patience's garden, she would look for a spot closer to the house.

"Be careful." Clay stopped as the path began a gentle decline. "It's slippery here." Though the change in elevation was only a few feet, it was enough that the lower area was still wet from last night's rain. He gave Sarah an appraising look, then before she knew what he intended, Clay covered the distance between them and swept her into his arms.

It lasted only seconds. Sarah knew it was nothing more than an attempt to keep her from falling, and yet her pulse began to race as she rested her head against his chest, inhaling the scents of soap and leather and something else, something that was uniquely Clay. For a moment, with his arms wrapped around her, Sarah felt safe. More than that, she felt cherished. It was silly, of course, and yet she could not stop the feelings from rushing through her.

"Thank you," she said when she was once more standing on dry ground. To Sarah's dismay, her voice sounded shaky. Oh, how she hoped Clay didn't notice.

It appeared he saw nothing amiss, for his voice was tinged with a bit of amusement as he said, "I'm afraid my gallantry was self-serving. With everything that's going on at the ranch, I don't need another patient."

Sarah seized the new subject gratefully. She was on firm ground here, both literally and figuratively. "The mothers are glad you're helping Dr. Adler. They said he suffers from frequent headaches."

The path had widened enough that they could walk side-by-side. Clay slowed his pace and looked at Sarah, his expression devoid of amusement. "It's more serious than that. Herman's going blind."

"Oh!" Sarah's eyes widened as she looked at the countryside, marveling at the tiny green leaves, the almost unbelievably blue sky with a few fluffy white cumulus clouds floating across it. What would it be like to know that one day she would no longer see them? Her heart reached out to both the doctor and the people of Ladreville who would be deprived of his services. "It's fortunate you're here," she said softly.

Clay shook his head again, and this time she thought she saw discomfort in his expression. "Only for a while." His lips tightened as he pronounced the words and quickened his pace, as if anxious to reach their destination. "We're almost there."

Though the path seemed to end at a dense thicket, Sarah saw a narrow opening. Holding her skirts close, she followed Clay through it, then stopped in amazement. "Oh, Clay!" Even though the space was badly overgrown, Sarah understood why Patience had chosen the location. The mesquite bushes formed natural walls, keeping the outside world away, turning the garden into a magical place. With the wild bushes surrounding them and providing a vivid contrast, the cultivated plants seemed even more special than they had in Mama's garden. And, though weeds had overtaken most of the beds, Sarah could visualize the flowers in bloom. "Oh, Clay, this is wonderful! Thea will love the secret garden."

And she did.

❦

School had been open for a month now, and nothing had changed. The German parents would not permit their children to enter the French church, and the French parents were equally adamant that their children not attend German classes.

"Surely you can see how this hurts the children." In desperation Sarah had approached Michel Ladre, reasoning that he was the one person in the town who could influence the others. "They're receiving only half the education they should."

Michel leaned back in his chair, as if distancing himself from her plea. "Half is better than none."

"But it could be so much better." Sarah folded her hands to keep from wringing them. "The townspeople respect you. Can't you persuade them?"

He pointed toward the maps on the wall. "These people have fought for centuries," he said, seeming to forget that he was one of them. "Sometimes I think they look for excuses to quarrel. Why would they change now?"

"Perhaps because this is America, not Alsace. Their children are Americans. They deserve the same education other Americans have."

The mayor's frown deepened. "There is nothing I can do."

Sarah left his office, unconvinced. Michel Ladre was a powerful man. If he'd wanted the children to attend school together, he could have persuaded the parents. She was confident of that. But for some reason he did not support her. She'd have to find another way.

That Sunday, Sarah believed she'd found the way, for Père Tellier's sermon spoke of loving thy neighbor. It was the perfect introduction.

"Good morning, Madame Berthoud," Sarah greeted one of the parishioners after the service. "Your son is doing well at school."

The woman preened. "He's a smart boy. Takes after his pa."

"Pierre could learn so much more if he went to class every week."

Her face flushed, Madame Berthoud stared at Sarah as if she'd uttered heresy. "Go to the German church? Never! It would be a sin to set foot inside there."

Sarah met the same reaction when she approached two of the German mothers. As she guided the wagon home, she tried not to frown, lest she worry Thea. The people of Ladreville claimed to be Christians. They attended church each Sunday and met for fellowship at least once during the week. The words were there, but the actions did not support them. Ladreville's citizens didn't love their neighbors. Even worse, they didn't seem to care that they were hurting their children. Something had to change. The problem was, Sarah had no idea what she could do to cause that change.

❧

The door was locked. If he hadn't seen Herman's buggy in the barn, Clay would have thought his friend was out on rounds, but that was clearly not the case. Why had he locked the house?

197

Clay rapped on the door.

"Who is it?" Surely it was his imagination that Herman sounded annoyed. Normally the man welcomed visitors.

"It's Clay."

"C'mon in." This time there was no mistaking the relief in Herman's voice as he slid back the bolt. "What brings you here?" he asked as Clay sank into a comfortable chair.

"Can't a man visit a friend?" Clay studied the older doctor, noting that while he was as well-groomed as ever, his eyes had begun to cloud over and he moved tentatively, as if he could no longer see the familiar furnishings and feared tripping.

"You're welcome any time. Any time, my boy. I just wondered if you had a particular reason for coming today."

Clay did, but he wouldn't admit it. Herman would hate knowing that he'd come to check on him, as if the doctor were one of Clay's patients. "How about escaping the ranch?"

"More fence problems?"

Clay shook his head. "No. Just the usual ornery cattle. I tell you, Herman, I hate that ranch and everything associated with it."

Laughter greeted his words. "That's because you're a doctor, not a rancher. Your brother loved the place."

"Yeah, and we saw what happened to him." When Herman rubbed his eyes, Clay regretted the choice of words. Even though he'd meant it figuratively, it was cruel to speak of sight when Herman saw less each day. "How are the headaches?" He'd already bumbled into the subject, so there was nothing to be gained by skirting it.

"Less frequent. And, before you ask, my eyes are about the same. Most people don't know I have trouble seeing, especially since you've been handling the difficult cases."

Thankfully, the majority of the calls had been for minor ailments which required Herman to do no more than listen to complaints and prescribe a potion or tincture. Only a few had been serious enough to warrant surgery.

"Do many patients still come here?" Clay had entered the building from the rear where Herman kept his residence rather than the front half which housed his medical office. When the town was first founded, most patients had visited the doctor, waiting in the small vestibule until Herman was able to treat them, but now Herman claimed the townspeople preferred him to travel to their homes.

The older doctor frowned. "More than normal come here, led by Mary."

"Mary Bramble? What's wrong with her?" Though he suspected he knew the answer, Clay tried to hide his amusement.

"She suffers from widowhood." Herman spat the words. "I hate to admit you were right, but it looks like I'm next on Mary's list of potential husbands. She comes here at least once a week. One time, I even found her snooping around this room, making herself at home."

Clay smiled as the reason for the locked door became apparent. "Don't laugh, my boy. It's not amusing." The doctor's protests, so like his own father's when Mary had set her cap for him, made Clay laugh out loud.

Herman's frown deepened. "When I asked her what she was doing, she told me she would need to find a new home when David married Sarah."

Clay's amusement faded. Herman was right. That was no laughing matter.

He was still not laughing that evening as he made his way

to the garden. While they'd eaten supper, Thea had begged him to accompany them, and though Clay had declined, the memory of the little girl's disappointment tugged at him. That was the reason—the only reason—why he found himself striding toward what Sarah called the secret garden.

"Papa Clay!" Thea shrieked with delight when he entered the small plot. "Me grow flowers! Look!"

Kneeling, Clay admired the tiny green sprouts that he suspected were weeds. "It appears to me that you two are enjoying digging in the dirt," he said as he rose and approached Sarah. Unlike her sister, she was carefully mounding soil around a plant rather than wriggling her fingers through the dirt.

"It's more than digging. We're coaxing plants into blooming." Sarah slid her trowel into the freshly turned soil. "I never realized how rewarding it could be to see seeds sprout."

Clay looked around, amazed at the changes she'd wrought in only a few weeks. "You've done more than plant seeds." She'd cleared the mesquite that had started encroaching on the flower beds, dug weeds, and pruned the rose bushes. He pointed toward the roses. "If they bloom, they'll be pink."

"Don't touch, Papa Clay. Horns!" Thea inserted herself between Clay and the bush, apparently believing he needed protection.

He smiled at his young guardian. "I think you mean thorns."

"That's what me said. Torns."

Sarah exchanged a conspiratorial smile with him. "I hope we get more than thorns. This is the first time I've worked with roses."

"They'll bloom." Martina had told him that the bushes had

been covered with flowers last year. "When they do, they'll smell sweeter than paper." Clay clenched his fists. Today was his day for saying stupid things. First he reminded Herman of his failing sight. Now he was raising memories of Austin and all that Sarah had lost.

Apparently unperturbed, Sarah said, "They may smell sweet, but I doubt they'll make my heart sing the way Austin's epistles do." She dusted her hands before rising. "Your brother should have been a poet. Every time I read his letters, I feel he's so close that I expect him to walk through the door."

Clay felt as if someone had punched him in the solar plexus. Those letters. Those infernal letters. It was clear they meant far more to her than he and Austin had intended. They were supposed to be part of a courtship, not a shrine to something she'd never have.

Clay shifted, staring into the distance. What would Sarah do if she knew he'd been the one who'd authored those missives? Would she tell him he was a poet? He wasn't. He was a doctor, a brother, and a man who'd poured his own longing onto paper. He was also a man who would never tell her the truth. He'd already made that decision.

"Have you thought any more about riding?" It was time to change the subject to something less painful.

But once again he failed. The blood drained from Sarah's face as she said, "I'm a coward, Clay. Every time I think about getting on a horse, my stomach knots and my hands shake. I can't do it."

And he was a heel to have even suggested riding. Would he ever learn?

༜

201

Today would be different, Sarah told herself. Today he would cooperate.

"Good afternoon, Pa." Now that she was confident Clay would keep her sister safe, Sarah no longer watched while they rode. Instead, she spent the extra time with Clay's father.

"How are you feeling?" Her question was greeted with a shrug. Though Sarah knew that Pa would speak to both Clay and Martina, he was careful not to utter a sound when she was in the room.

"Are you ready to beat me at chess?" As she'd hoped, he had proven capable of moving the pieces and seemed to enjoy their matches. "We'll play as soon as we finish your exercises." When Sarah reached for his right slipper, he shook his head. It was what she expected, the same reaction she got every day. Refusing to be discouraged, she began to massage Pa's foot. "I know you don't like this. I didn't, either." Stretching the muscles hurt. "You need to do this if you're going to walk again. You do want to walk, don't you?" He made no answer. "You can't give up."

But she was afraid he had and that once again she had failed.

10

The early June night was cool and clear, with hundreds, thousands, perhaps millions of stars twinkling overhead. Sarah walked slowly, savoring the muted sounds of evening. The crickets' chirping was slower now, the horses' whinnying less frequent. It was a time for rest. Perhaps, if she was fortunate, she would find the answers she sought, and then she, too, would be able to rest.

There had to be a way to resolve the dilemma. Though the older children had left for the summer, Sarah's class size had increased, for the parents had begun sending younger children to her, perhaps to keep them from being underfoot while their elders worked the crops. Pierre Berthoud was frustrated. She knew it, just as she knew that Anna Menger and Marie Seurrat suffered from the same malady. Those children learned quickly and yearned to attend classes every week. They could not, though, without facing their parents' disapproval. Pierre had dared to enter the German church one day and had been soundly thrashed for disobeying his father. Anna and Marie hadn't even tried. Recognizing their need, Sarah had given them assignments to work at home, but that wasn't enough. The children needed daily coaching, and that was something Sarah could not provide. There simply were not enough hours in a day, for she needed time with Thea and would not give up the hour she spent with Pa, no matter how little she appeared to accomplish with him.

"I didn't know you were a stargazer."

Sarah stumbled slightly as she turned, startled by the sound of Clay's voice. He'd moved so quietly that she hadn't heard him approaching.

"They seem closer here than in Philadelphia." That was only one of the many differences between her old and new homes.

Though there was no moon to light the night, Sarah saw Clay nod as he closed the distance between them. "The Texas sky is one of the few things I missed when I lived in Boston. When I was young, I used to lie on the ground and look at the constellations. I always wondered if there were people on those stars, staring in my direction."

"I tried to count them." Sarah smiled at the memory. Though, like Clay, she'd once lain on the grass to stargaze, today she was leaning on the corral fence. "Needless to say, I fell asleep before I got much past a hundred. Now I've given up counting them. I just look and admire. It may sound strange, but I find the sheer number of stars reassuring." Sarah kept her eyes fixed on Clay. Somehow, though she couldn't explain why, it was important that he understand. "When I realize how vast the universe is, my problems seem small, and sometimes being outside helps me solve them." That was one of the reasons she'd ventured to the paddock tonight.

"What's bothering you this time?"

Sarah was silent for a moment. She wouldn't tell Clay how little progress she'd made helping his father, for he would only be angered by the knowledge that she'd ignored his request. She certainly wouldn't tell him how often she worried about him and his desire for revenge, for he'd made it clear that nothing would sway him. "The school," she said, voicing her other problem. "I hate seeing eager children being held back. It's so unfair."

"I agree. Austin and I were fortunate." Clay's lips curved upward, and Sarah heard the smile in his voice. "Even though she had no formal training, our mother was a good teacher."

"Being in a classroom with other pupils is even better."

Clay nodded. "Once again, I agree, but it doesn't appear that that will happen in Ladreville, at least not with all the children."

"The strange thing is that most of the parents don't seem to object to their children playing together. The problem is using the churches." A sudden gust of wind loosened one of the hairpins securing her chignon. As a lock blew free, Sarah reached behind her head to push the errant curl back in place.

As if in response, Clay tugged his hat brim. "What you need is a neutral location."

"That's exactly what I thought. Ladreville should have a school building that both groups helped build."

"It's not a bad idea, and the town has plenty of open land. That big lot on the riverside corner of Rhine and Hochstrasse would be ideal. I'd support you. Of course, what you really need is Michel's support."

And that, Sarah learned the next day, was something Michel was unwilling to provide.

"It's a needless expense." Ladreville's mayor's crossed arms underscored his disapproval.

"I beg to differ." Sarah would not accept his refusal. Surely Michel would listen to reason. "Yes, there will be a cost to build it, but the school will be used for generations to come."

His frown deepened. "I'm not worried about future generations. I'm concerned about what will happen next year when you marry and the town no longer has a teacher. The schoolhouse will sit empty, reminding everyone of the money they squandered." Unspoken was the fact that the citizens might blame him.

"If that's your only concern, you need not worry. I have no intention of marrying."

"Bah!" The mayor fairly spat the word. "There are no secrets in this town. I am fully aware that two young men are interested in you. I can't vouch for David Bramble, but you'd do well to accept my son's offer." Before Sarah could protest that no one had proposed marriage, Michel continued, "Jean-Michel is an upstanding young man who knows his duty. Unlike David, he would let you raise your sister in his home."

Though Michel meant the words to be magnanimous, it was all Sarah could do to keep herself from shouting her outrage. How noble he made his son sound. Jean-Michel would permit her to raise Thea. Permit! As if she would even consider an offer of marriage given with so much condescension.

Sarah rose and left the mayor's office with no more than

a cursory good-bye, while inside she fumed. An upstanding young man. Duty. The word rankled. How could anyone consider Thea a duty? Sarah clenched her fists, then forced herself to relax them. One thing was certain: she would not marry Jean-Michel Ladre if he were the last man on earth. Thea deserved better than that. She deserved a man who'd care for her, who'd treat her like a father. She deserved a man like . . . Sarah paused as the image rose before her. Thea deserved a man like Clay.

~§

He hadn't counted on two other customers being there. Gunther cleared his throat as he entered the mercantile and saw them standing near the counter. Though he wanted nothing more than to vanish, he couldn't leave without causing comment, and that was the last thing he needed. No one was supposed to know that he'd come here today and certainly not why.

"May I help you?"

Though his heart pounded with dread at the conversation that would follow, Gunther managed a smile for the petite brunette behind the counter. Isabelle Rousseau might be shorter than most women, but she made up for her lack of height with the warmth of her smile. A man always felt welcome in the mercantile when she was waiting on customers. That was why he'd come today, when he'd known she would be here. Gunther shook his head in response to her question. "These ladies came first."

Five minutes later, when the two women had departed, not, Gunther noted, without sending half a dozen curious glances in his direction, he approached the counter.

Isabelle smiled again. "What can I get for you, Mr. Lehman?"

"I didn't know where else to turn. My parents did everything the last time. You're her friend. You're a woman." The words tumbled out in quick succession.

Her smile faded and her eyes darkened. "I'm sorry, Mr. Lehman, but you're not making sense."

How inept could one man be? Many had declared him the best miller in Alsace, and he hoped to become the finest in Texas. He knew his trade well, but it was obvious he was a complete failure where women were concerned. "*Dummkopf.*" As Isabelle flinched, Gunther let out a groan. He'd made yet another mistake. Was there no end to them? "My apologies, Miss Rousseau. I was speaking to myself. I'm the dumb one, not you." She was, he knew, a smart woman and a pretty one. What he didn't understand was why she wasn't married, but that, Gunther reminded himself, was not his problem. It was his own marriage that concerned him.

"I need some advice," he admitted, "and I hope you can provide it. I'll pay whatever you ask."

Though there was nothing remotely amusing about this conversation, Gunther thought he saw a glimmer of a smile in her eyes. "That won't be necessary," she assured him. "Advice is one of the few things we don't charge for."

The woman who held his future in her hands leaned forward, resting her elbows on the counter, as if she were eager to hear his question. Where should he start? He ought to have rehearsed this, but he hadn't. Another mistake. Gunther swallowed, trying to compose his thoughts. "Eva needs a mother," he said at last.

Nodding solemnly, Isabelle agreed. "Yes, she probably does."

Gunther waited. Was that all she was going to say? Surely she'd offer advice, now that she knew his problem. But all she did was sit there, apparently waiting for his next pronouncement. "Miss Dobbs is your friend."

Surely she knew what he wanted; surely she'd take the hint. Instead she simply said, "Yes, she is." Gunther groaned in frustration. Weren't women supposed to talk all the time? When Frieda had been alive, it had been difficult for him to articulate more than one sentence, or so it seemed. Miss Rousseau was not doing her part.

"Miss Dobbs would be a good mother for Eva." There! He'd told her what he needed. Gunther waited for advice to begin pouring from Isabelle's mouth.

"Oh!" Though her face flushed slightly, it appeared that the single syllable would be the extent of her reply.

"Do you agree?" Gunther tried to coax a reaction from her. He needed help, and this woman was his only source.

Removing her arms from the counter, Isabelle straightened her back. The action widened the distance between them, making Gunther sense her disapproval.

"It's not for me to agree or disagree," she said quietly. "It seems to me that that's for you and Sarah to decide."

"That's the problem. I don't know how to ask her. You know how it was done in the Old Country. My parents and Frieda's decided we should marry and arranged everything. Why, Frieda and I barely saw each other before the wedding. It's different here."

"Yes, it is. American women expect to be courted."

Gunther knew that. That was the reason he was here,

baring his soul before this pretty young woman. "I'll do anything to make Eva happy. The problem is, I don't know what to do." He knew how to grind corn and wheat and rye to make the best flours in the county. But women? They were an enigma.

Isabelle slid off her chair and came around the counter. "I'm not sure I can help you, because I've never been courted. My parents refused everyone who asked their permission. I think they frightened the others away." Her words were soft, though there was no one to overhear them, and Gunther sensed she was reluctant to admit her lack of suitors. What was wrong with the French men of Ladreville? Had they no courage? He would not have been so easily discouraged. Though he wished he could reassure her, Gunther reminded himself of his mission.

"Please!" She had to know what he should do. There was no one else he could trust. "You're Miss Dobbs's friend. You must know what she'd like."

Isabelle was silent for a moment, her pensive expression telling him she was trying to find a solution. "When Austin courted Sarah, he wrote letters. I know she liked them."

Letters! "Why would I write letters? I can speak to her." If he knew what to say, that is.

Nodding slowly, Isabelle acknowledged the truth of his protest. "Women like pretty words, but there must be something else." She tilted her head to one side, considering. "I've heard of men picking flowers for their sweethearts, and sometimes there are gifts."

At last she'd suggested something he could do. "A gift. That's a good idea. I gave Frieda a hog when we were betrothed."

Though she tried to control it, Gunther saw Isabelle's lips twitch. "You might want to start with something . . ." She paused, choosing the word. "Smaller."

Gunther looked around the store. Surely there was something here that Miss Dobbs would like. He spotted a display in a glass-topped cabinet and pointed toward it. "Frieda favored lace collars."

The amusement on Isabelle's face was replaced by horror. "Oh no, Gunther." She flushed before correcting herself. "I beg your pardon, Mr. Lehman."

"I would be honored if you would call me by my given name."

She hesitated, then nodded. "All right, Gunther. But you must not give Sarah any item of clothing. It would be most unseemly."

He shook his head, trying to understand why a lace collar was less acceptable than a hog. "There are so many rules. It was easier in the Old Country."

"But we're not in the Old Country any longer."

That was true. Gunther took a deep breath, considering everything Isabelle had said. It was true he would have to learn new things, but if Eva could do that, so could he. After all, she was the reason he was enduring this ordeal.

"Thank you, Miss Rousseau." He now knew where to start. Words, flowers, trinkets. Life had certainly been easier in the Old World.

༺

"I need your help, Wilhelm," Gunther said as he entered his friend's shop.

The blond carpenter looked up from the board he was

planing. "You'll have better luck if you remember my name's William."

"Sorry." This was definitely Gunther's day for mistakes. Soon after they'd arrived in Texas, Wilhelm Goetz had announced that he would henceforth be known by the American version of his name. "I wondered if we could trade services. I know you've got some corn you need ground."

"Are you looking for a new table or a chest?"

"Neither, right now. I need some pretty words."

William laid the plane on the bench and stared. "Pretty words? For what?"

There was no way around it. He'd have to tell his friend. At least he knew that William could keep a secret. "I need to convince a lady to marry me," he said, lowering his voice. "Everyone in town knows you read those fancy poets. I figured you could teach me some of the verses."

With two strides, William reached his side and clapped him on the shoulder. "You're fixing to court a lady." It was a statement, not a question. "Good for you. Who is she?"

Gunther shook his head.

"No name, no verses."

Why did this have to be so difficult? Who'd have thought normally affable William would drive such a hard bargain? "You can't tell anyone," Gunther said before he whispered a name.

❧

"What brings you here today?" the town's barber asked the next morning when Gunther entered his shop. "It's not Saturday."

"I need a haircut and shave." He settled into the chair.

"You goin' somewhere?"

"Nope."

The barber said nothing as he wrung out the hot towels, but as he laid one on Gunther's face, he was grinning. "Who's the lucky lady?"

Gunther flinched. "How'd you guess?"

"There's only one reason a man gets himself cleaned up in the middle of the week. So, who is she?"

The shop was empty, save for him. Lowering his voice again, Gunther said, "You can't tell anyone."

⁓

Sarah dipped the rag into the pail and began to wash the chalkboard. Though it was a task she normally delegated to one of the older students, today she'd dismissed class early and insisted she could straighten the schoolroom. The truth was, she needed time to think.

The first day, she'd believed him. He'd said he had an errand in town, and as long as he was close by, he thought he'd visit the school. It wasn't difficult to guess what the errand had been, for there was no mistaking the smell of fresh hair oil. As if that weren't enough, a few errant snips of hair on his shoulder confirmed that Gunther had visited the barber. Sarah had welcomed him and had tried to enlist him in her campaign for a new school. Though his statement that Eva had needs besides the school had raised concerns, Sarah had tried to dismiss them.

But then, in the space of little more than a week, Gunther had come three more times. Once he'd been clutching a bunch of flowers, claiming the classroom would be prettier with them. Another time he'd quoted Keats and Shelley. That had surprised her, for she hadn't realized he was interested in the romantic poets. Today she'd heard the sound of raised voices outside the school and had seen him apparently confronting David and Jean-Michel. Though she could not distinguish the words, she'd seen the two young men stalking away, their posture leaving no doubt of their anger. And then there was the note from Isabelle, inviting her to come for a cup of coffee. Something strange was going on, and Sarah feared she knew what it was.

~

"Come upstairs." Isabelle gave Thea a quick hug, then nodded at her mother. "Maman will watch Thea. She baked brioches."

"My favorite!" At least one thing was going well today. While Isabelle heated milk and coffee for *café au lait*, Sarah leaned back in the chair and tried to relax. She failed. "I don't know what to do," she told her friend. "I thought a separate school building was the answer, but every time I talk to the parents, they insist it's not a good idea."

Isabelle carried the two steaming pots to the table and began what Sarah considered the dangerous process of pouring coffee and milk simultaneously. "Perhaps it isn't a good idea," Isabelle said as she pushed the cup toward Sarah.

"I thought you were my friend."

"I am." Isabelle filled her own cup, then took the seat opposite Sarah. "I want what's best for you and Thea." She gestured toward the plate of rich pastries, urging Sarah to take one. "He's a good man," she said. "He'd make a fine husband and father to Thea."

Unsure why the conversation had drifted toward Clay when they'd been discussing the school, Sarah considered

214

her friend's statements. "I'm not so sure of that. He still mourns his wife."

"That's only natural. He loved her very deeply. That doesn't always happen with arranged marriages."

"I wasn't aware it was arranged." Though she knew Clay had married the daughter of his mentor, Sarah hadn't realized the marriage was anything other than voluntary.

"Most marriages in the Old Country were."

"The Old Country?" What did that have to do with Clay and Patience?

"Why, yes." Isabelle spoke slowly, as if she were explaining a concept to a not too bright child. "That's where Gunther and Frieda were wed."

"Gunther." She was talking about Gunther, not Clay.

"Of course. Who did you think I meant?" Isabelle smiled as she reached for a brioche. "I know it's supposed to be a secret, but everyone in Ladreville knows he's courting you."

"Gunther Lehman told people he's courting me?"

Isabelle smiled again. "Why do you think he comes to see you so often?"

The haircut, flowers, poetry. It was what she had feared. "I thought he was lonely. I thought he wanted company and conversation."

"He also wants a wife."

❧

Another fence. Clay balled his fists, wishing he could wrap them around the neck of whoever was responsible.

"It's all right, Shadow," he said, trying to keep the horse from sensing his mood. But it wasn't all right. He couldn't blame Karl for being angry. He was angry too. The truth was, Clay was angry most of the time. Part of the reason was the ranch. The Bar C was too much work for one man. Pa and Austin had shared the responsibility and hadn't hired a foreman, believing it an unnecessary expense. Now Clay was paying the price for that frugality. While Miguel was a good man, he wasn't a leader. That meant that the ranch hands looked to Clay for every decision. For Pete's sake, they couldn't even check fences without him telling them to.

He'd hated the ranch work and the way it consumed his entire life, even before he'd started taking over Herman's practice. But now that he spent at least half of each day treating Ladreville's ill, the ranch was suffering, and so was Clay. He couldn't continue this way.

Then there was Sarah. Though she said nothing, he knew what was happening. How could he not, when every time he went into town, some busybody greeted him with the news that Gunther was courting her? He shouldn't care. He didn't care. Of course he didn't care. It would be good for Thea to have a father, and any man would be lucky if Sarah were his wife. That was no reason to be angry. After all, it wasn't as if Clay had any interest in assuming those roles. He didn't. It was simply that he knew she could do better. Much better.

"What's wrong? You look like one of those thunderheads you're always warning me about," Sarah said that evening. They'd made a habit of remaining at the table for a few minutes after supper. Thea and Pa were at the opposite side of the room, Pa listening to Thea chatter about whatever subject caught her fancy, giving Clay and Sarah a chance for a private conversation. Normally he enjoyed the time. Tonight he did not. Tonight he did not want to talk about what was wrong.

"There's nothing wrong, unless you count another cut fence, three chickens being stolen from the Friedrichs' farm, and the fact that a day has only twenty-four hours." *Plus, of course, the fact that Gunther Lehman is courting you.* The sweet smile that had accompanied Sarah's words faded, and Clay had the sinking feeling he'd voiced his last words. Surely he hadn't.

"I wish I could help you." Sarah pushed her coffee cup aside, as if the coffee had suddenly lost its flavor.

No one could help. Clay knew that, just as he knew he should say nothing. Instead he heard himself ask, his voice full of sarcasm, "Why don't you follow your friend Isabelle's example and pray for me?" Austin always insisted that God answered prayers. Clay knew better. He also knew he'd made a mistake, for when he looked at Sarah, he saw tears in her eyes.

"It wouldn't help." She spoke so softly that he could barely hear the words. "God doesn't listen to me anymore."

11

"Man, Papa Clay." Thea dropped the reins to point at the stranger. "Man coming."

Instinctively, Clay grabbed Nora's reins and slid his arm around Thea while he castigated himself for his inattention. He'd been so intent on watching her that he hadn't seen the rider approaching. Tall in the saddle with hair so dark that it might be black, the man was a stranger, and strangers, Clay knew, could be dangerous. Though the dust that covered this one indicated he'd traveled a long distance, a supposition that his weary posture confirmed, all that could be a ruse.

"Lesson's over," Clay said, lifting Thea from Nora's back and keeping her in his arms. A man could not be too careful. "What brings you to these parts?" While he uttered the greeting, Clay assessed the stranger again. He appeared to be about his own age, yet the expression in his eyes, an expression that reminded Clay of the look he'd occasionally seen on his father's face, made him seem much older.

"Is this Robert Canfield's spread?" The stranger's voice cracked a bit, perhaps from disuse. That could happen to a man, particularly when he was traveling. The wind and dust took their toll on vocal cords, as did days with no human contact.

"It is." Clay confirmed the assumption. "I'm Robert's son Clay. Who might you be?"

"Name's Zach. Zach Webster." The name meant nothing to Clay, a fact that appeared to surprise the stranger. He paused, as if considering whether to elaborate, and closed his eyes briefly. When Zach Webster spoke, there was no mistaking the pain in his voice. "Your pa and I were together in Perote."

Startled by the reference to the notorious Mexican prison, Clay tightened his grip on Thea, relaxing only when she squirmed and batted his cheek in protest. It had been over thirteen years since his father had been incarcerated. Though Pa had recounted many of his war experiences, he'd rarely spoken of those months in Perote. Judging from Zach Webster's haunted expression, he'd been equally unable to forget what had happened there.

"Has Robert pass . . . er, is Robert still here?"

Zach's words reminded Clay that he'd not responded. It wasn't often that he found himself speechless, but it wasn't often that someone from his father's past appeared at the Bar C. "Pa's alive, but I'm afraid you'll find him much changed. He suffered an apoplectic attack a year ago."

"Dirty, Papa Clay. Man dirty." Thea, who'd been squirming in Clay's arms, pointed at the visitor.

"You'd be dirty too, if you rode a horse as far as this man has." Clay gave Zach a brief nod. "The least I can do is offer you a bath and a hot meal."

"I'd be mighty obliged for both, but if you don't mind, I'd like to see Robert first. When God sent me here, he told me to hurry, that I was needed."

God sent him? Clay raised an eyebrow. Though the sincerity in his voice told him the man believed it, Clay knew better. God had abandoned him and Pa. He was hardly likely to send an angel—or even a man—to help them. As for being needed, what the Bar C needed was a foreman, not someone who'd remind Pa of the horrors he'd endured during the war.

When Thea batted Clay's cheek again, demanding to be put down, he shook his head. "We're going inside to Pa."

The relief on Zach's face told Clay how important seeing Pa was to this man. For the first time, the visitor smiled. "That's a mighty cute daughter you've got. Robert used to say that the prospect of grandchildren was one of the things that got him through the dark days."

"She's not my daughter." Though the response was curt, there was no reason to explain Thea's presence. Zach Webster would be on his way tomorrow morning. He had no need to know that Sarah and Thea were here because Austin had sought to give Pa the grandchildren he longed for.

"This way." Clay lowered Thea to the floor as soon as they entered the house, letting her scamper toward Pa's room, while he led their visitor at a more sedate pace. As he'd anticipated, Pa was seated in his chair. What he hadn't expected was Sarah, perched on a hassock in front of Pa, apparently massaging his leg.

"Sarah!" The rush of anger surprised Clay with its intensity. How dare she defy him? Hadn't he specifically forbidden her to hurt his father?

She turned, startled. "I didn't expect you."

"Obviously." Before Clay could say more, he heard Pa mutter something and realized he was staring at Zach Webster. "Pa, do you remember . . ."

"Zach." Though the name was garbled, it was intelligible. Never taking his eyes from Zach, Pa gripped the arms of his chair and tried to rise, only to fall back in frustration. Clay stared, amazed. This was the first time in over a year that his father had attempted to stand.

"It's good to see you, Robert." Without waiting for an invitation, Zach pulled a chair close to Pa and shook his hand. "I haven't been able to forget all those stories you told about the Bar C. They made me want to see it for myself."

Though his smile was crooked, there was no doubt about it. Pa was grinning. Even Thea's antics had not coaxed this much of a reaction from him.

"The truth is," Zach continued, "I've got a hankering to settle down. I was hoping you might have a place for me here."

A place? Clay took a deep breath, trying to settle his thoughts. The last thing the Bar C needed was a freeloader, but he couldn't ignore Pa's obvious pleasure at being reunited with this man. Clay turned to Zach. "You ever herd cattle?" It was a long shot, but he had to ask.

To Clay's surprise, Zach nodded. "Most every day for the last six years. I was foreman of the Crooked L."

If it was true, those were impressive credentials. Though not as large as the Bar C, the south Texas ranch was known as a well-run spread. If Zach could manage the Crooked L, he might be able to solve one of Clay's problems. "You came here on the right day. It just so happens that I need a foreman," Clay admitted. "Let's give it a month's trial. If we're both happy at the end, you've got a job."

Clay extended his hand and was startled when Zach ignored it, instead bowing his head. "I thank you, Lord, for bringing me here," the Bar C's new foreman prayed. "Thank you for leading me to my friend. I ask you to show me your plan and to guide us all as we journey forward."

As Zach prayed, Pa closed his eyes, his face more at peace than Clay had seen it in months. Clay swallowed, trying to dislodge the lump that had taken residence in his throat. Though it might not be God's hand that had brought Zach Webster here, it was a mighty strange coincidence that the man had appeared one day after Clay had challenged Sarah to pray for him.

🙵

It was a decidedly unorthodox solution and only temporary, at best, but it just might work. Sarah smiled as she turned back to face the children. It was Friday afternoon and classes in the French church were about to end.

"Next week's lessons will be held in a different location."

Pierre Berthoud raised his hand. "We know, Miss Dobbs. The German church."

"No." She shook her head, giving the pupils another smile. "We're going to have school outdoors." Gasps and a few low comments greeted her words. "It will be a little different. For one thing, we'll sit on blankets under the oak trees." She wouldn't have a blackboard, and there would be new distractions for the children, but surely the result would be an improvement over the current situation. The grins that lit her pupils' faces told Sarah they approved of her plan.

"You all know those two big oaks near the river, the ones on the other side of Rhine from the post office." Heads nodded. "That's where class will be. I hope to see you there." As they filed from the school, murmurs turned into animated discussion.

"You seem pleased."

Sarah looked up as Clay's voice echoed through the schoolroom. She'd thought she was alone, for Thea was outside playing with Eva while Sarah gathered the materials she'd need for next week's classes. She'd been humming, unconcerned that her humming was as tuneless as her singing. Had Clay heard her? Sarah hoped not. To cover her confusion, she spoke quickly. "I didn't know you were going to be in town today."

Clay shrugged. "Patients are never predictable. As long as I was here, I thought I'd offer to take Thea home with me." He walked toward the front of the room, studying the children's paintings that she'd hung on the walls, nodding his approval.

"She'll ride on Shadow? Oh, Clay, you know Thea will love it." There were few things that pleased her sister more than horses and Clay's company.

"Now that that's settled, tell me what's making you smile so much."

Seeing you. But she couldn't tell him that, for that might lead to the admission of how often she thought of him. The simple fact was, thoughts of Clay were never distant. Sarah had been surprised when he'd said nothing about her trying to help Pa walk, for she'd seen his anger. Fortunately, that anger had faded quickly, melted by Zach's presence, and Clay had acted as if nothing was amiss.

Having Zachary Webster at the Bar C had changed so much. Though the man did not take meals with the family,

223

declining Clay's invitation on the grounds that his place was with the men he was expected to lead, his presence affected everyone. The lines of worry and fatigue that had marred Clay's face had lessened, probably because he'd been relieved of much ranch work. He smiled more often and lingered longer at the supper table, watching Thea play at Pa's feet while Zach and the older man conversed.

As for Thea, she regarded Zach as a new playmate, a dubious honor for him and the cause of concern for Sarah. Despite numerous reprimands, Thea refused to stay inside the house when either Clay or Zach was working with the horses. In desperation, Sarah had threatened to harness her sister like a horse and tie her to a chair. One afternoon of confinement had ensured Thea's obedience.

But the biggest change had been in Pa. He seemed more content and at the same time more frustrated. Though he still complained when she attempted to strengthen his legs, more than once Sarah had caught him trying to rise, only to fall back into his chair, his face contorted with frustration. The man wanted to walk. It was simply that he didn't want Sarah's assistance.

"If I'm smiling," she told Clay, "it's because I've decided to try something different with the school."

When she finished her explanation, he nodded. "Brilliant."

"It won't work on rainy days, but I'm hoping it'll help the parents realize how much their children gain by having classes every week."

Clay looked around the classroom, as if trying to envision how she'd teach outdoors. "Folks are still opposed to building a school. I heard that again today."

Sarah wasn't surprised. She met resistance everywhere. "I don't know what more I can do. The Rousseaus have tried to convince their French customers, and Gunther has approached many of the Germans."

A frown crossed Clay's face. "I heard Gunther was spending a lot of time here."

"Yes." She could no longer deny that he was courting her. What was more surprising was that he also appeared to be courting Thea. He came to the school almost every day, and when he did, he spent time talking to Thea. Her sister liked him. So did Sarah. The problem was, Gunther ignited no spark in her heart. He was a friend, nothing more.

"Gunther's doing what he can to convince people that the school is a good idea," she told Clay. "Only a few seem to listen. The rest act as if their children will somehow be contaminated if they study together."

"They speak of others' imperfections as if they had no blemishes of their own."

Sarah felt the blood drain from her face. It wasn't the sentiment Clay had expressed that startled her, but the words. They were almost identical to one of Austin's letters. She gripped a chair, trying to regain her equilibrium, trying to understand why Clay had used that particular phrase. Had he read her paper roses? Of course not. She would have known if anyone had disturbed them. It had to be coincidence, the result of being Austin's brother. Since they had grown up together, it was logical that they'd share many things, including more than one turn of a phrase.

"What a polite way to describe hypocrisy," Sarah said when she could once again breathe normally.

Clay reached for the satchel she'd filled with supplies. "I'm not certain hypocrisy's the problem. I suspect fear. Many people are afraid of those who are different."

Sarah was thankful they were walking toward the door and that he could not see her face, for his words raised unhappy memories. "Believe me, I know that. I wasn't exactly shunned by society because of my leg." The overt shunning came later, when her father's crimes were revealed. "But I had few invitations to parties and other social events. No one wanted to invite a girl who couldn't play all the games."

Clay placed his hand on Sarah's arm, turning her to face him. "In being so small-minded, they cheated themselves of the pleasure of your company." His eyes were dark with emotion.

"Unfortunately, they weren't the only ones who lost." Sarah wouldn't dwell on the years of loneliness and the times she'd cried when she heard other children playing outside. Those were all in the past, and nothing she could do would change them. "I'm determined that Thea will never be shunned."

"She won't. And I suspect that by the time you're done, neither will any of Ladreville's children."

Sarah wished she were that confident.

❦

"Look, Sarah. Flower!"

As they did many evenings now that the days were long, Sarah and Thea were working in the garden. Thea's working, of course, consisted primarily of walking around, poking her fingers into the dirt while Sarah weeded. Today Thea was pointing at the red blossoms of what Mary had told Sarah was a cedar sage.

Sarah's eyes widened at the sight of a dozen trumpet-shaped flowers that had opened on a single stem, and she bent down to touch one of the delicate blossoms. It was softer than she'd expected, almost velvety. As her fingers caressed the petals, Sarah pictured another garden. There had been nothing like this in Mama's plot, and yet she could imagine her mother smiling with pleasure at the sight of a flower in bloom. Sarah closed her eyes, remembering Mama's smile, and as she did, she felt warmth steal into her heart, chasing away the sorrow. For the first time, thoughts of her mother were not accompanied by tears. Sarah touched the flower again, savoring its soft petals. Perhaps Isabelle was right. Perhaps healing did come with time. Perhaps sorrow did fade.

"Me bleeding!" Thea rushed to Sarah's side, holding out the finger she'd pricked on a rosebush. "Hurt!"

It was only a drop of blood, nothing that should have triggered memories, but it did, transporting Sarah back to the day she'd found her parents' bodies. She started to shake as the image consumed her. There'd been so much blood, so horribly much blood. And then there was the look of shock frozen on Mama's face. Why, oh, why had he done it? Sarah bit the inside of her mouth to keep from crying out. Isabelle was wrong. Time did not heal everything. Sorrow might fade, but anger did not. She would never, ever forgive her father.

❦

As Mary opened the door, Clay caught a glimpse of a dress with too many buttons undone and a flash of gold. Tugging her bodice closed, Mary glared at him. "What are you doing here?"

Clay looked down at the medical bag in his hand, as if the

answer should be obvious. "You summoned a doctor. Since Herman is indisposed today, I came in his place."

Her buttons now securely fastened, Mary fisted her hands on her hips. "You can go right back where you came from, Clay Canfield. I ain't so ill that I'd let a young man I practically raised treat me. Why, it wouldn't be seemly." Before Clay could say anything more, she closed the door, leaving him standing on the front porch.

Clay grinned as he mounted Shadow. If he was correct—and he suspected he was—Mary wasn't ill at all. The call for a doctor had simply been another ploy to spend more time in Herman's company, like the visits she'd made to his house. Clay knew that when she set her mind to it, Mary was nothing if not determined, and she appeared to be determined to snag the town's senior doctor as a husband.

"C'mon, Shadow. Let's go home." Clay was still grinning when he crested a hill, but the grin faded at the sight of the wagon—his wagon—with a horse tied behind it. He tightened his grip on the reins as the details registered. Two girls were playing in the back, while a man and woman occupied the buckboard's seat. Though Clay wished otherwise, there was no doubt of anyone's identity. Gunther and his daughter were accompanying Sarah and Thea, and judging by the way Sarah leaned toward him, she was enjoying Gunther's conversation.

Two emotions slammed through Clay. He recognized anger, but it was mingled with something else, something that felt equally strong. Surely that something was not jealousy. Clay slowed Shadow as he took a deep breath, trying to conquer the need to send Gunther packing. The way he felt right now, he didn't trust himself to be near the man.

Relax, Clay told himself. *Think of something else. Something good.* There were indeed good things, for much had changed during the past few weeks, in great part because of Zach. If Clay were a praying man, he would have said that Zach was the answer to prayer. Zach had not exaggerated his experience. From the beginning, the men recognized him as a natural leader and no longer approached Clay for anything but the most critical decisions. No doubt about it, the salary Clay paid Zach was small recompense for the burden he'd lifted. Thanks to Zach, Clay no longer had to worry about the Bar C, and that was fortunate, for Herman now relied on him more frequently.

It wasn't only Clay who'd benefited from Zach's arrival. Though Clay wasn't sure how Zach found the time, he spent hours each day with Pa. The change in Pa had been remarkable. He seemed happier; he even slept better. Clay wouldn't be surprised if Pa were content to remain on the Bar C with Zach, even if Clay returned to Boston. Everything was going smoothly, except, of course, for that confounded Gunther and his courtship of Sarah.

Other things had contributed to Clay's newfound contentment. He'd been filled with a sense of relief the day he'd shipped Patience's trunk to her parents. Though at one time he had not thought it possible, cleaning the room they'd once shared had been the right thing to do. The door now stood open, and though Clay refused to sleep there, preferring instead to stretch out on the floor in the main room, the pain was gone, replaced by bittersweet memories. Clay knew he would always love Patience. He would treasure the months they'd spent together, and for the rest of his days, he would regret her life being cut short. But he had also accepted that Patience was part of his past. It was time for the future.

And that was the problem. The future that had once seemed so clear was now filled with ambiguity. Where would he go once he found Austin's killer? It disturbed Clay more than he wanted to admit that he was asking that question. When he'd left Boston, he had assured Daniel Morton that he would return to resume his practice there. But somehow the prospect of Boston and catering to the imaginary ailments of its wealthiest residents no longer held much appeal. Instead Clay pictured Leah Dunn and the child whose arm he'd splinted this morning. Instead of the large redbrick house he'd once shared with Patience, Clay's mind conjured images of the small cabin Austin had built for Sarah.

Something had changed, something fundamental deep inside him. Clay knew that. What he didn't know was why so much had changed. Surely it was not because of Sarah. Oh, it was true that he thought of her far too often, but that could be easily explained. It was proximity, nothing more. He saw her several times each day; that was why thoughts of her slid into his mind with alarming frequency. But that meant nothing. Sarah and her minx of a sister were not the reason Clay was suddenly reluctant to leave Ladreville. Only a fool would think that, and Clay Canfield was not a fool.

12

"All right, children. It's almost time. Quiet, now." Silence, Sarah knew, was an impossible dream, but she had to make the effort. She and her pupils had assembled on the Rue du Marché, directly across from the market that had given the street its name, waiting to take their place in Ladreville's Independence Day parade. Despite her admonitions, her students laughed, giggled, and shouted as they jumped up and down, barely able to contain their excitement. Though Sarah had no intention of jumping, she was almost as excited as they. The children's glee was easy to understand, for this was the first time they'd marched in the parade. In their minds, being included in the annual celebration made them adults, or so they'd told Sarah. Her own pleasure came from the fact that they would be walking as part of a single group with no regard for their last names.

"Quiet." This time she placed her finger over her lips, trying not to smile when the gesture accomplished what her words had not. Sarah had other reasons to smile. Conducting classes outdoors had been more successful than she'd dared hope. Each week more pupils came to the unusual schoolroom, possibly drawn by the novelty of lessons that included identification of birds and butterflies. At first, the children had sat in two distinct groups, separated by a large space. But as the weeks passed, the space had shrunk. Now anyone looking at the Ladreville students seated under the big oak trees would have seen nothing amiss, for there was only a single group of pupils. Though the parents had not changed their minds about building a school, and seemed unaware that their children studied in such close proximity, Sarah took comfort in the fact that her pupils' education was no longer being curtailed.

"All right, boys and girls. It's time." Time to march and time to prove she had not made a mistake. The youngsters would be walking three abreast, arranged by height with the shortest first. Though Clay had warned her she was playing with fire, having children of French descent walking next to Germans, Sarah had been adamant. Now she could only hope she'd not been wrong.

As the parade turned right onto Potomac Street, Sarah kept a smile fixed on her face. This was the children's moment. Surely no one would dare spoil it. No one other than participants had been allowed in the staging area, but anxious parents seemed to have crowded the first block of Potomac, eager for a glimpse of their offspring. Would they object to the marching order? Even worse, would someone pull a child out of the formation?

Sarah murmured words of encouragement to the youngest pupils, reminding them how important it was to smile.

What they needed, she soon realized, was not encouragement but an admonition not to skip and jump, for the sight of an audience appeared to fuel their excitement.

"*Mutti!*" one little girl shrieked.

As she started to run toward her mother, the boy next to her tugged her hand. "We're marching now," he reminded her.

"Good girl, Heidi," a woman with a heavy German accent called out. "Stay with your friend."

"That's my Jacques," the well-dressed woman standing next to Heidi's mother announced.

"*Sehr gut.* He's a good boy."

"Yes, he is." Jacques's mother smiled. "And your Heidi is quite pretty."

Perhaps she shouldn't have listened so intently, but Sarah couldn't help it, and her heart swelled with happiness at the sight of two women who, to the best of her knowledge, had never exchanged a civil word, and were now smiling at each other.

The scene was repeated several times as the procession made its way along Potomac, turning to travel the length of Hochstrasse and ending in the large field across the street from her makeshift outdoor school, and with each repetition Sarah's spirits rose. This was what she'd hoped for. Her pupils, from Olga Kaltheimer down to Thea, had had a wonderful time. Now they could enjoy the rest of the festivities.

Sarah looked across the field that would be the scene for most of the celebration. A platform had been erected for the speakers; everyone else brought quilts and blankets, which they'd spread on the ground. As the parade disbanded and the children raced to their parents, Sarah and Thea headed toward the Canfield quilt. Though Gunther had invited them to join him and Eva, Sarah had refused. It was one thing to realize the man was courting her, a far different thing to do something that would announce to the town that she favored his suit. For she did not. Marriage was not something Sarah wanted to think about, at least not anytime soon, and so she sat with the family that had given her a home.

The quilt would be crowded today. Though Sarah had assumed Pa would remain at the ranch, he'd insisted Clay and Zach carry him to the wagon. Now he was ensconced in the center of the blanket, flanked by Zach and Herman Adler. The doctor, Sarah noted with amusement, was studiously refusing to look to his left, lest he catch the eye of Mary Bramble and be forced to converse with her.

When she and Thea arrived, Thea flung herself into Clay's arms, acting as if they'd been separated for days rather than the space of an hour.

"No, Thea, you can't sit on Clay's lap." But neither her sister nor the man in question appeared to listen to Sarah's admonition. Instead, Clay wrapped one arm around Thea and patted the spot next to him, encouraging Sarah to sit there.

"The parade was nice," he said softly. "I've never heard so many proud parents."

As she arranged her skirts, Sarah nodded. If only she could convince those parents to take the next step and build a schoolhouse. But convincing them, she feared, was beyond her abilities. She had exhausted every argument, and none had worked. Though the townspeople were unfailingly polite, they were also adamant in their refusal. It would take a miracle or at least Michel Ladre's support to change their minds, and neither of those was likely to occur.

As the mayor and the other dignitaries climbed onto the

platform, Sarah took a deep breath. An instant later she realized she'd made a mistake, for instead of fresh air, she inhaled the scent of the man who sat so close she could almost hear his heart beat. Hair tonic mingled with soap and starch. The scents were all prosaic, and yet when Clay wore them, they seemed anything but ordinary, becoming positively delightful and far too distracting.

Sarah wanted to shift away from him, but if she did, she'd be on the Brambles' quilt, seated close to David. Since he and Jean-Michel were also reported to be courting her, Sarah couldn't do that, any more than she could sit with Gunther. And so she remained next to Clay, trying desperately not to notice how strong his arms were, how long and straight his legs were, or how right Thea looked sitting on his lap.

"Good morning, ladies and gentlemen, and welcome to our Independence Day celebration." At the sound of Michel Ladre's deep voice, the crowd fell silent. "Let us begin with a moment of prayer." First Père Tellier, then Pastor Sempert asked for God's blessing, reminding the townspeople how much God had already favored them by bringing them to a country filled with bounty and freedoms they'd never known. The prayers were greeted with fervent amens and a few cries of hallelujah. When the ministers had resumed their seats, Michel led the town in a patriotic song before he began his speech, a speech that enumerated the beauties of their new country and reminded the residents of Ladreville that they were now all Americans.

"It's this way every year," Clay murmured as everyone rose for another song. "For one day, the town is unified."

"Why can't it last longer?" Sarah looked around. This did not appear to be a cease-fire, a temporary lull between hostilities. Instead she sensed a common purpose. Why did that have to end when the sun set? She looked up at Clay. "Michel's right. We're all Americans."

"But we're also human, and humans aren't perfect. It's human nature to hate and to kill."

Though she suspected Clay was referring to Austin's murder, his words pierced her, reminding her of her father's crime, a memory that was sharper than a rapier. Sarah swallowed, trying to repress the painful images, trying to restore the moment of peace she'd found in her garden. She couldn't let the past destroy her future any more than she could let the townspeople's historical enmity destroy their children's chances for success.

Sarah closed her eyes for a second, picturing her mother. "It's also human nature to love," she said softly. "I'd like to believe that love will triumph over hatred."

Though everyone around them was singing, Clay continued their whispered conversation. "You're an optimist."

Was she? Sarah wasn't certain about that. What she did know was that someone had to act, and it appeared she was the only one willing. She wanted to—oh, how she wanted to—change their opinions. The question was, could she? Taking a deep breath, she straightened her shoulders. There would not be another opportunity like this.

"Where are you going?" The singing was so loud that Clay had no need to whisper when Sarah started moving toward the front of the crowd.

"To convince Ladreville that love is important." She heard murmurs as she picked her way between the quilts, and a few people started to speak to her, but she would not be deterred. This might be her only chance. By the time the song ended,

Sarah had reached her destination and was climbing the steps to the platform.

"Miss Dobbs. What do you want?" The mayor hurried to the side of the platform, apparently trying to discourage her from coming further.

"As Ladreville's schoolteacher, I would like to address the town." She was on the platform now, and judging from the buzzing in the audience, her presence had been noted.

"That's highly improper." Though Michel kept his voice low, there was no ignoring the anger in his eyes.

Sarah took another step toward the center, guessing that he would do nothing that could be construed as ungentlemanly. The man had a reputation to uphold, at least in public. "The town has never had a teacher before, so how can you say it's improper for one to take a part in the celebration?"

An expletive greeted her words. As if aware of the crowd's interest, Michel turned so he could not be overheard. "Women aren't supposed to give speeches. It's unseemly."

Though Sarah kept her smile firmly in place, she would not back down. "It would be more unseemly for me to start an argument here with everyone watching. Neither of us would benefit from that."

His fists clenched, his face red with anger, the town's mayor stared at her. "You'll regret this," he hissed. Then, wiping the anger from his face as easily as if he'd used a cloth to remove a speck of mud, he turned to the audience. "Ladies and gentlemen, Miss Dobbs has asked for a few minutes of your time." There was no mistaking the emphasis he placed on the word *few*. With a smile that could only be described as condescending, he added, "I beg you to indulge her fancy."

Moving to the center of the platform, Sarah flashed the

audience a smile. Though she was trembling inwardly, she could not afford any show of weakness. "I know you're all anxious to open your picnic baskets and sample some of the delicious food you've brought. I must tell you, my mouth was watering from the aromas as I walked up here, so I know there are treats in store for you." A ripple of laughter greeted her words. Excellent. She wanted everyone relaxed as she continued.

"I don't want to delay your meal, but what I have to say is important." The murmurs faded as Sarah's voice turned serious. "You know I believe it's important that all the children attend classes every week. I know you have reasons for not wanting to use the fellowship halls. There is a solution, ladies and gentlemen. Ladreville needs a school."

As Sarah paused, the low murmurs crescendoed. One man rose and shouted, "My son's not going to associate with those Frenchies."

On the other side of the field, a second man jumped to his feet. "I won't let my daughter near those Kaiser-lovers."

Though neither of those men had children old enough to attend school, murmurs of agreement swept through the crowd. It was as Sarah had feared. The town's one day of unity had lasted less than two hours. Though the parents thought they were protecting their children, their prejudices were depriving them of something important. Somehow, some way, she had to convince them that they were wrong. Sarah clasped her hands together as she tried to find an argument that might break through the centuries of hatred. She bit her lip as she realized there was only one. Could she do it? Could she tell them what she'd endured? She had no choice.

"Please listen to me." Sarah raised her voice, then waited

for the angry comments to subside. When she once again held the townspeople's attention, she spoke. "You all know that I have a limp. Some of you know that it's the result of being thrown from a horse when I was nine years old. What no one here knows is how badly I was hurt." Surely it was a good sign that the crowd remained silent. Surely that meant they were listening to her. "I don't mean the physical pain. That was bad enough, but there was something worse. Memories of physical pain fade, but other hurts remain. For months I was unable to walk. In fact, the doctors told my parents there was no hope." Sarah heard a gasp.

"Do you know what happened to me during that time? When they learned the news, my friends disappeared. No one wanted to be with a girl who couldn't play hopscotch." Several women looked down at their children, as if assuring themselves that they had suffered no injuries. "Even when I learned to walk again, I had no friends and received no invitations to parties. You see, my limp kept me from doing all the things others my age enjoyed. No one wanted to be with someone who was different, someone who had one leg shorter than the other."

Somehow she'd managed to keep her voice even, as if the story she was telling was someone else's. Somehow she'd managed not to reveal just how much she'd suffered during those years when books had replaced children as her companions.

Sarah looked out at the audience. She wouldn't look at Clay for fear of seeing pity in his eyes. Though Gunther nodded solemnly and Mary's expression was fierce, as if she understood what Sarah had endured, most of the people remained impassive. That was, Sarah tried to convince herself, better than outright condemnation. Behind her, she heard Michel shuffle his feet and cough, sure signs of his impatience. If she didn't finish quickly, he would interrupt.

She took a deep breath and continued. "I'm not telling you this because I want your pity. I'm telling you because I want you to understand what it's like for a child to be shunned or excluded. I thought it was my fault that no one visited me. I was convinced that if only I'd done something different, I would still have friends." Sarah heard the tremor in her voice as memories assailed her. "Don't you see? Children don't understand why they're excluded. They only feel pain. They think they're being punished for something they did, and that makes it so much worse."

When Sarah paused to let her words sink in, for the first time, she saw confusion on some of the faces. The fear of failure that had clutched her heart began to shrink as she realized they were listening. "I know you don't mean to hurt your children, but that's what you're doing. By forbidding them to play and study with others, you're denying them both friends and the education they deserve. The barriers you've created make it seem as if the children are being punished, and they don't understand why. How could they? The reason has nothing to do with anything they've done. They can't help the fact that their parents speak different languages any more than I could keep my horse from falling on me."

Though the men's expressions remained stoic, Sarah saw several women pale, and one lifted her handkerchief to dab the corners of her eyes. "Your children are suffering for things they can't control." Sarah paused for a second, gathering her courage. "I ask you. I beg you," she corrected herself, "to put aside your own feelings. Mayor Ladre reminded us

240

that we're all Americans. He's right. This is a new country and a chance for new lives. Please, I beg you, if you love your children, give them the lives they deserve. Let them all attend school together." Sarah heard Michel rise. Her time was over. "For their sakes, I hope you'll agree to build a schoolhouse." She looked at the audience one last time, trying to meet as many eyes as possible. When Michel reached her side, she said simply, "Thank you."

The mayor cleared his throat before he addressed his constituents. "I think you'll agree with me, ladies and gentlemen, that that was an unusual speech for Independence Day." He waited for laughter, but there was none. "Miss Dobbs has proven she's an unusual woman." This time, murmurs greeted his words. Sarah couldn't tell whether the townspeople were agreeing with him or not.

"She's got a point," one man said.

"She might be right," another agreed.

A red-faced man glared at Sarah. "Can't nobody convince me it's proper for our young'uns to sit with them others."

As the shouts continued, Michel pounded on the podium. "You'll have your say. As long as Miss Dobbs has raised the question, I propose we vote on the school. Any man who approves building one, stand up." His forbidding expression made it clear the mayor did not expect to see anyone rise.

Clay jumped to his feet, followed quickly by Gunther and Monsieur Rousseau. Sarah heard sounds behind her and turned to see both Père Tellier and Pastor Sempert rise from their seats at the back of the platform. Michel frowned. As the two ministers walked toward the audience, Sarah heard women's voices. Though the words were indistinguishable, the effect was not. Within seconds, dozens of men were on their feet.

"Humph!" Michel's displeasure was evident. He waited, perhaps hoping the men would back down, but no one did. "All right," he said. "You've spoken. Ladreville will have a school."

⌇

Clay watched Sarah make her way back to their quilt, stopping to talk to a few people along the way. She was quite a woman. It had to have taken courage to speak up like that, to bare her soul, as it were, but she'd done it, and she'd accomplished what she wanted. That was as close to a miracle as Clay had seen.

His eyes narrowed as she came closer. Though she continued to smile, her posture was rigid, her gait less steady than normal. Something was wrong. The woman who ought to be exulting over her victory was clearly disturbed.

"You did a good job." Clay watched as she settled onto the quilt next to him.

"I still can't believe I told them about my childhood." There was no doubt about it. The hands that were attempting to open the picnic basket were shaking.

"Hey, Zach." Clay punched the other man's arm to get his attention. "Keep an eye on Thea, okay?" He rose and extended his hand to Sarah. "Let's take a walk." Though he'd expected a protest, none was forthcoming. The feisty Sarah Dobbs he'd known seemed to have lost her spunk, for she acceded quickly, not even demurring when he placed her hand on his arm and covered it with his own hand.

As they walked slowly in deference to Sarah's leg, neither

242

of them spoke. It could have been an awkward silence, but it was not. Instead, Clay found himself noticing how dainty her hand felt beneath his, how her hair smelled like vanilla, and how her ragged breathing began to slow.

"Feel better now?" he asked when they reached the river. Though they were only a few hundred yards from the festivities, the din was muted by distance and the soft soughing of the oak trees. Knowing this was where she conducted classes, Clay looked around, marveling that she managed to keep her pupils' attention focused on lessons. He himself was distracted in no small measure by the woman at his side. Of course, the children would not have that problem. Sarah's students would see only their teacher, not a woman who'd defied the town's mayor and convinced its citizens to support her, a very attractive woman.

Sarah looked as if he'd asked her to solve the mysteries of the world, when all he'd done was pose a simple question. At last she nodded, then shook her head, clearly ambivalent. "I'm glad we'll have a school, but I can't imagine what my mother would have said if she'd seen me on that platform. She taught me that ladies never make a scene, and they never, ever refer to parts of the body. Mama would have been horrified if she'd heard me defy the mayor and actually say the word *leg* in mixed company."

Though her concerns might have made another man scoff, Clay did not. Marriage to Patience had taught him how differently men and women saw the world and how differently they were expected to act. Patience would not have climbed onto that platform; the thought would not have even occurred to her. But Sarah was different. Always in the past, even when he'd told her of Austin's death, she'd seemed strong and so resilient that he had believed nothing would break her, yet today she was vulnerable, needing reassurance. "Your mother would have been proud," he said firmly. "You did what was right. You convinced them to let love triumph over hatred."

"Michel didn't see it that way."

Clay couldn't disagree. "The man doesn't like anyone to challenge his authority. You and Austin both did that." Clay wondered if somehow his brother had sensed that the woman he'd chosen to be his bride had shared that trait with him. He would never know, just as it appeared he would never know who'd killed his sibling.

Sarah laid a hand against the tree trunk, perhaps to steady herself, perhaps simply to touch the rough bark. "I doubt Michel will help with the school raising."

"I'd say that's a good assumption." Clay knew how vindictive the mayor could be. After today, Sarah would be a focus for his enmity. "That won't stop you, though. The town will all pitch in. They've had more barn raisings than I can count. Compared to some of those barns, a school should be easy."

Sarah was breathing normally now, and the tilt of her head told Clay her earlier worries about the propriety of what she'd done were gone, replaced by concerns for the school. She looked up at him, her eyes bright with enthusiasm. "We need someone to plan everything, to order the supplies and then supervise the actual building."

A foreman. She was right, and it appeared she was looking to him for a suggestion. Though it pained him, Clay voiced the words. "Your friend Gunther might be able to do that." Clay suspected he'd jump at the opportunity, for it would give him another excuse to continue his courtship of Sarah.

She shook her head. "Gunther's not a leader. Besides, the French men wouldn't follow him."

An unexpected sense of relief flowed through Clay at the realization that Sarah was not seeking opportunities for more time in Gunther's company. "That logic would probably also eliminate Monsieur Rousseau."

Sarah nodded. "You're right." Though her lips quirked in what appeared to be the start of a smile, her voice was solemn as she said, "There's one person in Ladreville who commands everyone's respect."

"Who would that be?" Clay tried and failed to imagine someone who fit that description.

The smile blossomed. "You."

"Me?" A man's jaw wasn't supposed to drop, but his did. "Why would I build a school? I'm a doctor."

"You wouldn't have to do any of the actual construction," Sarah said, her voice as sweet as honey. Was this the way she convinced recalcitrant pupils to behave? If so, Clay suspected she had a model classroom. "You wouldn't have to build, although I know you can. Martina told me you and Austin raised your barn practically alone." Clay frowned. He'd have to talk to Martina about the stories she related. It appeared they were getting him in trouble. Now he would have to find a way to refuse, even though he hated to disappoint Sarah.

She was still speaking. "All that's needed is organization and leadership. You'd be perfect for that."

Clay was not perfect at anything, but now did not seem the time to announce that. What he needed was a simple refusal. Instead, he found himself saying, "Even if I were the right person, why would I want to lead the school raising? I have plenty of other things to do."

A light breeze sent Sarah's sweet scent to tantalize Clay's senses. Though he should take a step backward to evade it, he did not. Instead he stood as frozen as Lot's wife while she spoke.

"I need your help. The simple fact is, there's no one else in Ladreville who can lead this project." Sarah's smile said she knew Clay was wavering. He was, but she wasn't supposed to realize that. A man had his pride. He didn't like knowing a pretty slip of a woman could read his thoughts. "If you agree to help me," Sarah continued, "I'll help you."

That was a unique argument. "Just what do you propose to do?"

"Find Austin's killer."

Of all the words that could have come from Sarah's mouth, those were the last ones he would have expected. Clay felt as if he'd been kicked in the gut. When he could breathe again, he asked, "How do you think you can do that? I've talked to everyone who was with Austin that last day, and I've learned nothing."

Sarah nodded slowly, acknowledging his words and the frustration behind them. "My approach would be different. I'll have to visit each family, raising money and talking about the curriculum. When I'm in people's houses, I won't ask questions about Austin; I'll just direct the conversation that way. My experience is that when people are relaxed, they're more likely to reveal things they wouldn't in a confrontation."

Clay was silent for a moment, considering her plans. "You may be right. Every time I talk to anyone, it does become confrontational." He'd learned nothing. Absolutely nothing. If there was the slightest possibility that Sarah could help, how could he refuse?

Her eyes darkened as she looked at him. "Will you agree to help me?"

"You've got a deal."

Sarah held out her hand for the traditional shake to seal their agreement. As he took her hand in his, Clay felt tendrils of warmth begin to make their way up his arm. Her hand was small and soft, so different from his. All of Sarah was small and soft, all except her determination. That was as firm as his own, and it was—if he was being honest—one of her most appealing features. That and her outspoken tongue.

As the thought flitted through Clay's mind, his gaze wandered to her lips. Unbidden came the question, what would it be like to kiss her? Would her lips be as soft as they looked?

Abruptly, Clay dropped her hand. Where on earth had that thought come from?

13

Even the weather cooperated. Though Mary had predicted one of the summer rains that flooded the river, the day was clear and dry. All the supplies had arrived on schedule; the ground had been cleared; now everyone was gathered, ready to begin construction of the schoolhouse.

"I wish I could do more." Sarah looked around the tent where she and Isabelle had organized long tables soon to be laden with food.

"More?" Isabelle chuckled. "You've already done more than anyone dreamed possible. You convinced the town to work together. And, if that wasn't enough, you organized all the food."

"That part was easy." That hadn't required painful revelations. When she'd approached them, the women of Ladreville had proven eager to bring food, particularly when Sarah decided to capitalize on the town's natural rivalries and had mentioned that the culmination of the day would be the men's voting for their favorite dishes. That announcement had resulted in many women volunteering to bring both a main course and a dessert. No one would go hungry today.

Unfortunately, though providing food for the workers had been relatively simple, Sarah had been less successful in learning anything new about Austin's death. Each mention of his name had been met with shuttered expressions, making it clear that no one wanted to talk about Sarah's former fiancé. Perhaps they feared causing her more pain. Perhaps it was what Clay claimed, a conspiracy of silence. Whatever the cause, her failure to uncover even a single new detail weighed heavily on Sarah. Clay had done his part, but she had not.

Isabelle pulled another piece of oilcloth from her basket and extended it to Sarah. "What I find most amazing," Isabelle said, "is that you convinced Clay to take charge of the school. I know his family were the first settlers, but he's always remained aloof, acting as if he wanted no part of the town. Now he's helping Dr. Adler and working on the school. I don't know how you did it, Sarah, but since you came to Ladreville, Clay Canfield has been a changed man. Why, I even saw him start to smile once."

Sarah shook her head. "I'm not responsible for the changes. Maybe they're what you told me, the result of time."

"Or God's healing touch." Isabelle straightened the edges of the tablecloth. "Every day I pray that God will take the bitterness from Clay's heart."

Though Sarah no longer prayed, that was her most fervent hope. Sadly, she feared it was a hope that would not be realized. While Clay's sadness seemed to be subsiding, she knew his anger had not faded. "I'm afraid the only thing he cares about is finding Austin's murderer."

"Sarah!"

At the sound of Clay's voice, Sarah let her words trail off. He didn't need to know she and Isabelle had been discussing him.

"We're ready to start," he told her. "The ministers are both going to offer prayers. Afterwards, it would be good for you to say something."

She blinked in surprise. Though they'd discussed the agenda for the day, her making a speech was not on it. "You should have warned me."

"So you could refuse?"

"Exactly."

"Coward!" He accompanied the epithet with a grin.

Placing her hands on her hips, Sarah feigned indignation. "No one calls me a coward and lives to repeat it."

Clay's chuckle turned into a full-fledged laugh. "That's what I thought. Be ready in five minutes."

As he strode toward the group of men who'd gathered, their tools at hand, Isabelle touched Sarah's arm. "Clay Canfield laughing? You truly are a miracle worker."

The day passed quickly. Though speech-making was not Sarah's forte, she managed to welcome all the workers and thank them for their gift of time, and soon the air was filled with the sounds of hammers, saws, and busy men. While their labor was less strenuous, the women were no less busy as they supplied cool lemonade, tea, and hearty sandwiches. In less time than Sarah had thought possible the frame was erected, with the walls and roof following quickly. By nightfall, Ladreville had both its first school and a group of very hungry men.

"Don't forget to vote." As they entered the food tent, Sarah gave each of the men a ticket and pointed toward the tin cups she'd placed behind the platters. There had been friendly grousing that morning when she'd told the workers of the contest. Some men, she suspected, feared their wives' wrath if their dishes did not receive the blue ribbon. Though no names accompanied the various cakes and pies, it had not escaped Sarah's notice that many of the women had left clues, including specially fluted pie crusts and unusual swirls in the cake frosting.

"Which one did you make?"

Sarah shook her head as she handed Clay his ticket. "You know I can't cook." There had never been a need to learn, for her family had employed an excellent cook. Mama's responsibility had been to plan the menus, not translate those menus into delectable dishes. Mrs. Porter had done that. Had she been here, one of her light-as-air, beautifully decorated cakes would have been in contention for the top prize.

A pang of nostalgia swept through Sarah as she remembered the cake Mrs. Porter had made for her last birthday. Though it had been a visual masterpiece, almost too pretty to eat, Sarah, her family, and their guests had devoured it, laughing when the majority of Thea's piece remained on her face. There would be no cake this August, no wishes for another year of health and happiness.

Giving herself a mental shake, Sarah forced a smile onto her face. "Everyone says this peach pie is delicious."

"Is something wrong?" Clay lowered his voice. "You looked sad."

He wasn't supposed to notice. No one was. Sarah shook her head. "I must be more tired than I realized." Not wanting to continue that conversation, Sarah gestured toward the workers and their families. "I want to thank everyone personally."

"Mind if I come with you?"

The offer, though surprising, sent a wave of pleasure through her. "Not at all. This was your project as much as mine."

They walked slowly through the crowd, stopping to speak to each of the families. It might not qualify as a miracle, but for the first time, Sarah saw only smiles. Though the men were exhausted, their faces radiated pride, a pride shared by their wives. People gestured toward the schoolhouse, talking about the generations that would study there. They complimented Clay on the planning he'd done. They told Sarah their children were eager to attend school. Not once did she hear a disparaging comment. For one day at least, Ladreville was united.

She owed that to the man at her side. He'd arranged work assignments so that men with known enmities were separated, but he'd also placed men of German origin next to French-speaking workers. The result had been remarkably harmonious. While it remained to be seen whether the cooperative spirit would last, Sarah was reveling in the result: a beautiful new school and a seemingly happy town. If only she'd been able to help Clay, her day would have been complete, but the identity of Austin's killer remained a mystery.

❧

The first weeks in the new schoolhouse were a success by anyone's standards. Sarah had more pupils than ever before, a significant feat, considering that it was summer and the children were needed to work in the fields. Not only did the pupils attend school, but they appeared eager to learn. It was almost as if the dedicated schoolhouse made them realize that education was important. Sarah was delighted, and that delight grew when she noted the number of mothers who met their children after classes each day and who, while they were waiting for school to end, spoke with other mothers, regardless of their native languages.

Truly, life was good. And yet, Sarah could not dismiss the sense that something was missing. Though she was bothered by her failure to learn anything about Austin's death, Sarah knew that was not the cause of her malaise. Still, it made little sense. What more could she want? She had created a life for herself and Thea, a life where no one would know their past. Her sister was happy. Thea had friends, and so did Sarah. Isabelle was the truest friend a woman could want, and Clay . . . well, Clay made Sarah feel almost as if she were part of his family. Surely that was enough. Surely there was no reason for the emptiness that sometimes filled her.

If only she could identify the cause, she would be able to resolve it, but the reason was almost as elusive as Austin's murderer. Sarah wished there were someone she could ask. Though she and Clay discussed everything from the upcoming presidential election to the plight of slaves as depicted in Mrs. Stowe's *Uncle Tom's Cabin*, this was not a subject Sarah could raise with him or with any other man, for that matter. As her closest woman friend, Isabelle was the logical confidante, but Sarah already knew what Isabelle would say. She would claim Sarah needed God's presence in her life. While God might fill Isabelle's empty places, he was not what Sarah needed. She knew that, and so she resigned herself to living with the void.

"Sarah!" Mary's face brightened when she stepped onto her porch that afternoon, alerted by the sound of wagon wheels. "I figgered you'd forgotten me."

Regret that she'd neglected the woman who'd been so kind to her and Thea spiked through Sarah. "I haven't forgotten you," she assured Mary. "I've just been busy." She lifted Thea from the wagon, intending to spend more than a few minutes with their neighbor. This visit was well overdue.

"I surely wanted to be part of that school raising," Mary told her when they were seated in the front porch rocking chairs, a tray with buttermilk and cookies between them. Thea had already consumed two cookies and was racing back and forth in front of the porch. "I reckon it woulda shocked everyone," Mary continued, "if'n I grabbed a hammer and nails and helped put on that roof." She laughed at Sarah's raised eyebrows. "Us Western women are different from you Eastern ladies. We had to be. There weren't no one 'ceptin' Mr. Bramble and me when it came time to build that barn, so I climbed right up on the roof with him."

Sarah nodded. She'd heard tales of pioneer women's strength, but she hadn't realized just how literal that strength was.

"Can you shoot a gun?" Mary asked. "I reckon you oughta learn, if you're fixin' to stay here. When my husband was off fighting, if it hadn't been for my shotgun, David and I wouldn't have had meat for dinner most nights."

Though Sarah could not picture herself killing anything, even to eat, she forbore saying that. "I can't even cook," she admitted.

Mary gave her a long, appraising look. "We'll have to

change that. Next time you come, I'll show you how to fix biscuits. Now, tell me about the school. It's a nice building you got there."

"I have everything I need."

Mary flashed her an arch smile. "Not everything. You need a husband." When Sarah started to protest, Mary shook her finger at her. "You gotta excuse an old woman's meddling, but I know what I'm talkin' about. Gunther Lehman ain't the man for you. My David would make a much better husband."

What could she say? Sarah swallowed as she tried to formulate her words. "I'm certain they'd both be good husbands . . . for someone else."

"Balderdash! You can pretend, but you cain't fool me. I know you want a husband and a father for Thea."

"Someday, maybe." Where had those words come from? As Sarah shook herself mentally, another thought assailed her. Was that what was missing from her life? Did she secretly long for a husband?

"What do you know about Clay's new foreman?"

Mary's abrupt change of subject brought Sarah back to the present. "Zach? He doesn't talk about himself very much, but I know he fought in the war with Clay's father."

As she refilled Sarah's glass, Mary pursed her lips. "I wonder if he was treated as poorly as my Greg was. My husband sacrificed his life for his country, and what did they give him in return? Nothing!" She didn't try to hide her bitterness. "David ought to have the same inheritance that Austin did. His pa fought just the same as Robert Canfield. It ain't fair."

Sarah couldn't disagree. "It seems to me, life isn't fair."

❦

Clay strode toward the barn. He hadn't meant to pry, but when he'd seen Sarah's Bible on the table, he'd picked it up, intending to return it to the cabin she and Thea shared, and as he did, it had fallen open to the family pages. That's when he'd learned she would soon celebrate her birthday. Clay frowned, almost wishing he hadn't seen the entry. What did he know about birthdays other than that Patience had insisted they were important? Clay had never cared about his, and he couldn't recall Austin or Pa making a fuss about the day they were born. According to Patience, women were different. Clay certainly couldn't dispute that. He could pretend he didn't know, but his conscience would plague him. There was no way around it. He had to do something for Sarah.

"Hey, Zach." Thank goodness the man was there. Though he could not have predicted it the day the dusty stranger rode onto the Bar C, Clay had gotten more than a foreman. In just a short time, Zach had become a friend and confidant, a man with surprising depths of wisdom. If anyone would know how to resolve this new problem, it would be Zach. "Do you know anything about women's birthdays?"

The man who was almost as close to Clay as a brother looked up from the saddle he was cleaning, his lips twisting slightly as he said, "As I recall, they happen once a year."

"Even I know that." Clay had no time for humor. "Sarah's is in two weeks. I think we ought to do something."

"We?" Zach raised both eyebrows. "I'm a cowboy. Ask me anything about cattle, and I'll give you an answer. But women? The extent of my knowledge of women is that they don't think like us. Besides, why are you asking me? You're the one who was married. How did you celebrate your wife's birthday?"

That was the problem. "Her mother planned it all. The only thing her father and I had to do was promise to come to dinner on time."

Zach's lips twisted again, making Clay think he was trying to control a laugh. Surely he could see that this was no laughing matter. "All right," Zach said. "We're making progress. It appears dinner is involved. Martina can take care of that."

Clay thought about the fancy dinners his mother-in-law had arranged. Nothing Martina did could compare to that. She was a good cook, but meals tended to be plain, and Clay would bet she'd never considered cooking, much less eating, a snail. So much for gourmet food.

Clay tried to remember what else Prudence Morton had done for her daughter's party. They'd had a dozen guests . . . He frowned again. "I guess we need to invite some other people." Sarah didn't know the ranch hands, so they were not a good choice. Clay fixed his eyes on Zach. "You need to come." The man could provide support for Clay. It was becoming obvious he would need a lot of that. "I'll ask Mary and David and the Rousseaus." As Clay counted the guests, an unpleasant thought assailed him. "I suppose I have to invite Gunther and Eva too."

This time there was no doubt about it. Zach was on the verge of laughter. "You probably should," he agreed. "One more thing. I'm not an expert, but I've heard women like things like this to be surprises."

"I guess that means I can't ask Sarah to plan the menu." Clay plunked his hat back on his head and headed toward the door. Before he reached it, he turned and asked, "Do you really think I need to invite Gunther?"

Laughter was Zach's only response.

He didn't look like Austin. His voice wasn't similar. But Zach's laugh reminded Clay of his brother, and so he responded as he would have to Austin. "If you hadn't done that, I was going to tell you I was glad you came to the Bar C." Clay had even planned to give Zach a raise. Now he'd wait a week. After all, you shouldn't reward a man for laughing at another man's predicament.

"I'm glad I came." Zach nodded slowly. "It was God's will."

Clay's amusement faded. Austin would have said the same thing. The trouble was, both Austin and Zach were wrong. "I suppose it was also God's will that Austin die. If it was, you can keep your God. I have no use for him."

✎

"I want you to play very quietly," Sarah told her sister as they entered the mercantile. Thea had grown so much that she needed a new dress, and that meant buying fabric. Though it was a simple matter, Sarah wanted Isabelle's advice. Her friend had an excellent sense of fashion and would be able to select the perfect calico. But instead of the smiling woman Sarah had expected, she saw a woman with red-rimmed eyes sitting behind the counter.

"What's wrong?"

"Everything!" Isabelle began to sob, covering her face with her hands. "She was horrible, and now everyone knows, and nothing will ever be the same."

Though her leg throbbed and Thea began to whimper in sympathy, Sarah hurried behind the counter to wrap her arms around her friend. Until she knew why Isabelle was crying,

258

a hug was the only comfort she could provide. "Start at the beginning. What happened?"

"Frau Steiner never liked us." Isabelle turned and buried her face against Sarah. Though her words were muffled, Sarah understood them. "I remember how mean Frau Steiner was on the boat, always saying nasty things about my family. She hasn't changed. All she does is look for something bad, and then she tells everyone."

Sarah couldn't contradict her friend, for she knew Frau Steiner's reputation as the town busybody. "What is she saying now?"

Isabelle's sobs intensified. "I don't know how she found out, but she learned what happened in the Old Country, how Léon was in trouble with the law. She's spreading the story, and now he's being blamed for everything bad that happens here."

Sarah nodded slowly. There'd been another rash of thefts, and she'd heard Clay grousing about the continuing problem with cut fences. She could only imagine what life was like for Léon if he was being accused of the crimes.

"The only one who won't believe her is Karl Friedrich. He says he knows Léon didn't cut those fences." Isabelle raised her tear-stained face. "Oh, Sarah, I don't know what to do. This hurts Maman and Papa so much. They thought we could start anew here, and now they're afraid we'll have to move again."

Sarah's heart ached for her friend and the family that had been so kind to her. How she wished she could reassure Isabelle by promising that everything would be fine, but she couldn't. All she could offer was faint consolation. "The unpleasantness will die down. Rumors always do."

But Sarah also knew they were never completely forgotten. It was that knowledge that had led her to accept Austin's offer of marriage with its chance to begin a new life thousands of miles away from Philadelphia. It was that knowledge that kept her from telling anyone what her father had done. She couldn't risk letting Thea be hurt the way these good people were.

Isabelle wiped her eyes. "It's not fair."

"Life isn't fair." The phrase was becoming a refrain.

જી

Sarah winced as her comb caught a tangle of hair. That's what happened when you tried to rush; nothing went right.

"Pretty, Sarah." Thea fingered the lace-trimmed shirtwaist Sarah had laid out on the bed. Perhaps it was silly, wearing a new garment today. Technically she should still be in mourning, but for the past week Sarah had worn normal clothing to school, encouraged by her youngest pupils, who'd complained that she looked like a magpie in her somber black. It had been eleven months since Mama and Papa's deaths, and even though many observed a full year of mourning for a parent, Sarah knew her mother would not have minded that she was now in more cheerful garb. Mama herself had worn black for only six months after Grandmama died. But there was a difference between the serviceable clothing she'd worn all week and this delicate rose-colored shirtwaist. It was more suited for a special occasion, particularly since she faced the possibility that it might suffer the fate that had befallen one of her light gray dresses. That one had been irreparably stained when an overly exuberant pupil had signed his name with a flourish, sending drops of ink flying onto Sarah's skirt.

Though it might be foolish, Sarah slid her arms into the sleeves, enjoying the feel of the soft muslin. The fancy shirt-waist would remind her that this was a special day. Her birthday. A pang of nostalgia swept through her as she recalled the myriad ways her mother had turned birthdays into day-long celebrations for the entire family. This year would be different, for without Mama no one knew it was Sarah's special day.

"Me ready!" Thea pointed at her shoes, which she'd managed to put on to the correct feet this morning.

Sarah gave her sister a hug. How selfish she was, feeling sorry that there would be no birthday festivities. She had so many more important things to worry about, things like Thea's future and the unfair treatment Léon was receiving.

Admiring her sister's shoes, Sarah said, "You're a big girl now." And so was she. There would be no pouting. Instead she would enjoy all that she had: her sister, her pupils, her friends.

By the lunch recess, Sarah had almost forgotten it was her birthday. Classes had gone well. Not only were there no flying drops of ink, but—more importantly—Johann Steiner had recited the alphabet perfectly, and Marie Claude Moreau had missed only one number in today's multiplication table. Both students' eyes had lit with pleasure over their accomplishments, making Sarah feel as if she too had accomplished something. Now she sat at her desk, munching a carrot and reviewing her plans for this afternoon's lessons.

The sound of heavy footsteps startled her, for she'd expected no visitors—especially not a male visitor—today. As she looked up and recognized the man, Sarah's heart began to pound. Why was Léon here? Not only had he never come to the school, but he was supposed to be working on the Friedrichs' farm.

"Is something wrong?"

He grinned as he shook his head. "No. Karl gave me some time off." A wry smile lit Léon's face. "Much good it's doing me. Isabelle has turned me into her errand boy. That's why I'm here."

As her heart resumed its normal pace, Sarah copied Léon's playful tone. "You mean you didn't come to learn multiplication tables?"

"I'm afraid not. Isabelle asked whether you and Thea could stop by the store after school. She said she needs your advice on something."

But Isabelle seemed in no hurry to seek counsel. When Sarah and her sister arrived, Isabelle settled Thea on the floor with a basket of socks, turning sorting them into a game for her. While Thea played, Isabelle chattered. That was the only way Sarah could describe it. Though her friend spoke of a number of things, they were all inconsequential. Given the frequency with which she looked at the clock, she seemed more concerned about the passage of time than in seeking Sarah's advice.

At length, Isabelle said, "You're probably wondering why I asked you to come." As Sarah nodded, she continued. "I don't really need your advice, but I do need your help. I know you've seen the necklaces Frau Bauer makes out of pinecones." Sarah had indeed seen them and had admired the woman's skillful designs. She'd even suggested that the Rousseaus add them to their inventory, but the elderly German woman had insisted she preferred to sell them herself at the town's open-air market.

"As it turns out, Frau Bauer is at the market this week, and she has some new designs. I wondered if you'd select one for me." Isabelle wrinkled her nose. "I would have asked Léon, but he has terrible taste."

Though it was a simple enough request, and Sarah was always willing to help her friend, there was an easier solution. "Why don't I mind the store so you can go?" After all, Sarah had experience working in the mercantile, and that way Isabelle could choose her favorite design.

Isabelle shook her head. "Maman would be angry. I know she'd say I was taking advantage of you. Please, Sarah. I really want one of those necklaces." When Sarah looked down at Thea, Isabelle said quickly, "I'll watch her while you're gone. Just pick the one you like best."

The shopping excursion lasted longer than Sarah had anticipated. Apparently expecting her, Frau Bauer had a large selection of necklaces and seemed compelled to describe each one's advantages. Then when Sarah had finally chosen one, the shopkeeper insisted on wrapping it, even though it required the better part of five minutes to find a piece of cord to tie the package. By the time everything was ready, half an hour had gone by, and Sarah was anxious. If she didn't hurry, she and Thea would be late for supper. They'd already missed Thea's riding lesson.

When she rounded the corner, Sarah found the mercantile locked, a note stuck to the door. "Sarah," the note read, "Thea was fussy, so I took her home—Isabelle." Sarah shook her head, realizing Isabelle had gotten more than she'd bargained for when she'd volunteered to watch Thea.

As she headed back to the ranch, Sarah flicked the reins, urging the horses to quicken their pace. She could only hope

Thea had not developed a full-fledged tantrum. Though increasingly rare, they were alarming and might be beyond Isabelle's experience. The sense of relief that blossomed as Sarah entered the Bar C's lane turned to alarm when she saw four wagons, their horses hitched to the front posts. What was wrong? Though she'd expected the Rousseaus' buggy, she knew of no reason for the others to be here. Had something happened to Thea or Pa? As quickly as she could, Sarah dismounted and entered the house, her heart anxious, her palms moist with fear.

"Happy birthday!" Fear turned to surprise. Sarah froze, astonished by the cries that greeted her. As her eyes adjusted to the lower light, she saw the main room filled with people dressed in their Sunday best.

"Happy birthday!"

There was no doubt about it. Someone had learned that today was her birthday. Sarah's heart filled with warmth as she looked around the room. There was Thea, happily settled in Clay's arms, while Zach stood next to Pa's wheeled chair. Not only was the entire Rousseau family present, but close by were Gunther and Eva, and Mary and David. The Friedrich family completed the gathering.

"S'prise, Sarah. Papa Clay made s'prise." Thea punctuated her words with big grins.

Clay? Sarah's amazement grew as she tried and failed to picture her father or any of the men she knew planning a party. Yet Clay had done it. The proof was here. "How did you know?"

He shook his head. "Later. Thea tells me it's time to eat."

Keeping one arm firmly around Thea, Clay extended his other to escort Sarah to the table. Within minutes, they were all savoring the meal. Though Martina had prepared most of the dishes, each of the guests had brought something. A bowl of Frau Friedrich's cucumbers and sour cream sat next to a plate of Madame Rousseau's pâté. When Mary mentioned that she had made the biscuits, Eva proudly presented Sarah with a jar of peach jam that she'd helped make, insisting Sarah be the first to sample it.

Sarah's heart welled with happiness. Had it been only a few hours ago that she was feeling sorry for herself because no one knew it was her birthday? Now here she was, surrounded by friends, their smiles telling her they were as glad to be here as she was to have them.

"I know this is probably not as fancy as dinners in Philadelphia," Clay said softly.

She couldn't let him apologize, not when he'd done so much to make her day special. While it was true there was no crystal or china here, that mattered not a whit. "This is the most wonderful meal I can recall." The food was delicious, but the true appeal was being with people who accepted her for who she was, not for her last name or the size of her father's investments. The guests at last year's birthday celebration, people who had been her parents' closest friends, had all disappeared when they'd learned of Papa's disastrous investments. These people would not, for they were true friends. "Thank you, Clay." Though she whispered the last words, Sarah raised her voice and addressed everyone as she said, "I don't know how to express my feelings other than to tell you how happy I am to be here with all of you."

Isabelle leaned across the table, pitching her voice in a stage whisper. "The best is yet to come. We brought presents."

The gifts were simple but obviously selected with great

care. "Winter will come," Mary said when Sarah opened her package, revealing a lap quilt. Gunther's face reddened as he handed her a book, telling her he hoped she would enjoy this poet. Though Frau Friedrich dismissed the effort she had put into it, Sarah knew that the older woman's failing eyesight must have been taxed as she created a beautifully crocheted collar.

"I hope you brought our gift," Isabelle said when Sarah had opened the others. As Sarah gave her a puzzled look, Isabelle explained. "The necklace. I know it's unusual to ask someone to pick out her own gift, but I needed a way to delay you long enough that we could all get here."

Rising to retrieve the package she'd brought with her, Sarah smiled. Everything made sense now. Undoubtedly, one of Léon's errands had been to talk to Frau Bauer, encouraging her to take her time over the sale.

When she'd shown everyone the necklace, Clay handed her an awkwardly wrapped package. "I hope you'll like it."

Whatever was inside must be fragile, Sarah realized as she unwound many layers of paper, revealing a delicate china vase that she guessed was well over fifty years old. Urn-shaped, it boasted gold handles on each side and a slightly worn rose painted on the front.

"It's beautiful." Sarah traced the outline of the rose, marveling at the artist's skill at the same time that she wondered where Clay had bought it. The mercantile carried only new items.

As if he sensed her unspoken question, Clay said, "It was my mother's and her mother's before that. I know she'd have wanted you to have it."

Sarah shook her head, knowing she could not accept the

gift. "I can't keep this. It needs to stay in your family." If Clay remarried, this would be a gift for his wife, an heirloom for their children.

Clay's lips tightened ever so slightly as he refused to take the vase from Sarah. "You were supposed to be a Canfield. You should have this. Right, Pa?" Clay turned toward his father and waited until he nodded. "See? We all agree. Happy birthday, Sarah."

Tears filled her eyes as she smiled at Clay and rose to press a kiss on his father's cheek. She wasn't part of their family, and yet they were treating her as if she were. Friends and now an almost-family. What more could she want?

An hour later, after the guests had departed and Sarah had settled Thea in bed, she slipped out of the cabin and walked toward the paddock.

"Stargazing again?"

She turned at the sound of Clay's voice, the pounding of her heart telling her what she hadn't wanted to admit: that she'd hoped he would be here, that she had longed for a few private moments with this man who'd proved to be such a special friend.

"I am stargazing," she said, "but tonight I'm not trying to find answers. I came outside because I'm too excited to sleep." Her heartbeat accelerated as Clay came closer. This was what she wanted, a chance to tell him how wonderful he had made the day. Sarah stretched her hand toward him, reveling in the warmth of his palm as he clasped her hand. "I don't know how I can possibly thank you. This was the best birthday I've ever had."

"I'm glad." His voice was husky as he tightened his grip. "I wanted it to be a special day."

The crescent moon cast little light, yet there was enough to see him smile. Sarah wasn't sure how long they stood there, gazing at each other. She couldn't say who took the first step. All she knew was that she found herself in Clay's arms with his lips pressed to hers. It was the perfect ending to a perfect day.

14

He regretted it. She knew that from the moment the kiss
ended. He'd looked at her for a long moment, his eyes so
full of sorrow that Sarah wanted to cry, and then when she'd
thought she could not bear the silence any longer, he'd said
simply, "Good night, Sarah." The three words had echoed
through the darkness, leaving her alone and feeling oddly
bereft.

She frowned as she removed Pa's slipper and began to massage his foot. It was almost as if the older man understood
that something had happened between her and his son, for
he refused to answer her greeting. Perhaps this was where
Clay had learned the art of silence. Sarah hadn't seen him at
breakfast. That was not unusual, for he often left early either
to work on the ranch or to visit a patient. What was unusual
was the silence she'd encountered when she brought Thea
for her riding lesson. Clay had given Sarah no more than a
cursory greeting, then turned his attention to Thea, making

it clear that Sarah was the only one he wanted to ignore. The reason wasn't hard to guess: Clay regretted the kiss.

She did not.

Sarah fisted her hand, using the knuckles to massage Pa's leg. Surely it wasn't her imagination that his muscles were stronger. She could feel the sinews contract as she pressed them. They hadn't done that a month ago. Though he might resist her, his leg was responding.

She closed her eyes briefly, recalling those moments in Clay's arms. Her first kiss had been as wonderful as Mama had promised. Sarah knew she'd never forget the day she'd entered the parlor unannounced and had seen her parents kissing. When they'd broken apart, Mama's face had been flushed, and she'd looked prettier than Sarah had ever seen her—even prettier than the picture of a princess in one of her storybooks. Afterward, Mama had explained that when a man and a woman love each other, they kiss and that kissing was so wonderful it made a woman feel beautiful.

Mama had been right. When Clay had held her close, Sarah had forgotten her limp. She'd forgotten how the boys had called her a scrawny chicken. She'd forgotten every cruel taunt. For the first time in her life, she felt beautiful. Though Clay had turned away, the glow had lasted. As she studied Pa's leg, Sarah's mind whirled. For weeks now, she had felt as if something were missing from her life. Perhaps Mary had been right when she said Sarah needed a husband. Perhaps she'd been wrong to believe Austin's death meant she'd never marry. Perhaps Clay's kiss was the key, unlocking the door to her heart.

She'd had difficulty falling asleep, for she kept remembering her birthday and all that Clay had done to make it special, culminating with his kiss. When at last she'd slept, Sarah had dreamt of a man sitting at a desk, writing a letter. In the manner of dreams, one second she'd been standing in the doorway, in the next, she was at his side, with no memory of having crossed the room. As he continued to write, oblivious to her presence, she'd looked over his shoulder. She'd heard the rasp of the nib on paper; her nostrils had been filled with the scent of hair tonic; and her eyes had widened as she read the words he penned. This man, who seemed so strange and yet so familiar at the same time, was composing one of her paper roses.

In her dream, Sarah had stood for what seemed like hours, fascinated by the simple act of putting words on paper. She'd smiled, knowing this was the man she loved, the one who'd wooed her with his eloquence. And then he'd turned to face her, his blue eyes shining as his lips curved into a smile. Afterward, she knew she should have been surprised, and yet somehow she wasn't. Somehow it seemed right that the man at the desk was not Austin but Clay. After that, Sarah had slept dreamlessly, wakening with a smile on her face.

Morning's light had changed everything, for it brought the realization that her dream had been nothing more than a dream. The epistles she cherished had been written by a man with scrawling handwriting, the letters big with barely controlled loops. Clay's penmanship was far different, each letter small and carefully formed. No matter what Sarah's mind had conjured in the dream, Clay was not the man who'd written the paper roses.

Morning brought with it the reality that, though she cherished the memory, the kiss had meant nothing to Clay. Afternoon brought another, equally unpleasant reality: Pa did not want her to help him walk.

"C'mon, Pa," she said, trying to extend his leg. "I know it hurts, but you can do it. You can flex your foot. Try." His response was the same as it had been the previous four times: nothing. Tears of frustration filled Sarah's eyes.

"Will you let me try?"

Sarah's hand flew to her throat as she turned, startled by the unexpected voice. "I didn't hear you." Somehow, though he wore boots and spurs and the floor bore no rugs, she had been unaware of Zach's approach.

He shrugged and took a few steps further into the room. "Being silent was something we learned in prison."

For the first time that afternoon, Pa spoke. Sarah couldn't understand his words, but she knew they were directed at Zach.

"It was best if the jailors didn't notice us." Again Pa made a guttural sound. Zach gestured toward the door, then waited until Sarah rose. When they were out of hearing, he spoke. "What were you doing?"

There was no point in dissembling. "I know Pa wants to walk. To do that, he needs to strengthen his leg muscles, so I've been trying to show him how I learned to walk again. The problem is, he won't cooperate." Sarah looked at the tall man whom Clay's father seemed to respect. "Oh, Zach, it's so frustrating. I know how Pa feels, trapped in that chair, and I know he could escape it, if only he'd try."

Zach was silent for a moment, his expression thoughtful. "Perhaps he has trouble accepting help from a woman." When Sarah started to protest, he continued. "We're raised to believe we should care for women—not the other way around."

"That's ridiculous."

"I won't argue with you. All I'm saying is that a man's

pride is a powerful thing. It can even keep him from accepting gifts like the one you've been offering. Now, will you show me what you were doing and let me try?"

Reluctantly, Sarah nodded. It would be foolish to refuse help, especially if Zach could make a difference. What was important was getting Pa to use his legs again, not who accomplished that. Still, she couldn't help wishing she didn't feel like such a failure.

ॐ

She knew what he was going to ask. She knew what she would answer. It was Sunday afternoon, and he'd invited her to take a drive with him. Though his nervousness had been apparent from the way he held the reins, he said little while they were in the wagon. Instead, he waited until they reached a pretty spot where trees lined the riverbank. It was only when they'd left the wagon and stood at the water that he cleared his throat.

"I heard that ladies like flowery words." Gunther's voice quavered ever so slightly. "I tried to learn some, but they flew out of my head, so I'm afraid you'll have to settle for plain speaking." He cleared his throat again, then reached for Sarah's hand. When he'd captured it between both of his, he said, "I would be honored if you would become my wife."

It was what she'd expected, what she had in her darkest moments hoped he'd ask. Marriage to Gunther would solve so many problems. Isabelle kept reminding Sarah that Thea needed a father as much as Eva needed a mother, and that since Thea and Eva were friends and Sarah cared for Gunther's daughter, the marriage would be ideal for both children. Sarah knew that. She also knew that wedding Gunther would help her. It would give her one of the things she'd sought when she came to Ladreville: her own home.

There was no ignoring the fact that Sarah was no longer needed at the Bar C. Clay continued to avoid her, and Zach had taken over with Pa. She had no reason to remain and every reason to leave, for it was awkward sharing meals with Clay, realizing he did not want her there and that she provided nothing in return for her and Thea's room and board. If she married Gunther, Sarah would be needed. She would be the one who ran the household and raised both Thea and Eva. She would be useful, and she believed that would fill the empty spaces deep inside her. It was one thing to be needed at the school, something quite different to be part of a family. Though she hated the thought of giving up teaching, Sarah knew that with only a little more training, Olga Kaltheimer would be ready to replace her. The school did not need her the way Gunther and Eva did.

She looked down at her hand clasped between Gunther's. His hands were broad and strong. They would keep her and Thea safe; they would provide a good life for them. There was no reason—absolutely no reason—to remember another pair of hands, the fingers long and slender, and the shivers that touching them had sent up Sarah's arm.

She took a deep breath, trying to calm her thoughts. There was no point in thinking of things that would never be. She knew what she should do. She should accept Gunther's proposal. As she opened her mouth to give him the answer he expected, Sarah's heart balked. Something was missing. Something important. Gunther was wrong. It wasn't flowery words. Although she could not forget the beauty of Austin's paper roses, she didn't need them. What she sought was the

274

love Mama had described, a love that made a woman feel beautiful. Austin's letters had embodied that love. They'd made her feel special, just as Clay's kiss had made her feel beautiful.

Gunther was a good man. He was an excellent father. He needed Sarah, and it was possible she needed him. None of that could erase the simple fact that he didn't make her heart sing. No matter how many problems she might solve, Sarah couldn't do it. She couldn't marry Gunther.

She closed her eyes for a second, searching for words that would not hurt him. "I'm sorry, Gunther," she said at last, "but I can't marry you." As his eyes widened with surprise, he tightened the grip on her hand. Sarah winced but did not pull it away as she added, "You deserve a woman who can give you her whole heart. I wish I could be that woman, but I can't."

Gunther was silent for a long moment. "I don't know how I'm going to tell Eva," he said at last. "She'll be mighty disappointed."

And in that moment Sarah knew she'd made the right decision. Gunther only wanted a mother for Eva. He didn't love Sarah any more than she loved him. They both deserved more.

⌇

If he wasn't the dumbest man on the earth, Clay couldn't imagine who had managed to surpass him in stupidity.

"That's right," he said as Shadow whinnied, perhaps in protest over an overly vigorous currying. "I'm dumber than that comb."

What on earth had possessed him to kiss Sarah? What had

he been thinking? The truth was, he hadn't been thinking. When she'd stood next to him in the moonlight, she'd been so beautiful, so sweetly alluring, that he couldn't help himself. Before he knew what was happening, she was in his arms.

Clay clenched the curry comb, wishing he could clear his mind as easily as he removed snarls from Shadow's coat. Why couldn't he obliterate those memories? Why couldn't he forget how wonderful it had felt, holding Sarah close, pressing his lips to hers? The kiss they'd shared had been the sweetest he'd ever tasted. If Clay had had his way, it would never have ended. But it did, and when it did, reality returned, telling him how wrong he'd been. No matter how he felt, Sarah didn't love him. She loved Austin. Or, more precisely, she loved the man she believed Austin to have been, the man who'd wooed her with those cursed letters. In Sarah's mind, Clay was simply Austin's brother and the man who'd arranged her birthday party. That made her kiss one of gratitude, nothing more, and it made Clay the world's biggest fool if he let himself believe otherwise.

Besides, everyone in Ladreville knew Gunther was courting her. It would be unfair for Clay to interfere with another man's suit when he had no intention of marrying again. Marriage was not part of Clay's future any more than remaining in Ladreville was. As soon as he found Austin's killer, he'd take the first coach East.

No matter how you looked at it, it was wrong to have kissed Sarah, and yet Clay couldn't block the memories. They were there, sliding into his consciousness when he least expected them. He'd thought that not seeing her at breakfast and not lingering at the supper table for a few minutes' conversation would help, but they hadn't. Nothing had.

"Heard the news?" Zach climbed onto the fence rail, apparently content to watch Clay work. Without waiting for more than the shake of Clay's head, Zach continued. "The town's buzzing with the story that Gunther was seen walking with Olga Kaltheimer."

Clay didn't bother hiding his annoyance. He'd never cared about gossip and saw no reason to start now. "A stroll is cause for the grapevine to work overtime? That must mean there haven't been any thefts recently."

"It wasn't just a stroll. The story is, Gunther's courting Olga. It appears Sarah refused him."

Clay's heart skipped a beat. Quickly, he bent his head to inspect Shadow's foreleg, hoping Zach hadn't noticed the color that had risen to his face. "I always thought she could do better." By some small miracle, his voice sounded normal.

"So . . ." Zach drawled the word. "When are you going to start courting her?"

Clay turned, astonished by the question. "Me? Never!"

But if he wasn't courting Sarah, it appeared that a good portion of Ladreville's bachelors were. Clay couldn't venture into town without being told how many men had started hanging around the schoolhouse. Those announcements were invariably followed by his patients' assessments of each suitor's chances. According to gossip, Jean-Michel and David were considered the most likely to win Sarah's hand. It was ridiculous. For Pete's sake, you'd think they were discussing a horse race. Didn't anyone realize that Sarah was not a horse but a woman, a very beautiful, lovable woman?

Right now that woman looked perplexed. Though she normally spent the hours after supper with Thea, often going to the garden, tonight she'd followed Clay into the barn.

"Is something wrong?"

Sarah shook her head, then nodded. The indecision surprised Clay as much as her somber expression. "I'm not sure," she admitted, "but a couple things bother me. A silver bowl was stolen from Granny Menger last night."

Clay could imagine the midwife's distress. Like most of Ladreville's residents, she'd brought only a few valuable possessions from Alsace, and she treasured each of them. "It's unfortunate Granny was robbed again, but you know thefts have been a problem for over a year now."

"What seems strange to me is that the thief wouldn't take everything he wanted the first time. The risk of getting caught is much greater if you go back, because people are more alert."

Shadow and Nora, curious about the humans' conversation, ambled to the edge of their stalls. Though Clay scratched Shadow's nose, Sarah retreated a few steps. No matter what changes the months in Texas had brought, her fear of horses had not diminished.

Clay thought about what she'd said. "Perhaps the thief knows he's running a higher risk and enjoys the challenge."

"I considered that possibility. That's part of what's bothering me, because it made me look at Austin's murder in a new light."

"I'm afraid you lost me. I don't see a connection between petty theft and murder." Though he'd warned her that she was unlikely to succeed where he'd failed, Clay knew Sarah was bothered by her inability to solve the mystery of Austin's death. It appeared she was grasping at proverbial straws, trying to find a clue.

Those brown eyes that haunted so many of Clay's dreams

brightened with enthusiasm. "I know you haven't found Patience's locket, and you said Austin's watch was missing. What if they weren't lost but stolen? What if the thief took the locket and then decided he wanted something more from the Bar C? Maybe he demanded the watch and killed Austin when he refused to surrender it."

If anyone else had spun such a far-fetched tale, Clay would have laughed, but he couldn't hurt Sarah. As preposterous as the story was, it was obvious she believed it.

"I'm not an expert, but I've heard that criminals stick to a pattern. What happened to Austin doesn't fit that pattern," he said as gently as he could. "All the other robberies took place when the owners were gone or asleep. I don't think the thief would risk being seen, and I can't picture someone who sneaks around in the night confronting one of his victims."

Though the sparkle in her eyes began to fade, Sarah nodded. "When you put it that way, my theory wasn't logical. It's just that I wanted so badly to help you find Austin's killer."

"I know, but I warned you it wouldn't be easy. No one in this town will admit that anything is wrong." Clay clenched his jaw in a futile attempt to control his anger. He wouldn't—he couldn't—accept the possibility that the man who murdered his brother might never be found.

Sarah took a step closer, stretching out her hand, then quickly withdrawing it. Clay wondered if she'd been about to touch him, to try to soothe him the way he stroked Shadow or Nora when they were disturbed. In his current mood, he wasn't certain what he would have done, whether he would have drawn her into his arms and kissed her or pushed her away. It was best that she'd retreated.

"I know Michel Ladre and Austin had their share of

arguments. What about David?" Sarah was speaking. Clay forced himself to concentrate on her words rather than the image of her in his arms.

"David Bramble?" It was a silly question, for there was only one David in Ladreville. Still, Clay couldn't imagine why Sarah was asking about their neighbor. "David was Austin's closest friend. My brother spent almost as much time with him as he did with me." Though she nodded slowly, acknowledging she'd heard his explanation, Sarah didn't appear convinced. "Surely you can't believe David killed Austin."

"I don't, and yet . . ." She paused, her eyes dark with worry. "Some of the things he's said recently make me wonder whether he and Austin were such close friends."

This was the first time anyone had raised that question. Though it seemed almost as absurd as her earlier theory, Clay could not dismiss any possibilities. "What did he say?"

Sarah hesitated before she answered. "He told me I shouldn't mourn Austin, that he wasn't the saint I thought he was."

Clay let out the breath he hadn't been aware of holding. "Part of that is true. Austin wasn't a saint, any more than the rest of us are. As for the other part, it isn't hard to figure out why David wants you out of mourning. The man wants to marry you."

Sarah shook her head. Surely she wasn't denying David's courtship. Everyone in town knew Mary was doing her best to make a match between her son and the schoolteacher and that David was more than willing to enter the state of holy matrimony with Sarah.

"It wasn't just his words," Sarah said slowly. She looked at Clay, her eyes willing him to believe her. "The tone of his voice and his expression made me think he didn't like Austin very much."

Preposterous! Clay tried to keep his voice soft as he said, "It must have been your imagination, Sarah. They were almost as close as brothers. David would not have hurt Austin any more than I would have."

But that left Clay exactly where he'd been before: with no clues.

15

It was a miserable morning. Though the rain was no longer coming down in sheets, a drizzle remained. Sarah opened the cabin door, quickly shutting it against the damp chill that seemed to mock the calendar. August in Texas was not supposed to be cold and wet. Her brow furrowed as she considered how uncomfortable it would be, driving the wagon into town. This was a day to remain inside. She would, if only it were not Sunday.

Sarah wavered. Thea would not know they'd missed church. The problem was, Sarah would. Though she doubted there would be any thunderbolts from on high, Sarah didn't want to disappoint her mother. Mama had insisted that the Dobbs family attend services every Sunday. The only excuse had been serious illness, and even then the Sabbath had been a day of praise and thanksgiving along with prayers for healing. During the months Sarah had been unable to walk, Mama and Papa had worshiped in the family's church, then returned home to sing the day's hymns with Sarah. Each week the minister had visited on Monday afternoon, providing Sarah with an abbreviated version of his sermon.

"God has given us everything," Mama had told Sarah the first time she explained how important it was to attend services. "Surely we can give him one day a week." Though it had been more than fifteen years since Sarah had heard those words, her mother's voice echoed in her mind, and she knew her conscience would bother her if she and Thea stayed home. "All right, Mama," she said softly. "We'll go."

The drizzle turned back into steady rain, and by the time she and Thea reached the church, they were both bedraggled. Fortunately, Sarah's pretense that they were fish who loved water distracted Thea. Sarah's sister didn't mind a sodden hem or shoes that squished when she walked. In fact, Thea considered both a rare adventure. Sarah did not.

As they entered the sanctuary of the German church, Olga Kaltheimer approached them, her posture more confident than Sarah had ever seen it. Even her voice sounded more mature as she said, "You weren't here last week, so you may not know, but we're going to start a children's program today. I hope you'll let Thea join us." Though she used the plural pronoun, Sarah felt a rush of pleasure when she realized that Olga was in charge of the program. It wasn't the same as teaching every day, but it would be a valuable step toward Olga's dream of becoming a schoolmarm.

Before Sarah could speak, Gunther and Eva entered the church, shaking off raindrops like wet dogs. Sarah nodded briefly as Gunther removed his hat, then bent down to talk to Thea. This was the first time she'd seen Gunther since she'd refused his proposal, and she feared it would be awkward.

If the rumor mill was accurate and he was indeed court-ing Olga, he might be embarrassed at finding both women together.

Eva had no such qualms. "Come with me, Thea," she said, grabbing the younger child's hand. "Miss Kaltheimer prom-ised us something special."

"Be a good girl," Sarah admonished her sister, though there was little need. Thea was rarely fussy now. Just as Mary had predicted, Thea had adjusted, and if the appreciative looks Gunther was giving Olga were any indication, so had he. Only Sarah was still plagued by an emptiness deep inside her, an emptiness that seemed greater than ever today. She couldn't explain it, but she kept picturing her mother, her normally smiling face wet with tears.

Sarah took a seat in the far corner of the last pew, hoping no one would sit near her, for she wasn't certain she could manage even a casual greeting. Though she rose with the rest of the congregation to sing a hymn and knelt for prayers at the correct time, Sarah moved by rote, only dimly aware of her surroundings. *Oh, Mama*, she cried inwardly, *you should have lived. I need you. Thea needs you.* Sarah clenched her fists, fighting back the sorrow and anger that enveloped her whenever she thought of her parents' deaths. *How could you?* she demanded of her father as she had so many times before. *Didn't you know that killing is a sin?*

As the congregation settled back into their pews, Pastor Sempert took his place behind the pulpit. Sarah had always considered the tall, spare man with gun-metal gray hair and a face creased by wrinkles to be a grandfatherly figure. He opened his Bible and inclined his head. "Today's sermon is based on Exodus 20:12, one of the Ten Commandments."

"Which one is that?" Sarah heard the woman next to her whisper. A few other parishioners stealthily paged through their Bibles, searching for the reference.

The minister nodded, as if he knew that his congregation was trying to guess which commandment he'd chosen, before he intoned words Sarah had memorized as a child. "The Lord God has commanded us, 'Honor thy father and thy mother, that thy days may be long upon the land which the Lord thy God giveth thee.'"

Parents. Sarah cringed. Was it coincidence, or had Pastor Sempert somehow sensed her thoughts and decided to direct his sermon at her? Would he single her out by name as she'd heard some preachers did?

"It is not by chance that I chose today, the first day the youngest members of our congregation are not with us, for this text," he said, easing her worries. This was not a spontaneous sermon, but one he had planned. Thankfully, the pastor had not read her mind.

He leaned forward, his expression as open as if he were speaking to friends, and Sarah felt her tension begin to ease. That was one of the things she liked about him. Unlike the minister in Philadelphia, Pastor Sempert did not shout and thump his pulpit, nor did he act as if he were superior to the congregation. Instead, his counsel and guidance were delivered in a conversational tone.

"All too often when we hear this commandment, we believe it applies only to our children. It does not." Pastor Sempert paused for emphasis. "Many of you are already parents. Some of you have not yet reached that stage of your life; however, we all are children. We are God's children and also the children of earthly parents."

The pew creaked as the woman next to Sarah leaned forward to nod her agreement.

"Our Lord commands us to honor him," the minister continued. "That is his first commandment. But he also singles out our earthly parents, telling us to honor them. Why does he do this, and what does he mean?"

Sarah's heart began to thud. She did not want to think about parents and honor, not when her own father was so undeserving. No one—not even God—could expect her to honor a man who had killed.

"When a child is born, we often say that God has blessed the parents, that the infant is God's gift to them." A few people murmured their agreement. "We may not realize that the parents are God's gift to the child. Parents are his surrogates on Earth. They care for us; they nurture us; they teach us; they discipline us. They are the earthly manifestation of our heavenly Father's love. How often do we thank him for these gifts?"

Pastor Sempert's gaze moved from one pew to the next as he sought the answer from his congregation. When his questioning eyes approached her, Sarah lowered her head, lest he see her confusion. How could she—how could anyone—thank God for a murderer?

"For most of us, the answer is 'not often enough,'" the minister concluded. "How do we honor our parents? We begin by thanking God for them."

Sarah bit the inside of her cheek, trying not to cry. Pastor Sempert was wrong. He didn't understand what had happened and why she could not thank God for her father.

"Our earthly parents are not perfect. Only God is." The minister continued his homily. "Sometimes we see our parents' imperfections and believe they are not worthy of our honor or our love. How wrong we are! If our heavenly Father loves us—and we know he does, for he gave his Son so we might have eternal life—surely we should follow his example. We should forgive our parents their imperfections. We should love them for what they are: God's children, his creation and his gift to us." Pastor Sempert bent his head. "Let us pray."

In the distance Sarah heard the minister's voice as he led the congregation in prayer. Dimly, she was aware of the woman next to her saying "amen," but nothing else registered. Instead, Pastor Sempert's earlier words echoed in her head, each one sending shafts of pain through her. She had been wrong, so very wrong. Though she'd labeled them hypocrites for their self-righteous judgments, she had been worse than the parishioners in Philadelphia. She'd judged Papa, calling his sin unforgivable, acting as if she were spotless. She was not. She was a sinner, a worse sinner than Papa, for she'd broken one of God's holy commandments, not twice as Papa had, but countless times. Not only had she not honored her father, but not one day had passed when her heart had not been filled with anger toward her father—anger and worse: hatred.

When the service ended and the parishioners began to file out of the church, Sarah remained huddled in the corner of the pew, her head bowed as if she were praying. How would she ever lift her head again? Surely her shame was branded on her face. How could she continue to raise Thea when she was such a sinner?

"My child, you appear troubled." Pastor Sempert stood at the end of the pew, his voice low and filled with concern.

Unable to face him, Sarah murmured the words that haunted her. "I am the worst of sinners."

"Come with me." He placed his hand on her arm, urging her to rise, then led her to his study. The small room held a desk, a bookcase, and two comfortable chairs. Almost Spartan, the room had no rug on the floor, no curtains at the window. The walls were bare, save for a crucifix. Unlike the rough-hewn cross in the sanctuary, this silver cross and porcelain figure of Jesus had been crafted by skilled hands.

"Rest a moment," Pastor Sempert said when Sarah was seated.

The tears she had been holding back began to spill. "How can I rest when I know how much I've sinned?" She looked at the minister, expecting condemnation. Instead, she saw only concern.

"We've all sinned," he said.

"But my sin is unforgivable. I judged my father for his imperfections. I knew what he had done was wrong, and I . . ." Sarah lowered her voice, not wanting to admit the depth of her wrongdoing. "I hated him for it. I even prayed he would burn in hell." She covered her face, trying to hide her shame. "I'm the one who will burn, for I've broken God's commandments too."

Pastor Sempert reached for her hands, holding them in his. He waited until she met his gaze before he said, "Our Lord forgives us. All he asks is that we be truly repentant."

"I want to believe that. I do." But how could anyone, even God, forgive her sins?

"When I'm troubled, I lay my burdens at the foot of the cross. That is where Jesus gave us the most precious gift of all. He died so that we could be saved. Accept that gift, Sarah. Open your heart to him."

Could it be that simple? Sarah closed her eyes, then opened

them again. Pulling her hands free, she slipped from the chair and knelt, but instead of bowing her head, she fixed her eyes on the cross. *Oh, Lord, forgive me.* She stared at the figure of Jesus, crowned with thorns, his arms nailed to the crossbeams, his feet pierced with a spike. Crucifixion was a horrible way to die, and yet Jesus had gone to his death willingly, obeying his Father's command. Jesus had borne the suffering, the humiliation, the agony, and he had done it so all sinners could be saved. All sinners, even Sarah. Though she was unworthy, he had died that she might live. *Thank you, Lord.* Tears streaming from her eyes, Sarah bowed her head, accepting the gift he had given her, and as she did, peace filled her heart.

She wasn't certain how long she remained there, but when she rose, she turned to the minister. "I feel different."

His smile was warm and comforting. "You are different," he said. "You've given your life to Christ. That changes everything."

Sarah nodded, acknowledging the truth of his words. The Sarah who had entered this room was not the one who would leave. "I feel as if a great weight has been lifted from my shoulders, and yet one remains."

Pastor Sempert raised his eyes to the cross. "Our Lord bids us to forgive others, even as he asked his Father to forgive his executioners. Sometimes that seems the most difficult thing in the world, but it's necessary if we're going to find true peace. Anger and hatred hurt us, not the person we direct them at."

He was speaking of her father. She knew that. "I don't hate him any longer." She'd laid that burden at Jesus' feet, and he'd taken it from her. "I'm worried about my father's soul. I know God would forgive him if he repented, just as he forgave me, but what if Papa didn't?"

The minister nodded slowly, acknowledging her fear. "Do you remember the criminals who were crucified next to Jesus? The one repented, and Jesus promised, 'Today thou shalt be with me in Paradise.' We don't know what was in your father's heart in his last moments on Earth. We can only pray that he, like the crucified man, found peace."

"Papa was a good man, except for that day."

"Our Lord knows that. He hates the sin but loves the sinner. Can you do the same?"

Closing her eyes, Sarah began to pray for her father, and as she did, images rose before her eyes. She pictured him holding her on his lap, reading a story to her. She remembered the pain on his face when the doctor had predicted Sarah would never walk again and the joy he'd shown the day she'd taken her first steps.

"Oh, Papa," she whispered, "I love you. I pray that you are with Mama in heaven." As she pronounced the words, Sarah felt a warmth enfold her. The last weight was gone, and so was the emptiness that had filled her heart. The morning she had thought so miserable had become the best day of her life, for she had found what was missing from her life: her Savior's love.

16

Sarah's heart brimmed with happiness. If she hadn't experienced it, she would not have believed the sense of lightness that had enveloped her the moment she'd given her life to Christ. The emptiness was gone, replaced by the conviction that she was not alone, that she would never again be alone. The changes, she suspected, were more than internal, for Zach had given her several piercing looks yesterday afternoon, as if he'd discerned a difference but was reluctant to pry. She would tell him tonight, once she'd seen Isabelle. Since Isabelle had been the first to speak of faith and the difference that becoming a Christian made, it seemed right that she be the first to know.

When she'd finished writing the next assignment on the blackboard, Sarah walked to the door, intending to watch the children play. As she opened the door, her heart sank. Though she ought to be at work, Isabelle was approaching the school, her eyes red-rimmed, a handkerchief in one hand, ready to catch the next spate of tears.

"I don't know what to do," she said as Sarah led her back inside the schoolhouse. Her voice was listless, her shoulders slumped. Even the day Sarah had found Isabelle crying in the mercantile had not been like this. She had been upset then; now she was despondent.

"It's Léon, isn't it?" For the past week, Sarah had overheard mothers discussing the increased frequency of thefts in Ladreville. Without exception, everyone blamed Léon.

Isabelle nodded. "There were two more robberies last night. Michel came to the store first thing this morning and demanded to see Léon. He was already at the Friedrichs', but Michel searched his room. Now he's gone out to the farm to find Léon. Oh, Sarah, I think Michel's going to arrest him." As tears began to flow again, Sarah wrapped her arms around Isabelle, trying to comfort her.

Isabelle looked up, then scrubbed her cheeks with her handkerchief. "I know Léon couldn't have done it, because I heard him snoring all night. It was so loud, it kept me awake."

Sarah forbore mentioning that Michel might claim Isabelle had dozed long enough for her brother to leave the house. "Did Michel find anything when he searched?"

"No, but one of Léon's buttons was in a house that was robbed. That's why Michel's so sure he is responsible."

"Was the button one of those fancy gold ones?" It was common knowledge in Ladreville that Léon's Sunday coat sported unique buttons.

Isabelle nodded.

"It must be a coincidence," Sarah said firmly to assuage her friend's fears. "I noticed one of the buttons was loose when I saw you after church last week, but I forgot to say anything. The button probably fell off when Léon was visiting them." The Rousseaus, like many Ladreville families, paid social calls on Sunday afternoon.

This time Isabelle shook her head. "I wish it were that easy. The problem is, the button was found inside the Henkes' house. Léon has never been there."

Sarah closed her eyes and prayed for wisdom, for she did not like the direction her thoughts had taken. "If it wasn't coincidence—and it doesn't sound as if it was—putting the button at the Henkes' must have been deliberate." And that changed everything. Simple theft had suddenly become something much more sinister. "I imagine the button fell off elsewhere, maybe even in the churchyard, and someone saw it as an opportunity to blame Léon." Before this, there had only been rumors and suspicions; now there was evidence, even if it had been planted. Though she was confident she knew the answer, Sarah had to ask, "Do you have any idea who would do something so underhanded?"

Isabelle turned to face Sarah. "Everyone likes Léon. Everyone except Frau Steiner, that is." Isabelle's eyes were dry, and for the first time, she appeared angry rather than sorrowful. "It makes no sense. Léon never got into arguments the way . . ."

"Austin did." As she completed the sentence, Sarah frowned, realizing there were now two unsolved problems in Ladreville. "I wish I understood what makes people do things like this: murder, robbery, trying to pin the blame on someone else."

"Evil exists, but if we fight it, it won't triumph. I'm praying that the mayor finds whoever's responsible."

"So am I."

Isabelle's eyes widened, and a smile lit her face. "That explains it."

"What?"

She smiled again, as if the answer should be obvious. "The peace I see on your face. You found him." Isabelle nodded slowly. "No matter what happens to my brother, God answered my prayers for you."

"And he'll answer ours for Léon. He'll keep him safe. I know he will."

⸙

"I wouldn't want to be in Léon Rousseau's boots right now." Clay stared into the distance, hoping for the sight of an unbroken fence line. Though he'd given Zach responsibility for the ranch, today Clay was riding the line with his foreman. After everything that had happened, he wanted to assure himself that Bar C cattle were not devouring Karl Friedrich's crops. "The good people of Ladreville are ready to run Léon out of town."

Zach frowned, perhaps at Clay's sarcastic tone. He couldn't help it. Clay hated the mob mentality, where groups ganged up on an individual, usually a weak one. Léon wasn't weak physically, but he was vulnerable. If people believed him responsible for the rash of thefts, they might boycott the mercantile, hurting the people Léon loved most.

"If what Sarah said is true, he's innocent."

"I believe her." Though he didn't always agree with Sarah, this was one time Clay did. "Léon never struck me as sneaky, and that's what the thief has been. It's almost as if he's playing a game with the rest of us, and he keeps changing the rules so we have no chance of winning." Clay remembered

Sarah's concern when several houses became targets of multiple robberies. She'd been right in saying that was not a normal pattern. "I'm beginning to think the thief is doing this for the excitement, not because he needs money." And that was frightening.

"People like that are the most dangerous." Zach confirmed Clay's unspoken fear. "Their minds don't work the same way ours do, and that makes it very difficult to catch them."

Clay paused, debating how much to tell Zach. In the time he'd been at the Bar C, his advice had proven sound. Though this had nothing to do with ranching, perhaps Zach could provide a new perspective. "Sarah thought the thief might also be the person who killed Austin."

Zach's head swiveled so quickly Clay feared he'd injure a tendon. "Do you believe that?"

"At first I didn't, but now I don't know. I just know I have to find whoever's responsible. I want the thefts to stop, but mostly I want to see my brother's killer punished. Austin's death cannot go unavenged."

"Be careful, Clay. The Lord says vengeance is his."

Clay shouldn't have been surprised. Like his brother, Zach was in the habit of quoting Scripture, but he was surprised, for he had thought Zach would understand. Unlike Sarah, who'd been appalled by frontier justice, Zach had lived here his whole life. He ought to understand the realities of life—and justice—in a land with few lawmen.

"That may be so, but I haven't seen God capturing the killer. Michel Ladre is no use. He wouldn't call in the Texas Rangers, and I don't think he performed more than a perfunctory investigation." Though that wasn't a surprise, given the animosity between Michel and Austin, it still rankled. The town's mayor and self-appointed sheriff should have been able to put personal feelings aside. "Sorry, Zach, but it appears to me that I'm the only one who cares that my brother's murderer is still free. That means I'm the one who has to find him, and when I do . . ." Clay let the words trail off.

"Killing, even when you believe it is just, is not the answer." Though Zach spoke softly, his voice resonated with feeling. "That's one thing I learned during the war. Life is uncertain. It can end any day. Like the day the Mexicans decimated us."

Clay jerked the reins in an instinctive reaction to Zach's words. Decimation was truly the stuff of nightmares. Pa had mentioned that day only once and only then because his screams had roused both Clay and Austin. Frightened by their father's cries, both boys had rushed into his room. By then he'd wakened, but the sight of his haggard and gray face was almost as alarming as his shouts had been. In a low, broken voice Pa had described what he called the darkest day of his war service, the day a lottery determined which of the Americans would be killed.

It was a diabolical scheme, the "game," as their jailors called it, almost as terrifying as the ending, for each man knew that he held his fate in his hand. Literally. Their captors had placed beans in a large can, one black for every nine white ones. As each prisoner drew a bean, his fate was sealed. Those who'd chosen black would stand before a firing squad. The others would watch, knowing that the process might be repeated the next day or week or month, whenever the jailors felt the need for entertainment. Pa had survived, and so had Zach, but Clay knew neither man could have forgotten that day.

"I should have died," Zach said. "If it hadn't been for John

Tallman, I would have." This was part of the story Pa had not told. "I was a coward," Zach continued. "When I drew the black bean, all I could do was shake with fear. I wasn't ready to die. John wasn't either. He was only a couple years older than me, with a wife and a child at home. He had every reason to live, and yet he took pity on me. Before the Mexicans could see what was happening, he switched beans with me. John died in my place."

Zach's eyes reflected the anguish of the day. "Afterwards, I didn't know what to do. I was so ashamed of my cowardice that I wanted to die. At one point, I came close to taking my own life. It was your pa who stopped me. He told me not to let John's sacrifice be in vain, that I should live each day to the fullest, that I should love instead of hate."

Clay nodded slowly, trying to imagine how Zach must have felt in the face of such a sacrifice. It was no wonder Pa had given him the advice he had. Pa believed in love. At one time Clay had too, but Austin's death changed everything. "Unfortunately, that's easy to say, not so easy to do."

"The best things often aren't."

༄

Nothing was going right. Instinctively, Clay tightened the reins, then murmured reassuring words to Shadow. It wasn't the horse's fault that he was in such a foul mood. It also wasn't completely true that nothing was going right. The ranch was running smoothly, thanks to Zach, and Clay's medical practice was flourishing. More quickly than he'd expected, he had taken over almost all of Herman's patients, a state that seemed to bother the older doctor not one whit. In words reminiscent of Clay's conversation with Zach, Herman declared that he was going to enjoy each day of sight that remained. He'd added that he would not risk a patient's health to his failing eyesight and that it was best that Clay assume full responsibility for the town's health. Doing so had proven surprisingly satisfying. The rest of Clay's life, however, was filled with frustration.

Zach could preach all he wanted, but the fact remained: the need to find Austin's killer was intrinsic, as necessary to Clay as eating and sleeping. Furthermore, his continued failure was worse than an open sore. It had become a cancer deep inside him, consuming every vital organ. He owed it to Austin; he owed it to Pa; he owed it to himself to bring the murderer to justice. Each day Clay woke, convinced that would be the day he'd learn something. Each night he faced the fact that he had made no progress.

As if that weren't enough frustration for one man to endure, Clay was plagued with the constant presence of David and Jean-Michel. He could hardly take a step without tripping over them. One—sometimes both—of them came to the ranch each evening. They'd take Sarah for a ride, bring her a small gift, and—most annoying of all—sit there with foolish grins on their faces as they spoke of nothing more consequential than the weather.

It was ridiculous. Didn't Sarah understand that these were boys playing at courtship? Why, even Thea saw through their protestations of love. The child refused to let them carry her and had taken to hiding behind Pa's chair when they arrived. If Thea could see how false they were, why couldn't Sarah? She was smart and funny and oh, so lovable. Sarah deserved more than David and Jean-Michel could offer her. She deserved . . .

Clay blinked as the image flashed before him. She was standing in his arms, smiling into his eyes, and as she did, he knew that nothing in the world was more precious than that smile. Clay shook his head, trying to clear the image, but it remained. *When did it happen?* he demanded, not certain whether he was delighted or dismayed by the revelation. When did he stop viewing Sarah as Austin's bride-to-be? When had she become the woman he loved? Clay didn't know when it had happened. He didn't know how. He didn't know why. All he knew was that nothing would ever be the same.

He loved Sarah. He wanted to marry her. Those were incontrovertible facts. So too was the fact that if he didn't act quickly, she might make a mistake they'd both regret.

Filled with a sense of urgency, Clay urged Shadow into a gallop. The first step was to separate Sarah from her swains. He couldn't start too soon.

∞

"It seems to me you haven't been out to the garden lately." Clay pronounced the words as casually as if the thought had just occurred to him. The reality was, he'd carefully planned them, just as he'd planned to address them to Thea, not her sister. "What do you say? Shall we go pull some weeds tonight?"

As Thea clapped in delight, Sarah frowned. "You can't do that. Thea will pull all the wrong things."

Clay feigned surprise at the concept. "Would that be so bad? At least she'd have fun." Which he doubted was the case when the suitors tried to play games with her. Anyone could see that David barely tolerated Thea, just as it was obvious how Jean-Michel cringed at Sarah's limp. They were the wrong men—totally the wrong men—for Sarah and Thea. If all went well, Sarah would realize that at the same time that she realized Clay would be the right man to be her husband and Thea's father.

"Please, Sarah." Thea added her pleas to the cause. "Me wanna go to garden. Papa Clay take me."

From the corner of his eye, Clay saw Sarah waver. "All right," she said at last, "but I'm going too."

Success!

❦

If she didn't know better, she would have said Clay was courting her. Sarah bent at the waist as she continued brushing her hair, giving it the hundred strokes Mama had claimed were so important. He'd been different ever since that night he'd insisted on taking Thea to the garden. Though in the past he left the house early, almost as if he were avoiding her and Thea, now he joined them for breakfast each morning.

Previously many of the meals they'd shared had been silent, now he talked about everything imaginable. Clay didn't quote poetry, as Jean-Michel did, or compare her hair to acorns, which had been one of David's more memorable declarations. Instead, he asked questions, as if he wanted to discover the true Sarah. That was enjoyable, but even more so was the fact that he had begun to confide in her. He'd talked about his unwillingness to disappoint Daniel Morton by not returning to Boston while he explained his growing conviction that a wealthy urban practice no longer appealed to him. Though that was a dilemma Sarah could not solve, she felt honored that Clay had shared his concerns with her.

Memories of their breakfast conversations remained with

her all day long, popping into her head whenever there was a lull in the schoolroom. And then there were the evenings. Unless it rained, Clay would accompany Sarah and Thea to the garden each night. They'd settle Thea in her corner, where she was content to pull anything that poked its head through the ground. Slowly, Sarah and Clay would stroll through the garden, pruning and weeding when needed, but mostly talking.

Talking was wonderful; touching was even better. The first time it happened, she had thought it coincidence, but when it was repeated each night, Sarah knew better. It was a deliberate choice. Clay chose to stand so close to her that their hands brushed when they moved. They were casual touches, and yet they sent shivers up Sarah's arm, making her heart beat faster, making her long for more. She couldn't forget the touches. The truth was, she didn't want to forget them, any more than she wanted to forget the kiss they'd once shared.

Sarah stood, beginning the final stage of brushing, restoring her now-crackling hair to its normal smooth state in preparation for its nightly braiding. Braiding her hair was not the only thing she did each night. Once she drifted into sleep, Sarah dreamt of Clay, and each morning she woke with a smile on her face, knowing this was the beginning of another day she would spend with him. Though they were apart for many hours, Clay was never far from her thoughts. Memories, dreams, and daydreams were ready to surface at the slightest provocation.

Sarah smiled. She wasn't a doctor, but she had no trouble identifying the cause of those feelings. Mama had said Sarah would know when it happened, and Mama had been right.

Sarah was in love. She loved Clay, and if she could have her dearest wish, she would spend the rest of her life with him. When she'd refused Gunther's proposal, Sarah had known she wanted something more. Clay was that something more. He was the man who could make her happy, the one who could make ordinary days special, the one who could give her a love like Mama and Papa had shared. If only . . .

Sarah sank onto the side of the bed, her smile fading as she thought of the barriers that remained. Was she ready? She thought she was. Each night she prayed that God would give her a sign that Clay was the man he had chosen for her. There had been no voice, no lightning bolts, nothing but the conviction that she still had steps to take.

Sarah rose and opened the top drawer of her bureau to finger the letters she'd carried so carefully across the country. When she started to pull them out, intending to read them, her hand paused, and she drew back as if the envelopes were hot. She nodded slowly, knowing this was the first step. It was time to put the letters aside. "Good-bye, Austin," she whispered. Though she would never forget him or his letters, he was part of her past. Clay was her future. If only . . .

Sarah closed the drawer, knowing she would not open it again. That felt right, as did her love for Clay. But all was not right. She took a deep breath, trying to settle her thoughts. One day when they had been discussing marriage, Isabelle had talked about the need for Christians to be evenly yoked, explaining that that meant they should choose mates who shared their beliefs. At the time Sarah had paid little attention, though it had explained why Isabelle was still single. At the time Sarah had believed the concept had no relevance to her. Now she knew that she had been wrong. The day in

Pastor Sempert's study had changed everything. She could no longer consider marrying a man bent on vengeance, a man who planned to kill, a man who didn't trust God. All she could do was pray that the man she loved would find his way to God before it was too late.

⳥

"Oh, Sarah, they're lovely. Thank you for thinking of an old woman." Mary smiled as she arranged the sheaf of flowers Sarah had brought from her garden.

"You're not an old woman," Sarah countered. Though Mary was ten years older than Sarah's mother had been, Sarah never thought of her as elderly. "You're my friend, and I thought you might enjoy the flowers. After all, you're the one who told me about Patience's garden. If it weren't for you, they'd be growing wild."

Mary bent her head over the blossoms, studying each of the stems, snipping a few to make the bouquet symmetrical. "You'll have to forgive a mother for saying this, but I'm mighty disappointed. I had high hopes for you and my David, and now the rumor mill claims you're fixin' to marry Clay."

Marriage was not a subject Sarah wanted to discuss, but the manners Mama had instilled demanded she reply. "He hasn't asked me." Nor had David, but saying that would only prolong the discussion.

"Perhaps he won't." Though Mary's tone was conversational, her eyes were unnaturally bright. Surely those were not unshed tears. Sarah knew Mary was encouraging a match with her son, but she'd never acted as if it were of paramount importance. Mary lowered her gaze to her lap as she said, "It 'pears to me Clay's still mourning his wife."

303

Though Clay's first wife was not the barrier to remarriage, that was another topic Sarah preferred to avoid. Instead, she stated the truth. "Clay is focused on discovering who killed Austin. I've tried to help him, but no one seems to have any idea who the murderer might be."

Apparently satisfied with the arrangement, Mary placed the bouquet on the table. "Some mysteries are never solved. That's just the way it is. Life ain't fair. If it was . . ." She broke off, then shook her head. When she spoke again, she surprised Sarah by the change of subject. "I hope Michel arrests Léon soon. Them thefts gotta stop." Mary reached inside her collar and fingered a gold chain. "We ain't been robbed yet, but I ain't taking no chances. I keep my valuables close to me."

Sarah guessed that the gold chain held the locket Mary's husband had given her. The older woman treasured it the way Sarah did her earrings. Instinctively, she touched her ears.

"Them are mighty pretty earbobs you've got." Mary leaned closer to admire them. "You'd better be careful with 'em."

"I'd hate to have anything happen to them. They were a gift from my parents on my eighteenth birthday."

"Then don't take them off," Mary advised. "Now, tell me what Thea's been up to. I surely miss having her here. You be sure and bring her the next time you come."

⌘

She was later than usual. Both David and Jean-Michel had been waiting outside school, insisting they needed to speak with her. Short of being rude, there was nothing Sarah could do but listen as they extolled the beauty of her hair and eyes, each one trying to outdo the other. When David had handed

304

her a packet of seeds, saying his mother thought she might like them for her garden, Jean-Michel had announced that his mother had a cutting from a rosebush for Sarah. It seemed that everyone in Ladreville knew of Sarah's garden and how much time she and Thea spent there. The place she'd named the secret garden was anything but secret.

David and Jean-Michel continued their litany of praises. Although she'd tried to discourage both of them, they were immune to subtlety, and Sarah was loath to hurt them with a blunt dismissal. Today she wished she had, for she had planned to stop at the Lazy B on her way home, giving Mary a chance to visit with Thea. Now there was no time. She would barely be able to reach the ranch and get Thea's hands washed before Martina served supper.

"Sing, Sarah. Me wanna sing with you." Oblivious to Sarah's mood, Thea bounced on the wagon seat and tugged on her sister's arm.

"What do you want to sing?"

"Pretty song."

That didn't narrow the field too much. Sarah thought for a moment, then began to sing one of the tunes her mother had taught her, a silly song about flowers in a garden. Thea didn't mind that the lyrics didn't rhyme well or that Sarah sang off-key. She grinned and began to clap and sing.

Sarah tightened her grip on the reins. This was a particularly bumpy part of the road, with huge potholes from the last downpour. She ought to slow the horses, but if she did, they would be late. She and Thea would simply have to endure the jolting.

Crack! Without warning, the wagon lurched to the side, sending Thea tumbling into Sarah. Instinctively, Sarah grabbed her sister at the same time that she gripped the side of the wagon to steady herself.

"It's all right, sweetie," she said, trying to calm Thea's sobs. "We're all right." But they were not, for when Sarah looked down, all she could do was gasp. The wagon wheel was gone.

17

It was an accident. Clay knew that accidents happened and that it wasn't always possible to determine what had caused them. Still, he had to check. That was why, once he assured himself that Sarah had suffered nothing more than blisters from walking home, he had questioned Miguel and why he was now in town, talking to the man who ran the livery. As he'd expected, Klaus reiterated what Miguel had said, that the wagon had been in perfect shape. Klaus added that he would have noticed if one of the wheels were loose, because he checked the wagon each afternoon before he hitched the horses for Miss Sarah. "A man cain't be too careful when there's young'uns," he told Clay. It was Klaus's theory that the rough road had somehow loosened the bolts.

Clay leaned against the livery door, feeling relief wash through him. If the wheel had had to fall off, it was fortunate that the accident happened where it did. Sarah had been less than a mile from home. More importantly, she'd been on dry land. If she'd lost the wheel in the middle of the river, there was no telling how long she and Thea would have been stranded there. Though there would have been little danger of drowning, with the river as high as it was after the recent rain, Sarah would not have been able to climb out and carry Thea through the water, and they would have been forced to wait until someone noticed their predicament and rescued them. Indeed, they'd been lucky.

"Thanks, Klaus. You're a good man."

Though the comment required no response, Klaus's lips twitched, as if he wanted to say something but wasn't sure how to begin. That was odd, for the livery owner's taciturnity was legendary in Ladreville. Clay counted himself fortunate that Klaus had even postulated a theory. Perhaps he had another explanation for the loose wheel.

"You fixin' to marry Miss Sarah?"

Instinctively, Clay straightened and fisted his hands, then relaxed as he reminded himself this was not a fighting matter. It was ridiculous for him to be so touchy where Sarah was concerned. Still, marriage was the last topic Clay would have expected Klaus to introduce. "What makes you think that?"

"Folks been talkin'. They figure something's up, cuz she keeps asking questions about Austin." The livery owner gave Clay a long look. "I reckon you both want the past settled afore you start a new life."

"There's nothing wrong with that, is there?" It appeared there was no point in denying he wanted to marry Sarah. A protest would only fuel more rumors.

Klaus weighed the question. "Cain't say it's wrong. I just know what I hear." He scuffed the floor with his boot toe.

"Folks get nervous over questions. I reckon they don't like being reminded of a killing."

"Or maybe someone has a guilty conscience."

❦

Lines of strain etched Isabelle's face. "It's getting worse," she told Sarah a few days later. "It was only words before, but now I'm afraid they'll do something awful."

They were speaking of Léon. Sarah knew that without asking. "Surely not. There's no proof." Unfortunately, Sarah knew that mobs needed no proof. Allegations were often sufficient to incite them to anger, and angry men were unpredictable.

Thea tugged on Sarah's skirt in a play for attention. "Just a few minutes longer," Sarah told her. "I need to talk to Isabelle." Surely there was a way to comfort her friend. Sarah had prayed that God would reveal the thief, but so far he had not. Last Sunday Père Tellier had spoken of God's timing, reminding the congregation that it was perfect, at the same time that he urged patience. The advice might be sound, but it was difficult to be patient when loved ones were threatened.

"Evidence or proof—I'm not sure anyone in Ladreville thinks there's a difference." Bitterness colored Isabelle's words. "The evidence keeps mounting. The button was bad enough, but there's more. Yesterday Monsieur Ferrand discovered his new saddle was missing. He also found Léon's glove in the barn."

As Thea continued to fuss, Isabelle handed her an empty spool, showing her how to roll it along the floor. "This morning I overheard two women talking. They weren't whispering, so I'm sure they wanted me to hear what they were saying.

They claimed it was time the town took matters into its own hands." Isabelle's face crumpled. "Oh, Sarah, they want to lynch my brother."

"But he's innocent." Sarah knew that with every fiber of her being. Léon had put his past behind him; he would not steal.

"Not in their eyes. Whoever's doing this has convinced everyone Léon's guilty."

There was only one solution. "We have to find the real thief."

"How?"

Sarah wished she knew. It was easy to pronounce the words; turning them into actions was far more difficult. The last few months had proven that. When she'd enlisted Clay's help to build the school, Sarah had been certain she'd be able to learn something about Austin's death. She had not. Subtle questions had elicited no information, and so she'd changed her tactics, asking directly. That had accomplished nothing, save annoying some of the townspeople. They'd regarded her questions as personal affronts rather than what they were: an attempt to glean the truth. Sarah had believed she would harvest something, at least a few grains of truth among the chaff, but she had nothing, not even chaff. She had failed miserably in her efforts to help Clay. What made her think she would succeed this time?

Before she had a chance to say anything more, the doorbell tinkled, announcing the arrival of a customer. Isabelle struggled to fix a smile on her face.

"Good afternoon." Jean-Michel fairly strutted as he entered the store. Sarah watched, surprised by both his jaunty walk and the bright smile he wore. This was not the same

Jean-Michel who'd spent so much time with her this summer. That Jean-Michel had been courtly but more subdued, and he'd never smiled at her the way he did at Isabelle.

"How fortunate I am, to have two of the most beautiful ladies in Ladreville in the same room."

Though the fulsome compliment startled Sarah, Isabelle simply raised her eyebrows. "You see, Sarah," she said in apparent response to Jean-Michel's words, "I told you you and Thea were beautiful."

Jean-Michel feigned chagrin. "I stand corrected. The three most beautiful ladies in Ladreville are here." He looked down at Thea. "I can't ignore the little one." Unbidden, the memory of Jean-Michel's father telling Sarah his son knew his duty and would care for Thea flashed through her mind. She tried not to frown, then noticed that Isabelle seemed equally ill at ease.

"Can I help you find anything?" Isabelle kept her voice polite but distant, the tone she used with new customers.

"Not today." Jean-Michel leaned on the counter, directing his attention to Isabelle. "I came to offer my assistance." Though his pause said he expected Isabelle to respond, she remained silent. Jean-Michel cleared his throat before he said, "I heard some unpleasant rumors and want you to know that I don't believe them." This time Isabelle stiffened, but still she made no response.

"Your brother and I had our differences in the past and I imagine we will again, but I know he's not responsible." Though Sarah expected Isabelle to say something, if only to thank Jean-Michel for his faith in Léon, she did not. Jean-Michel flushed. "If there's anything I can do to help you, you need only ask." Isabelle nodded slowly. Though Jean-Michel might construe her nod as agreement, Sarah suspected she was only acknowledging his offer, not accepting it.

"Well, then." Clearly dissatisfied by the reaction to his offer of help, Jean-Michel took his leave.

"Does he come here often?" Sarah asked when the store was once again devoid of customers. The encounter between Isabelle and Jean-Michel had been an unusual one and one which made Sarah's mind whirl.

"Almost every day. Why?"

Sarah nodded. "I thought so. I saw the way he looked at you. The man is smitten."

"But he's courting you." Isabelle appeared appalled by the idea of Jean-Michel as her suitor. "Everyone knows that."

"I've never encouraged him, or David, for that matter." In both cases, Sarah had been convinced the men were acting in response to their parents' wishes, not their own inclination. While that might have been the favored approach in the Old Country, it was not enough for Sarah.

"I never thought Jean-Michel's heart was engaged." Though he'd said all the right things, the words had not rung with sincerity. That was one of the reasons Sarah had never considered him a serious suitor. She'd been polite to him, nothing more. "Now I know why."

Isabelle flushed with indignation. "The whole idea is pre-posterous. Jean-Michel and me? Never!"

"Why not? Surely your parents would approve." After all, Jean-Michel was of French descent, and his father was the most highly regarded man in the town.

"Maman and Papa would approve, and even Léon might be persuaded that Jean-Michel would care for me," Isabelle admitted. She stared into the distance for a moment, as if composing her thoughts. "It's difficult to explain, but I don't trust him. It's not what he says as much as the way he says it." She looked at Sarah, a question in her eyes. "Does that make any sense?"

It did, indeed, for that was the way Sarah felt about David. And the thought that Ladreville was home to two men who couldn't be trusted troubled her almost as much as the problems Léon was facing.

"There must be a way to discover who's responsible for the thefts," she said at supper that night. Though she'd been unable to think of anything, perhaps Clay and Zach would have ideas. That was why she'd asked Zach to join them.

"I'm not so sure there is a way." Clay accompanied his words with a frown. "I'm constantly reminded that this town is very good at keeping secrets."

"I hate secrets." The second the words left her mouth, Sarah blanched. She was a fine one to talk. Wasn't she keeping a secret—a large one—of her own?

Though he gave her an odd look, Zach said nothing. It was only after supper that he took her aside. "I know you said you don't like secrets," he said when they were out of earshot, "but I'm hoping you'll keep what I'm about to tell you in confidence."

Her curiosity aroused, Sarah nodded agreement.

"You were right." A smile of pure happiness split Zach's face. "Those exercises you showed me for Robert were the right ones. He stood today."

Sarah's heart leapt with joy. This was what she'd hoped for, what she prayed for each day. "That's wonderful! Does Clay know?"

"No. Robert wants to wait to tell him until he can actually

walk. That's why I'm asking you to keep this secret. I think Robert doesn't want to raise Clay's hopes in case he never goes beyond this stage. It was only a few seconds, but he stood on his own."

"That's the first step." Sarah remembered the thrill she'd felt the day she'd been able to put weight on both legs. That day had been a turning point for her, for it had proven that, no matter how painful the exercises were and how frustratingly slow her progress seemed, she was healing. "Pa will walk again. I know it. And you're responsible. It's because you're here that Pa wants to walk." Sarah knew Zach's presence had given him the incentive he needed to persevere.

Sarah was reveling in the thought of Clay's father walking again as she made her way to the garden that evening. For once, Clay and Thea were not with her. Nora had been off her feed that morning, and Clay wanted to check on the mare one more time. When he'd invited Thea to join him, there had been no question. Though Sarah's sister enjoyed digging in the dirt, nothing compared to being with a horse. Promising he'd bring Thea to the garden in half an hour or so, Clay had headed for the barn, leaving Sarah to traverse the path alone.

She didn't mind. In fact, she was grateful for the solitude, for it gave her a chance to rejoice in the news. She knew the happiness bubbling up inside her must be evident and that if he saw it, Clay would try to find the cause. Perhaps by the time he joined her, Sarah would have her elation under control. But for the present, she could think of nothing save the fact that Pa would walk again. If she could have skipped, Sarah would have. As it was, she alternated between singing and humming, all the while murmuring prayers of thanksgiving.

It wasn't her doing or even Zach's that was responsible for Pa's being able to stand. It was God's mercy.

The path was at its narrowest here, with mesquite bushes lining both sides. Idly, Sarah noted the leaves that obscured the ground. Though it wasn't the season for leaves to fall, they must have blown down in the last storm, carpeting the path. If Thea were here, she would have shuffled through them, kicking them out of her way. She might have even lain down, waving her arms to make the autumn equivalent of snow angels. Sarah would do none of those, lest she somehow injure her leg. She merely walked, but after the months of fearing she would not walk again, that was enough. She smiled as she took another step.

There was no warning. One instant she was walking, her feet crunching on the dry leaves. The next, she was falling. Sarah heard the crack as branches broke, followed by the sickening thud as she landed at the bottom of a deep hole. She smelled the pungent odors of crushed leaves and fear. She saw the darkness of the pit. But mostly she felt. Pain shot through her as her leg crumpled beneath her. Shock stole her breath. Fear dried her mouth. She had fallen into a trap.

Traps were common. Sarah knew that. Only not on the path. Only not this deep. This one had not been dug for an animal. Sarah's blood chilled at the realization that she was the prey.

❦

Clay could not recall ever being this angry. Not even Austin's death had provoked this fury. Someone had tried to hurt Sarah. Twice. The words echoed through his brain. There was no doubt of it. If he was right, and his instincts shrieked that he was, the wagon wheel had not fallen off by accident. Though there had been plausible reasons for believing that an accident, there was no way anyone could mistake the pit in the path as chance. Someone had known Sarah walked this path almost daily. That same someone had dug a hole deep enough that she could not climb out. Someone wanted to trap her, to injure her, to . . . Clay refused to even consider the third alternative.

Whoever had done it had been clever. After he'd dug the pit, he'd placed branches over the opening, camouflaging them with leaves. Thea would not have fallen in, for the branches would have borne her weight. There was no question; Sarah was the intended victim.

Clay took a deep breath, reminding himself Sarah had been fortunate and had suffered no serious injuries. Though painful, her leg had been strained, not broken again, and she could walk—hobble—with the assistance of a cane. That was the only good thing Clay could say about the evening.

If he lived to be a hundred, he would never forget the fear he'd felt when he'd heard Sarah's cries. He and Thea had been coming down the path, their progress reminding Clay of a jackrabbit. Thea would scamper for a few seconds, then pause, distracted by a flower or a butterfly or even a fluttering leaf. The child found joy in everything. She'd tried to convince Clay to sing, and when he refused, undaunted, she'd proceeded to sing—if you could honor the sounds which emerged from her vocal cords with that word—as loudly as she could. That's why Clay didn't hear Sarah until they were almost at the pit.

If he'd ever doubted that he loved Sarah, the sight of her standing there, obviously in pain but determined to escape, would have destroyed his last doubt. He loved her; he wanted to protect her; he wanted to marry her. But first he had to discover who had tried to hurt her.

"I don't understand it," Clay said, venting his frustration on Zach. Once he'd assured himself that she had no broken limbs, Clay had insisted Sarah return to the cabin and rest. She'd had her hands full, quieting Thea, for the child had been distraught over the sight of her sister in the pit, but eventually Thea's eyes had closed. If they were fortunate, they would both sleep now. Clay knew he would not. He paced the main room of the ranch house, ranting at Zach. "God must be punishing me by taking everyone close to me."

Though Clay had expected a vigorous remonstrance, Zach's expression was calm. "God didn't kill Austin. A human did that," he said quietly, adding, "I thought your wife died of food poisoning."

"She did. Although . . ." Clay's thoughts began to race again as he thought of the day Patience had died. "I wonder if the poisoning was deliberate. It seems strange to me that the only other person who was ill was Mary." He'd heard how the other women hadn't wanted to taste the fish chowder. At the time Clay had been too distraught to question the story. Now he did. Didn't courtesy demand that everyone sample each dish, even if the serving were small? Perhaps the chowder hadn't been to blame. Clay grabbed his hat and headed toward the door.

"Where are you going?"

"Into town. There are some questions that need answers."

"And they can't wait until morning?"

"No."

Zach appeared resigned. "I'm going with you."

"You don't need to."

"I think I do."

Within minutes, they had saddled their horses and were heading toward town.

"She's a wonderful woman." Though they'd been riding silently, Zach seemed to feel the need to talk while they forded the river.

"Sarah?" As far as Clay was concerned, there was only one wonderful woman in the state of Texas. "I thought Austin was crazy when he decided she was the bride for him. A woman responsible for a small child, a woman who can't ride a horse—I couldn't picture such a woman on the Bar C, but Austin insisted. Now I can't imagine life without her."

"You love her." Zach made it a statement rather than a question.

"The whole idea fills me with guilt." Clay didn't bother denying that he loved Sarah. Zach knew him well enough to recognize a lie. "Sarah was supposed to be Austin's wife, not mine." And that was the crux of the matter. Though Clay had written the letters, he'd done that for Austin, not himself. It was Austin who should have been Sarah's husband and Thea's father.

Zach was silent for a moment before he said, "From everything I've heard about him, your brother would have wanted you and Sarah to be happy."

Clay couldn't deny that any more than he could deny his feelings for Sarah. "It still seems wrong, as if I'm cheating both of them." That was why he'd made no mention of love to Sarah, no matter how often he'd longed to make his courtship official.

Zach gave him a sidelong look as they left the river. "I'll pray that you find the answer."

He should have been used to it by now. Zach talked about God and prayer as much as Austin had. Perhaps on another day, it wouldn't have bothered Clay, but today wasn't another day. Today was the day someone had tried to harm Sarah. "A fat lot of good that will do." He spat the words at Zach. "You and Austin put a lot of store in your God. Look what that got Austin: killed. He was so sure God meant Sarah to be the Canfield bride that . . ."

As the words echoed, Clay lost his train of thought. Was it possible? Had Austin somehow known he wouldn't live to wed Sarah? Surely not! Clay searched his memory, trying to recall the times Austin had spoken of Sarah. "That's how he always described her," he mused. "The Canfield bride. Austin called her the Canfield bride, never his bride. I wonder . . ."

Though Zach appeared thoughtful, he shook his head. "You'll never know why he said that. Don't even try to find a reason. You'll only make yourself crazy."

Clay accepted the wisdom of Zach's advice. "You're right. I have more important things to do. Somehow, I will learn who killed my brother and who hurt Sarah."

When they reached Herman's house a few minutes later, Clay pounded on the door.

"I'm going blind, not deaf," the older doctor groused as he opened the door, admitting Clay and Zach. "C'mon in. I can use the company." He pointed toward a couple chairs. "Although, judging from the thundercloud on your face, this is not a social visit."

"I wish it were." Briefly, Clay explained what had happened to Sarah. "There have been too many accidents," he

319

concluded. "I can't believe they're coincidence. That's why I want to talk to you about the day Patience died."

"It was food poisoning. The fish chowder was tainted."

"Possibly. My question is, what if it wasn't bad fish? Could the poison have been deliberately added to Patience's portion?"

Blood drained from the older doctor's face. "It's possible," he admitted. "The only other person who said she ate the chowder was Mary."

"Did she exhibit the same symptoms as Patience?"

"I can't say. I didn't see her until the next day, and she was apparently recovered by then."

"Mary didn't summon you immediately?" Though Clay had not been with Patience that afternoon, Herman had described the symptoms as severe. He couldn't imagine anyone in such agony not calling the doctor.

Herman shook his head. "That woman was never ill a day in her life. You know the reason she's summoned me so often over the past year has nothing to do with her health. I went to the Lazy B the next day, simply because one of the other women told me Mary had eaten a bowl of the chowder and I wanted to check on her. Judging from her condition, she must have ingested far less than your wife."

Clay did not like what he had heard. "So someone could have deliberately killed Patience."

"Based on what you've said, I can't dismiss the possibility."

Though Herman spoke softly, to Clay the words sounded like nails in a coffin. The anger he'd been struggling to control raged like a wildfire, filling every sinew of his body.

"Patience, Austin, and now Sarah." Clay looked at Zach. "I swear by the God you hold so dear that I will find whoever's responsible, and I will make him pay."

18

She couldn't sleep. Every time she closed her eyes, she felt as if she were falling again. It had taken only an instant to reach the bottom of the pit, and yet in her mind she was tumbling for minutes, perhaps hours, before she crumpled in a heap. Shock, fear, and regret mingled with the pain that shot through her leg. Shock that she had fallen. Fear that she might not live to care for Thea. Regret that she had not told Clay she loved him. Over and over, the images haunted her.

It was useless. Sarah tossed the blankets aside and swung her legs over the edge of the bed. Sleep wasn't simply eluding her; it had fled and was probably miles away. Sliding her feet into slippers, she reached for the cane Clay had given her. Though the injury had made her limp more pronounced, she was able to walk so long as she placed most of her weight on the cane. Slowly and deliberately she made her way into the cabin's main room and sank into the rocking chair. Perhaps the rhythmic motion would soothe her nerves. Perhaps it would help her make sense of what had happened.

She closed her eyes, and this time she saw Clay's face as he reached the hole. When she'd landed, she'd soon realized that escape was impossible. Though the pit was only seven or so feet deep, that was enough that she could not reach the top. Whoever had dug it had been careful to remove rocks and roots that might have helped her climb out. The trap had been meticulously planned and constructed, with only one flaw. The digger must not have known that Clay accompanied Sarah to the garden most evenings. It was the knowledge that he would be coming soon and that he would be able to pull her out of her prison that kept Sarah from panicking.

She'd heard them coming. Thea was singing the garden song at the top of her lungs, and Clay was laughing as she mangled the words. If she hadn't been so worried that Thea might tumble into the pit, Sarah would have laughed too. As it was, she shouted to Clay to hold her sister.

A second later, he was staring into the trap, his eyes dark with anguish. "Sarah! What happened?" His expression softened somewhat when he pulled her out and assured himself that she had broken no bones, but there was no mistaking Clay's barely controlled anger. He'd lifted her into his arms and carried her to the ranch house, walking slowly so Thea could keep pace. And as he'd walked, he'd recited a litany of reassurances. Sarah wasn't certain whether they were for Thea's benefit, hers, or his own. All she knew was that they rang false. When he told Thea it was an accident and that Sarah would be safe, Clay was mouthing words he didn't believe.

He'd wrapped her ankle and found a cane somewhere.

Though Sarah longed to talk to him, he'd cut off every attempt, nodding in Thea's direction as if reminding Sarah that her sister needed reassurances, not questions.

"Just rest tonight," he said as he carried her to the cabin. "Everything else can wait." The fact that he and Zach had ridden out only minutes later gave lie to his words. As for resting, that was something Sarah could not do. It had taken close to an hour to coax Thea into sleep, and now . . . now even rocking was doing nothing to soothe Sarah's worries.

Someone wanted to hurt her. There was no denying that. Though Clay had refused to discuss it, she'd heard him mutter "wheel" and suspected his thoughts had taken the same path as hers, reaching the conclusion that someone had tampered with the wagon's wheel. The reason wasn't difficult to find. The only thing that had changed recently had been Sarah's approach toward Austin's death. She'd seen discomfort on several of the townspeople's faces when she'd asked what they knew about the day he died. Though they denied having any idea why someone would have wanted to kill Austin, Sarah didn't believe them. Someone knew something. And what happened today told her she was getting close to uncovering the murderer.

When her ankle began to throb, sending waves of dull pain up her leg, Sarah slowed the rocking. She closed her eyes and leaned back in the chair, considering the possibility that she would soon know who had killed Austin. If that happened, tonight's pain would have served a valuable purpose, for if the killer were brought to justice, Clay would be able to rest. Sarah bowed her head and said a silent prayer that she would be the one to unmask the murderer. That was the only way she knew to prevent Clay from exacting vengeance. "Please, Lord, let me help him."

Once more at peace, Sarah rose and entered Thea's room. Her sister was sleeping. If only she could do the same. She thought for a second, then wrapped a light cloak around her. When she'd been young and had difficulty sleeping, her mother had given her warm milk. Perhaps the childhood remedy would work tonight.

She was in the main house kitchen, stirring milk, when she heard Clay and Zach return. Though she thought they might come into the kitchen, they were evidently so engrossed in their conversation that they didn't see the light or attributed no significance to it. She would not interrupt them. As soon as the milk was ready, she would return to the cabin. There was no reason for Clay and Zach to know she was here. But . . . Sarah's hand paused as the words echoed through the kitchen, the men's voices so loud she couldn't help overhearing.

Oh no! Please, God, no!

❧

"We need to talk." Zach grabbed Clay's arm and propelled him toward the ranch house. Though he'd been silent on the ride back from town, Clay had sensed his friend's disapproval.

"There's nothing to say. I know what I have to do, and I'm going to do it." The anger that had been surging through him all evening continued unabated. One way or another, he was going to stop these attacks on people he loved.

Zach sank into a chair and gestured Clay toward another. Clay knew he might as well sit. One thing he'd learned about Zach was that, for a normally taciturn man, he could be surprisingly long-winded when he was agitated. He was agitated now.

"Finding Austin's killer is one thing," Zach said. "Imposing your own idea of justice on him is something else."

Clay stared into the distance. While it was normally true that he valued Zach's opinion, he had no desire to listen to a sermon tonight, and that appeared to be what Zach had in mind.

"Killing is wrong," Zach said in a voice that belonged in a pulpit. "It doesn't matter whether you call it just deserts or vengeance, it's still killing, and it's still wrong. If you go ahead with your plan, you'll be as much of a murderer as he was. Is that what you want?"

It wasn't the first time Zach had voiced this opinion, but it was the first time he'd been so vehement. Clay fixed his eyes on the man who was more friend than foreman. "I want him to pay for my brother's death. Is that too much to ask?"

"No, it's not." Zach's capitulation surprised Clay. When Zach continued, Clay realized he should have known his friend wasn't finished. "The killer *will* pay. God tells us that. He also tells us that vengeance is his." Zach leaned forward, his eyes darkening with emotion. "Let God take care of Austin's killer. He will."

It was a familiar refrain. Clay knew what was coming next. "I suppose you're going to tell me I should forgive the murderer." Austin had spoken of forgiveness too, but it had always been for minor offenses—an insult, a sharp word, never murder. Some acts were unforgivable.

"I believe you should forgive him," Zach agreed. "But it's for your sake, not his."

"Right." Clay let the sarcasm roll off his tongue. "It'll help me if I let a killer go free."

Zach shook his head. "That's not what I said. I never said

the killer should go free. Find the man and bring him to justice. You need to do that. But once you find him, let the Texas Rangers take over. Let them apply the law of the land." Zach closed his eyes and pinched the bridge of his nose. It was a gesture Clay had seen several times, always when Zach was concentrating, trying to frame his next sentence. "Forgiving the killer is different. You do it for yourself, not him."

Zach had said that before. Clay hadn't understood him then, and he didn't now. Oh, he understood the words. They were simple English words. It was the meaning behind those words that made no sense.

"You and Sarah talk a lot about forgiveness. So did Austin. Forgive me for saying this," Clay said, deliberately using the word, "but it's easy for you to talk. Don't misunderstand, Zach. I'm not belittling what you endured. I know being in that prison was horrible, and I can't begin to imagine how you felt during the decimation. Pa wouldn't even talk about it." Clay leaned forward, gripping the chair arms as he tried to control his emotions. Somehow, some way, he had to make Zach understand why forgiveness was impossible. "I can almost understand how you could forgive your jailors. I know it can't have been easy, but this is different. Someone hurt the people I love. For me that's much, much worse than anything that could happen to me."

Clay glanced down and was surprised to see white knuckles on his hands. Taking a deep breath, he forced himself to relax his grip. "Zach, this is different. You and Sarah can talk about forgiveness, but you don't understand what it's like to have one—maybe two—of your closest family members killed. I cannot forgive that."

Furrows appeared between Zach's eyes. "You're right. I don't understand exactly what you're feeling."

"I do." Though soft, the words echoed clearly through the room.

Clay jumped to his feet, his heart pounding with alarm. "Sarah! What are you doing here?" She stood in the doorway to the kitchen, an expression of almost unbearable sorrow on her face.

"I didn't mean to eavesdrop, but I was warming some milk and couldn't help overhearing."

She shouldn't be out of bed. She shouldn't be putting weight on her leg. The thoughts ricocheted through his mind at the same time that her words reverberated. *I do.* What did she mean? Why did she think she could possibly understand what he felt? First things first. Clay led Sarah to the chair next to him and settled her into it, pulling out a footstool to prop her leg.

"I'm sorry I interrupted, Clay, but I had to. I couldn't let you make the same mistakes I did." Her gaze moved slowly from Clay to Zach and back again. "Zach is right." Though her voice was low, Sarah enunciated each word carefully. "Forgiveness helps you. It opens your heart to love."

Her eyes searched his face, as if hoping to see understanding. He couldn't give her that, for he did not understand Sarah any more than he did Zach. Clay didn't doubt the sincerity of their beliefs. It was simply that he didn't share them, just as they had never shared his experiences. As for mistakes, Clay had made plenty of those, but he failed to see how Sarah's peccadilloes had any bearing on his life.

"I know what I'm telling you is true," she insisted. "I know how you feel, because it happened to me."

"You can't know what I feel." Clay was tired; he was angry; he most definitely was not in the mood for a sermon, particularly not from Sarah. Though he knew she wanted to help him, she could not, for she didn't understand. It was true her parents had died, but death from illness was very different from murder. Clay had felt no need to avenge his mother's death; instead, the fact that she had succumbed to yellow fever had been one of the reasons he'd decided to become a physician. By doing that, he hoped to prevent others from suffering the same losses.

Sarah closed her eyes, and Clay sensed that she was praying. When she looked at him again, her expression was determined. "I never wanted anyone to learn what happened in Philadelphia." The slight tremor in Sarah's voice told Clay how much the revelation would cost. "I thought silence was the only way I could protect Thea, but I was wrong. You need to know."

Zach rose. "I'll leave you two alone."

Sarah shook her head. "Please stay. The time for secrets is over." She turned back to Clay, her hands clasped tightly in her lap. "I wasn't completely honest in my letters to Austin. I told him my parents were dead, but I never explained how they died."

"It wasn't influenza?" Clay couldn't recall the exact wording, but he'd thought she'd said that.

"No." The word was almost inaudible. Sarah swallowed deeply, her expression telling Clay she was mustering every resource she possessed to tell her story. When she spoke, her voice was surprisingly calm. "It wasn't influenza. It's true there was an influenza epidemic at the same time. I mentioned that in one of my letters, hoping Austin would believe that was what had killed my parents. What really happened is Papa made a series of disastrous investments. When they went bad, he lost every dollar he had. Even the house and Mama's jewelry had to be sold to repay the debts." Her letters had alluded to a reduced economic situation. Presumably this was what she meant.

Sarah took a deep breath before she spoke again. "Their friends deserted them. When even the parishioners shunned them, it was too much for Papa. He couldn't bear the shame, and so one night he killed Mama before he turned the gun on himself." Sarah's eyes darkened with remembered pain. "I heard the shots, but by the time I got there, it was too late."

Clay felt the blood drain from his face. "Oh, Sarah!" Though her voice had quavered only slightly as she'd told the story, what she endured must have been unspeakably horrible.

"I'm not telling you this because I want your pity, Clay. I want you to know that I understand how you feel. I know what it's like to have your closest relatives killed." She unclasped her hands, transferring her grip to the chair arms. "When I saw what Papa had done, do you know what I felt? Not sorrow but anger and hatred. I hated my father for what he'd done."

Clay heard Zach sigh. If Sarah heard him, she gave no sign but kept her gaze fixed on Clay.

"I saw that as proof that God had deserted me. After that day, I wouldn't trust him any more than I would forgive my father." Sarah's eyes filled with anguish, telling Clay how much she regretted her actions. "Oh, Clay, I was so wrong. God never abandoned me. I was just too stubborn to ask for his help. When I did ask him, he gave it to me. He helped me understand Papa."

Though her eyes still reflected sorrow, the intense pain was gone. "I spent almost a year mired in anger and hatred. I even prayed that Papa was burning in hell. Not once did I try to understand what had caused him to use his gun until I prayed for help. Then I realized how much Papa loved my mother. He knew how important their role in society was to her and wanted to spare her the shame of being shunned. That was why he killed her. And then, because he couldn't bear the thought of living without her, he killed himself."

Sarah shifted slightly to include Zach in the conversation. "Zach was right when he told you that killing is always wrong. Papa was wrong, but so was I. My hatred was as much of a sin as what he did. The difference was, my sin hurt me, not anyone else." Sarah turned her gaze back to Clay. "This may sound strange, but I felt that I was empty inside, while on the outside I was weighed down, almost as if I was carrying a load."

"I understand." Though he had not taken the time to analyze his feelings, what Sarah described applied to Clay too. He'd been wrong when he thought no one could understand what he'd endured. Sarah did. She understood, but—more than that—she had overcome it. "What changed?"

"I did. I forgave my father, and then I prayed that God would forgive me. When he did, he lifted an enormous burden from my shoulders. It may sound melodramatic, but I felt like a new person."

Clay nodded as a piece of the puzzle that was Sarah fell into place. "That's why you've seemed so different the past few weeks." He'd thought the new school was the reason for her happiness, but it appeared he had been wrong.

"I found peace." There was no ignoring the light shining

from her eyes or the serenity of her expression, an expression that reminded him of Austin. Gone was the pain Clay had seen on Sarah's face. Gone, too, was the tension in her arms. No longer did she grip the chair. Instead, she sat with her hands in her lap, the fingers soft and relaxed. "I'm not exaggerating when I tell you it's the most wonderful thing in this world. That's why I pray that you will find it too."

Looking at the woman he loved, seeing the glow on her face, Clay knew there was nothing he wanted more than to share her experience. He wanted to fill the emptiness inside him, to put aside his burden. The problem was, though Sarah made it sound simple, Clay knew it was not. "I don't think I can forgive."

Sarah leaned forward. Placing one hand on his, she said, "With God's help you can." She turned to face Zach. "I'm so new at this that I'm feeling lost. Help me, Zach. Help Clay."

Zach nodded. "It's the easiest, the most difficult, and the most important thing you'll ever do. Open your heart to God. Let him fill it."

They made it sound easy, but it couldn't be. It couldn't be that simple. Nothing important was. "I don't know how."

Sarah tightened her grip on Clay's hand, but it was Zach who spoke. "God is waiting for you. All you need to do is talk to him. Invite him in. He'll do the rest."

Clay looked at the man who'd become his best friend and the woman he loved. Though their faces were somber, they were filled with a peace he could not ignore. He wanted that, and yet he feared it would never be his. "I need to be alone."

Clay rose and strode to the empty bedroom, the room he

and Austin had once shared, the room that had been his and Patience's. Closing the door behind him, he began to speak. "I don't know what to say, Lord. If Zach is right, you can see what's in my heart. Show me what I need to do."

There was no answer. Those stories he'd heard about voices were just that: stories. The reality was that he was alone, as he'd been for so long. Clay walked slowly around the room, laying his hand on top of the bureau as he passed it. And as he did, he remembered how Austin had kept his treasures in the bottom drawer. In all the time they'd shared this room, Clay had never opened that drawer. He wouldn't open it now.

He took a few more steps, reaching the chair that had once been his mother's but which Pa had insisted Patience take. Clay's wife had placed it next to the window and, no matter how busy she was, always found time to spend a few minutes there each day, looking outside. She'd called this her daydreaming chair. Clay touched the chair back as he stared out the window. He wasn't certain how long he stood there or when the tears began. All he knew was that his face was wet and his heart was full.

This room held so many memories; it had seen joyous moments; it had witnessed almost unbearable sorrow. Those memories were the reason he no longer slept in this room. They were also the reason he'd come here tonight. Tonight he wept for the lives that had been cut short. He wept for Austin, for Patience, for Pa's infirmity. And as he wept, Clay felt the anger that had been his companion for so long begin to dissolve. When his tears were spent, so was his anger. The cold fury that had propelled him was gone, replaced by warmth. The emptiness deep inside had disappeared, and in its place came a feeling of completeness. The burden he had carried was gone, shouldered by the One who had borne so much more. Clay was no longer alone.

He wiped his eyes and looked around the room. The bureau and chair stood where they always had. The coverlet on the bed had the same wrinkles it had yesterday. Nothing had changed, and yet everything had, for he had changed. He saw the room and the world with new eyes. Was this peace? Clay wasn't certain. All he knew was that it was the most wonderful feeling of his life.

He sank to the floor and knelt, his head bowed reverently. "Thank you, Lord."

༜

His hands weren't shaking. Men's hands didn't shake, or—if they did—a man didn't admit it. What Clay would admit was that he was nervous. He could not recall feeling this way the last time. Perhaps he'd forgotten. That must be the case. After all, weren't things supposed to be easier the second time?

Four days had passed since the night his life had changed. They'd been four days of almost constant conversation. He and Sarah and Zach had spent hours talking about their Lord and the plans he had for their lives. Some of those hours had been spent reading his Word and offering prayers of thanksgiving. Others had been hours of quiet contemplation. But the majority had been a joyous sharing of experiences. Clay had recalled amusing moments from his and Austin's childhood, while Sarah had recounted pleasurable days spent with her parents. Even Zach, who rarely spoke of his life before the war, had contributed an anecdote of growing up in a small East Texas town.

With each story he told, each recollection he heard, Clay felt the healing continue. As a physician, he knew how healing occurred. The surgeon cleansed the wound in what was often a painful process. Next came the sutures and dressing. That was all that could be done on the outside. The rest was internal. God had been the surgeon. He'd cleansed and sutured. He'd provided Zach and Sarah as sterile dressings to protect the wound. And now he was working inside Clay, healing him, draining away the poison of hatred, growing firm new flesh in place of cancerous sores.

If he hadn't experienced it, Clay would not have believed it possible for a man to change so quickly and so completely. But it had happened. Through God's grace, he no longer felt the need to wreak vengeance. He'd memorized the verses Zach had shown him from Romans 12, admonishing him to overcome evil with good. Each day Clay prayed that, if he did find Austin's killer, God would give him the strength to repay evil with good. Today, however, his thoughts were focused not on killing or revenge but on love. His love for Sarah.

Though he hadn't told Zach what he was planning, he suspected the man knew and that was why he'd concocted a scheme to occupy Thea. While Zach took Thea into town to watch the blacksmith make horseshoes, Clay would have time alone with Sarah. Everything was prepared, except, that is, for Clay himself. Somehow he had to keep his hands from shaking.

"We haven't been to the garden in a few days," he said as casually as he could. "At this time of the year, the weeds may have taken over. Do you think you can walk that far?" Though he would gladly have carried Sarah, he knew she'd refuse. The woman was nothing if not independent.

"We'd have to go slowly."

They did. Somehow Clay managed to speak of inconsequential things, though his heart was pounding and his mouth dry. Nerves could do that to a man. When they reached the spot where Sarah had fallen, he laid a hand on her arm to stop her. Though he'd had the hole filled in, and the men had assured him everything was firmly packed, he wouldn't let Sarah precede him. It was only when he'd crossed it safely that Clay allowed her to cross.

"Thank you," she said softly. "My mind told me everything would be fine, but I'm glad I didn't come this way alone. I'm not sure my legs would have obeyed my brain. I might have turned around."

Clay shook his head. "You're a brave woman, Sarah. You'd have continued." Her courage was one of the things he admired about her. Why mince words? It was one of the things he loved about her.

When they entered the garden, Clay's heart accelerated. Would she like what he'd done? There was only one way to know. He led her toward the far corner where the roses were planted. As they rounded the final bend in the path, she stopped abruptly.

"When did this . . . ? Who did . . . ?" Sarah turned to face Clay, her eyes sparkling with warmth. "Oh, Clay, did you do this?" She pointed toward the carved wooden bench that now sat amid the rose bushes, the bench that William Goetz had finished only this afternoon. Though Clay had been pleased with the result, what mattered was Sarah's reaction.

"Do you like it?" He countered her question with one of his own.

"Yes, of course." She took another step, then reached out

to touch the roses carved into the bench back. "This is beautiful."

"In that case, I'll admit I'm responsible."

Sarah raised one brow, a skeptical expression crossing her face. "And if I hadn't liked it . . ."

"I would have pretended I had no idea how it got here." Clay accompanied his words with a smile. "I didn't think I'd have to resort to lies, though. You spend so much time here that I thought you should have a comfortable place to sit." Though she never complained about sitting on the ground, Clay had noticed how awkward it was for her to rise.

Sarah traced the carving one more time, then settled onto the bench. "This is wonderful," she said, placing one hand on the wooden arm. "You should try it." She patted the spot next to her.

Clay shook his head. The time had come. In a few minutes, he would have his answer, but first he had to ask the question. "I prefer to stand. This way I can watch you." He had to see her face, to be certain she was not acting from pity or even compassion. Though she said nothing, a furrow appeared between Sarah's eyes as she tried to make sense of his words. "I brought you out here for a reason," he told her.

"To show me the bench."

"That was one reason, but not the only one." Clay took a deep breath as he tried to compose his thoughts. "When Patience died, I believed my heart had died too. I never thought I would love again." Sarah nodded, her gesture telling him she understood. "This is one time when I'm glad to say I was wrong."

Clay bent one knee in the classic posture. As he did, he realized that his eyes were level with Sarah's. Those eyes were

336

widening, as if she recognized the significance of his bended knee but didn't understand why he was doing it. Surely she had to know how deeply he cared for her. "I love you, Sarah. I think I loved you from the moment I saw you standing in front of the *cabildo*. I love your strength, your determination, your faith. I love all of you, and I want you and Thea to be part of my life."

Her eyes widened again, and as Clay saw the glint of tears, his heart began to thud. It appeared he had been wrong in thinking she returned his love. "I'm not asking you to forget Austin," he said quickly. "I know you'll always love him, and I won't try to change that. I can accept being second in your heart, even though you are first in mine. I love you, Sarah, and I want you to be my wife. Will you marry me?"

Sarah shook her head, nodded, then brushed a tear from her cheek. "Oh, Clay, I'm sorry."

It was what he had feared. She didn't love him. She wouldn't marry him. Clay's face must have reflected his dismay, for she said quickly, "I'm not as confused as I seem. It's just, you're right and you're wrong."

"I don't understand. How can I be both right and wrong?"

"You're right that I'll never forget Austin. He was the first man I loved. You know how I fell in love with his letters. But I know now that Austin was not the man God intended me to marry." Sarah laid her hand on Clay's arm. "You're that man. You're the one God chose for me."

Clay believed that too. These past four days had shown him the rightness of loving Sarah. Before that, he'd wanted her as his wife. Now he knew she would be more than that. She would be his soul mate.

"How am I wrong?"

She smiled, a smile so full of love that Clay's heart skipped a beat. "You're wrong to think you'll ever be in second place. I love you, Clay. I always will."

Sarah's words erased the doubt that had encased his heart. "Will you marry me?"

Her smile widened, and her eyes brimmed with love. "If only you knew how often I dreamt of being your wife and how I feared that day would never come. Now my dream is coming true. Yes, Clay, I will marry you."

19

"But, Clay, this would be the perfect opportunity." Sarah gripped his hand, hoping that if her words did not convince him, her touch would. A light rain was falling, keeping them from their nightly walk to the paddock. Instead, they were seated on the porch of Sarah's cabin, nestled close to each other on the courting swing.

"I'm close to finding the answer. I know I am." She and Clay had agreed that the questions she'd been asking about Austin were the likely reason for someone trying to harm her. "Our engagement will give me another reason to talk to people. Someone will say something important. I feel certain of that."

"No." Clay's eyes darkened as he pronounced the word. "I won't let you risk your life to learn who killed Austin. God will take care of that."

"But, Clay." That phrase seemed to be becoming a refrain. Though Sarah was happy that he no longer sought vengeance, she knew that until the killer was unmasked, Clay would always be searching. He might deny it, but the doubts and worries would remain, coloring even the most casual encounter with suspicion. "I can help. I know I can."

"The answer is still no." Though he tried to soften his words by threading his fingers through hers, she saw the anguish in his eyes. "I've already lost two people I love. I can't let you risk your life."

He wouldn't change his mind, and Sarah wouldn't cause him additional worry. She leaned back, lulled by the soft plunk of raindrops on the steps and the clean scent of moist soil. On a night so filled with peace, it was difficult to believe that a murderer still roamed free. She had prayed that she could help Clay. Though it wasn't what she'd envisioned, perhaps the help she could provide was to abandon her search.

"All right. I promise I won't ask any more questions about Austin." The look of relief on Clay's face told Sarah her decision was the right one. "There is something else, though. I want to help Isabelle and her family. There must be a way to discover who's responsible for all the thefts."

Clay shook his head, but this time Sarah sensed he wasn't disagreeing, simply trying to clear it. "I've never felt like this before," he admitted. "My head and my heart are at war, and I don't know who's winning. I know how you feel about the Rousseaus, but at the same time, I want to wrap you in cotton and keep you safe until we're married." Clay's lips curved in a wry smile. "I suspect you wouldn't like that."

"Your suspicions are correct." Sarah chuckled at the image. "Three months is a long time to be wrapped. I'd probably suffocate." Figuratively, if not literally. After the initial giddiness of admitting their love, she and Clay had turned to practicalities and had decided to be married three days after Christmas. Though Sarah had no family other than Thea, Clay wanted Patience's parents at his side. Three months would allow enough time for them to travel from Boston to Texas.

Clay smiled and raised Sarah's hand to his lips, pressing a kiss on her fingertips. "You wouldn't be the woman I love if you weren't worried about your friends." He stared into the distance for a moment. "I'd like to find the thief too. Maybe then the town can get back to normal. For a while I thought the school was uniting the town, but the suspicion of Léon has undone most of the good."

Sarah nodded. "The unpleasantness has hurt the Rousseaus in so many ways. It's not just the lost business that bothers them. Worse than that is the fear that they may have to move. They don't want to think about uprooting themselves again."

"And they shouldn't have to."

Sarah wondered how Clay—loving, protective Clay—would react to her next words. "I want to do more than ask questions. I need to find a way to force the thief into the open."

"You're talking about a trap." When Sarah nodded, Clay began to protest.

"It may not be the only way, but it's the quickest," Sarah told him. "And this way, we'd control everything."

"We?" Clay gave her a stern look. "We will plan it, but I'll be the one who catches him. Don't even try to argue, Sarah. I told you before that I can't bear the thought of losing you. Besides, you don't know how to shoot a gun, do you?"

It was only when Sarah conceded the point that Clay agreed to help her. "We need the right location." He thought for a moment. "Gunther hasn't been robbed, and his house is far enough out of town to be perfect. I'll ask him tomorrow."

Gunther agreed. In fact, Clay reported, his only regret was that he wouldn't be present for the unmasking of the thief. They'd chosen the location; now it was time to set the bait.

Clay arrived at the mercantile at the busiest time of the day and made sure that several of the town's women overheard him asking Madame Rousseau to order a cut glass bowl for Sarah's wedding present.

"I want one about the same size as Frieda Lehman's," Clay explained. "Eight inches in diameter." He shrugged his shoulders in a self-deprecating gesture. "Patience never had much use for fancy glass, but Gunther told me the bowl was his wife's favorite gift. That's why he's saving it for Eva."

The story was pure fabrication. Frieda Lehman had never owned a cut glass bowl, and the one that was now displayed in Gunther's house was an inexpensive piece Martina had found in the back of a cupboard. Clay and Sarah were betting that the thief knew nothing about crystal and would not notice the difference, particularly in the dark. They were also betting that the story of Clay's gift and the reason for it would spread quickly, attracting the thief's attention. All that remained was to provide him with the ideal time to steal the bowl.

After church the next Sunday, Sarah approached Gunther, drawing him away from a group of men.

"I'm still nervous about it," she said, pitching her voice so it could be easily overheard. "This will be the first time Thea's been separated from me, but it's such a good opportunity for her. So, if you're still willing, I agree that Thea can go with Eva when you visit her cousins."

Gunther grinned. "Eva will be mighty pleased. You know how she dotes on that sister of yours."

They spoke for a few minutes longer, confirming the details of the overnight trip that would leave the Lehman house empty.

"Do you think it will work?" Sarah asked Clay as the day approached.

He nodded. "I doubt the thief will be able to resist the bait. A prized possession in an empty house." Clay shook his head slowly. "The only thing that worries me is that we may have made it too easy for him. I hope that's not the case."

"I wish Thea didn't have to go away." Though they'd tried to devise other schemes, Sarah and Clay had realized it was important for Sarah to have a reason to be talking about Gunther's trip.

"She'll be fine. Besides, she needs to get used to being away from you occasionally." Clay pressed a playful kiss on Sarah's nose. "As much as I love your sister, I don't want to take her on our wedding trip."

"You know I don't need a wedding trip."

"It's not a matter of needing anything. I'm selfish. I want a few weeks alone with you. Besides, I think you'll like New Orleans."

"I know I will. It's just . . ."

"You worry about everyone." Clay completed her sentence.

"That's right. I'm worried about you being at Gunther's house."

"Don't worry." Clay punctuated his words with a kiss. "I won't be alone."

❦

But he was restless. Clay shifted, doing his best to make no sound as he wondered how long he would have to wait. Perhaps this was part of God's plan to teach him patience. That was one virtue he had in deplorably small quantities. Though he'd entered the house three hours earlier, slipping in the back door while Gunther and Eva made a noisy exit through the front, Clay knew the thief was unlikely to come before dark. Since the sun had set only an hour ago, it was unrealistic to have expected a visitor before now. Perhaps the man lived with others and could sneak out of his house only in the middle of the night. It didn't matter. Whenever he came, Clay would be waiting. The Lehman house was completely dark now, with Clay stationed in Eva's room, the door ajar. This way, he could watch the man, unseen until the time was right.

At last! Clay heard the front door open and footsteps cross the main room. The man made no attempt at stealth. Why would he? Gunther had no close neighbors. There was no one to see or hear an intruder. A shaft of light told Clay the man had uncovered the lantern he'd been carrying and had begun his search. The sound of drawers being opened and closed was accompanied by low mutters. *Look at the table*, Clay urged silently. They'd left the bowl in plain sight.

"Well, what do you know? It was here all along."

There was no mistaking the voice. Clay realized he shouldn't have been surprised, for all the signs had been there.

"Find what you want, Jean-Michel?" Pulling his six-shooter from the holster, Clay moved into the room.

If the situation hadn't been so serious, Clay might have been amused by the thief's shocked expression. "Clay? What are you doing here?" Jean-Michel stared at the gun.

"That should be obvious. I've been waiting for you." Clay gestured toward the bowl in Jean-Michel's hand. "I suspect your father will be surprised when he learns who's been robbing the townspeople."

Jean-Michel's eyes shifted from Clay's gun to his face. "You have no proof." Surprise had changed to belligerence.

"What would you call the bowl in your hand?"

"I'll break it. Then you'll have nothing."

Clay shrugged, as if unconcerned by the loss of a supposedly priceless bowl. "That won't change anything." He looked at the man who'd created such havoc in the town, trying to imagine why he'd chosen to steal. It couldn't be because he needed money, for he did not. Though he wanted for nothing, Jean-Michel had stolen from his neighbors and then tried to cast the blame on someone else.

"What's this?" A piece of white cloth hung from Jean-Michel's pocket. Clay tugged the handkerchief loose and inspected it. Like the other "evidence" Jean-Michel had planted, the handkerchief bore Léon's initials.

"I don't know how it got there."

A flash of annoyance speared Clay. "I'm not stupid, Jean-Michel, and neither is your father."

A reasonable man would have admitted his guilt. Jean-Michel was not reasonable. His eyes narrowed as he said, "My father won't believe you. Everyone knows he didn't like Austin."

The two sentences had no bearing on each other, unless . . . Clay tightened the grip on his gun. "Is that why you killed him? To make your father happy?"

The man blanched, and he lowered his eyes. "I didn't kill Austin. I swear to God I didn't kill him." Though his voice rang with truth, Clay said nothing. Jean-Michel might not be a murderer, but he'd done something almost as evil: he'd tried to destroy another man's reputation.

When the silence grew uncomfortable, Jean-Michel continued, "I'll admit I took a few things." He laid the glass bowl back on the table, as if making reparations.

"And cut a few fences?" Though Clay was confident that the same person was responsible for the vandalism as well as the thefts, he wanted there to be no doubt when he approached Michel Ladre. It would be difficult for the man to admit that his son, of whom he was so proud, was a criminal.

"Yeah." The word came out reluctantly.

"Why did you do it?"

Jean-Michel's reply confirmed Clay's thoughts. "For the fun. I liked seeing everyone worried and knowing I was responsible."

"Then why blame Léon? Why let him get the credit for what you'd done?"

"So Isabelle would marry me."

Clay stared at the man, wondering if he'd heard correctly. "What made you think Isabelle would marry someone who'd destroyed her brother's reputation?"

"It was the only way. Léon didn't like me. He said I wasn't good enough for his sister." Clay couldn't disagree with that assessment. "If everyone hated Léon," Jean-Michel continued, "he would have to leave Ladreville. Then I'd be free to marry Isabelle."

Though the reasoning was twisted, Clay could understand how it might make sense to a man as cosseted as Jean-Michel. He saw everything from his own perspective, never considering how others might react. "I suppose you courted Sarah to make Isabelle jealous."

Jean-Michel nodded. "When that didn't work, I had to find another way."

"By stealing and blaming Isabelle's brother. What were you going to do when someone learned the truth?"

Jean-Michel shrugged. "No one would. I'm smarter than they are."

Clay forbore mentioning the obvious fallacy of that statement. "We'll see what your father says."

Once more Jean-Michel assumed a belligerent stance. "I told you that he won't believe you. It's just my word against yours."

Clay shook his head and turned toward the window he'd so carefully opened earlier that day. "That's not true. Zach, you can come in now." Jean-Michel blanched. "That's right. Zach heard everything you said. I have no doubt that your father will believe him." Clay gestured with his gun. "Put your hands behind your back. We're going to tie you up."

"You can't do this to me."

"I can and I will." Clay watched as Zach tied the thief's hands. "I'm also going to tell your father that I believe you killed Austin." That was a bluff. Jean-Michel was a sneak and a thief, but he was also a coward. A coward might have shot Austin in the back, but he would not have had the courage to face him as he pulled the trigger. Jean-Michel might not have killed Austin, but the way his eyes had shifted when Clay had accused him told Clay he knew more than he'd admitted.

"I didn't kill him. I swear I didn't." Jean-Michel looked from Clay to Zach, his eyes moving wildly as he tried to convince them. "You've got to believe me. I didn't do it, but I think I know who did."

Though his pulse quickened, Clay forced a sarcastic tone to his words. "Let me guess. You're going to try to pin it on Léon."

"No." A vehement shake of Jean-Michel's head accompanied the word. "If you want to find the murderer, you should look closer to home. When we heard what happened, we all agreed not to tell anyone that one man left our poker game right after Austin did. No one asked where he went, but he was gone long enough to have killed him."

A sense of vindication rushed through Clay. This was what he'd believed from the beginning, that the killer was one of the men Austin knew best. Though there were others in Ladreville whom Austin trusted enough to let approach him, no one else would have known the exact time he'd left the barn that night. No one else would have been close enough to intercept him on the way home. "Who was that?"

"David."

The word echoed in the room. Clay heard a gasp and wasn't certain whether it came from himself or Zach. "David?" That wasn't possible. "David was Austin's closest friend."

The look Jean-Michel shot Clay was almost pitying. "That's what he wanted everyone to think. The truth is, he always resented your brother. Austin had everything David wanted: a father, an older brother, a prosperous ranch. Soon he'd have a wife."

Zach gave Clay a quick look, his expression confirming Clay's thoughts. As unpalatable as it was, Jean-Michel was telling the truth.

"My guess is that seeing Sarah's miniature that night sent

him over the edge," Jean-Michel continued. "He didn't like the fact that Austin would have not just a wife but a beautiful one. I think that's why he killed him."

"I don't want to believe it." For almost as long as he could recall, David had been part of Clay's life. How could the man who'd been so close to Austin have killed him? It didn't make sense. And yet Clay couldn't forget Sarah's concerns. She'd been the first to tell him that David resented Austin. It had been Clay's foolish pride, his belief that he knew David better than Sarah could, that had caused him to dismiss her worries.

"You always said the murderer was someone Austin trusted," Zach reminded him.

"You're right. I've been blind." He holstered his gun and took a step toward the door. "Will you take Jean-Michel to his father? I've got another visit to pay."

20

"Sarah! Sarah, where are you?"

Sarah blinked at the unexpected sound of a human voice. Clay and Zach had left before supper, and all the ranch hands were spending their night off in town. With Thea gone, that had left only Sarah and Pa. Though she'd tried to play chess with him, he'd proven a poor companion, falling asleep unusually early. Sarah knew she would be unable to sleep until Clay returned, and so she had gone back to the cabin, hoping that the book she was reading would distract her. It had not. She'd been staring at the same page for several minutes. Instead of caring about the plights befalling Mr. Dickens's characters, she envisioned Clay inside Gunther's house, waiting for the thief. Had the man arrived? Was he even now occupying Ladreville's one jail cell?

"Sarah!" the cry came again.

"I'm here." Sarah reached for her cane and made her way onto the porch. It was frustrating, moving so slowly when she was needed. Though she had barely recognized her neighbor's voice, there was no mistaking the urgency. "Oh, Mary!" The cabin light spilled onto the porch, revealing the older woman's flushed face. "What's wrong?"

"You gotta help me." Mary doubled over, clutching her stomach. When she raised her head again, her eyes were glassy, their expression one Sarah had never seen. Even though her experience with illness was limited, Sarah knew something was desperately wrong.

"Take me home."

Sarah's heartbeat accelerated as she tried to remember what her mother had said about glassy eyes. They were a sign of a fever, weren't they? "You're ill. You should lie down here." Sarah turned to open the door.

"No, I gotta go home. Herman gave me a tincture. It's there." Mary grabbed Sarah's hand. "Take me home."

Sarah flinched as Mary tightened her grip. "Did you ride?" If they had only the one horse, Sarah could not imagine how she could get the other woman to her home. She couldn't ride, and the ranch hands had taken the Bar C's wagon.

"No." Mary shook her head. "I brung the wagon."

Thank goodness. "All right. I'll drive it." Sarah kept one arm around Mary's waist, supporting the ailing woman while she gripped her cane with the other. When they reached Mary's wagon, Sarah frowned, wondering how she could possibly hoist the older woman into it. It was difficult enough lifting Thea, and Mary outweighed Sarah by thirty or forty pounds.

"I don't know . . ."

"Don't fret," Mary said as she climbed in with surprising ease. "Just get me home."

"Why did you come to the Bar C?" Sarah asked as she guided the wagon off the ranch. If she had been as ill as Mary, Sarah doubted she would have left her bed.

Mary gripped her stomach again. "No choice. I needed a doctor, and there weren't no one to take a message. Everyone's gone." Though the words made sense, Mary's voice was devoid of emotion, almost as if she were reciting phrases she had memorized.

"Clay will be able to help you, but I don't know when he'll be back from town." Sarah wouldn't tell Mary what he was doing. Instead, she said a silent prayer for his success.

"Don't matter. You're what I need." Mary reached a hand toward Sarah, then drew it back. "It won't be long now."

It was a sign of her illness that Mary's words were no longer making much sense. "Won't be long until what?"

The older woman stared at Sarah, as if puzzled by the question. "Until we reach the ranch," she said at last. "I can wait."

Sarah's alarm increased. She'd had little experience with illness, but Mama had said that people were sometimes incoherent when they had high fevers. That must be what ailed Mary. Thank goodness, they were close to the Lazy B and whatever Dr. Adler had prescribed. Sarah breathed a sigh of relief as she turned off the main road. Just another minute or two.

As she stopped the wagon in front of the house, a man emerged from the barn. Sarah gave Mary a quick look. Hadn't she said all the ranch hands were gone tonight? Perhaps the fever had addled her brain.

"Oh, you're still here, Jake." Mary's voice was sharp with reproof. "Unharness the wagon, and then you can go into town."

"But, ma'am—"

"Do as I say."

He nodded and reached for the horses. "Yes, ma'am."

"Let's get you inside." The fever must be increasing. That was the only way Sarah could explain Mary's uncharacteristic actions. She led her into the house and opened the door to Mary's room. "You need to lie down. I'll find your medicine."

Mary sank onto the bed. When Sarah reached for her feet, intending to unlace Mary's boots, Mary slapped at her hand. "I ain't dead yet. Fetch the pills." She pointed toward her dresser. "And then make a cup of tea."

Sarah nodded. Though Mary hadn't asked, she would also bring a ewer of cold water. Cool compresses had been Mama's cure for fevers. Realizing she'd need both hands to carry the tray, Sarah hung her cane over the doorknob and hobbled into the kitchen. Poor Mary! Whatever had caused the fever, it was obviously severe, for it had turned her friendly neighbor into a stranger.

As she waited for the water to boil, Sarah kept her head cocked, listening for sounds from the bedroom. There were none. Surely that was a good sign, for it must mean Mary had fallen asleep.

Walking as quietly as she could, Sarah returned to the bedroom with the tray. If Mary was sleeping, she'd wait until she wakened before she gave her the medication. Sleep, Mama had said, was the best cure. Sarah was so intent on not spilling anything and on not waking her patient that it was only when she was inside the bedroom that she realized Mary was no longer on the bed. Laying the tray on a small table, Sarah turned.

"No!"

It was easier than he'd dared hope. David was nothing if not a creature of habit, and habit said he would spend Saturday evening in the saloon. There he was, one boot on the rail, an elbow on the bar. Though he wanted nothing more than to drag him out and pummel his face, Clay had no desire to involve the entire town in his argument. He tapped David on the shoulder. "You've got some explaining to do."

David raised an eyebrow as he drained his glass. "What's going on?"

"That's what you're going to tell me." Rather than wait any longer, Clay pulled a coin from his pocket and tossed it onto the bar. "Let's go outside."

"What's the matter?" David demanded when they were far enough away from the saloon that they would not be overheard by patrons. "Can't a man have a drink with his friends?"

The air was warm and moist, presaging a storm. Powerful as they might be, the natural elements were no match for the fury inside Clay.

"Not the man who killed my brother."

David took a step backward, recoiling from Clay's anger. "Are you loco?"

Clay grabbed David's shoulder. The man was not going to escape, not tonight, not ever. He'd pay for what he'd done. "You might as well admit it. Jean-Michel told me how much you hated Austin."

David leaned toward Clay and made a show of sniffing. "Nope. It ain't whiskey that's addled your brain. I reckon you're just plumb loco if you think I hated Austin. I didn't hate him, and I sure as shootin' didn't kill him."

David's voice sounded sincere. Perhaps it was only a trick of the moonlight, but his face appeared guileless. Clay released his grip. It was clear the man was not preparing to flee.

"I reckon I oughta smash your face for even thinkin' it. Why would I hurt him? Austin was like a brother."

Was it possible Jean-Michel had been lying? "Do you deny telling Jean-Michel that you resented Austin, that you wanted to best him at everything?"

David shook his head slowly. "I reckon part of that's true. I always wanted to do better than him. That ain't no crime, Clay. Austin was the same way. He spent his life tryin' to prove he could do things better than you."

Clay frowned. He'd never thought of his brother as a competitor, but Austin, it appeared, had felt differently. If Clay had been oblivious to that, what else had he missed?

"Sure, I wanted to outdo Austin," David admitted, "but it was friendly-like. I would never have hurt him."

David's words rang with truth. Though Clay wanted to believe them, there was still the matter of David's prolonged absence from the barn.

"Where did you go the night Austin was killed? Jean-Michel said you left the barn soon after Austin and were gone a long time. Long enough to have killed him."

Two patrons left the saloon and staggered toward Clay and David. David waited until they were past before he answered. "I went back to get more food for us." Once again, David's words rang with honesty. "You know Ma don't like my friends settin' foot in the main house." Clay nodded, remembering the restrictions Mary had imposed on him and Austin when they'd visited.

"I knew she baked a couple pies that day." David continued.

"I figured I'd better ask before I took them. Didn't want to get no tongue-lashing in the mornin'. Problem was, she weren't there." David shrugged. "I reckon she went to the outhouse. I waited a bit afore I went back empty-handed. You know, Clay, I had some mighty riled friends when I didn't bring no pies."

The hair on the back of Clay's neck began to prickle. He wanted to believe David's story, and in fact he did, but believing it raised a disturbing possibility. "Do you know where your mother was?"

David shrugged again. "Like I told you, I figured she was in the outhouse. By the time the men left, I heard her back in her room."

Clay clenched his fists as his thoughts continued to whirl. Had he been wrong? He'd always believed the killer to be a man, but what if he'd been mistaken? Austin trusted Mary. That meant he would have let her come close enough to shoot him. She had had the opportunity, for according to David, she'd been gone at the critical time. Clay knew she was an excellent shot and strong enough to have lifted Austin onto Nora's back. If she had had a reason, Mary could have killed Austin. The question was, what possible reason could have made her shoot Clay's brother?

When Clay clapped David on the shoulder, it was a friendly gesture, not a restraining one. "I believe you."

He mounted Shadow and headed for home, deep in thought. As difficult as it was to believe Mary was a murderer, everything pointed to her. As for the reason, from the beginning Clay could not understand why anyone would have wanted Austin dead. But humans were not necessarily logical, as his conversation with Jean-Michel had proven.

Only a twisted mind would have believed the way to woo a woman was to destroy her brother's reputation. Was Mary equally disturbed? Clay didn't know. What he did know was that tomorrow would be soon enough to confront her. That would give Clay time to think, time to phrase his questions, time to tell Sarah everything he'd learned.

Soon after he passed the Lazy B, Shadow began to whinny. "What's wrong, boy?" Clay patted the horse's neck. There must be a reason for his restiveness, for his stallion was not easily spooked. Shadow tossed his head and strained, clearly unhappy with Clay's pace. Something was definitely wrong. Clay looked around. Nothing seemed amiss. He listened. The evening sounds were ordinary, the hoot of an owl, the rustle of a rodent. Clay sniffed, then stiffened as he realized what Shadow sensed. Something was burning.

Fear brought a burst of energy along with the realization that he had to help. Fire was every man's enemy. No matter what animosities existed, when a man's livelihood was threatened, everyone helped. If Karl Friedrich's house was on fire, Clay would be there, pouring water onto the flames. Shadow needed no encouragement to gallop. As they crested the hill, Clay's fear turned to sheer terror. It wasn't the Friedrichs' house. The Bar C was burning!

"Let's go!" Clay bent low as Shadow increased his pace. There was no telling how long the fire had been burning. All he knew was that he had to reach the ranch. Sarah needed him. She was alone with Pa, and with her injured leg, she would need help getting him to safety.

"C'mon, Shadow. Faster." Clay's heartbeat was quicker than Shadow's hooves as he raced toward the ranch. Soon. They'd be there soon. His eyes scanned the road mechanically, looking for snakes and holes. He listened for the sound of predators. Nothing could delay him. He had to reach Sarah.

"Just one more hill," he told Shadow. "Then we'll be there." But when they reached the top, Clay's heart stopped. *No! Please, God, no!* It couldn't be!

21

Sarah felt the blood drain from her face. Standing a mere five feet away was Mary, a pistol in her hand. What was she doing? The woman was ill. She should have been in bed.

"What's wrong?" Sarah gripped the edge of the table, trying to steady herself. Had Mary heard an intruder? Did she fear that Ladreville's thief had come to take her valuables? Mary had no way of knowing that even now Clay was at Gunther's, attempting to catch the thief.

"You're what's wrong." Mary took a step closer, keeping the barrel of the gun pointed at Sarah. "Give me your earrings."

Something was desperately amiss. Though Mary had appeared ill a few minutes ago, unable to stand without assistance, now her posture bore no sight of frailty. Only her eyes glinted with unusual brilliance. What was happening? Sarah thought quickly, remembering the oddities she'd attributed to Mary's fever. She'd claimed she'd gone to the Bar C to find Clay, and yet she already had medicine from Dr. Adler. She'd claimed all the servants were gone, but Jake was here. And now she was demanding Sarah's earrings.

"I won't give them up."

Mary shook her head. "You will. They'll be mine, just like the locket and the watch." With one hand, she pulled a gold locket from inside her collar. Mary had been wearing it the day Sarah had met her. Sarah's heart sank as she recalled how she'd admired it, how Thea had wanted to play with it, how Mary had claimed it was a gift from her husband. Mary had lied.

She didn't have to examine it, for the sickening feeling deep inside her told Sarah this was Patience's locket. Bile rose to her throat as she considered how it must have come to be in Mary's possession. Sarah clutched the edge of the table as waves of horror washed through her. The locket and the watch, Mary had said. Only one person in Ladreville had lost a watch.

"How did you get them?"

Mary laughed, a laugh that sent shivers down Sarah's spine. "I think you know." She laughed again. "Look in there." Mary gestured toward a carved wooden box on top of the bureau. "The baubles were little enough compared to all that I lost."

Her legs weak with fear and horror, Sarah moved to the bureau. As she expected, the box contained a man's watch open to reveal her miniature. "How did you get this?" she asked again. Surely what she feared wasn't true. Surely Mary wasn't the person who'd killed Clay's brother.

"The same way I'll get your earbobs. When we're done here, you'll put my little pills in the cup and drink that tea. They worked for Patience; they'll work for you. The only difference is, she didn't know what was comin'. You will." Mary waved the gun as she shook her head. "I liked you, Sarah. I really did. If you'd agreed to marry David, I wouldn't have to do this. But you wanted to be a Canfield bride, so now you've gotta die just like the others."

The woman was mad. It was the only explanation. Sarah gripped the edge of the bureau as her leg began to buckle. "What did they do to deserve this?"

"They took what shoulda been mine. Now they've gotta die. All of them." Mary waved the gun again. "You're next."

Help me, Lord. Sarah said a silent prayer. Somehow, some way she had to escape. But how? With her injured leg, she couldn't go far, especially without the cane. She had no choice. She had to get out of here. She had to find Clay. Perhaps if she distracted Mary, she could reach the cane.

"I don't understand," Sarah said as she inched toward the edge of the bureau. "What was stolen?"

"Land!" Though nothing was amusing, Mary laughed. "All the land oughta been mine and David's. Mine, not theirs."

Sarah nodded, hoping Mary would focus on her face, not her legs.

"It weren't fair. My husband died in the war. He oughta been rewarded, but he weren't. Robert Canfield got the land." Mary's voice rose until she was shouting. "It weren't fair. I deserved that land. Michel Ladre shoulda paid me for it, not Robert."

Sarah took another step toward the cane. "I understand." She used the voice that calmed Thea's tantrums. What Sarah understood was that Mary's grievance, which should have been directed at the State of Texas, had taken on maniacal

361

proportions, and she had turned Clay's family into scape-goats.

"It shoulda been mine," Mary repeated. "I knew that. That's why I tried to get Robert to marry me. He refused. The old fool refused me." The laughter that burst from Mary chilled Sarah. "He got his punishment. Look at him now, helpless as a baby in that chair."

Sarah nodded slowly as she took another step. All doubts about Mary's sanity had disappeared. The woman was mad, and that made her doubly dangerous, for there was no pre-dicting what she would do. There was also no stopping her, for she would not listen to reason. It was only by God's grace that Mary didn't appear to realize Sarah was moving.

"When Robert refused me, I knew what I had to do. If I couldn't become a Canfield, I would make sure the blood-line died." She fingered Patience's locket again. "I couldn't let Clay's wife give him a child. She had to die before the baby was born. That's why I poisoned her bowl of chowder. I thought that would be the end. But then Austin decided he'd marry, and it was his time to die." Mary let out another blood-chilling laugh. "It was easy to kill him. Even when he saw the gun, he didn't try to escape. He was as much of a fool as his father. Nobody figgered a woman could kill. They were wrong."

Mary waved the gun. "Clay weren't no problem at first. He was going back to Boston. But now he's fixin' to marry you and stay here. I can't let that happen. I didn't want to kill you. You were s'posed to get scared by the wagon wheel, but you didn't. That's why I had to dig the hole." She looked at Sarah, bewilderment in her eyes. "Why didn't you leave? You were s'posed to."

362

Mary gestured toward the bottle of pills. "It's too late now. Put the pills in the tea, Sarah. It'll soon be over. Then only Clay will be left."

"And his father." If Mary killed her, at least Clay would have Pa. But she wouldn't let Mary kill her. Somehow she would escape. Another two steps was all she needed to reach the cane.

Mary shook her head. "Robert will be dead in minutes. I left him a little present when I visited the Bar C. By now the cheroot shoulda set the whole house on fire." She glanced at the window. "If this faced east, you'd see the flames. I thought of everything. In an hour, Clay won't have nothing. No house, no father, no wife." Mary laughed.

Sarah closed her eyes. *Please, God, help me. I can't let Clay lose everything.* She opened her eyes and took the final step, wrapping her hand around the cane, then moving through the door.

"Stop!"

But Sarah would not. This was her only chance. She had to escape. She had to reach the Bar C. She had to save Clay's father. Sarah ran. Though she feared the sound of Mary's finger on the trigger, it never came. Another yard and she'd be outside. She heard footsteps and felt Mary's hand grip her arm. No! She would not remain here. Sarah raised the cane. With every ounce of strength she possessed, she brought it down on Mary's head. The older woman crumpled to the floor, moaning. *Please, God, make her stay there.*

Though her leg throbbed with each step, Sarah ran toward the barn. She had to reach Pa. She had to. And that meant . . . a horse. Sarah tried not to cringe at the thoughts, but the images rushed in. Flying through the air. The sickening thud when she'd hit the ground. The unbearable pain when Daisy landed on top of her. The months of lying in her bed, certain she would not walk again. She couldn't. She couldn't ride a horse. But she had to.

I can't do it alone. Sarah's hands were trembling as she opened the barn door. *Help me, Lord. Give me strength.* She took a deep breath and felt peace flow through her. Resolutely, she opened the stall and walked inside. Horses sensed a person's fear. Sarah knew that, and so she willed herself to show no fear. Somehow, she managed to get the bit into the mare's mouth. There was no time for a saddle. Though she'd never done it before, she would have to ride bareback. Somehow she found herself mounted. An instant later, she was out of the barn. *Thank you, Lord.* Sarah bent low over the mare's neck, urging her to gallop. They had minutes, perhaps only seconds, if they were to reach the Bar C before it was too late.

The air was still, but there was no mistaking the smell of smoke and burning wood. Mary had not lied. *Please, God, let Pa still be alive. Let me reach him in time.* Sarah gripped the reins tighter, urging the horse forward. Soon. Soon she'd be at the ranch.

And then she heard it, the unmistakable sound of hoofbeats behind her. She wouldn't look, for if she turned, she might lose her balance and fall. She couldn't risk that, not when Pa's life depended on her. The horse was closer now. Perhaps the rider was Clay. But it was not. A second later, the horse was beside her. A hand snaked out and grabbed Sarah's reins, tugging her horse to a stop.

"Get off. Now." Mary had caught her.

❧

Clay had heard people claim their blood chilled. As a physician, he had thought it an impossibility. Now he knew otherwise. Blood drained from his face and pooled around his heart, forming an icy shroud as he stared at the scene before him. While two horses grazed peacefully, Mary Bramble held Sarah at gunpoint in the middle of the road. Clay's last doubt vanished. This was the woman who'd killed his brother, and now she was threatening the woman he loved.

"Sarah!" He let out an anguished cry as he drew his six-shooter. Mary had to be stopped. She couldn't hurt Sarah. A bullet in the arm would keep Mary from shooting Sarah. He was too late. Before he could aim, Mary grabbed Sarah, pulling her in front of her, a human shield. Clay's heart sank as he considered the possibilities. Though Sarah had the advantage of age, Mary was bigger and stronger and was not burdened by an injured leg. The woman he loved had no chance of escape unless Clay could find a way to disarm Mary. His gaze moved quickly, searching for a weakness he could exploit.

"Go, Clay! Save your father." Sarah's words echoed through the night. Though his heart remained frozen with terror, warmth began to spread through his veins at the realization that this woman—this wonderful woman—cared more for Pa than her own life. "I'll be all right," she said.

"That's right, Clay. Go." Mary's laugh chilled his blood another ten degrees despite the warmth Sarah's love had generated. "I'll take care of your bride." Mary's laugh left no doubt how she proposed to care for Sarah.

"I can't do that." The acrid stench of smoke burned his eyes, filling his heart with pain at the thought of what his father was suffering. *Dear Lord, spare Pa the agony*, he prayed silently. He had made his choice. No matter how high the cost, he could not leave Sarah with this woman.

I love you, Pa. He sent the thought winging toward the Bar C. *I know this is what you would have wanted.* The day he'd returned from the war and stood at his wife's grave, Pa told Clay and Austin that the future belonged to the next generation. Sarah was Clay's future. If he were given the choice, his father would tell him to save Sarah, even though it meant his own death sentence.

Clay's eyes narrowed as he tried to find a way to free Sarah. "Let her go, Mary."

Mary laughed again. "If you want her, toss me your six-shooter. If'n you don't, I'll shoot her."

There was no choice. Mary had killed once; Clay knew she'd do it again. He dropped his gun.

"Good." Mary cackled. Keeping her arm tightly wrapped around Sarah, she trained her gun on Clay. "Now, get off the horse."

Again, there was no choice. As he slid from Shadow's back, Clay measured the distance between him and Mary. Without a weapon, he would have to tackle her, but only when Sarah was safe. He looked at Sarah. Though her eyes were filled with fear, she managed a small smile for him, as if she sought to reassure him that everything would be fine. It wouldn't, unless he could find a way to overpower Mary.

When Clay was on the ground, Mary smiled, a smile devoid of all mirth. "This is more than I coulda hoped for. Now I can be rid of all of you." She laughed. "First Patience, then Austin, now you, your father, and your pretty bride."

For a moment, the words did not register, but when they did, rage deeper than anything he'd ever known slammed

366

through Clay. This woman was evil, pure evil. She had killed his brother and his wife and their unborn child, and now she threatened Pa and Sarah. Mary was a murderer. Worse than that, she was a monster who enjoyed killing, and there was nothing so horrible on the face of the earth. With every fiber of his being, Clay knew she could not be allowed to live.

I will repay, saith the Lord. The words Clay had memorized echoed through his brain. He clenched his hands, wanting nothing more than to wrap them around Mary's throat. He could not, not without disobeying his God. *Help me, Lord. Give me strength.*

As the rage began to subside, Clay stared at Mary. Perhaps if he convinced her to talk, Sarah would be able to break free. "Why are you doing this? I thought you were our friend."

Mary's lips curled with anger. "The land shoulda been mine. You Canfields don't have no right to it."

Dimly Clay recalled her complaining that she hadn't received a land grant to match the one the state had given Pa. It appeared that the slight had festered and that she now blamed his family for everything that had gone wrong in her life. Clay couldn't change that. He wouldn't even try. All that mattered was saving Sarah. If Mary wanted the ranch, she could have it, so long as she freed Sarah.

Clay's thoughts whirled. There had to be a way to distract Mary long enough for Sarah to break free. He looked at the woman he loved, hoping she could read his expression, hoping she knew why he shifted his eyes to the right. "Killing us won't give you the Bar C," he told Mary. "Only I can do that." Though Mary kept her gun pointed at him, Clay saw her eyes flicker with confusion. "Let Sarah go." Sarah nodded almost imperceptibly. "If you do, I'll deed the ranch to you. That's the only way you'll get it. If I'm dead, it will go to the state."

"How do I know I can trust you?"

Clay glanced to the side again, not daring to look at Sarah, lest he alert Mary, but hoping she would understand. "What have you got to lose?" As he pronounced the final word, Clay bent down, as if reaching for his gun. Enraged, Mary took a step forward. The distraction was momentary, but it was all Sarah needed. She lurched to the side and broke free. *Thank you, Lord.*

The instant Sarah was safe, Clay lunged. Wrapping his arms around Mary's legs, he dragged her to the ground, then pulled her arms behind her. Though she was kicking and struggling, she could not escape.

Clay twisted his head and looked at Sarah. "There's a rope on Shadow. Will you get it?" The woman he loved might limp, but she moved toward the stallion with confidence. Gone was the fear that had characterized her interactions with horses. Suddenly the implication of the two horses he'd seen grazing at the side of the road hit him. "You rode," he said, wonder in his voice.

Sarah acted as if overcoming her fear was of little importance. "It was the only way to save your father."

"It's too late now." Mary cackled as she pronounced the words. "Too late. Too late. Too late."

She was mad. As a student, Clay had seen enough patients to be certain of the diagnosis. Though she'd hidden her illness for years, Mary had stepped over the brink tonight. There was no turning back.

Clay wrapped a length of rope around her wrists, then tied her ankles. For her own safety as well as others', Mary could not be allowed to escape. A deep sadness filled him at the thought that this woman who had once been a friend would spend the rest of her life in an asylum, a tragic, pitiful figure.

"It's over," he said softly. "The killing is over." Mary's only response was another mad laugh. The poor, poor woman. Clay swallowed and prayed for strength, knowing there was more to be said. She wouldn't understand it, but that didn't matter. Zach and Sarah were right. Clay was doing this for himself. He took another deep breath as he looked at the struggling figure on the ground. "I forgive you for what you've done." As he pronounced the words, Clay pictured Austin's smile.

❧

Sarah's legs buckled, and she sank to the ground. Perhaps it was relief; perhaps it was fatigue; perhaps it was sorrow over Pa's death. She didn't know the cause. All she knew was that she could no longer stand. She'd handed Clay the ropes, and then she'd collapsed. Sarah watched while Clay restrained Mary. Though he was speaking, she could not distinguish the words. All she saw was his bowed head and then the confident way he straightened his shoulders as he bent to pick up Mary. Something had happened, but Sarah did not know what it was.

Clay draped Mary over the horse's back, tying her so she could not fall off. When he turned and saw her, Sarah read alarm in his eyes. "What happened?" Clay cried as he crossed the distance to her in a few long strides.

"It's nothing. My leg gave out from the strain. That's all." Though she knew tonight was indelibly etched on her brain, it was one of God's miracles that she had not been harmed.

"Oh, Sarah, I couldn't bear to lose you too." As tenderly as if she were a child, Clay gathered her into his arms and carried her to Shadow. "I'll keep you safe," he promised as he mounted in front of her.

The horse that bore Mary walked next to them. It was a pitiful sight, the once strong woman broken, her words reduced to babbling. Sarah said a prayer for the woman who'd done so much harm and for the man who'd lost so much.

When Sarah shuddered, thinking of the scene that awaited them, Clay spoke. "It's just a little longer. Then we'll be home."

But there would be no home. Sarah knew that. "I'm sorry about Pa. I thought I could save him."

"No one could." Clay's voice broke. "Maybe this was a blessing. Pa wasn't happy this past year, trapped in his body. Now he's with Ma and Austin."

Sarah laid her head against Clay's back, trying to comfort him. "I know, but we'll miss him."

As they approached the Bar C, the smoke lessened, telling them the fire was over. That too was a blessing, for Clay would not have to battle flames as he searched for his father. Sarah tried not to cry when she saw the burned-out shell of what had once been Clay's home. The roof was gone, leaving only a few charred beams and the stone chimney. His parents' dream was gone, destroyed along with his father. Sarah bit back tears. Though Clay had gotten his wish and had learned the identity of Austin's murderer, the price he'd had to pay had been unbearably high.

She tightened her arms around him, turning her head to the side, and as she did, something moved at the corner of the house. It must be an animal, come to investigate. But as it moved again, Sarah's heart leapt. No animal moved like that.

"Clay, look!" She unwrapped one arm and pointed toward the house. "There, in front."

"Pa!" An instant later, both Clay and Sarah were on the ground, and he was running toward the figure. "Pa! You're alive!"

❧

"It's strange. In all the times I visited, I was never inside the parlor." Clay wrapped his arm around Sarah's shoulders as they entered the Lazy B's ranch house. The long night with its endless explanations was over, and dawn was painting the sky. Though she doubted anyone had managed to sleep, Zach had taken Pa to the Friedrichs.

Sarah looked at the place that had been the sight of so much terror, the same place that would be her temporary home. Though she would never forget what had happened here tonight, at least Clay and Pa and Thea had no such memories to haunt them. "It was kind of David to offer us his home."

"The poor man." Clay looked around the parlor. "His world has crumbled. I know he blames himself for not realizing his mother was mad."

No one had, for Mary had been careful to hide her illness. "What will happen now?"

"Mary will be put in an asylum. David's going with her, but he's not sure he wants to return to Ladreville." Clay opened the doors to the two first-floor bedrooms. "Pa can have this one. I'll take the other."

Sarah breathed a sigh of relief that she and Thea would sleep upstairs. Those rooms held no memories.

"David offered to sell me the ranch," Clay continued. "I refused, but I told him I'd lease it for a year. That'll give him a chance to think."

Sarah nodded her agreement. "A lot can happen in a year." It had been little more than that since her parents' deaths.

"In another year, Jean-Michel will be back from his exile." Despite Jean-Michel's claims to the contrary, his father had not excused his crimes. Michel planned to send him to Houston to work for an empresario, declaring that the hard physical labor was what his son needed. He'd further stipulated that Jean-Michel's wages would be sent back to Ladreville to repay the people he'd robbed.

As they entered the room where Mary had threatened her, Clay tipped Sarah's chin up so that she was looking at him. "In another year, we'll be living in our own home." As they'd waited for the sun to rise, Clay and Sarah had made plans, plans that included building a new, larger house on the same site his parents had chosen. Though Sarah nodded, she said nothing. "You're unusually quiet." Clay sounded worried. "Is something wrong?"

She shook her head. Though she had dreaded setting foot in this room, now that she was here, she realized it was a room—nothing more. "Nothing's wrong. I was thinking how much is right." Sarah looked around, her eyes resting on the carved wooden box that held Austin's watch. Silently she opened it and handed the watch to Clay.

As tears glinted in his eyes, he nodded. "We'll save this for our first son."

Sarah nodded. Taking Clay's hand, she left the room and closed the door behind her. "Did you ever think about God's plan for us?" When he shook his head, she said, "I didn't either. But now I see it. At first I didn't believe Isabelle when she told me God could make all things work for good, but it's true. If my parents hadn't died, I would never have come here. I would never have met you."

Clay looked at her, his gaze moving from the top of her head to her toes. "If you hadn't broken your leg, you would not have known how to help Pa. He would have died in the fire."

"It's only Austin's death that puzzles me. I don't see how that brought anything good."

"It did. It brought you to me. I can't think of anything more wonderful than having you as my wife." Clay was silent for a moment, as if he were weighing his words. When he spoke, those words surprised Sarah. "I suspect that's what Austin had in mind from the beginning."

"I don't understand."

Clay led her back to the porch. It was only when they were both seated on the swing that he continued. "There are things I haven't told you about my brother, but tonight has convinced me there should be no secrets between us." Sarah remembered the night she had said something similar, the night her revelations had helped Clay find his Savior.

His eyes darkened. "The truth is, Austin wasn't ready to marry. When Pa was stricken with apoplexy, we both searched for something that would give him a reason to live. We knew how much Pa wanted a grandchild, so it seemed like the answer to Austin's prayers that Patience was with child. You know what happened."

Clay looked into the distance for a moment. "After Patience died and I was in mourning, Austin wouldn't give up the idea of grandchildren. That's why he decided to look for a bride. I tried to talk him out of it, but he was adamant." Clay threaded his fingers through Sarah's, the warmth of his palm reassuring her, though his expression was solemn. "When he read your first letter, Austin told me you were the woman God meant to be the Canfield bride. I disagreed, but once again he would not be swayed. I didn't recognize it at the time, but when Austin talked about you, you were always the Canfield bride. It was almost as if he didn't believe he would marry you, for he never once referred to you as his bride."

Sarah shook her head. She couldn't let Clay believe his brother had had a premonition of his death. "Yes, he did. Austin's letters called me his bride-to-be." Though the letters had burned with everything else in the house and cabin, Sarah knew she'd never forget the wonderful words she'd memorized.

She'd hoped to comfort Clay, but it appeared she'd had the opposite effect. Clay shifted his weight and looked into the distance as if he were seeking an answer. Surprised by his reaction, Sarah saw indecision on his face, then a tightening of his jaw. He took a deep breath before he said, "Austin didn't write those letters."

The words were spoken so softly that for a second Sarah thought she'd imagined them. "Then who . . . ?" Shock turned to certainty. Of course. It was no wonder that so many things Clay had said reminded her of the letters. It was no wonder that when she dreamt of a man inscribing the words that had touched her heart, that man was Clay. "You did." She looked at the man she loved so dearly. "You wrote them. You're the man who gave me my paper roses."

"I'm also the man who loves you with all his heart." Though love shone from Clay's eyes, she also saw regret. "I was wrong. I should have told you sooner. Oh, Sarah, can you forgive me for deceiving you?"

Sarah leaned forward and pressed her lips to his. "There's nothing to forgive. Don't you see, Clay? It was all part of God's plan."

Author's Letter

Dear Reader,

More than any book I've written, *Paper Roses* was a journey. Normally, once I have the idea for a story, it becomes reality within a year or two. Not so with this one. I started it more than ten years ago. As I think back on all that happened, I'm reminded of the parable of the sower (Matt. 13:3–8). There were definitely thorns along the way, in the form of other books that competed for my attention and choked the seedlings. I suspect some birds consumed the early ideas too. But the biggest problem was that when I first started, I was sowing in shallow ground.

From the beginning, I knew that Sarah would be a mail-order bride and that Clay was the author of the letters. I even referred to this as my mail-order-bride-meets-Cyrano-de-Bergerac book. The problem was, as much as I loved that premise, the story didn't feel right to me. The characters were simply that—characters. They weren't real people with real problems. They weren't characters I cared about enough to finish writing the book, and they certainly weren't characters you would have fallen in love with.

The change came the summer that a dear friend from college entered the final stages of leukemia. Though we were separated by thousands of miles, that summer brought us closer than we'd ever been. Knowing we had only a few months left together, we spoke of many things. For the first time in the more than thirty-five years we'd known each other, we spoke of what was truly important: faith, love, and hope. In our lighter moments, we spoke of the final gift she had for me. Though she was referring to a piece of French porcelain, what she gave me was of far greater value, for her last months on Earth brought me a stronger faith and the realization that it was time for me to write about God's love.

By the end of the summer, I had changed and so had my writing. I'd found the deep soil where seeds could take root and flourish. Sarah and Clay had become real people.

I hope you enjoyed their story and that, like me, you're eager to return to Ladreville. The second book in the trilogy will be available in January 2010. As it continues the story of Texas dreams, it will give you a chance to reconnect with old friends like Zach, Isabelle, and Gunther as well as to meet some new people—people whose stories I hope will touch your heart.

Until we meet again, I send you blessings.

Amanda Cabot